Watching the Dark

Watching the Dark

Peter Robinson

HARPER LUXE

An Imprint of HarperCollinsPublishers

WATCHING THE DARK. Copyright © 2013 by Eastvale Enterprises, Inc. All rights reserved. Printed in the United States of America. No part of this book may be used or reproduced in any manner whatsoever without written permission except in the case of brief quotations embodied in critical articles and reviews. For information address HarperCollins Publishers, 10 East 53rd Street, New York, NY 10022.

HarperCollins books may be purchased for educational, business, or sales promotional use. For information, please e-mail the Special Markets Department at SPsales@harpercollins.com.

FIRST HARPERLUXE EDITION

HarperLuxe™ is a trademark of HarperCollins Publishers

Library of Congress Cataloging-in-Publication Data is available upon request.

ISBN: 978-0-06-222291-6

13 14 ID/RRD 10 9 8 7 6 5 4 3 2 1

To Sheila

1

On nights when the pain kept her awake, Lorraine Jenson would get up around dawn and go outside to sit on one of the wicker chairs before anyone else in the center was stirring. With a tartan blanket wrapped around her shoulders to keep out the early-morning chill, she would listen to the birds sing as she enjoyed a cup of Earl Grey, the aromatic steam curling from its surface, its light, delicious scent filling her nostrils. She would smoke her first cigarette of the day, always the best one.

Some mornings, the small artificial lake below the sloping lawn was covered in mist, which shrouded the trees on the other side. Other times, the water was a still, dark mirror that reflected the detail of every branch and leaf perfectly. On this fine April morning, the lake was clear, though the water's surface was ruffled by a cool breeze, and the reflections wavered.

Lorraine felt her pain slough off like a layer of dead skin as the painkillers kicked in, and the tea and cigarette soothed her frayed nerves. She placed her mug on the low wrought-iron table beside her chair and adjusted the blanket around her shoulders. She was facing south, and the sun was creeping over the hill through the trees on her left. Soon the spell would be broken. She would hear the sounds of people getting up in the building behind her, voices calling, doors opening, showers running, toilets flushing, and another day to be got through would begin.

As the light grew stronger, she thought she could see something, like a bundle of clothes, on the ground at the edge of the woods on the far side of the lake. That was unusual, as Barry, the head groundsman and general estate manager, was proud of his artificial lake and his natural woodlands, so much so that some people complained he spent far more time down there than he did keeping the rest of the extensive grounds neat and tidy.

Lorraine squinted, but she couldn't bring the object into clearer focus. Her vision was still not quite what it had been. Gripping the arms of her chair, she pushed herself to her feet, gritting her teeth at the red-hot pokers of pain that seared through her left leg, despite the OxyContin, then she took hold of her crutch and made her way down the slope. The grass was still wet with dew, and she felt it fresh and cool on her bare ankles as she walked.

When she got to the water's edge, she took the cinder path that skirted the lake and soon arrived on the other side, at the edge of the woods, which began only a few feet away from the water. Even before then, she had recognized what it was that lay huddled there. Though she had seen dead bodies before, she had never actually stumbled across one. She was alone with the dead now, for the first time since she had stood by her father's coffin in the funeral home.

Lorraine held her breath. Silence. She thought she heard a rustling deep in the woods, and a shiver of fear rippled through her. If the body were a victim of murder, then the killer might still be out there, watching her. She remained completely still for about a minute, until she was certain there was nobody in the woods. She heard the rustling again and saw a fox making its way through the undergrowth.

Now that she was at the scene, Lorraine's training kicked in. She was wary of disturbing anything, so she kept her distance. Much as she wanted to move in closer and examine the body, see if it was someone she knew, she restrained herself. There was nothing she could do, she told herself; the way he—for it was definitely a man—was kneeling with his body bent forward, head touching the ground like a parody of a Muslim at prayer, there was no way he was still alive.

The best thing she could do was stay here and protect the scene. Murder or not, it was definitely a suspicious death, and whatever she did, she could not screw up now. Cursing the pain that rippled through her leg whenever she moved, Lorraine fumbled for her mobile in her jeans pocket and phoned Eastvale police station.

There was something about Bach that suited the early morning perfectly, DCI Alan Banks thought as he drove out of Gratly toward the St. Peter's Police Convalescence and Treatment Center, four miles north of Eastvale, shortly after dawn that morning. He needed something to wake him up and keep his attention engaged, get the old gray cells buzzing, but nothing too loud, nothing too jarring or emotionally taxing. Alina Ibragimova's CD of Bach's sonatas and partitas for violin was just right. Bach both soothed and stimulated the mind at once.

Banks knew St. Peter's. He had visited Annie Cabbot there several times during her recent convalescence. Just a few short months ago he had seen her in tears trying to walk on crutches, and now she was due back at work on Monday. He was looking forward to that; life had been dull for the past while without her.

He took the first exit from the roundabout and drove alongside the wall for about a hundred yards before arriving at the arched entrance and turning left on the tarmac drive. There was no gate or gatehouse, but the first officers to arrive on the scene had quite rightly taped off the area. A young PC waved Banks down to check his ID and note his name and time of entry on a clipboard before lifting the tape and letting him through.

Driving up to the car park was like arriving at a luxury spa hotel, Banks had always thought when he visited Annie. It was no different today. St. Peter's presented a broad south-facing facade at the top of the rise that led down to the lake and surrounding woods. Designed by a firm of Leeds architects, with Vanbrugh in mind, and built of local stone in the late nineteenth century, it was three stories high and had a flagged portico, complete with simple Doric columns at the front and two wings, east and west. Though not so extensive as some other local examples, the grounds were landscaped very much in the style and spirit of Capability Brown, with the lake and woods and rolling lawns. There was even a folly. To the west, beyond the trees and lawns, the outlines of Swainsdale's hills and fells could be seen, forming a backdrop of what the Japanese called borrowed scenery, which merged nature with art.

The forensic team had got there before Banks, which seemed odd until he remembered that a detective inspector had made the initial call. Kitted out in disposable white coveralls, they were already going about their business. The crime scene photographer, Peter Darby, was at work with his battered old Nikon SLR and his ultramodern digital video recorder. Most SOCOs—or CSIs, as they now liked to be called—also took their own digital photos and videos when they searched a scene, but though Peter Darby accepted the use of video, he shunned digital photography as being far too susceptible to tampering and error. It made him a bit of a dinosaur, and one or two of the younger techies cracked jokes behind his back. He could counter by boasting that he had never had any problems with his evidence in court, and he had never lost an image because of computer problems.

DI Lorraine Jenson, a lone, hunched figure resting her weight on a crutch by the water's edge and jotting in her notebook, stood with two other people about five or six yards away from the body. Banks knew her slightly from a case he had worked a few months ago that crossed the border into Humberside, where she worked. Not long ago, he had heard, she'd had a run-in with a couple of drug dealers in a tower block, which ended with her falling from a second-floor balcony. She had sustained multiple fractures of her left leg, but after surgery, the cast and physio, she would be back at work soon enough.

"What a turn-up," she said. "Me finding a body."

Banks gestured toward the CSIs. "I see you've already called in the lads."

"Judgment call. I thought it best not to waste any time. The divisional duty inspector made all the decisions." She turned to introduce the others. "By the way, this is Barry Sadler, estate manager, and Mandy Pemberton, the night nurse."

Banks greeted them, then asked them if they would mind returning to the main building, where they would be asked for statements. Still in shock, they headed up the slope.

"Who's the crime scene manager?" Banks asked Lorraine.

"Stefan Nowak."

"Excellent." Stefan Nowak was one of the best. He would protect his scene to the death, if necessary, but he was still a delight to work with, Banks found, a charming, witty and intelligent man. Banks glanced toward the body, slumped forward by the tree line. "Know who he is?"

"Not yet," said Lorraine. "But I might when I see his face. If he's from here, that is."

It was too early for Dr. Glendenning, the Home Office pathologist, who lived in Saltburn, so the police surgeon, Dr. Burns, knelt over the body making notes in his little black book. Banks squatted beside him and watched, hands on his knees.

"Ah, Alan," said Burns. "I'd like to get him turned over, if I may?"

"Peter Darby finished with his camera?"

"Yes."

Banks studied the body for a few moments and, finding nothing particularly interesting or unusual about it except for its odd position, helped Dr. Burns. Carefully, they turned the body over on its back. As soon as they had done so, they exchanged puzzled glances. Banks stood up. He heard Lorraine Jenson, hovering over them, give a faint gasp.

Something was sticking out of the man's chest. On first appearances, it resembled the kind of wooden stake that Van Helsing wielded to kill vampires in the old Hammer films, though it had feathers on the end, like an arrow. But it was too deeply embedded to be an ordinary arrow. "Looks like a crossbow bolt," said Banks.

"I think you're right," Dr. Burns agreed.

"We don't get many of those around these parts." In fact, Banks couldn't remember ever investigating a crossbow murder before.

"I can hardly say it's my area of expertise, either," said Dr. Burns. "I'm sure Dr. Glendenning will be able to tell you more, once he gets him on the table." Dr. Burns stood up. His knees cracked. "From the position and angle, I'd say it almost certainly pierced his heart. He would have died almost instantaneously. Of course, he might have been poisoned first, but there are no apparent signs of strangulation, bruising or other physical trauma."

"Do you reckon he was killed here, or was he moved after death?"

Dr. Burns unbuttoned the man's shirt and examined the shoulders and chest area. "These are lividity marks, hypostasis, which means he's been in this position for some time, and the blood has pooled here. But I can't say for certain. Not until Dr. Glendenning does the PM. It certainly seems as if he dropped to his knees, then keeled over and fell forward, so that his head rested on the ground. You can see there are traces of blood on the grass there, approximately where his heart would have been directly above it. That's consistent with his injuries. There isn't much blood. Most of the bleeding will have been internal." Dr. Burns pointed toward the woods. "The shot probably came from where those CSIs are working around that tree, say fifty, sixty feet away. Hard to miss at that range, but it means your shooter could also stay hidden by the trees, in case anyone from the center happened to be watching out of a window."

Banks glanced at Lorraine Jenson, who was still staring, horrified, at the crossbow bolt in the man's chest. "He seems vaguely familiar to me," said Banks, "but I've met a lot of coppers in my time. Do you recognize him now, Lorraine?"

Lorraine nodded slowly, a little pale. "It's Bill," she said. "DI Bill Quinn. He was a patient here, too."

"Bloody hell," said Banks. "Bill Quinn. I thought I recognized him."

"You knew him, too?"

"Only in passing. He worked out of Millgarth, in Leeds, with DI Ken Blackstone." Banks paused and turned back to Dr. Burns, who was busy with his thermometer. "Time of death?"

"As usual, I can't be really precise. You've seen the lividity. Rigor's started, but it isn't complete yet. Judging by the temperature, I'd say he's been dead about seven or eight hours. I'd guess that he was killed no later than one in the morning, say, and no earlier than eleven last night. Of course, that's only an estimate. You might do better pinning down his movements, such as when he was last seen. It shouldn't be too difficult in a place like this."

"Just hoping you might be able to save us some time."

"Sorry. Perhaps—"

"Actually, you have," said Banks. "Two hours is a pretty good window to work with. Wouldn't it have been too dark for the killer to shoot?"

"As I said, the killer was probably pretty close," Dr. Burns answered. "Maybe even closer than I estimated. It was a clear night, and there was a bright three-quarters moon, very few clouds. The victim would have made an easy enough target against the backdrop of the building, especially if the killer knew his way around a crossbow. I don't think it would have been too difficult at all."

Banks squatted again and went through the dead man's pockets. He found nothing and decided that that, in itself, was odd. When he mentioned it, Dr. Burns said, "Maybe he left his stuff in his room? You don't usually need your wallet and mobile if you're just nipping out for a quick walk before bedtime."

"If that's what he was doing. And people these days tend to be glued to their mobiles. They're like a lifeline or something. Then there are the keys."

"What about them?"

"There aren't any."

"Maybe he didn't need them."

"Maybe not. Or maybe someone took them. We'll find out."

A black Toyota swung through the arch, and the officers on the gate let it through after their usual checks. DS Winsome Jackman jumped out, all six feet something of her.

"Not like you to be late, Winsome," said Banks, glancing at his watch. "Wild night last night, was it?"

Winsome looked aghast, then smiled. "No, sir. I never have wild nights. You should know that."

"Of course not," said Banks. He explained the situation. "Will you go up to the house and get the practicalities organized?" he asked. "A murder room in the main building, phone lines, civilian personnel, the usual."

"Yes, sir," Winsome said.

"You'd also better organize a thorough search of the buildings and grounds as quickly as possible, before everyone gets wind of what's going on down here. We're after the murder weapon, a crossbow. Can't be that easy to hide."

"Including the patients' rooms?"

"Especially the patients' rooms. They won't like it. They're cops, like us. But it has to be done. They ought to understand that much, at least. This is one of our own that's been killed. It could be an inside job, and if this place is as wide open as it appears, then anybody could come and go as they please. Set up interviews, too. You can start with the two who were just here. Barry . . . ?" Banks glanced at Lorraine Jenson.

"Barry Sadler and Mandy Pemberton."

Winsome headed off. Lorraine fell in beside her. She moved well, he noticed, despite the crutch. She made some comment, and Banks spotted Winsome glancing over her shoulder and laughing.

Banks gazed down at the body again. Though they had only met once, at a retirement do with DI Ken Blackstone, he remembered lanky Bill Quinn, prematurely gray-haired, with his stained and crooked teeth, smiling quietly in his seat through the ribald speeches, a small whiskey in his hand. "Bill Quinn," he muttered to himself. "What have you been up to?" He looked around at the lake, the trees and the big house on the hill, sniffed the air, then set off after Winsome and Lorraine, up to the main building.

"You'll be treating me as a suspect, then, as well as searching my room?" Lorraine said as she put her crutch aside and settled down in her armchair. Her bedsit resembled a pleasant hotel room, Banks thought, with a single bed in one corner, en suite bathroom and toilet, a writing desk, and three arm-chairs arranged around an oval table. There were also tea- and coffee-making facilities on the top of the chest of drawers, a spacious wardrobe, and a flat-screen television fixed to the wall. A combination radio, CD player and iPod dock completed the setup.

"Don't be silly," Banks said. "Why would you think that?"

"I discovered the body. It's always the person who discovers the body."

"Or the nearest and dearest," added Banks. "What have you been doing here, reading too much Agatha Christie?"

"It just stands to reason."

"Did you do it?"

"No, of course not."

"Well, we've got that out of the way, haven't we?"

"You should suspect me. I would if I were you. We're all suspects. All of us here."

Banks gazed at her with narrowed eyes. Early forties, looking older and more frail since her injury, once-plump body wasted by the recovery process, pale skin sagging, shrewd eyes with bags underneath, a ragged fringe of dark hair. "We'll talk about that later," he said. "For now, you're just a witness. We'll want a full written statement later, of course, but all I want now is a few basics, your immediate impressions, what you knew of the victim. That sort of thing. I saw you making notes, so it's probably still fresh in your mind. Let's start with what you were doing outside so early, and what made you walk down to the lake."

"I'm not sleeping very well because of the pain," Lorraine said after a brief hesitation. "Most days I get up early, when it starts to get light, and I feel claustrophobic. I need to get out. It's peaceful sitting there before the place comes to life. And I can enjoy a cigarette."

"What drew you to the lake?"

"I saw something down there, at the edge of the woods. That's all. A bundle. It seemed unusual. Out of place. The grounds are usually immaculate."

"And when you saw what it was?"

"I kept my distance and phoned it in."

"You didn't touch anything?"

"No."

"Did you notice anything else?"

"Like what?"

"Anything odd, apart from the bundle itself."

"No, not really. I stood and listened. I saw a fox. The sound startled me. I thought the killer might still be in the woods, but it was only a fox."

"You couldn't see the crossbow bolt at this point, could you?"

"No. He was practically facedown on the ground. You saw for yourself."

"But you just said 'killer.' What made you assume he'd been killed, rather than just, say, dropped dead of a heart attack or something?"

"I don't know. It was just the way he was lying, kneeling. It looked suspicious. It was instinct, a hunch. I can't really think of any logical explanation."

Banks knew how easily witnesses got confused and how easy it was for the questioner to take advantage of that, to make them even more nervous and defensive. Question anyone for a few minutes, and pretty soon they all sounded as if they were lying. Cops were apparently no different. "I just wondered whether there was anything in particular that made you feel that way, that's all," Banks said. "You didn't see or hear anyone running away, a car starting out on the road, or anything like that?"

"No. Just the fox. And birds, of course. The birds were already singing. Why are you asking? When do you think he was killed? He must have been there for a while. Surely he can't have been killed just before I found him?"

"Did you know Bill Quinn well?"

"No, not really. I'd talked to him, chatted briefly in the lounge over a nightcap, that sort of thing, but I wouldn't say I knew him. We're both smokers, so we'd meet up outside occasionally by chance and pass the time of day. We're all pretty civil here, but we don't really socialize all that much."

"You weren't involved in any sort of relationship?"

"Good God, no." She held up her left hand. "The only people I'm in a relationship with are my husband and my two children."

"Did you ever witness DI Quinn arguing with any of the other patients, or hear anyone making threats toward him?"

"No. It's a pretty peaceful place here, as you might have noticed. He was quiet most of the time, abstracted. I didn't see much of him. I didn't witness any arguments at all."

"Noticed anyone hanging around? Anyone who shouldn't be here?"

"No."

"When did you last see Bill Quinn alive?"

"At dinner last night."

"When was that? What's the routine?"

"Dinner's usually at half past six, then three nights a week there's quiz night at eight. After that, about half past nine, people either meet for a drink or two in the library bar or head off to their rooms to watch TV."

"And when there's not a quiz night?"

"There's a film sometimes, usually a quite recent one, in the gym, or people just amuse themselves, play cards, read, whatever."

"No karaoke?"

Lorraine laughed. "Hardly. Though I think sometimes it might liven things up a bit."

"How did Bill Quinn appear at dinner last night? Did he seem agitated, distracted, edgy?"

Lorraine frowned with the effort of memory. "Maybe a little. I'm not sure. He didn't say much, but then he rarely did. He was always a bit distracted and edgy. Not agitated, mind you, just in another world, as if he was carrying a burden. It's far too easy to read things into a situation with hindsight."

"What would you read into his behavior last night?"

"That he seemed maybe a bit more anxious than usual, that's all, as if he had something on his mind. He didn't stick around to chat over coffee, for example, and he didn't go to the library bar for an after-dinner drink."

"Did he usually stay for a chat and go for a drink?"

"Yes. A small malt. Just the one, as a rule. He also missed quiz night, which was not like him at all. He enjoyed quiz nights." Lorraine paused. "He wasn't easy to know. Hard to get a handle on."

"Any idea who might have killed him?"

"I doubt if it was anyone here," Lorraine said. "We've all been thrown together by chance and circumstance, and there hasn't been really much of an opportunity to form grievances and vendettas so far." She gestured toward her crutches. "Besides, most of us are incapable."

"Even so," Banks said. "An old grudge suddenly confronted?"

"Bit of a coincidence, though, wouldn't you say? I reckon you'd be better off checking out the villains he brought down, rather than cops he was spending a couple of weeks' rest and recuperation with."

"Fair enough." Banks glanced around the room. "Nice digs," he said. "And you can get a decent single-malt here, too?"

"It's not a health spa, you know, or a fitness center."

St. Peter's, Annie Cabbot had explained to Banks, was a charity-run convalescence center for injured police officers, those recuperating from operations or suffering from stress and anxiety, job-related or otherwise. It offered a range of treatments, from physiotherapy to Reiki, including massage, sauna, hydrotherapy and psychological counseling. The general length of stay was two weeks, but that was flexible in some cases; Annie had stayed for three weeks and still returned regularly, as an outpatient, for physio and massage therapy.

"Did you hear anything during the night?" Banks asked. "You said you don't sleep well."

"I usually take a pill when I go to bed. That knocks me out for a few hours, then I can't get back to sleep again, so I get up early. But from ten o'clock, when I usually go to bed, until about three or four, I'm dead to the world."

"So you didn't hear anything after you woke up early?"

"No. Only the birds."

"Where did Bill Quinn go instead of staying for a drink and participating in quiz night?"

"I've no idea. I wasn't keeping tabs on him. To his room, I suppose. Or out for a late smoke. All I know is I didn't see him again."

"And you didn't hear him leave the building after you went to bed?"

"No. As you can see, my room's right at the back, on the second floor, and he's on the third floor at the front. The ground floor is all offices and treatment rooms, along with the dining room and library bar. Then there's a basement, with the gym and swimming pool. I wouldn't even have heard Bill Quinn if he'd had a wild orgy in his room. I wouldn't necessarily hear anyone leaving through the front door. He could have gone out during quiz night for all I know. As I said, I didn't see him at all after dinner."

"You were at quiz night?"

"Yes."

"OK. We'll ask the others. Someone might have seen something. What's the security like here? Is access easy?"

Lorraine snorted. "Security? There isn't any, really. I mean, it's not a prison, or even a hospital. More like a posh hotel. Maybe there are a few expensive bits of gym gear or medical equipment around, but they don't keep drugs or cash on the premises. As you know already, there's a big wall, but no gate, so I suppose anyone can walk or drive in and out whenever they want. We can. It would be easy enough for someone to slip into the woods by the gate without being seen and just wait there. The nearest village is a mile and a half away, and sometimes some of the people here nip out for a jar or two in the pub. There's no sentry post, no porter's lodge, no curfew, no book to sign. There's the night nurse on duty—you met Mandy—and she might have noticed something, but even she was probably fast asleep by then. We come and go as we please."

"Was Bill Quinn in the habit of going down to the woods at night?"

"Not that I know of, no. Whenever I saw him outside, he'd be having a smoke by the front door."

"Is there CCTV?"

"I don't think so. You'd better ask one of the staff. I mean, why would there be? We're all honest coppers here, right?"

"Hmm." Banks stood up. "I'll be off, then. Thanks for your time, Lorraine. I might be back."

As he left, two uniformed WPCs entered Lorraine's room. "Damn," he heard her say. "If you must go through my knicker drawer, try not to make too much of a mess."

Banks walked down the broad wooden staircase to the reception area, letting his hand slide along the dark polished banister. A stair lift had been fitted on one side for those patients who had difficulty climbing the stairs. Annie had used it, he remembered. The whole place was crawling with police now. Banks spotted DC Doug Wilson and asked him if Winsome was still upstairs searching Bill Quinn's room.

"As far as I know she is, sir," said Wilson. "It's twenty-two B, west wing. I'm just getting the guest interviews organized. It'll take us a while. We're using one of the staff meeting lounges as the murder room. It's being set up now."

"Excellent. How many patients in all?"

"Only twelve, sir. Then there's the staff, mostly part-time. We'll use the library bar and the ground-floor offices and treatment rooms for the interviews. That way we can conduct more than one at a time and get finished sooner."

"Fine," said Banks. "Got enough help?"

"I've got Gerry, sir. I mean DC Masterson."

DC Geraldine Masterson had just finished her probationary period and was shaping up very well. She was young and still had a lot to learn, but that wasn't such a bad thing. More important, she was bright and keen, and showed above-average aptitude for grasping things. She also had a degree in IT.

"I'll see if I can manage to draft in some help," Banks said. "Until then, just do the best you can."

"Yes, sir."

"And get a couple of officers asking around the general neighborhood, the village, find out if anyone was seen hanging around here lately, last night in particular. A car, anything suspicious."

"It's pretty isolated, sir."

"That's why someone might have noticed something. You can get the word out to the media, too. No information about DI Quinn's murder, especially about method of death, but we want to talk to anybody who passed by St. Peter's between, say, ten o'clock last night and two in the morning. The press will be here soon, so make sure you warn the men on the gate to keep them at bay. Did DS Jackman mention anything about searching the grounds and rooms?"

"Yes, sir. We're trying to get it done as quickly and discreetly as possible."

"Carry on, Doug," said Banks.

"OK, sir." Doug Wilson strode off.

"Sir? Excuse me. Just a minute, sir. Are you in charge of all this?"

Banks turned toward the new voice. The woman behind the reception desk was calling out to him. The area reminded him of a hotel reception, with the rows of pigeonholes on the wall behind her for keys and messages, a laptop computer on a pullout shelf, filing drawers, printer, fax and photocopy machine. The woman was perhaps a little older than Banks, gray haired, matronly, and her name badge read "Mary."

"I'm DCI Banks," he said, offering his hand. "Sorry for all this upheaval, Mary. What can I do for you?"

"Well, I was just wondering, you know, about the regular schedules. The patients. I mean physio, massage and suchlike. We do have our routines and timetables."

"A police officer has been murdered," said Banks. "I'd say normal operations are pretty much suspended for the moment, wouldn't you? I'll let you know when they can be resumed."

Mary reddened. "I'm sorry. But what should I tell people? I mean, one of our physiotherapists drives all the way over from Skipton, and her first appointment isn't till two this afternoon. Should I phone and cancel?"

"I'm afraid not," said Banks. "We'll want to talk to everyone connected with the place as soon as we possibly can, including the staff. That means we'll need the names and addresses of any personnel who won't be coming in today. Were you here all night?"

"No, sir," said Mary. "I live in Eastvale. The desk isn't staffed twenty-four hours a day. No need. I'm usually gone by six or seven at the latest, depending on how much catching up I have to do. I start at eight, as a rule. In fact, I just arrived. I can't really believe what's going on."

"Are you a police officer, Mary?"

"No, sir. Registered nurse. Retired."

"No need to call me 'sir,' then."

"Oh. Yes. Of course."

"I'm sure it's a shock," Banks said. "Apart from the patients and the nurse, is there anyone else who stops here for the whole night?"

"There's Barry."

"Barry Sadler?"

"Yes. Head groundsman, porter, jack-of-all-trades. He lives in the flat over the old stables, but he's here to help if there's ever a need for heavy lifting or anything, and he does most of the odd jobs himself. Of course, he has a small staff to call in, as and when he needs them. Cleaners, gardeners, a lawn trimmer and topiarist and so on. But they don't live here."

"I'll need a list of their names, too," said Banks. "Do you have a security system?"

Mary paused. "Well, yes, sort of. I mean . . ."

"Yes?"

"The rule is that the front door's locked at midnight, and the burglar alarm is activated."

"But?"

Mary gave Banks a lopsided grin. "You know what it's like. It's a pretty laissez-faire sort of place. If someone wants to go out for a smoke, or stops out late at the pub, you don't want to be turning the burglar alarm on and off, do you?"

"Right," said Banks, who used to smoke back in the days when it was possible to light up almost anywhere. He could hardly imagine the hassle these days, standing out in the cold in winter. Another reason to be grateful he had stopped. "So what you're saying is that there isn't much in the way of security?"

"I suppose that's true."

"And no CCTV?"

"Afraid not. St. Peter's is a charity-run establishment, and the board decided that CCTV was too expensive to be worth it. Also, people don't like being spied on. Especially police officers."

Banks smiled and thanked her for her time. Mary blushed. As he walked away, Banks figured he'd made a conquest there. His charm seemed to work especially well on the over-sixties these days.

Banks turned right at the top of the second flight of stairs, following the sign on the wall to rooms 20 to 30B. The door to Bill Quinn's room was open, and Winsome was still systematically searching through the drawers and cupboards.

Banks stood in the doorway. "Anything for us?"

"Nothing yet," said Winsome. She dangled a ring of house keys. "Just these. They were on the desk. A few clothes in the wardrobe. Toiletries. No mobile. No wallet. No room key."

The room was a mirror image of Lorraine Jenson's. Banks noticed a fishing rod and tackle in one corner and a stack of *Angling Times, Trout & Salmon, Gardeners' World* and *Garden News* magazines on the coffee table. An outdoorsman, then, Bill Quinn. Banks hadn't known that. Still, he hadn't known much about the man at all, a situation that would have to be rectified as quickly as possible. The solution to the crime, he had come to believe over the years, more often than not lies in the victim's character. "I think we'd better send a couple of officers over to search his house. Where does he live?"

"It's already taken care of, guv," said Winsome. "He lives alone in a semi in Rawdon, Leeds, up near the airport."

"Alone? For some reason, I thought he was married with kids."

"He was. His wife's dead, and the kids have flown the coop. They're both at university, one in Hull, the other at Keele. The local police are trying to track them down. His parents, too. They live in Featherstone."

"I didn't know that," Banks said. "About his wife, I mean."

"I found out from his boss, sir. It was very recent. Only a month. Massive stroke."

"Is that what he was in here for? Depression? Grief counseling?"

"No. Neck problems. Physio and massage therapy."

"OK, carry on," said Banks. He stood in the doorway watching Winsome work her way through Bill Quinn's room.

When she had finished, neither of them was any the wiser.

"There doesn't seem to be anything of a personal nature here," said Winsome. "No diary, journal, notebook. Nothing."

"And no note signed by the killer saying 'Meet me by the lake at eleven o'clock tonight'?"

Winsome sighed. "I wish."

"Did it seem disturbed at all when you first came in? I suppose if someone could get into the woods to kill him and take his key, they could also get in his room."

"No signs of it," said Winsome. "Anyway, it might be a bit riskier, actually entering the building."

"Not according to what I've just heard from Mary," said Banks. "There's about as much security here as a kid's piggy bank. Do we know if he had a mobile?"

"I'd be surprised if he didn't," said Winsome. "I mean, these days . . ."

"Well, he doesn't appear to have one now," said Banks. "And that's very peculiar, wouldn't you say?"

"Yes, I would. I always take mine with me when I go out."

"Better make sure we ask his fellow patients, or guests, or whatever they are, and the staff. Someone should remember if he had one. Same with a laptop or a notepad." Banks slipped on the protective gloves he always carried with him to crime scenes and picked up a heavy book Winsome had found in a drawer. *Practical*

Homicide Investigation. Bill Quinn's name was written in the flyleaf. "And this is his only reading material, apart from the fishing and gardening magazines?"
Banks flipped through the book. "It hardly looks like
the sort of reading you'd want to do if you were here
recuperating for a couple of weeks, does it? Some of
these pictures are enough to turn your stomach."

"Well, he was a detective, sir," Winsome said.
"Maybe he was doing a bit of studying?"

"I suppose we can check if he was doing any
courses."

Banks flipped through the rest of the book, but
nothing fell out. He examined it more closely to see if
anything was cellotaped inside, or rolled up and shoved
down the spine, but there was nothing. Nor were the
pages cut to hold a package of some sort, the way he
had cut out *The Way to Keep Fit* to hide his cigarettes
when he was fourteen. It hadn't worked, of course.
His mother had noticed what an unusual title it was,
mixed in with James Bond, the Saint, the Toff, the
Baron and Sherlock Holmes. There was no denying
from which side of the family Banks had inherited his
detective abilities. He had fared about as well with his
copies of *Mayfair, Swank* and *Oui,* too, hidden under a
false bottom in the wardrobe. God only knew what had
tipped her off to that one.

But Bill Quinn's secret wasn't hidden in a hollowed-out book or under the false bottom of a wardrobe; it was between the hard book cover and a loosened endpaper, which had only been very superficially smoothed and pasted back down.

Banks peeled back the edge of the flap and managed to prize out a small, thin buff envelope with the tips of his gloved fingers. He sat down by the coffee table; took the envelope, which was closed but not sealed; and shook out its contents onto the table's surface. Photographs. He turned them all the right way up and set them out in a row. Three four-by-six color prints, run off an ink-jet printer on cheap paper. There were no times or dates printed on them and nothing written on the backs. But they were of good enough quality to show what was happening.

The first one showed Bill Quinn sitting in a bar enjoying an intimate drink with a very beautiful, and very young, woman. She hardly looked old enough to get served, Banks thought. Quinn was leaning in close toward her, and their fingertips were touching on the table. Both had champagne flutes in front of them. The figures in the background were blurred, as were the details of the room, and it was impossible to make out any faces or decor to identify where it had been taken.

In the second photograph, the couple seemed to have moved on to a restaurant. They were sitting in a booth, and the decor seemed darker and more plush, brass, wood and red velour. On the table in front of them, on a white linen tablecloth, were two plates of pasta and two half-full glasses of white wine beside a bottle placed upside down in a metal ice bucket. Their faces were close, as if in intimate conversation, and Quinn's hand rested on top of the woman's thigh.

The third photograph was taken slightly from above and showed Quinn on his back with the young girl, naked now, straddling him, her small breasts jutting forward, nipples hard, dark hair hanging over her shoulders. Quinn's hands rested on her thighs. The girl had an expression of ecstasy on her face, but it was impossible to tell whether it was genuine. Probably not, Banks thought, because the odds were that Bill Quinn had passed out, or had been drugged, by this time. He couldn't be certain, of course, but there was something about the pose, the way Quinn's head rested slackly on the pillow, his body slumped and his hands lying passively on her thighs. Maybe he should have been squeezing her breasts, rearing up and sucking them, kissing them, doing *something*, at any rate. The surroundings were in darkness except for an oblong blot of pale light that must have been a window, and one or two pieces of furniture in the shadows. A hotel room, Banks guessed.

"What do you think?" he asked Winsome, who was perching on the arm of the chair beside him, peering at the photos.

"Escort," she said without missing a beat.

"Perhaps it was more than just a sexual transaction?" Banks suggested. "She's not dressed like a hooker. Those are more like student clothes, not slutty or expensively stylish at all. Could she have been a lover, maybe? He seems a bit out of it in the room, doesn't he? What do you think?"

"She could be a high-priced escort," Winsome said. "I imagine you can order them dressed any way you wish. Maybe he had a thing about student chic. And you're right, guv. There's definitely something odd about that picture in the hotel room. His position. He's sort of inert, when you wouldn't expect him to be."

Banks raised his eyebrows. "Winsome, you surprise me. What should he be doing, do you think?"

"He just seems too passive, that's all," she said. "I'd say that if a man his age was lucky enough to be in bed with a girl her age, a girl as beautiful as her, then he should probably be enjoying himself."

Banks laughed. "Good point, Winsome. Thanks for sharing that." He stood up. "Lots of questions that need answers. Whichever way you look at it, it seems as if our DI Quinn has been a naughty boy. Bit of a dark horse. OK, let's get these photos over to Photographic Services and have some copies made before they get to work on them. It would be interesting to find out when they were taken and who the girl is. Perhaps we can isolate her face so we can show it around without giving away what Quinn was up to. Will you seal off this room, Winsome, and make sure no one enters? I especially don't want any of the media getting a scent of this. They're bound to find out eventually—they always do—but let's keep it under wraps for as long as we can."

"Yes, guv."

Banks glanced at his watch. "I'd better be getting back to the station. I'm sure the boss will be chomping at the bit, wanting to know what's going on, and I need a few favors from her."

2

Since the reorganization, which meant more meetings, recently promoted area commander Catherine Gervaise had added a low round table and four tubular chairs to her office. There was plenty of room for them, and they allowed for a more informal meeting space than the boardroom, where the full team briefings were carried out.

Banks felt the tubes holding up his chair give gently as he sat and leaned back, carefully placing his coffee mug on a rose-patterned coaster on the glass table. The coffee was from Gervaise's personal filter machine, and it was good and strong. There was no doubt that Gervaise had brought a feminine touch to what used to be Superintendent Gristhorpe's very masculine office, though she would never thank anyone for telling her so.

Photographs of her husband and children adorned her desk and the top of the filing cabinet; the walls were painted in muted pastel shades of blue, complemented by a couple of well-framed water lily prints. The whole place seemed somehow more airy and light, with everything neat and in its place.

Most of the books were legal or forensic texts, rather than the rows of leather-bound literary classics Gristhorpe had kept on the shelves, though there was the telltale Stella Rimington autobiography that Gervaise had clearly forgotten to hide. The books were in neat groups, separated by the occasional cup or plaque for archery, dressage or fencing, which had been Gervaise's passions when she had had more time to indulge in such pursuits.

The window was open about three inches, and Banks could hear sounds from Eastvale's cobbled market square—delivery vans, children's squeals, shouted greetings—and the smell of fresh-baked bread from Bob's Bakery made his mouth water. It was going on for nine o'clock. He had been up since just after five, and he hadn't eaten anything yet. Maybe he'd grab a pasty or a sausage roll from Greggs after the meeting.

AC Gervaise was as fresh and businesslike as ever in her navy blue suit and crisp white linen blouse, a little red, blue and yellow needlework around the collar adding a touch of color to its strict lines.

"Is everything in hand?" she asked, sitting opposite Banks and smoothing her skirt.

"It is," said Banks.

The mechanics of a murder investigation could be quite overwhelming, and it was as well to get everything set up and running, make sure everyone knew what his or her job was, before information started arriving in the form of forensics reports, witness statements, alibis and the like. Computer systems such as HOLMES and SOCRATES needed to be set up, and that job would probably fall to DC Gerry Masterson these days, with her IT background, but there was still so much reliance on actual paper in police investigations that plenty of good strong cardboard boxes and large filing cabinets would also be needed. And even though officers used their mobiles most of the time, dedicated landlines had to be set up, and the public needed to be made aware of numbers to call if they had information.

"Did you know DI Quinn personally?" Gervaise asked.

"I met him once," said Banks. "Seemed like a nice enough bloke. But I can't say I knew him. You?"

"Same thing. He was awarded a medal for bravery about three years ago. I was at the presentation."

"I didn't know that."

"Distinguished service record. I don't get this at all, Alan. From everything I've heard so far, it certainly doesn't seem like a random act of violence, or even an old enemy lashing out in anger."

"No," Banks agreed. "The choice of weapon. It all seems very deliberate, as if it were planned. And then there are the photos."

Gervaise's eyes widened. "The what?"

Banks explained about the photographs he'd found in Quinn's forensic textbook. "They should be with Photographic Services by now, though I don't imagine there'll be a lot they can tell us."

"You'd be surprised. Quinn with a young woman, you say?"

"Very young."

"What do you make of it? Blackmail?"

"That seems most likely." Banks paused. "Winsome told me his wife died just a month ago," he went on, "which makes me think that if the photos had been used for blackmail before then, there's a good chance they'd be quite useless after."

"What about his children?"

"It's not the same, is it? Besides, they're grown up. At university."

"Doesn't matter. I know that I wouldn't want my kids to know . . . you know . . ." Gervaise reddened. "If I'd done anything like that."

"I suppose you're right." Banks imagined what Tracy or Brian would say if they knew about some of the things he'd done over the years. Not that infidelity had been a habit, but once was enough. There were other things he'd done, things he wasn't proud of, down in London when he was undercover and living on the edge, or over it sometimes. "But the blackmail still loses a lot of its sting, doesn't it? I mean, your kids can hardly haul you through the divorce courts and take everything you've got, can they?"

Gervaise gave him a look that would freeze a volcano. "You mean take what they're entitled to, surely, Alan?"

"Sorry, ma'am. Yes. Of course."

Gervaise inclined her head regally. "I should think so. And less of the 'ma'am.' It does nothing to excuse your sexist attitudes." She paused. "All I'm saying is that the threat of blackmail might have still been there, if not as strong. Kids. Parents. Even bosses, work colleagues. And it's hardly a good thing for a police officer's career to admit that he left himself open to blackmail. There's been rumors lately, too. A rotten apple. Just rumors, mind, but even so . . ."

"So I heard," said Banks. "You think it was Quinn?"

"All I'm saying is that we need to keep an open mind. Back to the girl. You say she's young?"

"Yes."

"Underage?"

"Just young."

"But if it even *appeared* that way, he could have lost his job," Gervaise pointed out.

"I still think that for Quinn the biggest fear would have been his wife finding out. Anything else he could have brushed off or dealt with. There's no proof the girl's underage. And she's certainly a very attractive woman. Any man would be proud to be seen with her. Christ, some of his mates at work might even have envied him."

Gervaise rolled her eyes.

"What?"

"Never mind. Why do you think he kept the photos with him?"

"I don't know. In my experience, people hang on to the strangest things for the strangest of reasons. Can't complain. It makes our job easier in the long run. Maybe he was proud of himself for pulling her, and they were some sort of trophy? Maybe he was in love with her, and they were all he had left? Maybe he'd just got hold of them? Maybe he was going to pass them on to someone? Quinn obviously didn't expect that he would never return to his room at St. Peter's last night, and that someone else would find them, unless . . ."

"Yes?"

"Unless that was why he left them there. As some form of insurance against something happening to him."

"You mean he was *expecting* to be killed?"

"No, not that. Expecting trouble, maybe, if he'd agreed to meet someone he was wary of, to pay off the blackmailer, say. But I doubt very much that he expected to be hurt or killed. He may have left the pictures in his room as a form of insurance, in case something went wrong. They weren't very well hidden. Quinn was one of us. He knew we'd find them on the first pass. Which means they may be important now that something *has* happened to him. Not just insurance, but evidence. *She* may be important. We need to find her."

"It's not much to go on, though, is it? A handful of photographs?"

"I don't know," said Banks. "I suppose we can get someone to trawl through the escort agency file photos, check the online dating services, see if she turns up on one of them?"

"So you think he was meeting someone he knew out there last night, maybe about something connected with the girl and the photos?"

"I don't know. Perhaps he even thought he was meeting the girl herself? That would cause him to be less on guard."

"Maybe he did meet her," suggested Gervaise. "Maybe she killed him."

"It's possible," Banks agreed. "But it's far too early to speculate. One way or another, I think the pictures are connected with his murder, which is what makes me think of blackmail, that they must have been taken while his wife was still alive to be of any use to anyone." Banks paused. "Any chance of a few extra bodies?"

"You know what it's like these days, Alan. But I'll ask ACC McLaughlin, see what I can do. And I'll take care of the media. I should bring our press officer in on this. One of our own. A high-profile case. I'll set up a conference."

"Appreciated. Winsome and the others are already working on the staff and patient interviews at St. Peter's, but we also need to go over Bill Quinn's old cases, talk to his colleagues, see if anyone had a grudge against him big enough to kill him, any hard men recently released from jail, that sort of thing. I'll start by paying DI Ken Blackstone a visit in Leeds before I head out to Rawdon to check out Quinn's house. Ken knew Bill Quinn fairly well, so he should be able to tell me a bit more about what sort of copper he was. We also need his mobile phone records. Credit card and bank statements, too." Banks glanced over at the trophies on the bookcase. "Er . . . by the way, I noticed a few archery awards there. You don't happen to know anything about crossbows, do you?"

"Afraid not," said Gervaise. "I'm strictly a long-bow person. And I think you'll find that most serious archers disdain crossbows. They're hunters' weapons, mostly, not for sporting competitions."

"Well, they're pretty easy to get hold of," Banks said. "No questions asked, as long as you're over eighteen. They're quiet, and just as deadly as a bullet from the right distance. We need to canvass the shops and Internet sites where people buy these things."

Gervaise scribbled something on her pad. "What else does the choice of weapon tell you?" she asked.

"Well, I don't know much about the mechanics of crossbows, but I assume they could be used just as easily by a man or a woman. They're efficient, anonymous and cold. And quiet. I don't know about the range, but it was a moonlit night, and the killer was obviously able to get close enough and stay hidden in the trees. The bolt had buried itself deep in the chest, pierced the heart, according to Tom Burns. He thinks it was shot from about fifty or sixty feet away. If the killer was hiding behind a tree and wearing dark clothing, the odds are that Quinn wouldn't have known he was there. Or she. Dr. Glendenning will be able to tell us more."

"It sounds to me suspiciously like a hit."

"That's one possibility," said Banks. "Which is why we need to find out if anyone had a reason for making a hit on Bill Quinn. We all make enemies on this job, but it's rare that any of them follow through with their threats, especially in such a cold-blooded way."

"Maybe there was another reason?" Gervaise suggested. "Maybe DI Quinn had got himself into deep trouble. Maybe he'd been sleeping with the enemy. It happens. The gray area. Money. Corruption. Gambling debts. Drugs. Or a woman. The girl in the photograph, for example? She must be somebody's daughter, if not someone's wife or girlfriend. A jealous husband or lover, perhaps? Maybe Quinn thought he was in love with her, and that's why he kept the photos? As you say, a trophy or memento. All he had left of her. A midlife crisis? Perhaps he was hoping to rekindle the romance after his wife had died and he was suddenly free. Maybe we're dealing with a love triangle?" She put her pad down and rubbed her eyes. "Too many questions, too many possibilities. How's DI Cabbot doing, by the way?"

"Fine," said Banks. "She's in Cornwall staying with her father."

"She's due back Monday, right? Clean bill of health?"

"Far as I know," Banks said. Annie Cabbot had been recuperating from a serious operation to remove bullet fragments from an area close to her spine. The wait for surgery had been a long one—she had first had to regain strength from a previous injury to her right lung before the operation on her back could be carried out—but it had been a success in that the fragments had been removed and Annie still had the use of all her limbs. Her recovery had been very slow, however, and involved far more excruciating pain than the surgeons had expected, followed by a great deal of physical therapy, some of it at St. Peter's. The spinal cord was intact, but there had been some disc, muscle and vertebrae problems they hadn't foreseen. Annie had coped well with the pain and uncertainty, Banks thought, getting stronger every day, but he knew that the shooting had also left her with internal demons she would have to deal with eventually. She would be unlikely to go to a psychologist or psychiatrist because of the stigma involved. Rightly or wrongly, seeking professional help for mental problems was viewed as a weakness in the force. Many coppers still maintained that it was bad for the career, and perhaps it was.

"I was thinking of putting her on desk duties for a while, until she gets her sea legs back again. What do you think?"

"For what it's worth, I think Annie should be given a chance to dive right in. It will do her confidence no end of good to start working on a real case again. Even the doctor says her main hurdles now are psychological. She's been through a lot. First she gets shot, then she thinks she's never going to walk again, then she suffers from chronic post-op pain."

"I'm simply pointing out that there are a lot of reasons why DI Cabbot, when she comes back next Monday, should keep a low profile on light duties for a little while and catch her breath before attempting to dash off and solve murders."

"She can be useful. We need her. Annie's bright, she's—"

"I know all about DI Cabbot's qualities as a detective, thank you very much." Gervaise ran a hand across her brow. "Let me think on it," she said. "I know you need more officers on the case. I'll have a word with ACC McLaughlin when I talk to him about the personnel issue. I'll see what he says about DI Cabbot's future here. It's the best I can do."

Banks held her steady gaze. "OK," he said finally. "Thanks."

"Anything else you'd like, while you're at it?"

"Well, a twenty percent pay raise would be nice. And a bigger office."

"Out!" Gervaise picked up a heavy paperweight and threatened to toss it at Banks. "Out, before I throw you out."

Smiling to himself, Banks left the office.

Banks munched on his Greggs sausage roll as he guided the Porsche toward the A1, the fourth movement of Mahler's *Resurrection Symphony* playing loudly on the powerful stereo system. It helped that this was a vocal movement. He had always liked Mahler's lieder, and he had only recently been getting to like the symphonies a lot, having spurned them as boring and bombastic in the past. Was this something that happened when you got older? Failing eyesight, mysterious aches and pains, enjoying Mahler? Would Wagner be next?

The last time Banks had been to Leeds, he remembered, it was to help his daughter, Tracy, move a few months ago. She had shared a house in Headingley with two other girls, but it hadn't worked out. Tracy had suffered a number of traumatic events around the time Annie had been shot, and after a brief period of depression and withdrawal, she had decided to change her life.

That first meant moving from Leeds to Newcastle, which was a little further from Eastvale, but not so much as to make a big difference. It also meant leaving a dead-end job and getting back onto a career track again. She had got a part-time administrative position at the university and enrolled in the master's program in history, with a view to moving into teaching once she felt a bit more secure in her qualifications.

It was also time to live alone, she had told Banks, so she had rented a tiny bedsit close to the converted riverside area, and both Banks and his ex-wife Sandra were helping her with the rent until she got on her feet. Her brother, Brian, whose band the Blue Lamps seemed to be going from strength to strength, had also been most generous. In an odd way, Banks thought, they were starting to act like a family again, though he knew that the gap between him and Sandra was unbridgeable. He had visited Tracy once already in Newcastle and had taken her across the river to the Sage to see the Unthanks in concert, then for a drink after. They had had a good time, and he was looking forward to doing it again.

The A1 was a nightmare. Mile after mile of roadworks, down to one lane each way from Leeming to Wetherby, and a fifty-mile-per-hour limit, which everyone obeyed because the cameras averaged out your speed over the whole distance. As a result, it took well over an hour and a half before Banks approached the eastern outskirts of Leeds. The Porsche didn't like it at all; it had never been happy at fifty miles per hour. He had been thinking of selling the car ever since he had inherited it from his brother, but for one reason or another he had never got around to it. Now it was getting a bit shabby and starting to feel comfortable, like a favorite old jacket, jeans or a pair of gloves, and the sound system was a corker, so he reckoned he would probably keep it until it bit the dust.

Millgarth was an ugly, redbrick fortress-style building at the bottom of Eastgate in Leeds city center. DI Ken Blackstone wanted to hang around his tiny, cluttered office no more than Banks did, so they headed out into the spring sunshine, walked up the Headrow as far as Primark, then turned left down Briggate, a pedestrian precinct crowded with shoppers. There used to be a Borders near the intersection, Banks remembered fondly, but it was gone now, and he lamented its passing. There was a Pizza Hut in its place.

Blackstone was a snappy dresser, and today he wore a light wool suit, a button-down Oxford shirt and a rather flamboyant tie. With the tufts of hair over his ears, and his wire-rimmed glasses, Blackstone had always reminded Banks more of an academic than a copper. In fact, the older he got, the more he came to resemble some of the photos Banks had seen of the poet Philip Larkin.

Banks and Blackstone decided against the posh Harvey Nichols café in the Victoria Quarter and plumped for Whitelocks, an eighteenth-century pub in an alley off Briggate, near Marks & Spencer. The alley was narrow and high, with the pub stretching down one side, much longer than it was deep, and a row of benches down the other side, against the wall, with a few tables and stools where space permitted. Not much light got in at any time of the day, but it was always a popular spot with the city-center workers and the student crowd. It was lunchtime, so they were lucky to get space on the bench next to a group of office girls discussing a wedding one of them had just attended in Cyprus.

"You hang on to the seats, Alan," said Blackstone. "I'll get us a couple of pints and something to eat."

"Make mine a shandy," said Banks. "I've got to drive. And steak-and-kidney pie and chips."

He reached for his wallet, but Blackstone brushed the gesture aside and headed into the pub. He had to stoop to get through the old, low door. People were much shorter in the eighteenth century. Banks remembered that the food was served canteen-style behind the counter beside the bar, so when Blackstone came back he carried the drinks first, then went back for the plates of steaming pie and chips.

"And Josie got so drunk we had to take her to hospital," one of the office girls said. "She nearly died of alcohol poisoning." The others laughed.

"It's terrible news," said Blackstone, pushing his glasses up the bridge of his nose. "First Sonia, then Bill. I can hardly bloody believe it. Not only one of us, but Bill."

"Sonia was his wife, right?"

"Twenty-five years. I was at their silver wedding anniversary do last December."

"How old was Bill, exactly?"

"Just turned forty-nine."

"How did he take her death?"

"How do you think? He was devoted to her. He was devastated, naturally. This neck business that got him into St. Peter's was a bit of an excuse, if you ask me. Not that he hadn't been having problems on and off for years. But I'd have said he was on the verge of a breakdown. Depressed, too. Couldn't sleep."

"Winsome said it was a massive stroke."

"Sonia was always a bit frail. Heart problems. I think that was why Bill was especially protective of her. Some people said he was too much under her thumb, but it wasn't really like that. He adored her. It was sudden, a stroke, yes."

They both paused for a moment. Banks didn't know about Ken, but he often felt a brief stab of worry about his own mortality these days. He contemplated his steak-and-kidney pie. He'd already eaten a sausage roll for breakfast. Not one vegetable all day, unless you counted the chips. Hardly the healthy diet he'd been promising himself since his last visit to the doctor. Still, he had stopped smoking years ago, had cut down on his drinking a bit recently, and he hardly ever put on any weight. Surely that had to be a good thing?

"Poor sod," said Banks.

Blackstone raised his glass. "I'll drink to that. And to life."

They clinked glasses. One of the office girls smiled at Banks. "Birthday?"

"Something like that," he said. The girls moved on to boasting about drunken exploits in Sharm el-Sheikh, paying no further attention to Banks and Blackstone, who spoke quietly anyway. A gust of warm wind blew along the alley and carried just a hint of the summer to come.

"There are a couple of things I'd like to know," said Banks, glancing around. "First off, it looked very much like a professional hit." Banks described what they had deduced so far about the crime scene.

Blackstone thought for a moment. "Well, if access was as easy as you say, anyone could have done it, though it would have had to have been someone who knew Bill was there, I suppose, someone who knew his habits and the lie of the land, or somehow managed to lure him down to the edge of the woods. And what professional hit man uses a crossbow? Have you considered an inside job, or helper, at any rate?"

"Naturally," said Banks. "We're open to just about anything at the moment, and we'll be checking everyone out. But there are a few problems with that theory. How would someone on the inside get rid of the murder weapon, for example? As far as I'm concerned, the most likely scenario is that it was someone Quinn put away, a criminal with a grudge and a taste for revenge."

One of the office girls lowered her voice, but not quite enough. "And the last night we were there Cathy pissed herself right in the main street. It was simply dripping down her legs. Like something out of *Bridesmaids.* Talk about embarrassed! Laugh? I nearly died. Jenny said we should find a Boots and buy her some adult nappies."

"Why do it at St. Peter's?" Blackstone asked. "Have you thought about that? If someone wanted Bill out of the way, there must have been better opportunities, surely?"

"Not necessarily, especially if timing was an issue. My guess is that it was easier. He was a sitting duck at St. Peter's. It might have been a bit harder to isolate him in the city. More chance of witnesses there, too. And I wouldn't be surprised if there was an element of bravado. It probably appealed to the killer's warped sense of humor to kill a cop in a place full of cops, even though they were disabled, or geriatric, for the most part." Banks paused. "But that begs a few questions."

"Like what?"

"Like how did the killer find out Bill Quinn was at St. Peter's in the first place?"

"It wasn't a secret. I mean, anyone could have known, not only people on the inside with him, but others, friends, family, even his coll—" Blackstone stopped, and his eyes hardened. "Wait a minute, Alan. Are you saying what I think you're saying?"

"We have to consider it, Ken. The possibility of a mole in Quinn's team, someone in the department. There have been rumors, you know."

"You think it's Bill? So what's going to happen now? The works? Suspend operations, seize all the files? Send in Professional Standards or the Independent Police Complaints Commission?"

"I hope it won't come to that," said Banks. "We're not sure about anything yet. All I'm saying is that it's an angle we have to consider along with all the others until we can rule it out. Someone knew where to find him."

"Any trace evidence? Forensics?"

"None yet. His pockets had been emptied, and his mobile is missing. We're tracking down the provider, then at least we'll have a list of calls to and from. The CSIs are working on the usual—footprints, fabrics, DNA, fingerprints. The area near the tree where they think the killer stood looks promising."

"So what do you want from me?"

"Area Commander Gervaise will be asking for full details of Bill Quinn's cases from the brass, and for a list of villains he's put away, along with their release dates, but I thought I'd just pick your brains in the meantime, get a head start."

Blackstone rubbed his cheeks. "Another drink first?"

"Not for me, thanks, Ken."

Blackstone studied the remains of his pint. "No. I suppose I can make do with what I've got left, too. Where to begin?"

"Wherever you want."

"Well, Bill's been around for a while. You'll have quite a job on your hands going through the minutiae of his career."

"Let's start at the top, then. Any counterterrorism investigations?"

"We try to leave that sort of thing to Special Branch. Of course, West Yorkshire can't avoid getting in on the peripheries at times, especially in Bradford or Dewsbury and some parts of Leeds, but nothing comes immediately to mind. Surely you don't believe this was some sort of a fatwa, do you?"

"Just casting flies on the water."

"Aye. One thing I can tell you, though. It was Bill helped put away Harry Lake nearly twenty years ago. He was a young DS then, and it didn't do his career any harm, I can tell you."

Banks whistled between his teeth. Harry Lake was famous enough to have had books written about him. He had abducted, tortured and killed four women in the Bradford area in the early nineties, cut them up and boiled the parts. Like the even more infamous Dennis Nilsen, he was only caught when the body pieces he'd flushed down the toilet blocked the drains, and a human hand surfaced in one of his neighbors' toilet bowls.

"He can't be out yet, surely?" said Banks.

"I don't think he'll ever get out. He's in Broadmoor. But it's worth checking. He always swore revenge, and maybe he persuaded some sick follower to do his dirty work for him? You know what it's like. People like him get marriage proposals, offers of continuing his work for him. According to the prison governor, he gets plenty of those."

Banks made a note. "There must be more?"

"I suppose his other most famous case was his biggest failure. Well, not his really."

"Oh?"

"The Rachel Hewitt business."

"Rachel Hewitt? Isn't she that girl whose parents keep cropping up in the news, the girl who disappeared in Latvia, or wherever?"

"Estonia, actually. Tallinn. Six years ago. Yes. And they were in the news again not too long ago. That phone-hacking inquiry. You might have heard. They've been complaining about being hounded by the media, phones tapped, private papers and diaries stolen and published. The sister went off the rails, apparently, and the press had a feeding frenzy."

"Bill Quinn worked that case?"

"Bill worked this end, such as it was. Family and friends. Rachel's background. The Tallinn police worked the actual disappearance. But Bill spent about a week out there liaising quite early in the investigation. Rachel was a West Yorkshire girl, from Drighlington, part of City & Holbeck Division, and he drew the short straw, depending on how you look at it. But with the local police running the investigation, and in a foreign country with different ways of doing things, he didn't stand much of a chance. It was more of a show of strength and solidarity, really, and a bit of a PR exercise, if truth be told. Otherwise they'd have sent in a team."

"They didn't?"

"No. The British embassy was involved, of course, but they don't carry out criminal investigations in foreign countries. It was strictly Tallinn's case. Nobody expected Bill to solve it where the locals had failed. That was back in the summer of 2006. As expected, he got precisely nowhere, but he did get his photo in the papers quite often, and he did a few press conferences with the parents of the missing girl."

"The Hewitts have had to use the media to keep their daughter's name in the public eye, haven't they?"

"It's a two-edged sword. You don't get owt for nowt from those bastards."

"And what role did Bill play?"

"As I said, he was just a glorified consultant, really."

"He's not been implicated in the hacking business?"

"Bill? Good lord, no. Though some days it seems we've all been tarred with the same brush."

"So it's unlikely to be connected with his murder?"

"I can't see how it could be. Nothing's changed. Rachel still hasn't been found. Her parents insist she's being kept alive somewhere, but we're all pretty certain she's dead. Thing is, it haunted Bill. I don't think he ever quite got over not solving it, not finding her. He was convinced she was already dead, of course, but I think he wanted to provide the parents with some sort of explanation, proof, some positive outcome. A body, for example."

"Anything else I should be looking at?"

"Just the usual. Dozens of petty villains, domestic killings. What you'd expect from a long career in detective work. He's put away burglars, murderers, muggers, embezzlers, gangsters and hard men. None of them stand out much except for Harry Lake, and maybe Steve Lambert, that big property developer, the one who paid someone to murder his wife about three years ago."

"I remember that one," said Banks. "Didn't he claim someone broke in, and she was stabbed while interrupting a robbery?"

"That's right. Appeared to have a watertight alibi, too. The usual citizens above suspicion. But Bill stuck at it, followed the money trail, found the bloke he'd hired, along with a strong forensic connection to the scene. It was a solid case in the end, and Lambert went down swearing revenge."

"But he's still inside, isn't he?"

"If he hired someone to kill his wife . . ."

"Long tentacles?"

"Possibly."

"I'll bear it in mind. Mostly what we should look at first, though, is anyone he put away who's actually come out recently, and anyone he's pissed off who's still wandering free."

"There'll be a few. I'll see if I can narrow things down a bit for you."

"Appreciate it, Ken."

"All this . . . Sorry. Bill was a mate, that's all. It's getting to me."

"I know, and I'm sorry, too. What about more recently? What was he working on when he died?"

Blackstone finished off his drink and stared at the empty glass. "Well, as you know, he was off duty for a couple of weeks with his neck problems before he went into St. Peter's, and before that he had a couple of weeks' leave after Sonia . . . you know. Before that he was working with a specially formed citywide team of detectives on a long-term surveillance and intelligence-gathering mission."

"What was it?"

"Just the tip of the iceberg. It started with a gang of loan sharks. They operate around the poorest estates in the city, mostly targeting new immigrants, as often as not illegals, asylum seekers or unregistered migrants who still owe a bloody fortune for their staff agency fees, transport, lodgings and food. And, in some cases, for the risk of smuggling them in. Some of them live in dormitories in converted barns, or what have you, outside the city, but a lot of them have managed somehow or other to get hold of council houses, illegal sublets from fellow countrymen, mostly. Of course, the jobs they were promised and had to pay so much for didn't materialize, or they ended up cleaning out pig sties or public conveniences for ten quid a week. Unless they're attractive girls, of course, and then . . ."

"I get the picture," said Banks. He thought once more of Quinn's photographs, the young girl, and how she reminded him of a young girl some years ago, involved in the case during which his brother had been murdered. That girl had been trafficked from Eastern Europe, along with many others. It still went on.

It was going to be tricky, broaching the subject of Quinn's infidelity and susceptibility to blackmail to Ken, but it had to be done, gently or otherwise. Sometimes, Banks felt, it was best to jump right in and dodge the retaliation, if it came. "We found some photos of Bill Quinn with a young girl—and I mean young, Ken—hidden in his room."

"Sexual?"

"Well, they weren't taken at a vicar's tea party."

"And what do you make of this?"

"I'm not sure, but blackmail comes to mind."

Blackstone thrust his head forward. "Are you suggesting that Bill was in someone's pocket?"

"No. I'm asking you if you think it possible that he was being blackmailed. I assume that he wouldn't have wanted his wife to know, and I doubt that he'd have said anything to his friends."

"Sonia? She'd have kill— No, he wouldn't have wanted her to know. Sonia was a naïve, trusting soul. Bill was always very protective toward her. He genuinely loved her. Something like that . . . well, it would have devastated her. And if you're asking does it surprise me that he had a bit on the side, yes it does. Very much."

"Nobody's judging him, Ken."

"But they will. You're starting already."

"Ken, I'm investigating his *murder*. I need to know. Surely you, of all people, can understand that?"

Blackstone ran his hand over his sparse hair. "Shit. OK. I know. It just . . ."

"Did he play away from home?"

"No. I was only away from home with him once. A conference in Lyon, France. Interpol. Christ, he was only human. He'd look, like the rest of us. Married, but not dead. He'd watch them walk by, sitting at a café or somewhere, look a bit wistful. We both did. For crying out loud, there are lots of pretty girls in Lyon."

"But he didn't get up to anything?"

"Not that I know of."

"Would you have known?"

"I wasn't his keeper, if that's what you mean. We didn't share a room. We weren't together twenty-four hours a day. But no, I don't think he did. I think I would have known. When were they taken, these pictures?"

"We don't know. Has he been anywhere since his wife died? Any conferences, holidays?"

"Are you bloody joking, Alan? It was only a month ago. The man was shattered. A wreck. There's no way anything like what you're talking about happened between Sonia's death and now."

"OK. Appreciate it, Ken. Was he working under-cover on this loan-sharking case?"

"No, it was all quite open and aboveboard. The chief villain's a bloke called Warren Corrigan. Small-time crook, really, or at least he started that way. Has his office in the back room of a pub called the Black Bull in Seacroft. Fancies himself as a sort of latter-day Kray. You know, man of the people, pillar of the community, tray of tea from Mum. We've got him down for a few assaults, demanding money with threats and so on, but nobody will talk. Everyone's too scared. We've got two bodies already that we're not entirely sure he didn't have something to do with, but we can't prove anything."

"Bodies?"

"Yes. Suicides. They finally cracked under the pressure of their debts, according to friends and family. But more than that, nobody will say. The most recent was a trafficked Romanian girl with needle marks up and down both arms. Fifteen years old. The girl. She couldn't turn enough tricks to pay the interest. We've been trying to contact her parents."

"Shit," said Banks. He thought of the girl in the photographs again. At least from what he had been able to make out, she seemed healthy enough, and most likely older than fifteen, though sometimes it was hard to tell. No visible needle tracks, but then the quality of the photo wasn't that sharp. "Does this Corrigan have any connection with the people-trafficking, the drugs?"

"Not that we can prove," said Blackstone. "But it seems more than likely. It's one of the things Quinn and the team were checking out."

"Would he have had a good reason for wanting Quinn dead?"

"I can't see it. Killing a cop seems a bit extreme."

"Did Corrigan know the team was on to him?"

"He knew. At this stage, it was all a bit of a cat-and-mouse game to him."

"Are you working this case, too?"

"No. Bill and I chatted about it once in a while over a pint. Shop talk."

"Who's on his team?"

"Nick Gwillam's probably the one you want to talk to," said Blackstone. "Trading Standards, Illegal Money Lending Unit. There's a bloke from SOCA and a couple of DCs, too, but Gwillam's your best bet. He worked closest with Bill on it."

"Can you fix up a chat? Just informal at this stage."

"He's off until Monday, but I'm sure I'll be able to arrange something. I'll let you know."

"Thanks, Ken. I know this is tough for you. Has Corrigan uttered any threats against Quinn specifically, or against any members of the team?"

"Not that I know of. He's too smart for that. At least, Bill never mentioned it. We've had him in for questioning a couple of times, so he knows he's on our radar, and I helped out on one of the interviews. Played the good cop. It didn't work. Slippery bastard. Cocky as hell. I wouldn't put anything past him. But he may be a bit . . . I don't know . . . too overconfident to feel the need to eliminate Bill. I would imagine Corrigan always believes he'll come out on top without having to do anything but intimidate his powerless victims on the estates. Or get someone else to do it. He's not exactly a hard man himself. And if he did do it, you can be sure he's got a solid alibi. Probably having dinner with the mayor or someone."

Banks had come across villains like Corrigan before. They were bottom-feeders, parasites who exploited the poorest, most vulnerable members of society. His victims were unskilled laborers or jobless workers far from home, often from very poor communities, with no means of returning and nowhere else to go; they were frightened people who didn't even speak the language or understand the terms of interest being offered, living constantly under the threat of violence to themselves or their families. And people like Corrigan always seemed to get away with it.

"Can you put together a preliminary file on this Corrigan for me?" Banks asked. "Links to Quinn, to any informants, undercover officers, members of the trafficking chain, that sort of thing. If you think it's just the tip of the iceberg, it could be a big operation, and there could be enough at stake to drive someone to murder a copper."

"I'll see what I can do."

"Thanks, Ken. Is there any way this Corrigan could have known Quinn would be at St. Peter's for two weeks?"

"Not unless somebody told him. For all I know, Bill might have told him himself. Or one of the team members."

"Why would anyone do that?"

"Like I said, it was all a bit of a game to Corrigan, and Bill played along sometimes in the hopes of getting some titbit out of him. You know, how's the family, how's that bad neck of yours coming along. All very pally, the veneer of civilized conversation." Blackstone snorted. "Sometimes I think we should have just gone in with the rubber hosepipes."

"Maybe," said Banks. "But one way or another we'll get to the truth."

"And if anyone on Bill's team *was* responsible for tipping off Corrigan as to his whereabouts," Blackstone went on, "I'll have his balls, civilized conversation or not. Have you considered that it might have been the girl herself? The one in the photographs you told me about? As I remember, there was a girl with a crossbow in a James Bond movie once. Not that I use those things as my yardstick for real life, you understand, but it's a weapon that could be as easily used by a woman as a man."

"We're keeping an open mind. *For Your Eyes Only.* That was the movie."

"I can never remember titles. You'll keep me posted on developments?"

"Will do."

Blackstone glanced at his watch. "I'd better get back." He touched Banks's shoulder briefly. "Take care."

Banks's conversation with Blackstone had depressed and exhausted him. It was a sudden and unwelcome reminder of the filth and sewage he had so often had to wade through in his job. The depth of man's inhumanity to his fellow man never ceased to amaze and appall him. It had been a quiet winter, and since the escapade with Tracy and Annie, life and work had generally been ticking along at a manageable, if rather dull, rate. Now this: a potentially compromised cop murdered, a thug running riot with the law. Still, this was what he had signed up for, not sitting at a desk making budget cuts or fudging crime statistics.

He finished his drink and realized that he had better call in at Bill Quinn's home in Rawdon before heading back to Eastvale. Before he went, though, he felt he needed a treat, the way his mother always used to buy him a toy soldier or a Dinky car after a visit to the dentist. He had no one to buy it for him—his mother was in Peterborough, unless she and his father had taken off on another cruise—but he could do it himself. He bought a lot of stuff online these days, given that he lived in such a remote place, but it was always a treat to go into a real record shop or bookshop and browse around the piles of special offers and racks of new releases. This time, after half an hour in HMV, he came out with Kate Royal's *A Lesson in Love*, Martin Carthy's *Essential* two-CD set and a DVD box set of the first season of *Treme* on sale for fifteen quid.

Banks pulled up outside Bill Quinn's home in Rawdon early that afternoon. There was quite a mix of houses in the area, he had noticed, trying to find his way after the satnav had given up. Bungalows rubbed shoulders with brick terraces, and they, in turn, stood alongside detached and semidetached houses with lower halves of exposed stone and upper halves fake Tudor, dark beams and white stucco. Quinn's semi must have cost a bob or two, Banks thought, but it probably wasn't out of his price range if he had bought at the right time and if his wife had also worked. Two kids at university wouldn't help, though, especially these days. Still, it was too soon for theories about Quinn's financial situation; they should have his bank account details as well as his mobile phone log before too long. For now, they were interested in anything that seemed out of place.

The search team was already at work, and Banks recognized DS Keith Palmer, the officer in charge, who was standing in the doorway. "Anything yet?" Banks asked.

Palmer led Banks into the house, where officers were busy searching through the sideboard drawers in the front hall. "Not yet," Palmer said, leading him to the kitchen at the back. "But you might find this interesting."

One of the small glass panels on the door had been broken, and the door itself was an inch or so ajar. It had to be connected with Quinn's murder, Banks thought, otherwise it would be too much of a coincidence. Banks glanced at the floor and saw the glass fragments scattered over the fake wood finish. "There's no mess, except in Quinn's study," Palmer went on, "and even that is pretty orderly. Whoever did this probably knew what he was looking for. Want the guided tour?"

"Sure." Banks glanced around the kitchen. Washed dishes were piled neatly in the metal rack on the draining board, small sandwich plates, cups and glasses. The rubbish bin was full of discarded takeaway containers, and the green box by the door held mostly empty Bell's bottles. Banks followed Palmer.

The living room was neat and tidy, as Palmer had indicated, though there was a thin layer of dust on the mantelpiece, and Banks guessed that while Quinn had kept things more or less in order, he hadn't taken much of an interest in housework since his wife's death. There was a small bookcase in the hall that held a number of angling, football, gardening and cooking DVDs, a few movies that had been given away in the Sunday papers over the past year or so and several books, mostly on Quinn's hobbies, but mixed in with book club novels with titles like *Twiddling My Fingers in Timbuktu*, *Dwarf Throwing in Darwin* or *Blowing Eggs in Uzbekistan*, nestling beside a couple well-thumbed Mills and Boons.

Upstairs were four bedrooms, the smallest of them set up as a study. The cabinets and drawers stood open, covered with fingerprint powder. A cheap ink-jet printer sat on the desk. Banks glanced down at the power-socket bar and saw one charger plugged in that wasn't connected to anything. "Laptop?" he asked Palmer.

"Looks that way. If so, it's gone."

"Any signs of a desktop?"

"No. That was it."

"Bugger. No files, no e-mails, nothing."

"We could access the server. There could be e-mails stored there. But someone's been thorough. If there were any portable storage devices, flash drives and the like, they've also been taken."

"Any prints?"

"Only Quinn's."

"I'll have a closer look here later. Let's move on."

Two of the bedrooms were obviously the children's and had been for a number of years. Now that they were both grown up, they probably just stayed there when they came back from university for the holidays. One was a light airy space containing a storage unit stuffed with old dolls and a bookcase full of classics. Banks pulled out a copy of *Middlemarch* and saw the inscription, "To Jessica with love from Auntie Jennifer on your 15th birthday." Banks whistled between his teeth. Reading *Middlemarch* at fifteen was pretty good going; reading *Middlemarch* at any age was pretty good going. Like most people, Banks had watched it on TV.

The second room, which bore a plaque marking it as "Robbie's Room," was much darker in color scheme and had little sign of childhood memorabilia other than a collection of model boats, but there were a few festival and concert posters on the walls: Green Man Festival 2010, Glastonbury 2009, Elbow, Kaiser Chiefs, Paolo Nutini. Banks noticed the electric guitar resting against a small amp in one corner. It reminded him of his own son, Brian. No doubt Quinn's son owned at least one other guitar, probably acoustic; he wouldn't go off to university for weeks on end without one. There was also a compact CD player but very few CDs. He probably downloaded most of his music. As for books, there were a few science fiction and fantasy titles, old copies of *Mojo,* and that was it.

The third bedroom, the largest, clearly belonged to Quinn and his wife. Like the living room, it was tidy, the bed made, no discarded clothing on the floor, but there was more dust on the windowsill. The wardrobe held a hamper full of dirty laundry. Banks wondered what would happen to it now that its owner was dead. Would it ever be washed? Maybe one of Quinn's children would wash it and give it to Oxfam.

"Better go through that lot, too," Banks said to DS Palmer. "You never know what people leave in their pockets and put in the wash."

"Don't worry," said Palmer. "We have. Not even so much as a used tissue or bus ticket. And there are no signs of disturbance in any of the bedrooms."

Banks and Palmer returned to the study. Set aside at the edge of the desk was a small heap of file folders. "We picked those up off the floor," Palmer said. "It's mostly just a lot of general correspondence, day-to-day stuff, bills and so on. We'll take it all in and go through it in detail, but these may be of more immediate interest."

Banks doubted it. Not if someone had already been through the place first. He picked up the first folder.

Harry Lake. Like most good detectives, Quinn sup-
plemented his official notes and reports with his own
observations. These often consisted of intuitions, gut
feelings and imaginative ramblings that wouldn't make
it past his SIO's scrutiny. They might be worth taking
back to the station and studying, but Banks wouldn't
give them a high priority. If there had been anything
of interest to him in Quinn's study, it would be gone
now. He flipped through the stack. There was nothing
on Warren Corrigan or Stephen Lambert he noticed,
but also very little on Rachel Hewitt, the failure that
had apparently haunted him. If Quinn had been in the
habit of keeping personal files on all his cases, or at least
his major cases, then what was missing would probably
reveal far more than what was present, even though a
clever villain would know to take a few irrelevant files
along with the important one, just to muddy the waters.

Banks picked up some more folders and flipped
quickly through them. He found a mix of handwritten
notes and printed pages, yellow stickies and file cards,
along with the occasional photocopy—a parking ticket,
train ticket, passport photo, the usual odds and ends
of an investigation. As a matter of routine, he checked
the undersides of the drawers and backs of the filing
cabinets to see if anything had been taped to them, but
found nothing.

One thing he did find, in a folder stuffed with old Visa bills, was a photograph. Either the burglar had seen it and decided it was of no interest to him, or he had missed it. Curious, Banks pulled it out. It was of a young girl, aged about eighteen or nineteen, cropped from a group shot. Her arms were stretched out sideways, as if wrapped around the people on either side of her, both of whom were represented only by their shoulders.

At first Banks felt a tremor of excitement because he thought it might have been the girl in Quinn's photos, but it clearly wasn't her, even allowing for the possibility of disguise. This girl had fine golden-blond hair down to her shoulders. It looked as if it had been braided, then left free to tumble. She had a small nose in the center of an oval face, an appealing overbite and light blue eyes, set in the most delicate porcelain complexion. The girl in the photo with Quinn was darker-skinned, more exotic, with fuller lips and dark eyes. This one was an English rose. So who was it? She seemed familiar, a face he had seen, perhaps more than once, and he guessed that she was Rachel Hewitt. Keith Palmer couldn't help him. Just in case Banks was completely out on a limb he took the photo downstairs and checked it against the framed family shots he had noticed on the sideboard. It certainly wasn't Quinn's daughter. She had coarser brown hair, was carrying far more weight, and could by no means be said to have a porcelain complexion.

And when he looked up from the family photo, he got the shock of his life to see the same face, this time in the living, breathing flesh, standing right in front of him, a red-faced PC behind her, saying, "I'm sorry, sir, I couldn't stop her. She says she's Jessica Quinn, DI Quinn's daughter. She lives here."

"I came as soon as I could," said Jessica, brushing past Banks and going into the living room. "What's going on? What are all those people doing here? Have they been searching the house? Have they been in my room?"

Her voice was rising to a hysterical pitch. Banks put his arm on her shoulder, but she shook him off. "Jessica—"

"You can't do this. You just can't do this. It's an invasion of privacy. My father will . . . my father . . ."

And suddenly she crumpled and fell in tears on the sofa. Banks sat down opposite her in an armchair. It was best to let her cry, he thought, as the great chest-racking sobs came from her, even though she buried her face in a cushion. He gestured for DS Palmer to leave the room and carry on with the search. Jessica was still a little overweight, as she was in the family photo, and the baggy jumper and shapeless peasant skirt she wore didn't flatter her. Her face, when Banks saw it again, was pretty enough, but dotted with teenage acne as well as streaked with tears. Her tangled hair hadn't been washed or brushed for a few days. She seemed to be what his old politically incorrect colleague DS Jim Hatchley would have described as "a hairy-legged eco-feminist," though Banks could vouch for neither the legs nor the eco-feminism.

"Jessica," he said when she had been quiet for a while, "I'm sorry. I'm sorry you had to walk in on this. But it has to be done, and quickly."

Jessica reached into her shoulder bag for a tissue and rubbed her eyes and nose. "I know. I'm sorry, too," she said. "It was just driving up here all by myself, knowing about Dad . . . it got to me. I just got into a terrible state. I couldn't stop thinking about it. I was lucky I didn't have an accident."

"One of our cars would have brought you."

"No, I wanted to drive myself. Really. I needed . . . just to be alone. The last place I wanted to be was in the back of a police car. I used to think it was exciting when I was young, when Dad . . ." She started crying again, more softly this time, and took out another tissue. "You must think I'm a terrible softie."

"Not at all," said Banks. "Where's your brother?"

"Robbie's on his way. We talked on the mobile. He was just leaving when I got to my turn-off. You know Keele. It's in the middle of bloody nowhere, and he doesn't have a car. I just had to drive along the M62." Her eyes filled with tears again. "I can't believe this. How could it happen? First Mum, and now Dad. My God, we're orphans now." She cried again.

"I know it's a terrible shock," said Banks, "but I do need to ask you some questions. How about a cup of tea before we start? It's a bit of a cliché, but I could really do with one myself."

Banks followed Jessica into the kitchen. He offered to make the tea, but she told him to sit down, she knew where everything was. Banks sat at the solid pine table while Jessica set about boiling the kettle and putting two tea bags into a white teapot with red hearts all over it. The kettle didn't take long. As she poured the boiling water, Jessica looked at the sink and rubbed her sleeve across her eyes. "Typical Dad. He just lets things pile up like that. All neat and tidy and clean, of course, but honestly, I mean, who else would just leave a dish rack full of dishes if he knew he was going away for two weeks? And I'll bet he didn't think to empty out the fridge. I don't even dare open it."

"It's not too bad," said Banks. "There's a bit of green stuff here and there, but at least it doesn't smell. The milk's off." His own fridge went like that occasionally, too, with things changing color and starting to smell a bit, but he saw no point in admitting that to Jessica.

"*Men*. Just sugar do, then?"

"Please. Two teaspoons."

The tea ready, Jessica poured, set the two mugs down on the table and slumped in a chair, resting her chin in her hands. "I just can't get my head around this." She gave Banks a sudden sharp glance. "What happened? Will I have to identify the body?"

"Somebody will," said Banks. "You or your brother. Don't worry. The family liaison officer will deal with all that. She should be here soon. Didn't they tell you what happened?"

"Only that he was dead."

"He was murdered, Jessica. That's why we're here. That's why there are men searching the house."

"Murdered? Dad? But he wasn't even at work. He was—"

"I know. He was killed in the grounds of St. Peter's. It was quick. He wouldn't have suffered."

Her eyes brimmed with tears again. "They always say that. How do you know? I'll bet you suffer a lot if you know you'll be dead in even a split second."

There was no reply to that. Banks sipped the hot, sweet tea. Just what he needed.

"There's been a break-in here," he said. "We think it's connected. They've been through your dad's study. Maybe you can help us determine what's missing."

"I'm only here in the holidays. I wouldn't know what's supposed to be where, especially in Dad's study. None of us were allowed in there."

"Do you know whether your father owned a laptop?"

"Yes."

Well, that was one question answered, but it begged another. "Did he use it much? I'm wondering why he didn't take it with him to St. Peter's. I mean, laptops are small and light enough to carry around. That's what they're for. As far as I know, they had Wi-Fi available up there."

Jessica gave him a sad, indulgent smile. "Dad was such a Luddite when it came to things like that. Oh, he had one—he could just about do e-mail and stuff like that—but it was always me or Robbie who had to sort it out for him whenever we came up. He was always messing it up, getting viruses, ignoring error messages. If something didn't work immediately, he just kept pressing the 'enter' key or clicking the mouse. Honestly, he'd have about ten copies of Internet Explorer open at the same time, and he wondered why it was running so slowly. He was hopeless."

"Did he use it for writing or anything else? Facebook?"

"Writing? Dad hated writing. Reports were the bane of his life. And Facebook . . . well, I'd blush if I had to tell you what he thought about social networks. No, if anything, he probably used it a bit for surfing the Internet, you know, fishing and gardening sites, that sort of thing. And he did manage to work out Skype so we could talk for free during term time. Half the time he couldn't get the video bit working, though, so it was voice only."

"Games?"

"I doubt it. He wasn't much of a one for computer games. Now trivia, that's another thing. He probably used Wikipedia a lot."

Banks smiled. He supposed, then, that there wasn't much, if anything, of value on Quinn's laptop, except, perhaps, for some e-mails. Whoever had taken it had probably done so as a safety measure, just in case there was something incriminating on it or because he believed it contained information he wanted. In either case, he was probably out of luck. If Quinn wasn't a big computer fan, they had a far better hope of finding something interesting in his phone call logs than in his e-mails, Banks reckoned. "Do you know of anyone who might have wanted to harm your father?" he asked.

"No. I mean, really. I suppose maybe some of those villains he caught. But he was well liked. He didn't have a lot of close friends outside of work. He was a bit of a loner, bit of an anorak, if truth be told. He liked being off by himself fishing and bird-watching. And working on his allotment. I used to go with him and help him sometimes when I was younger, especially on the allotment, but you know . . . you change . . . lose interest . . . grow apart. Robbie used to go to the tarn sailing model boats with him. He used to build them himself. Lovely, some of them, the detail. Now we just tease him about being an old anorak." She put her hand to her face and stifled a sob. "Sorry."

Banks could feel sympathy. His own children had been the same, interested in whatever seven-day wonder he had been passionate about at the time until they were about thirteen, and then they didn't want to know; they just wanted to be off with their friends. He made a mental note to ask Keith Palmer's lads to check out Quinn's allotment. The odds were that he'd have at least a little gardening shed there. It might be just the sort of place to hide something, and the burglar would probably not have known about it.

Jessica's expression had become wistful, and Banks got the impression that she wished she hadn't lost interest in the things that bound her to her father, that she had continued to help him on the allotment and accompany him on fishing trips and bird-watching expeditions, that they hadn't grown apart. But it happens to everyone. There was nothing he could say to her to make her feel better. It was too late now.

His own father had been a keen cyclist in his younger days, Banks remembered, and many was the day Banks had accompanied him on rides beside the Nene, or across the Cambridgeshire flatlands, when he was eleven or twelve. But like his own children, and like Jessica, the older he had got, the less interested he had become in going with his father on bicycle rides. All he wanted to do was hang around with his mates listening to the latest Beatles, Bob Dylan or Animals record. There had been no room for adults and their boring interests in his world. He was lucky his father was still alive—at least they had been able to rebuild a few bridges in the past few years—but they wouldn't be going on any bicycle rides together again.

"It was most likely to do with his work," Banks said. "Do you know if he received any threatening letters or phone calls recently?"

"No. But I've been at university since Christmas, except I came home when Mum died, of course, and he didn't mention anything then. He never talked about that stuff at home. His job. Well, hardly ever.

Sometimes he'd tell us funny stories about things that happened at the station, but I think he liked to protect us from the bad stuff."

Exactly as Banks had done with Brian and Tracy. "So you can't think of anyone who wanted to harm him? He didn't get any threats or anything?"

"Not that I know of." Jessica cradled her mug in both hands and took a sip.

"I did find one thing you might be able to help me with," Banks said, going back into the living room for the photo he had left there. He brought it through to the kitchen and turned it around on the table so that Jessica could get a good look. "Is this Rachel Hewitt?"

"That's Rachel. She's so beautiful, isn't she?" Jessica bit her lower lip, the tears flowing over. "He could never let it go, you know. Never let *her* go. It's like she was his only failure, and he had to beat himself up with it every time he got a bit down. It used to drive Mum crazy."

"It wasn't his fault," said Banks. "They still haven't found her."

"That's because she's dead," said Jessica. "She was dead right from the start. And if you don't mind my saying so, you're being terribly naïve if you think saying it wasn't his fault ever did any good. As far as he was concerned, it *was* his fault. He wasn't entirely logical about it. We tried to tell him, time after time, but it didn't work. Why couldn't they all just believe that she was dead? Why couldn't *he* just believe it? Besides, can you imagine what her life would be like if she'd been abducted by some pervert and kept in a cellar as some sort of sex slave? Or forced into prostitution?"

"Even if he had believed that she was dead," said Banks, "it wouldn't have stopped him from doing his job, or from blaming himself. If he was a good copper, he would still have needed to know what happened to her, and why."

She gave Banks a sharp glance. "*A good copper.* What's that supposed to mean? Anyway, why do you want to know about this? What does any of it have to do with Dad's death?"

"I've got no idea. Probably nothing. The photo was just sitting there in a folder full of Visa bills, with no identification or anything. The name came up before. She seemed familiar . . ."

"She should be. Her face has been plastered over the papers often enough these past six years or so. Still is every now and then, when her parents step up the campaign again."

Banks could hardly imagine how he would feel if his own daughter disappeared completely without a trace in a foreign country, but he had always felt a deep sympathy for the Hewitts and their ongoing grief. They had suffered at the hands of the media, too, and were now caught up as victims in the never-ending phone-hacking scandal, which must have made it hurt all over again. Banks was suspicious of "closure" and all it implied, thought it was some sort of modern psychobabble, but he knew that in their case there could be no rest, no peace, until their daughter's body was recovered and returned home.

"Did your father have much contact with Rachel's family?"

"None. Except when she first disappeared, I suppose."

"He didn't stay in touch?"

"No. Why would he?"

"No reason. They didn't . . . you know . . . blame him, or anything?"

"He didn't need them to blame him. He managed that all by himself."

Banks realized that Jessica was probably right. The Rachel Hewitt connection was interesting, but that was all it was, just another item to drop in the bulging file, along with Harry Lake, Stephen Lambert and Warren Corrigan. Soon they would have even more material from West Yorkshire, and a whole host of other names from Quinn's past to sift through. There was nothing more Banks could think of, so he stood up to leave. "Where are you staying?" he asked Jessica at the door.

"Here. Why? It's not a crime scene, is it?"

"Well, it is, really . . . technically . . . the break-in . . . It's obviously connected with what happened to your father. But the CSIs have already gathered all the evidence they can, and they'll be taking the rest of his papers away. They should be finished here soon."

"Well . . . ?"

"I just thought . . . I mean, are you sure you want to stay here? Is there someone I can call for you? A relative? Boyfriend?"

"Thank you for your concern, but I'll be fine. Really. Robbie will be here soon. We'll probably just get pissed."

A very good idea, Banks thought, but he didn't say so.

3

Banks arrived in his office early on Friday morning after a quiet evening at home listening to Kate Royal, watching the first episode in the *Treme* series and sipping the best part of a bottle of Rioja. So much for cutting back.

He had phoned Stefan Nowak, the crime scene manager, as the team was packing up at St. Peter's around sunset the previous evening. They had finished their search of the woods and lake and had found no sign of a weapon. They had, however, found a cigarette end close to the body, some synthetic fibers and traces of what might have been blood from a scratch on the tree trunk where they thought the killer had leaned. There was also a fresh footprint that definitely wasn't Bill Quinn's. Their expert said that, at first glance, it was a common sort of trainer you could buy anywhere, but they might be able to get a bit more detail from it. There was often a correlation between shoe size and height, for example, and measurements could give them at least a working estimate of how tall the person who wore them was and how much he or she weighed. Any distinguishing marks on one or both of the soles could be as individual as a fingerprint.

DS Keith Palmer and his team had finished searching Bill Quinn's house and allotment in Rawdon, including his garden shed. They had even dug up a good deal of the allotment but had found nothing.

Banks linked his hands behind his neck, leaned back in his chair and listened to Ravel's *Gaspard de la nuit* on Radio Three's *Breakfast*. As he glanced around his office, he realized that he had been in the same room for over twenty years and that it had only been redecorated once, as far as he could remember. He didn't much care about the institutional green walls, as they were covered in framed prints and posters for concerts and exhibitions—Hockney's Yorkshire scenes, Miles Davis at Newport, Jimi Hendrix at Winterland, a Chagall poster for the Paris Opera—but he certainly needed a newer and bigger desk, one that didn't require a piece of wadded-up paper under one of its legs. He could do with another filing cabinet, too, he thought as his gaze settled on the teetering pile of paper on top of the one he had already. A couple of shelves and an extra bookcase wouldn't go amiss, either, and perhaps a chair that was kinder to his back than the antique he was sitting in now. No wonder his neck was starting to play up after long days at the office, especially with all the extra paperwork he seemed to have these days. He'd be in St. Peter's soon, himself, if he wasn't careful. At least the heater worked, and the tatty old Venetian blinds had been replaced.

But now was not the time to ask for such things, he knew. He should have made his demands a few years ago, when the police were getting almost everything they asked for. Those days were long gone. Like everywhere else, Eastvale had been recently plagued by 20 percent cuts across the board and a drastic county reorganization designed to implement some of those cuts. The three "Areas" had been replaced by six "Safer Neighborhood Commands." Changes at county HQ in Newby Wiske also meant that the Major Crimes Unit, or Homicide and Major Inquiry Team as it was now known, still operated out of Eastvale but covered more ground.

The team came under Assistant Chief Constable (Crime) Ron McLaughlin, known as "Red Ron" because of his leftist leanings, but it was run on a day-to-day basis by Area Commander Catherine Gervaise, and it was now responsible not just for the defunct Western Area but for the whole county—with the same team strength and no increase in civilian support staff.

It was time for the nine thirty briefing, and the team gathered in the boardroom, which, despite its modern glass writing board, along with the white-board and corkboard, still managed to retain some of its old-fashioned appearance, with the large oval table at its center, high hard-backed chairs and portraits of eighteenth- and nineteenth-century wool barons on its walls, red-faced, pop-eyed men with whiskers and tight collars.

Banks took his place nearest the writing boards as the others drifted in, most of them clutching mugs or Styrofoam cups of coffee as well as files and notebooks. AC Gervaise had managed to borrow a couple of DCs, Haig and Lombard, from county HQ, but it wasn't a big team, Banks reflected, nowhere near big enough for a major investigation into the murder of a fellow police officer. It would have to be augmented if the scope of the investigation ballooned, as Banks expected it would, unless they caught an early break. He would be especially glad to see Annie Cabbot back, but DS Jim Hatchley, one of the officers Banks had known the longest in Eastvale, had retired as soon as he had done his thirty years, as Banks had always known he would. He missed the lumbering, obstinate sod.

First, he shared what he knew with the team, then asked if they had anything to add. The short answer was that they didn't. Scientific Support were still working on the footprints, Photographic Services had the photographs, and the DNA results from the cigarette end and blood didn't come back anywhere near as quickly as they did on *CSI*. All the specialist was able to tell him so far was that the brand of cigarette was Dunhill, which a few quick inquiries on Winsome's part ascertained was Bill Quinn's brand. There were no other cigarettes found in or near the woods. Obviously the groundsman did a good job.

There was nothing new on the murder weapon, or on the state of Bill Quinn's body, as Dr. Glendenning, the Home Office pathologist, was not due to perform the postmortem until later that afternoon. A list of possible enemies would be on its way up from West Yorkshire sometime later in the day, if they were lucky, and Quinn's bank statements, credit card details and home and mobile call logs should also be arriving before the day was out, again with luck. It was a Friday, so there was always a possibility of delays. Inquiries were being made in the village nearest to St. Peter's, as well as at the nearest petrol stations and any other places where strangers were likely to have been spotted. Uniformed officers were canvassing the neighborhood of Quinn's Rawdon home to find out if anyone had noticed an interloper recently. The interviews at St. Peter's had been concluded and had revealed nothing of interest except that Quinn was in the habit of going outside for a smoke before bed each night.

"So it would seem," Banks said, summing up after the team had digested all this information, or lack of it, "that we need to get our fingers out. We're no closer than we were when DI Jenson found the body yesterday morning."

"We do have the photos, sir," Winsome pointed out. "Photographic Services say they're digital, printed on a common or garden ink-jet printer, so nothing new there. They're analyzing the ink content and pixels for comparison with Quinn's own printer, but it's not an entirely accurate process."

"Their thinking being?"

"That Quinn may have received the photos as JPEG images and printed them out himself. Which also means there might be more."

"And we might be able to trace them to a sender?"

"If we had them," said Winsome, "then it's possible they could be traced to a specific computer."

"But we don't."

"No."

"Well, that's one dead end," Banks said. "I don't think it really matters whether he printed them himself or someone sent them by post, unless we have the envelope and it has a postmark and prints on it, which we don't."

Winsome stood up and started handing out eight-by-ten prints. "They also came up with this enhanced blowup image of the girl from the restaurant photo," she said. "It was the best they could do. They're still working on the background to see if they can get any points of reference."

"Any prints on the photos?"

"Only the victim's."

Banks examined the blowup. It was a little grainy, but Photographic Services had done a great job, and he believed that someone could recognize the girl from it. "Excellent," he said, then addressed the two young DCs on loan. "Haig and Lombard, I want you to make it your priority to check the photo of this girl against escort agency files, Internet dating services and what-ever else you think is relevant. You can use the spare desks in the squad room. We've no idea when or where the pictures were taken, of course, but my thinking is sometime over the last two or three years."

"It sounds like a long job, sir," mumbled Haig, the bulky one.

"Better get on with it, then. You never know, you might even find you enjoy it. But be careful. If either one of you comes back with a smile on his face and a cigarette in his mouth, he'll be in deep trouble."

Everyone laughed. Haig and Lombard exchanged dark glances, took two copies of the photo and left the room.

"Anything else?" Banks asked Winsome.

"We've just about finished interviewing the patients and staff at St. Peter's," she said. "Nothing so far. Barry Sadler and Mandy Pemberton were the last up, but neither of them saw or heard anything."

"Are they telling the truth?"

"I think so, sir. I interviewed Barry Sadler, and he's very cut up. He's an ex-copper. The nurse has a clean record and a spotless reputation. Of course, we can always have another go at them if something else turns up pointing in that direction, but I think it's doubtful."

Banks took the photograph of Rachel Hewitt from his briefcase and stuck it on the glass alongside the blowup of the unknown girl with Quinn. He still didn't understand why the deputy chief commissioner had seen the necessity of spending close to £500 on a glass writing board when the whiteboard worked perfectly well. Basically, you could write and rub out and stick pictures on it, which was all you needed to do. He'd probably seen one on *Law & Order: UK* or some such television program and thought it was a necessity for the modern police force.

"This may mean nothing at all," Banks said, "but Bill Quinn worked on the Rachel Hewitt case for a short while in the summer of 2006, not long after she was reported missing, and he had this photograph in a file in his study. Quinn spent a week in Tallinn helping with the investigation there and carried out background checks into Rachel and her friends. Both DI Blackstone in Leeds and Quinn's daughter said the case haunted him."

"Was it ever closed?" asked Winsome.

"No," Banks said. "Just inactive. Officially, Rachel Hewitt is still a missing person, but there haven't been any fresh leads for six years—there weren't any leads at all—so until new information comes in, there's nothing more can be done, and the investigation has been mothballed. She'd be twenty-five now."

"Surely she's dead?" said Doug Wilson.

"In all likelihood. But families don't give up that easily, Doug. Think of the McCanns. Little Madeleine's been gone for years now, but they won't let themselves believe that she's dead, even though, compared to the alternatives, some might say death would be a blessing. They can't. Rachel Hewitt's family is the same. They won't give up. They won't accept that their daughter is dead. Anyway, as I said, it's probably nothing, but at some point we'll have to talk to the parents and friends. In the meantime, I'd like one of you to put together a dossier on Rachel Hewitt. Clippings, photos, names, whatever you can find on the investigation. There should be plenty. Gerry, maybe you can get started on that?"

DC Geraldine Masterson scribbled something down on her pad. "Yes, sir."

Banks turned to Winsome. "I think in the meantime you and I should get back to St. Peter's and see if we can wrap up there," he said. "The rest of you all have your actions and TIEs to be getting on with. Doug, I want you here when the list of Bill Quinn's possible old enemies and his phone records arrive, and I want you to head the examination. Coordinate with DI Ken Blackstone at Millgarth. Ken mentioned a bloke called Corrigan. Warren Corrigan. He's got his finger in a few pies, all of them nasty, but basically he's a loan shark. Ask around. See if he has any sort of presence in these parts. We want to know who Quinn has been talking to lately, and who's been talking to him. Keep an open mind about the old cases. Something might leap out at you, but you can't rely on that. You can probably forget the junkies and alcoholic wife-beaters—they probably wouldn't even remember making threats, let alone have what it takes to stalk and kill someone with a crossbow—but give them all at least a passing glance. Anything that strikes you as odd, interesting, possible, make a note of it. Gerry here will give you a hand in her spare time. If she has any."

"Yes, sir." Doug glanced over at DC Masterson, who tapped the end of her pencil on her notepad.

"And we also need to find out if Bill Quinn had ever worked with or had any close connection with anyone staying at St. Peter's. Or if anyone there had a connection with someone he put away, someone who threatened him, had a grudge. You might as well include the staff, too. I realize this all adds up to casting a very wide net indeed, but we've got to either rule all these things out or find a link to Quinn's murder somewhere, if we're to narrow it down to a viable line of inquiry. I shouldn't have to remind you that Bill Quinn was one of our own and that we'll be under extreme scrutiny on this. Clear?"

Everyone nodded, glum expressions on their faces. They knew what it meant: say good-bye to the weekend, and all leave is canceled.

"Sir?" said Winsome.

"Yes."

"Well, I've just been thinking. The choice of weapon, the murder in the woods . . . Could we be looking for someone with hunting experience? Hunting and tracking? We know that Quinn himself was into outdoors stuff—angling and gardening, specifically—so he might have known people who were hunters, who belonged to the same clubs or societies he did."

"That's a good point, Winsome," said Banks. "Doug and Gerry, you should keep an eye open for anything like that, too. Any hunters, flag them. Check on Quinn's friends outside the force, too, if he had any, and any organizations he belonged to. Also," Banks went on, "one of you will need to check sources for crossbows and bolts, including online. And I want someone to search for any similar crimes, anything involving a crossbow, in fact, over, say, the past five years. OK?"

"Yes, sir," said DC Wilson.

Before the meeting broke up, the door opened and Area Commander Gervaise walked in with another woman behind her. Late thirties or early forties, Banks guessed, a tall attractive blonde, elegant suit, the skirt ending just above her knees, black tights—no Primark for her—a trim, lithe figure with gentle curves, a smattering of freckles across her small nose, intelligent green eyes, regal bearing. Her blond tresses were piled and coiled on top, giving the impression of casual simplicity, though Banks guessed the haircut was expensive and the arrangement took a lot of time. She seemed a little nervous, he thought.

"If you'd all just hang on for a minute," Gervaise said, avoiding Banks's gaze, "I'd like to introduce Inspector Joanna Passero. Joanna is from Professional Standards, and she'll be working with you all very closely on this case."

"The rat squad," Banks muttered.

Gervaise raised an eyebrow. "What was that?"

"Nothing," said Banks. "Welcome to the squad. Pleased to meet you, Inspector Passero."

"Likewise," said Inspector Passero. "Call me Joanna."

Even in those few words, Banks thought he noticed a hint of a Scottish accent, which went quite against her Italian surname, as did her blond good looks. Still, he thought, remembering Bill Forsyth's *Comfort and Joy*, with its Glasgow ice-cream wars, a lot of Italians had settled in Scotland over the years.

"In my office, Alan," said Gervaise. "The rest of you can get back to work."

Banks gestured for Winsome to wait for him and followed Gervaise and Joanna Passero down the corridor.

The three of them made themselves comfortable around Gervaise's circular glass table and drank coffee made from Gervaise's machine. Banks felt lucky; it was his second cup in two days. On the other hand, when he realized why Inspector Joanna Passero was present, he didn't feel so lucky after all. She crossed her long, black-stockinged legs and leaned back with the mug in her hand as if she were at her book club or a Women's Institute coffee morning. A half smile played around her full pink lips. Perhaps she was enjoying Banks's obvious discomfort, he thought, or perhaps she had noticed his stolen glances at the swell of her breasts under the finely tailored jacket, or the shapely ankle of her crossed leg.

There was a Nordic aspect to her beauty, despite her Italian surname and Scottish accent. All that lovely blond coolness, Banks thought. Alfred Hitchcock would have loved her. And tied twenty birds to her clothes with long nylon threads.

"You could have given me some warning," Banks said to Gervaise. "You made me look a right twat back there at the briefing."

"That wasn't my intention," said Gervaise. "The decision's just been made. I've been at a breakfast meeting with ACC McLaughlin and the chief constable over at county HQ, and we are all agreed that, given the circumstances of DI Bill Quinn's murder, and what was discovered in his room, we need a representative from Professional Standards on board. ACC McLaughlin suggested Joanna, who is relatively new to the county but comes along with an excellent pedigree from Thames Valley. I brought her back here with me. I'm sure she'll be a valuable addition to the team."

"Valuable in what way, ma'am?" Banks asked.

"I've told you, less of the 'ma'am.' We can be informal in here."

"Valuable in what way?"

Gervaise deferred to Inspector Passero. "Joanna?"

Joanna Passero held Banks's gaze as she leaned forward and set her coffee mug down on the table. There was a pink lipstick stain on the rim. Banks realized that he was being outflanked by two strong women, one above him in rank, and the other with a cool demeanor and any number of little feminine wiles up her sleeve. He also realized that there was probably nothing he could do about any of it. Once Gervaise's mind was made up, that was it, and she had the backing of ACC McLaughlin and the chief constable. This meeting was a mere formality, a courtesy, perhaps. Banks wasn't going to get Joanna Passero sent back to Newby Wiske or Thames Valley, no matter how much he might try. About the only thing he could hope to get out of this meeting was to escape with his dignity intact and maybe gain a few minor concessions. But he wasn't going to give up without a struggle. He listened as Joanna Passero spoke in her lilting Edinburgh accent.

"I'm sure you'll agree with me," she began, "that in the light of the compromising photographs you found in DI Quinn's possession, implicating him in the possible corruption of a minor, not to say grave dereliction of duty, this investigation goes somewhat beyond the norm."

"There's no evidence that the girl was a minor."

"Oh, for goodness' sake." She gave an impatient twitch of her head. "Look at her. Just look at her."

"It's possible that DI Quinn was being blackmailed because of those pictures," Banks said. "It's also possible that he was set up."

"In what way?"

"If you look at the way he's lying in that bedroom photo, you can see he seems quite out of it. Maybe he was drugged?"

"Or drunk."

"Possibly. But—"

"He didn't appear drugged in the bar, or in the restaurant. In fact, he seemed to be very much enjoying himself."

"And where's the law against having a drink or a meal with an attractive young woman? If he was drugged, have you considered that the restaurant or the bar may well have been where the drug was administered? In his drink or his food? She may even have been as much a victim as he was. We just don't know. This is all a bit premature, in my opinion."

"There's no point you two arguing back and forth about this," Gervaise said, glancing first at Banks. "Alan, you have to admit that the whole business is extremely fishy. The photos, the murder method, everything. You said yourself that you think DI Quinn might have been blackmailed because of the girl."

"But we're just starting out on our investigation," Banks argued. "We don't really know anything yet. These are just theories."

"That's why I want Joanna in right at the beginning."

"To do what?"

"My job," said Joanna. "What do you think? I'm happy to tag along and observe and ask what questions I think necessary. Believe me, DCI Banks, I have no intention of getting in the way of this investigation, or of slowing it down in any way. I want the same as you. A result. I also want to know if there is any hint of wrong-doing on the part of the police. Is that so unreasonable?"

"Not when you put it like that. But this is already a complex investigation, and I don't want to be in the position of having to describe or explain my every move and decision to someone else. I also don't want someone looking over my shoulder and judging my methods all the time."

Banks didn't think he had anything to fear from Professional Standards. Whatever his methods, whatever corners he cut and instincts he followed, he stayed within the boundaries of the law. Usually. He noticed once again the intelligent pale green eyes, the expensive blond hair, the freckles, straight nose, full lips lightly brushed with pink lipstick. She held his gaze without flinching. She would probably be formidable in an interview room, or at a poker table.

"I understand that," said Joanna, picking up her coffee again, flicking him a Princess Di upward glance, "and I can only repeat that I have no intention of slowing things down or of looking over your shoulder. I know all about your methods, DCI Banks. They're legendary at county HQ. But you're not my brief. DI William Quinn is."

"But you will slow things down, whether you intend to or not. Your presence will affect my whole team."

"I can only repeat: neither you nor your team is my brief." She paused and shot him a cool glance. "Why? What have you all got to hide?"

"Oh, come off it. You know perfectly well what I mean. When the taxman calls, you don't expect it's about a rebate, do you? We're working at cross purposes here. I'm after the person who murdered Bill Quinn. Period. You want the dirt on Quinn. You'll be trying to prove him corrupt or perverted, or both. I'm not saying you shouldn't be, or that his reputation doesn't deserve to be trashed if you find evidence he was bent. I have no more tolerance for bent coppers than you have. But as yet, there's no evidence that Bill Quinn was crooked, and plenty that he was murdered. We're not searching for the same thing at all."

"I had hoped you would be more understanding, Alan," Gervaise chipped in. "Quite frankly, I'm disappointed in you. I realize that some of your arguments are not without merit, but no matter what you say, you will do this. There's no point in getting off on the wrong foot. This thing is going to happen. I say it's going to happen. ACC McLaughlin says it's going to happen. The chief constable says it's going to happen. The purpose of calling this little tête-à-tête right here and now was to see that it happens in the spirit of cooperation and amicability. Is that too much to ask? If Bill Quinn were alive, and you found what you found hidden in that book in his room, with all its implications, what do you think would happen then?"

"I presume there would be an investigation by Professional Standards, probably in the form of Inspector Passero here. But that's not the case. Bill Quinn was *murdered*. That changes things. Please excuse me if I sound dismissive, but that makes it a fully fledged murder investigation, not a hunt for a bent copper."

"But it's both," argued Joanna. "And they may be connected. Can't you see that?"

"Right at the moment, all I can see is that the murder investigation takes precedence, and I want everyone on my team to have some expertise in that particular area. Have you ever been involved in a murder investigation before, Inspector Passero?"

"I don't see how that's relevant." Joanna paused, licked her lips and inclined her head slowly. Her voice softened. "Of course, I understand what you're saying," she went on. "Don't think for a moment that I don't know what you all think of Professional Standards. I've heard all the insults you could possibly imagine, and more. Aren't we the 'rat squad,' which you called me just a few minutes ago? It's not very nice or polite, but I can live with it. Like you, we have a job to do, and it's an important job, even if it is an unpopular one. In this case, we have a murdered detective who may or may not have been having sex with an underage girl, but who most certainly had in his possession proof that he was sexually involved with someone other than his wife. And that proof, as you have already pointed out yourself, suggests that he was subject to blackmail. Whether he paid this blackmailer in cash or in inside information, it makes no difference. We're talking about possible police corruption here, and what one man does taints us all." She glanced at AC Gervaise, and Banks noticed Gervaise give an almost imperceptible nod. "There's been rumors, as you probably know," Joanna went on. "Rumors of corruption, of a 'bent copper,' as you call it. Now this. No smoke without fire, I say."

"So that's why you're here," said Banks.

"It's one reason. All I'm saying is that his murder and the discovery of the photos makes that possibility more . . ."

"More possible?"

"I was going to say more realistic."

Banks held his hands up. "Fine," he said. "Fine. I agree. As I said, I'd no more turn a blind eye to police corruption than you would. But can't we give the poor sod the benefit of the doubt? He's not even in his grave yet, and we're already acting as if he were a criminal. What about his children?" He glanced toward Gervaise, who remained expressionless. "If I find out anything that points toward Quinn being the one involved in corrupt or criminal activities, the first whiff of a scandal, you'll be the first to know. And Inspector Passero here. I promise. All right? Now can't you just leave us alone to get on with our murder investigation? It's complicated enough already."

"There's no negotiating on this," said Gervaise. "I told you. Respect my honesty and directness in calling this meeting, and respond with a little generosity of your own. You know it's the right move."

"What about Annie? DI Cabbot. Where does she fit in with all this?"

Gervaise sighed. "DI Cabbot will be back at work on Monday, as I told you yesterday. According to all the reports I've read, she's fit for duty, so that's exactly what she'll be doing. Her normal duties."

"Not deskbound?"

"ACC McLaughlin has met with her doctors, and they have assured him that she's ready for a full return to duty. Personally, I still think she should take it easy for a while and get some counseling, but that's only me."

"She's been taking it easy for six months."

Annie would be livid about Joanna Passero, Banks thought. She would be convinced that the Professional Standards officer was being set up as her replacement on the team, perhaps even that they were going to get rid of her after she'd almost sacrificed her life for the job. Not just for the job, but for Banks's daughter, Tracy, who had also risked a great deal herself to save Annie's life.

For the moment, though, Annie wasn't the main issue; Joanna Passero was. Banks knew that he couldn't trust her, that he would have to be constantly on guard, but he also knew, as he had known going into the meeting, that he had no choice in the matter. It would never do to be too nice to Professional Standards, certainly not in public, and there might be one or two times ahead when he would want to hold his cards close to his chest, and he would do so. He wasn't going to make things easy for her. At least she was a great improvement on that old fat bastard Superintendent Chambers, who had retired due to ill health after Christmas, thank God. It was politic, he thought, to offer a tentative olive branch.

"OK," he said. "Let's assume that we work together."

Joanna Passero's expression indicated that there was no "let's assume" about it but that she was willing to listen to what he had to say for the sake of politeness.

"How's it going to work?" Banks asked. "I mean, I'm still senior investigating officer on this case, right?" He glanced at Gervaise. "What does that make Inspector Passero? Deputy?"

"No," said Gervaise. "DI Cabbot will be your DIO, as usual. As I said, Inspector Passero is on board to investigate Bill Quinn. She's attached to your team as an adviser and as an observer."

"That certainly complicates things," said Banks.

"No, it doesn't," said Joanna. "It means I won't get under your feet. Why don't we just see how it works out

first before coming to any conclusions? If my partici-
pation causes problems that jeopardize your investigation, or interferes in any way with the swift progress or
smooth running of the operation, then we'll reevaluate
and find some other way of uncovering the bad apple."

Gervaise looked at Banks. "Can't say fairer than
that, can you, Alan?"

Banks sat for a moment, feeling neither defeated nor
victorious, then he leaned forward, fully aware he was
inviting the wolf into the fold, and offered Joanna his
hand. "Welcome to the team," he said. "You'd better
come and meet the others, get up to speed."

"You know," Banks said, turning down the volume
on Anna Calvi's "Baby It's You" as they approached
the roundabout before St. Peter's, "I've been thinking. Our killer obviously didn't walk here, and I very
much doubt that he parked his car out front."

"Which means," Winsome said, "that he must have
found a nice, quiet out-of-the-way spot to leave it not
too far away."

"Exactly. Preferably somewhere that couldn't be
seen from the road. The center's less than a hundred
yards past this roundabout, which is an easy enough
walk. There are no major roads feeding into it, they're
all B roads, so let's go and see what we can find."

"But what about Inspector Passero?" Banks was driving Winsome in his Porsche, and Joanna Passero was following in a red Peugeot.

"I'm sure she'll be able to keep up with us."

Instead of taking the exit to St. Peter's, which was the first one off the roundabout, Banks took the third, which headed in the opposite direction from the center entirely. He saw Joanna's Peugeot in his rearview mirror. She started to turn off at the St. Peter's exit, then swerved when she saw what he'd done, skidded and did a 180-degree turn back to the roundabout to follow him, barely missing a white delivery van, which was going too fast. Its horn blared.

The Peugeot seemed to stall in the roundabout for a few moments, then it started up again and followed them.

There were no hiding places along the stretch of road Banks had chosen, and after about a quarter of a mile, he used a lay-by to do a U-turn and headed back toward the roundabout. Joanna Passero whizzed by on the other side, and he saw her slow down behind him, then pull into the lay-by and turn around to follow. Winsome didn't seem very amused. "What's wrong?" Banks asked. "Aren't you having fun?"

"If you want my opinion," Winsome said, "this is very silly, dangerous and childish. Sir."

"Ouch. That puts me in my place." Banks turned into the roundabout and took the only other exit he hadn't explored, again the third, which took him away at a right angle from the road on which the center was located, a continuation of the road he had first come in on.

Winsome folded her arms. This time, less than twenty yards along the road, on the opposite side, Banks saw a rough track leading off at a sharp angle. There were high trees on both sides, and the lane was so narrow that it would have been impossible for two cars to pass without one backing up. There was nothing coming on the road, so Banks turned into the lane, blocking the entrance with the Porsche. He hadn't seen Joanna behind him and assumed that she either hadn't reached the roundabout yet or had given up and gone on to St. Peter's by herself.

Banks didn't want to drive any further in, just in case this was the right place and there were tire tracks or other evidence. He and Winsome got out of the car and walked carefully along the edge of the rutted track, beside the hedgerow. There was no drystone wall on either side. When they stopped a few yards in, they couldn't see, or be seen from, the road at all, but they could see some tire tracks. The uneven surface was just stones and dirt, no doubt intended for farm vehicles, though there was no farmhouse in sight. It would have made the perfect hiding place for the killer's car after dark. Farmers don't usually drive tractors around country lanes at that time of night. Banks wasn't even sure whether tractors had headlights.

"A hundred yards' walk from the center," he said, "hidden from the road by trees, very little traffic. I think we've found the spot, Winsome. It would have been very bad luck indeed if he'd been spotted here, and we can assume that he probably had a contingency plan. Professionals usually do. No prints. Car rented under an assumed name."

Banks heard a car screech to a halt on the road behind his Porsche, then the sound of a car door slamming. Joanna Passero appeared in the entrance to the lane and started walking toward them. About the same time that Banks held up his hand and called to her to stay back, she went over on her ankle and cursed, then grabbed on to a roadside tree branch to keep her balance and cried out again. Thorns. Banks started to walk back toward the main road, still keeping close to the hedgerow. It wasn't long before he came up to a fuming Joanna Passero standing, or rather hopping, at the entrance to the track, one leg bent up behind her, like a stork's, grasping a shiny black shoe in one hand and wobbling dangerously. "Banks, you bastard! You just made me break a bloody heel! Do you know how much these shoes cost? What the hell do you think you're playing at?"

"Just doing my job," said Banks. He approached her gingerly and explained about the need for the killer to hide his car, and this being a likely spot.

As he talked, she visibly relaxed and leaned against his car, keeping her stockinged foot just above the rough surface. "You could have bloody warned me," she said. "That road surface is lethal."

"I'm sorry. I only thought of it when we got to the roundabout. It's like that in a real investigation sometimes. Anyway, I think we should get the CSIs down here. We found some tire tracks, and there may be footprints. We'll stay here and protect the scene. Would you mind driving on to St. Peter's and asking the lads to send someone over ASAP?" He glanced down at her foot. "Sorry about the heel. I've got some old wellies in the boot, if that's any help, though they might be a bit big for you. How's your ankle? Not sprained or anything, I hope? Can I help you back to your car?"

Joanna glared as if she wanted to throttle Banks. She turned and hopped back to her Peugeot with as much dignity as she could manage and drove off in a spray of roadside dirt and gravel.

"See what I mean?" said Winsome, standing behind him, arms folded. "Childish."

"Who?" said Banks with a straight face. "Me or her?"

The mortuary, along with Dr. Glendenning's recently modernized postmortem suite, was in the basement of the old Eastvale infirmary. Banks thought it would be a good idea to take Inspector Passero along. She probably wouldn't learn anything of relevance to her case, but if she was working with Banks, it was time she got used to the late hours. And the blood and guts. It was after five on a Friday afternoon, and a Professional Standards officer would likely be well on her way home by now, if not sitting back with her feet up in front of the telly with a large gin and tonic. Or was Joanna more the cocktail-party-and-theater type? Probably.

She turned up in a new pair of flat-heeled pumps that she had clearly bought that afternoon at Stead and Simpson in the market square. No fancy Italian shoe shops in Eastvale. The new shoes didn't make as much noise as Banks's black slip-ons as the two of them walked down the high, gloomy corridor to their appointment. The walls were covered in old green tiles. DC Gerry Masterson had told Banks earlier that Robbie

Quinn had been brought in to identify his father's body that morning, so the formalities were done with for the moment. Dr. Glendenning had the coroner's permission to proceed with his postmortem.

Banks gave a slight shudder, the way he always did in the Victorian infirmary, and it wasn't caused by the permanent chill that seemed to infuse the air as much as by the smell of formaldehyde and God only knew what else.

"Something wrong?" asked Joanna, her voice echoing from the tiles.

"No. This place always gives me the creeps, that's all. It's probably haunted. There never seems to be anyone else here. And I can just imagine all the patients back in Victorian times, the primitive instruments and lack of anesthetic. It must have been butchery. A nightmare. Corridors of blood."

"You've got imagination, I'll give you that," Joanna said. "But you must have been misinformed. They had anesthetics in Victorian times. At least they used chloroform or ether from the 1850s on, and I think it said over the door this place wasn't built until 1869. I also think you'll find the instruments were perfectly adequate for their purposes back then."

"University education?" Banks said.

"Something like that."

"Well, it still gives me the creeps. Here we are."

They donned the gowns and masks provided by one of Dr. Glendenning's young assistants and joined the doctor, who was just about to begin.

"Tut tut, tardy again, Banks," said Dr. Glendenning. "You know how I hate tardiness. And me working late on a Friday especially to accommodate you."

"Sorry, Doc. You know I'm eternally grateful."

"Who's your date?"

Banks glanced toward Joanna. "This is Inspector Joanna Passero. Professional Standards."

"In trouble again, Banks?"

"She's here to observe."

"Of course." Dr. Glendenning scrutinized Joanna, who blushed a little. "Ever been to a postmortem before, lassie?"

"No," she said. "I can't honestly say that I have."

"Aye . . . well, at least you're a fellow Scot, by the sound of you."

"Edinburgh."

"Good. Excellent. Just try not to be sick on the floor."

"Now you've got the Scottish mutual-admiration society well and truly off the ground," said Banks, "do you think you could get started, Doc? We've still got a murder to investigate."

Dr. Glendenning scowled at Banks. "Sassenach." Then he winked at Joanna, who smiled. He adjusted his microphone, called over his first assistant and took the scalpel she handed him. Quinn's clothes were already lying on a table by the wall. They would be searched and put into labeled paper bags—not plastic, which didn't breathe and caused mold to grow on moist fabrics—and sent over to Evidence, signed for at every stage of the way to ensure chain of custody.

Before beginning his incision to get at Quinn's insides, Glendenning studied the external details of the body and had his assistant take a number of photographs, then he leaned over and slowly pulled out the crossbow bolt, which had already been tested for prints, to no avail. There was no blood, of course, as Quinn's heart had stopped pumping some time ago, but the sucking sound it made when it finally came out made Banks feel queasy, nonetheless. He glanced at Joanna from the corner of his eye. She wasn't showing any reaction. She had to be pretty good at hiding her feelings, Banks thought, though maybe you didn't need feelings to work for Professional Standards.

Dr. Glendenning laid the bolt down next to a ruler fixed to one of the lab tables. "A twenty-inch Beman ICS Lightning Bolt," he said. "Carbon, not aluminum, in my opinion. That's fairly common, I should say."

"How do you know the make?" Banks asked.

"It says so right there, down the shaft. Now, a lot depends on the power of the crossbow your man was using, but you're generally talking a hundred-and-fifty-pound draw, maybe even as much as two hundred pounds these days, so I think if I take the measurement of how deep it went into him and an average of the bow's pressure, then we might get an approximation of the distance it was fired from."

"We think it was about fifty or sixty feet," said Banks.

Dr. Glendenning stared at him. "Is that scientifically accurate or just pure guesswork, laddie?"

"Well," said Banks, "it's about the distance between where the evidence shows the shooter was standing and where the victim fell. He might also have nudged the bolt on the ground when he fell forward and pushed it in a bit further. That's why it always pays to attend the scene."

Dr. Glendenning narrowed his eyes. "You can't miss at that range if you know what you're doing and have a decent weapon. Even in the dark. I'll let you know when the calculations are done." He went back to the body, measured and took swabs from the wound, probed it and muttered his findings into his microphone.

A lot of what happened at postmortems, Banks often found, was simply a matter of restating the obvious, but once in a while something knocked you for six, which was why it was a good idea for the SIO to attend. This time, however, everything was pretty much as he had expected it to be. Dr. Glendenning sorted through the stomach contents—chicken casserole, chips and peas, followed by apple pie and ice cream—and agreed with Dr. Burns about time of death, placing it at between eleven p.m. Wednesday evening and one a.m. Thursday morning, on the basis of digestion. The internal organs were weighed and sectioned for tox screening. Apart from Quinn's tarry lungs, on which Glendenning could hardly comment, being a smoker himself, and his liver being a bit enlarged, on which Banks certainly wouldn't be so hypocritical as to pass judgment, everything was in tip-top shape. Quinn was no athlete, but he was fit enough, and his heart had been in good working order until the crossbow bolt had pierced it. Both kidneys, and all the other various important bits and pieces Dr. Glendenning had removed, had also been up to par. If he hadn't been murdered, Dr. Glendenning ventured, he would probably have lived another thirty years or more if he'd stopped smoking. Every once in a while, Banks would sneak another glance at Joanna, but she seemed quite impassive, fascinated by the whole thing, if anything, and as icily cool as ever.

"So the cause of death is?" Banks asked as Dr. Glendenning's assistant closed up.

"Oh, didn't I say? How remiss of me. Well, barring any surprises from toxicology, he died of a crossbow bolt through the heart. It pierced the aorta, to be exact, just above the pulmonic valve. Death would have been as instantaneous as it gets, the chest cavity filled with blood, breathing impossible, no blood flow. A matter of seconds. You'll have my report in a day or two. Tox should take about a week."

"Thank you, Doc," said Banks.

"My pleasure. And charmed to meet you, ma'am," the doctor said, giving a little bow to Joanna, who put her hand to her mouth to stifle a giggle, or perhaps a gagging reaction, Banks thought. She seemed anxious to get out of the postmortem suite, at any rate.

"Fancy a drink?" Banks asked when they were back in the corridor. "I must admit, I always do after a PM. Or is that an arrestable offense in Professional Standards?"

"Why not?" said Joanna, glancing at her watch. "The sun's well over the yardarm. You obviously don't know me very well."

The Unicorn was just across the road. It wasn't one of Banks's favorite pubs, but it would do, and luckily it was still too early for the noisy crowd that filled the place on a Friday and Saturday night. At least the landlord served a passable pint of Black Sheep, if Banks remembered correctly.

"What would you like?" he asked Joanna at the bar.

"I'll have a brandy please. No ice."

Banks's eyes widened. He'd pegged her as a white-wine-spritzer kind of woman, and definitely not on duty, even if she turned a blind eye to him. Then he realized they weren't on duty. "Soda?"

"Just as it comes, please." She seemed amused by his surprise but said nothing except, "You bring the drinks and I'll take that table over there by the window, shall I?"

Banks paid for the drinks and carried them over.

"I see you got some new shoes," he said, sitting down.

Joanna stretched out her legs. Banks admired them, as he thought he was intended to do. "Had to, didn't I? It's such a hard job to dress for. You never know what sort of garden path you're going to be led up from one day to the next. Or country lane."

"What do you mean?"

Joanna took a sip of brandy and leaned forward, her elbows on the table. "Oh, come off it, DCI Banks. Don't play the innocent with me. You spin me around the roundabout, you make me break my heel, then you drag me off to a postmortem thinking it'll make me sick all over the nice tiled floor. Isn't that true? Wasn't that the idea?"

"But you weren't sick, were you? You didn't even flinch."

"Don't sound so disappointed." She sipped some brandy and grinned. "My mother's a cardiovascular surgeon—was, she's retired now—one of the best in the country. She often invited me to watch her operate when she thought I was old enough. I've seen more operations than you've put villains away."

"But you said—"

"I said this was my first postmortem. That's true. But I've seen plenty of bypasses, valve replacements and even a couple of heart transplants. Beats telly. There was a time when I seriously thought of becoming a surgeon myself, but I don't have the hands for it." She held them up, but Banks had no way of telling what was wrong with them. They didn't seem to be shaking or anything. He tried to stop his jaw dropping, then he started to laugh. He couldn't help it.

She let him laugh for a few moments, tolerant and slightly bemused, then, when he had finished, she said, "Can we please just stop it now? Bury the hatchet. Whatever. It's been a crap day so far. Do you think you could just lighten up a bit and stop treating me as your enemy? We both want the truth behind DI Quinn's murder, right? If he was the rotten apple, I'm sure you want to know as much as I do. So why can't we work together? I honestly can't afford a new pair of shoes every day, for a start. And I'm not trying to replace Annie Cabbot. I'm sorry she got shot, but it wasn't my fault. At least she's still alive. I had a partner I grew to trust and like very much once, before I came to Professional Standards. Can you just give me the benefit of the doubt? If Quinn was bent, I'll need to report it. I won't lie about that. If he's innocent, then his memory remains unsullied, he has a hero's funeral, twenty-one-gun salute, whatever, and his reputation has nothing to fear from me. How about it?"

"Your partner? What happened?"

Joanna paused and sipped some more brandy. "He died," she said finally. "Was killed, actually. Shot by a bent cop trying to avoid being exposed. Ironic, really. It was someone Johnny trusted, someone he was trying to help."

Banks remained silent and drank his beer. There wasn't much to say after that.

Joanna's mobile hiccupped. A text. She took it out of her bag and glanced at it, frowned briefly, then stuck it back in her handbag without replying.

"Anything important?" Banks asked. "Bad news? Your husband?"

Joanna shook her head and finished her drink. "What now?" she asked.

Banks looked at his watch. "I don't know about you," he said, "but I'm going to call in at the station and see if there are any developments, then I'm heading home."

She got to her feet. "I'll come with you," she said. Then paused. "At least, as far as the station."

Banks was sitting on a wicker chair in the conservatory, feet up on the low table, sipping a Malbec and listening to June Tabor sing "Finisterre." Only one shaded lamp was lit, and its dim orange-tinged light seemed to emphasize the vast darkness outside. A strong breeze had whipped up, and now it was lashing rain against the windows. April showers. Fortunately, the CSIs had finished their investigation of the St. Peter's grounds and covered over the lane where Banks and Winsome had found the tire tracks.

Banks thought about Joanna for a moment, how she had become more human to him when they had a drink together in the Unicorn and she told him about her mother the surgeon and her partner who got shot. Was it all just a ploy to gain his sympathy, to lull him into being careless and weak? He didn't know. There was something likable about her. Annie Cabbot, he remembered, had worked Professional Standards for a while a few years ago, and it hadn't turned her into a monster.

Banks tried to put Joanna Passero and the case out of his mind for the time being. June Tabor was singing "The Grey Funnel Line," the dark warmth of her voice filling the room. He sipped his wine and abandoned himself to the music. It was easy enough to imagine that he was out at sea, here in the semidark surrounded by glass, the wild night outside, the wind howling and rain lashing.

He had just reached for the bottle to refill his glass when the doorbell rang. It made him jump. He glanced at his watch. Close to ten. Who on earth could be calling at this time? Worried that it was probably not good news, Banks put his bottle down and walked through the kitchen, hall and study to the front door. When he opened it, he was surprised but relieved to see Annie Cabbot standing there without an umbrella.

"I was just thinking about you," said Banks. "When did you get back?"

"Yesterday. Can I come in? It's pissing down out here."

Banks stood aside as she stepped past him, and closed the door on the chilly rain. Annie hung up her coat and shook her hair like a wet dog. "That's better. Any chance of a cuppa?"

"I've got wine."

"Why doesn't that surprise me? But a simple cuppa would work wonders right now."

Banks walked through to the kitchen, Annie following. He turned his head. "Regular, green, chamomile, Earl Grey, decaf?"

"Chamomile, please," said Annie. "My God, where did you come up with all those choices?"

"California," said Banks. "They like their fancy tea in California. I learned to appreciate green tea there, especially. They have lots of different kinds, you know. Sencha, gyokuro, dragonwell."

"I'd forgotten you'd been there. I've forgotten most things around that time. Ordinary chamomile will do fine for me."

"How was St. Ives?"

"Wonderful. Beautiful. I got back into sketching and painting. Did a lot of walking on the cliffs."

"And Ray?"

"He's fine. Sends his regards. He's got another floozy. She can't be a day older than me."

"Lucky Ray." Banks had spent a lot of time with Annie's father during her illness and recovery, and they had got along remarkably well. Ray had even stopped over at the cottage a few times after they had opened that second bottle of wine, or hit the Laphroaig.

Banks put the kettle on. He decided to have some tea himself. He was trying to cut back on the wine intake, after all, and chamomile was particularly relaxing late at night. It might help him sleep. Annie leaned her hip against the counter. He was about to tell her she could go through to the conservatory and he'd bring the tea when it was ready, but he realized it would be tactless. He could even see it in her face under the toughness, a vulnerability, an uncertainty about whether she really should be facing the conservatory right now.

Several months ago, while Banks had been enjoying himself in sunny California, Annie had been shot in his conservatory. When he had first found out, he had wondered whether he would be able to go back in there again himself and enjoy it the way he had done before. But he hadn't been there when the shooting happened. The cleanup team had done a great job before he returned home, and Winsome had even had the sensitivity and good taste to refurnish the whole place for him. New carpet, new paint job, new chairs and table, new everything. And all sufficiently different in color and style from the originals. It was like having a new room, and he had felt no ghosts, no residual sense of pain, fear or suffering. He had lost a table, chairs and a carpet but not, thank God, a dear friend.

He was apprehensive after what had happened to Annie there, though, worried that it might bring on a panic attack or something. It was her first visit since the shooting.

They chatted in the kitchen until the kettle boiled, then Banks put the teapot and cups on a tray. "Want to go through?" he asked, gesturing toward the conservatory.

Annie followed him tentatively, as if unsure what effect the room would have on her.

"It looks different," she said, sitting in one of the wicker chairs.

Banks set down the tea tray on the low table and took the chair beside her. He looked at her, trying to gauge her reaction. Annie was in her early forties now, and Banks thought she had never looked so good. During her convalescence, she had let the blond highlights grow out and her hair had returned to its previous shoulder-length chestnut cascade. Banks decided he preferred it that way. "If you want, we can sit in the entertainment room," he said.

Annie shook her head. Toughing it out, then. "No, it's fine. I was expecting . . . you know . . . but it's fine. It's really nice, and it's very cozy with that warm light and the wind and rain outside." She hugged herself. "Let's just stay here, shall we? What's that music?"

"June Tabor," said Banks. "This one's called 'The Oggie Man.' Want something else on?"

"No. I'm fine. Really." That made a change; she was always complaining about his tastes in music. "What's an oggie man?"

"A pasty seller," said Banks. "It's a song lamenting the disappearance of street pasty sellers in Cornwall in favor of hot-dog stands. An oggie is a Cornish pasty. You ought to know that, being a good Cornish lass."

"Never heard of it. Sounds like a very sad song for such a silly little thing."

"Folk songs. You know. What can I say? I don't suppose it was silly or little to them at the time. It's about loss, the passing of a tradition."

"You know," Annie said suddenly, "I *do* remember that night. I remember when everything was fading to black, and I was feeling so cold and tired. I thought this was the last place I would ever see in my life, and for a moment, that was what I wanted." She glanced at Banks and smiled. "Disappearing like the silly oggie man. Isn't that funny?"

"I don't know. I don't think so."

"But I'm seeing the room again. That's the point. I know everything's different and all, but now it feels like . . . like being reborn. I didn't disappear. I didn't die. It wasn't the last thing I saw. It's the same room, but it's different. Not just the way it's been refurnished or decorated. Oh, I can't explain myself. I'm not good with words. I'm just saying it's a special place, that's all. For me. And the memories start now. I'm back, Alan. I want you to know that."

Banks gave her hand a quick squeeze. "I know you are, and I'm glad. But that's not why you came, is it?"

"No, it's not. I heard about DI Bill Quinn getting killed at St. Peter's. I want you to bring me up-to-date so I can jump right in on Monday morning. I've got to be more than a hundred percent on this one, or I'll be out."

"Don't be daft," said Banks.

"It's true. I'll bet you Madame Gervaise doesn't think I'll be fit enough, mentally or physically. I'll bet you she thinks I've lost my mojo. She'll be trying to drive me to resign."

"I think that's going a bit too far, Annie."

"Is it? Then what about that other woman in there with you? Your new partner. Miss Professional Standards. She's very attractive, isn't she? What's her name again? I've had a word with Winsome. She told me most of what's been going on, but I've forgotten the damn woman's name."

"Inspector Passero. Joanna Passero. She's just tagging along to nail Quinn. Or his memory."

"Are you being thick, or naïve?"

"Aren't you being a little bit paranoid?"

"Just because you're paranoid, it doesn't mean they're not after you."

"Fair enough. You worked Professional Standards for a while. You know what it's like. You didn't let the job swallow you up or change your basic attitude."

"It fucks you up, whether you fight it or not."

"I'm sure it does. But you're all right now, aren't you? What do you know about Inspector Passero?"

"Not much, but I do have my sources at county HQ. She lived in Woodstock, worked for Thames Valley, got an Italian husband called Carlo. And she's an icy blonde. I don't trust icy blondes. You never know what they're thinking."

"As opposed to feisty brunettes? All what you see is what you get? Jealous, Annie?"

Annie snorted. "Something's going on. Mark my words. I'd watch my back if I were you. I hear the sound of knives being sharpened."

"Don't worry about me. What are you going to do?" he asked.

"What do you mean?"

"You think Gervaise wants you out. What are you going to do about it?"

"I don't know. My options are a bit limited at the moment."

"Going off half-cocked and trying to prove you're better than everyone else won't work."

"Look who's talking."

"I'm being serious, Annie."

"So am I. I like my job. I'm good at it. And I want to keep it. Is that so strange?"

"Not at all," said Banks. "I want you to keep it, too."

"So you'll help me?"

"How?"

"Any way you can. Trust me. Give me decent tasks. Don't sideline me."

Banks paused. "Of course. I'll help you all I can. You should know that."

Annie leaned forward and rested her hands on her knees. "Use me, Alan. Don't keep me in the dark. I know I might seem like a bit of a liability at first, that I might seem a bit wobbly, and it'll take me a while to get back to normal, but it doesn't mean I have to be left out in the cold. Keep me informed. Listen to what I have to say. If I have a good idea, make sure people know it's mine. I'm resilient, and I'm a quick learner. You already know that."

"Across the Wide Ocean" ended, and with it the CD. Rain beat against the windows, and the wind howled through the trees. Annie sat back, shuddered and sipped some tea. "I enjoyed that," she said.

"I'm glad."

" 'The Oggie Man.' I'll remember that. Poor oggie man. I wonder what happened to him. Did they kill him? Was he murdered? The rain softly falling and the oggie man's no more." She shifted position and crossed her legs. "Tell me about Bill Quinn."

"Not much to say, really," said Banks. "According to everyone I've talked to, he was a devoted family man. Devastated by his wife's death. No trace of a reputation for womanizing or anything like that."

"But there are some pictures of him with a girl. I've seen them. I dropped by the squad room after a visit to Human Resources this morning, while you were out. The copies arrived while I was there. She looks like a very *young* girl."

"She wasn't *that* young."

"She was young enough. But that's not what I was thinking. Men are pigs. Fact. We all know that. They'll shag anything in a skirt. Quinn did it, and he got caught."

"Or set up."

"All right. Or set up. But why?"

"We don't know yet. Obviously blackmail of some kind."

"He didn't have a lot of money, did he?"

"Not that we know of. We haven't got his banking information yet, but there's nothing extravagant about his lifestyle. Nice house, but his wife worked as an estate agent, and they bought it a long time ago. Mortgage paid off. Kids at university before the fee increases."

"So he wasn't being blackmailed for his money."

"Unlikely."

"Then why?"

"To turn a blind eye to something, or to pass on information helpful to criminals," said Banks. "That's what Inspector Passero believes. She said there were rumors. But when Quinn's wife died, their hold over him was broken, all bets were off, and that caused a shift in the balance of power. Quinn became a loose cannon. All that has happened since resulted from that. At least, that's my theory."

"I should imagine right now you're casting your net pretty wide?" said Annie.

"We have to. There are a lot of questions to answer. Quinn worked on a lot of cases. I must say, though, that unless we're missing something, or the girl herself killed him for some reason we don't know about yet, it seems professional, organized."

"Cut to the chase. He wouldn't have kept those photos with him if there wasn't something important about them. Far too risky, even hidden as they were."

"His house was broken into," Banks said.

Annie shot him a glance. "When?"

"Probably around the time he was killed, maybe even long enough after for it to be the same person. We're not sure. They took his laptop and some papers. And we've got some tire tracks from a farm lane near St. Peter's that might help identify the killer's car."

"Why don't you bring me up to speed with the rest of it?"

Banks shared the last few drops of tea and told her what little he knew.

"One of the first things that came into my mind when I saw those photos," said Annie, "and what seems to be even more relevant now, after finding out that Quinn was supposedly a devoted family man, was what would make him do what he did with the girl?"

"Like you said, men are pigs."

"They let the little head do the thinking, right? Given the right circumstances, they'll shag anyone. But they've still got oodles of the old self-preservation instinct. They don't only lie to their families; they lie to themselves, too."

"Meaning?"

"Meaning that a man like Bill Quinn—devoted family man, as you say—was very unlikely to shit on his own doorstep, if you'll pardon my French. It's harder to lie to yourself about that if you smell it every day, to pursue the metaphor. Meaning you need to check out any conventions he went to, any holidays he took without his wife and kids—a trip to Vegas with the lads, for example, or a golfing holiday in St. Andrews. The further away from home, the better. Something so far away that it made it easy for him to pretend that he was on another planet, and everything that happened there had nothing to do with his earthly life, nothing to do with everyday reality, nothing to do with the family he was devoted to."

"Fishing. With Quinn it was more likely to be a fishing trip."

"Right, then. Whatever. Any period when he was away from home, either alone or with other like-minded blokes, staying in a hotel. You can't tell much about the place from the photos, but you might get one of the digital experts in Photographic Services to see if he can blow up a few beer mats and bring a sign or two into focus."

"We're working on it."

"Good. Because that might tell you whether we're dealing with a trip abroad. In my limited experience of such things, the further away from his own nest a man gets, the freer and friskier he feels, and the more likely he is to stray. It's like the wedding ring becomes invisible. Some men take it off altogether for the duration. And the shackles, the inhibitions, they conveniently fall off with it."

"You sound as if you're speaking from experience."

"I did say it was limited experience. And don't ask."

"But Quinn got set up."

"Indeed. What is it? What are you thinking?"

Banks hadn't realized that his expression had so clearly indicated a sudden thought. "Two things," he said. "A conference in France—Lyon—with Ken Blackstone, among others, and the Rachel Hewitt case."

"The girl who disappeared from the hen weekend in Tallinn?"

"That's the one."

"I've been to Tallinn once," said Annie. "Lovely city."

"I didn't know that."

"You don't know everything about me."

"Obviously not. When was this?"

"A few years ago. After Rachel Hewitt disappeared."

"Hen party?"

"Do I *look* like a hen?"

"What, then?"

"Dirty weekend."

"The married man?"

"Mind your own business."

"Anyway, there might be other trips Quinn made abroad, in addition to Lyon and Tallinn. We'll ask around. Thanks for the tip. That's a good line of inquiry, and I'll see it gets priority and that your name is mentioned in dispatches."

Annie put her mug down and stretched. "All I wanted to hear. And now I'd better go."

"You sure? No more tea? One for the road?"

"I'm tired. I really think I'd better get going. I've got a massage appointment at St. Peter's tomorrow afternoon." Annie stood up, took a long look around the conservatory, then headed for the front door. Banks helped her on with her coat. It was still raining outside, but not so fast now, and the wind had dropped. "See you on Monday," she said. "Maybe I can help run down Bill Quinn's trips abroad?" Then she gave him a quick peck on the cheek. "Remember, watch out for the blonde," she said, and dashed outside. He watched until her car disappeared down the drive, waved and went back inside. She'd given him a lot to think about, he had to admit. In the initial flurry of questions, information and possibilities, he had neglected to zoom in on the important psychological details the way Annie had.

It was just after eleven o'clock on Friday night, and he didn't feel like going out. Helmthorpe would be closing down for the night, anyway, unless they had a lock-in at the Duck and Drake. But Banks didn't feel like company. Instead, he made a detour through the entertainment room and pressed "play" again with *Ashore* still in the CD player. "Finisterre" piped through the good-quality speakers in the conservatory, where the rain was now no more than a pattering of mice's feet. The tea had been nice, but he poured himself another glass of Malbec and settled down to listen to the music and think about what Annie had said. He did his best thinking when he was listening to music and drinking wine.

4

"Are you sure this is the right place?" asked Banks. "According to the phone company, yes."

"But it's—"

"I know," said Winsome. "Apparently, it's won prizes, though."

Banks gave her a quizzical glance. "Prizes?"

"Yes. It's quite famous. A tourist attraction."

Banks opened the door and glanced inside. "Bloody hell, I can see what you mean."

"That's why it's famous," said Winsome, smiling.

The old red telephone box abutted the end wall of a terrace of cottages in the village of Ingleby, not far from Lyndgarth. The paintwork and the windowpanes were as clean as could be, not a scratch or a greasy fingerprint in sight. Inside, there was a carpet on the little square of floor, a vase of fresh-cut pink and purple flowers on the shelf by the directory, a box for donations, and an empty wastepaper bin. Banks shook the donations box. It rattled with coins. The whole place smelled clean and lemony, and all the surfaces shone every bit as much as the outside, as if recently polished. There was even a functioning telephone, as shiny black as could be, and no doubt sanitized, too. In almost every other telephone box Banks had seen over the past few years, the cash box, if there was one, had been broken into and the phone ripped, or cut, from its connecting wire. The donations box wouldn't have lasted five minutes, either.

What was more, Bill Quinn had received two telephone calls on his mobile from this very box over the past ten days, the last one on Tuesday evening, the day before he had been killed. There were other calls, of course, including several to and from his son or daughter, and one from an untraceable mobile number on the morning of the day he died, but this one seemed really odd. The team was already checking to find out what other calls had been made from the telephone box in the past ten days, especially around the same time as the calls to Bill Quinn.

Ingleby was a beautiful village, slate roofs gleaming in the morning sunshine, still a little damp from last night's rain; limestone cottages scrubbed and rinsed clean by the wind and rain; the gardens neat and already colorful, though it was still only late April, ready to burst forth in spectacular fashion as soon as summer arrived. Smoke curled up from one or two of the chimneys, as there was still a slight nip in the air. Behind the village, the daleside rose steeply through green and sere slopes to the rocky outcrops that marked the beginnings of the moorland. A narrow track wound up the hill, then split and ran along the daleside in both directions, about halfway up. Cloud shadows drifted slowly across the backdrop on the light breeze.

Banks felt as if he were in a place where nothing had changed for centuries, though the telephone box was clear evidence that they had. No signs of vandalism; neat gardens, obviously tended with pride. No wonder Ingleby had won the prettiest-village award more than once. There were people in the cities who didn't know, or even believe, that such places existed. Everybody believed in the urban landscape, with its no-go areas, dodgy council estates, riots, looting, terrorist hotbeds, street gangs, people who would mug you as soon as look at you and people who would kick the shit out of you if you so much as glanced at them. But this was something else. This was Arcadia.

Banks remembered the stories in a book he had read recently about wartime evacuees sent from the cities to the country panicking when they saw a cow or an apple tree because they had never experienced such things in their natural environment before. They thought that cows were no bigger than dogs or cats and that apples grew in wooden boxes. Of course, there were other people, mainly in America, who believed that all of England was like this. The fact was that, while such pastoral idylls did exist in many pockets of the country, even in places as picturesque as Ingleby appearances could be deceptive; even in the prettiest villages there were things under the surface that didn't bear close examination. As Sherlock Holmes had once observed about the countryside in general, there were stones you didn't want to turn over, cupboards you didn't want to open.

Banks took a deep breath of fresh air. "We'd better get the CSIs to come and check out the telephone box," he said. "I doubt we'll find anything, the way it's been cleaned and polished, but it's worth a try."

"I suppose we'd better start asking a few questions, too," Winsome said. "Shouldn't take long, a place this size. Should we ask her to help?" She nodded in the direction of Inspector Passero, who had insisted on accompanying them from Eastvale and was now standing back, checking her mobile for texts.

"I don't think so," said Banks. "Let's just keep her at a distance for now. She can tag along, but I don't want her taking any leads." At least Joanna was wearing more appropriate clothing today, Banks had noticed, though even to someone as unversed as he was in matters of style and design, its quality and fashion cred were unmistakable. With her skintight designer jeans disappearing into tan leather boots a little below her knees, and the green roll-neck jumper under the light brown suede jacket, all she needed was a riding cap and crop and she would be ready to set off on the morning gallops out Middleham way.

"Please yourself," said Winsome with a shrug. "You're the boss."

There were several cottages clustered around the small square facing the telephone box, and Banks had noticed the net curtains twitching in one of them while they had been standing there. "Let's start with that one," he said. The cottage he pointed to had a gate of blackened iron railings and worn steps leading up to the arched stone porch around the door. Creeping vegetation covered almost the entire front of the building like something from a horror movie Banks remembered seeing many years ago.

A few seconds after Banks rang the bell, an elderly woman answered the door. She reminded him of

Margaret Thatcher; at least her hair did. The rest of her was plump and matronly, like a cook from a television costume drama, and she was dressed for gardening, in baggy trousers and a shapeless jumper. Banks showed his warrant card and introduced Winsome. Joanna lingered at the bottom of the garden, inspecting the herbaceous borders, as if not quite sure what to do. Banks identified her for the woman anyway, just for the record.

"Gladys," the woman said. "Gladys Boscombe. Please, come in. I saw you looking at our telephone box, and you don't seem like the usual tourist types we get." She had a hint of a Yorkshire accent, but it sounded to Banks as if she had worked at adding a veneer of sophistication to it over the years.

Banks and Winsome followed her first into the hall, then through to the living room. Joanna didn't seem at all sure what to do, so Banks gestured for her to accompany them. It was a small room, and it seemed crowded with the four of them in it, but they each found somewhere to sit, and Gladys Boscombe dashed off to make tea. Nobody had refused her offer. The front window was open a couple of inches, despite the chill, and the silence was punctuated only by birds singing. The room smelled of lavender. The velour sofa and armchairs were covered with lace antimacassars, and even the hard-backed chair Banks sat on had a covered seat cushion. Knickknacks stood on every surface and filled every alcove: delicate porcelain figurines of piping shepherds or waiting princesses, whorled seashells and pebbles, silver-framed family photographs, a carved ivory and ebony chess set.

That gave him a sudden, sharp memory of Sophia, who had been his girlfriend until a few months ago. She liked to collect shiny pretty things, too, and he had been partly responsible for some of them being vandalized. She had never forgiven him for that; in a way, it had helped precipitate the end of their relationship. He still missed Sophia, despite everything, and sometimes he thought he should try to get in touch with her again, try to rekindle the spark, which he was certain was still there. Then he remembered how she had ignored his calls and e-mails before, and he didn't want to risk rejection again. Her "dear John" e-mail had been banal, chatty and brutal. He remembered how low it had made him feel, and how he had half-drunkenly responded with some gibberish he could hardly remember now. He wished he had acted in a more grown-up manner, been more accepting and kind. Clearly such happiness as he had known in those few brief weeks they had been together was not meant for him. Sometimes he felt dragged down by the recent past, and he wanted desperately to get beyond it, to be OK with Annie, with Tracy, with Sophia, even, though he realized he would probably never see her again. Right now, there was nobody in his life except family and friends, and that was just fine for the moment. He had nothing to give anyone else.

Gladys Boscombe came back with the tea service on a silver tray, delicate little rose-patterned china cups rimmed with gold, matching saucers and teapot. She put the tray down on the low table in front of the fireplace and beamed at them. "We'll just let it mash a few minutes, shall we? Giles will be sorry to miss you. That's my husband. He's always been interested in detective stories. Never missed a *Midsomer Murders*. The proper ones, you know, with John Nettles. But he's out walking the lads on the moor. Perhaps he'll be back soon."

"Your children still live with you?" She looked far too old to have children young enough to take for a walk, but Banks thought it best to be polite.

Mrs. Boscombe patted her hair. She ought to be careful or she'd cut herself, he thought. "Oooh, don't be silly, young man. Both our children are long grown up and moved away. No, I mean the lads, Jewel and Warriss, the Jack Russells."

"Ah, of course." Banks managed to suppress his laughter at the thought of two Jack Russells named after a pair of music hall comedians. Jimmy Jewel and Ben Warriss; he hadn't thought or heard of them in years. Must be dead now, he supposed, along with their contemporaries Mike and Bernie Winters. "Right. Thanks, Mrs. Boscombe. We're here about the telephone box, as you might have gathered."

Mrs. Boscombe eased herself down on the sofa beside Winsome. "Yes, I couldn't think for the life of me why you were all standing around it chatting, then examining it like some museum exhibit. I can't imagine why on earth you would be interested in that old thing," she said, a note of distaste creeping into her tone. "True, I suppose it is famous in its way, but it's still an eyesore. And some of the people it seems to attract . . ." She gave a mock shudder.

"Actually," said Banks, "that's what we're interested in. The people it attracts."

"Tourists, mostly. A lot of foreigners. They leave their litter in the street and keep their car engines running, filling the air with that dreadful carbon monoxide. Some of them even stand and smoke cigarettes. I suppose we should think ourselves fortunate it doesn't draw the younger generation, or it would soon be vandalized, no doubt, but even so . . ." Mrs. Boscombe poured the tea, offering milk and sugar to all who wanted it. When Banks lifted the cup to take his first sip, he felt that he ought to stick his little finger in the air. Joanna did so, he noticed. She caught him glancing and blushed.

"Do the villagers use it often?"

Her eyes widened. "Villagers? Why would we? We all have proper telephones. Some of the newcomers even have mobiles."

What year was it here? Banks wondered. And just how new were the newcomers? He was surprised that mobiles even got coverage in such a remote area, but there were towers all over the place these days. Still, the fact remained that Bill Quinn had received two telephone calls from the very box in question over the period he had been at St. Peter's. That certainly didn't smack of passing tourists; it indicated deliberation, rather than chance. "Perhaps for privacy, or a fault on the home line?" Banks suggested. "Have you noticed anyone you know using that public telephone over the past week or two?"

"I haven't noticed anyone I know using it for the past year or two," Mrs. Boscombe replied.

"Are any of the cottages rentals?"

Mrs. Boscombe bristled. "I should think not. We have strict rules about that sort of thing in the village. Besides, who'd want to rent a cottage here? There's no pub, no general store, nothing. You'd have to go all the way to Lyndgarth for anything like that."

"Perhaps someone who likes the country air, a walker, bird-watcher, naturalist? Some people enjoy the solitary existence, at least for a while."

"Perhaps. But there are no rental cottages available in the village."

"Mrs. Boscombe," Banks said, hoping not to betray in his tone the desperation and frustration he was feeling. "It's very important. We have information that someone we're investigating received two telephone calls from that box within the past ten days. Now, does that sound like a tourist to you?"

Her face lit up. "No, it certainly doesn't. The tourists rarely use the telephone, or if they do, they use it only once. Mostly they just take photographs of their husbands or wives pretending to use it. Is it a true mystery then? Has there been a *murder*? Oh, I do so wish Giles were here." She checked her watch. "Perhaps if you could just stay for another half hour or so? He's usually not so long. More tea? I have fresh scones."

The prospect of spending any longer in the cramped living room surrounded by twee knickknacks and a garrulous old woman had about as much appeal as a poke in the eye with a sharp stick. Winsome and Joanna were looking twitchy, too, Banks noticed. "Can you think of anyone?" he asked. "You have the perfect view of the place. If the locals don't use it, and the tourists don't use it, then who does?"

"Only the Gypsies, I suppose, if you care to count them."

"Gypsies?"

She waved her hand in the air. "Oh, you know. Gypsies, Travelers. Whatever they call themselves. They don't stop anywhere long enough to have proper telephones installed, do they, and I don't suppose they can afford mobiles, anyway. Not when they're all on the dole."

"Who are these people?"

"I'm afraid I have no idea. I've just seen them in the village occasionally, a man and a woman, separately. It may be terribly superficial of me to jump to conclusions, but there it is. Greasy hair, dirty clothes, unshaven face. And you should see the man."

It took Banks a moment, but he glanced at Mrs. Boscombe and saw the glimmer of a smile on her face. She'd cracked a joke, knew it and was proud of it. He laughed, and the others laughed with him. "So did you see this Gypsy man or woman use the telephone recently?" he asked.

"Yes. A couple of times in the past week or two," Mrs. Boscombe said.

"But they weren't together?"

"No."

Banks took out the photo of the girl with Bill Quinn. "Is she anything like the woman you mentioned?" he asked.

She shook her head. "I didn't get a good look at her, but I would say the one I saw was older, and she had a bit more flesh on her bones. No, it wasn't her."

"OK," said Banks, feeling disappointed. If the photo had been taken a few years ago, the woman might have changed, he thought. "What about the man? What can you tell me about him?"

"I'm afraid I don't know anything about him, or about any of them."

"Are there any others?"

"I don't know. I only saw the two of them use the phone, and it was always after dark. I could only see what I did because the box is well lit, of course."

"Do you remember what days?"

"Not really. I think the man was last here on Tuesday about nine, because I'd just finished watching *Holby City,* a little weakness of mine. The woman . . . it might have been Sunday. Or maybe Saturday. The weekend, I think, anyway."

"Can you describe him?"

"I could only see him in the light from the telephone box. About your height, perhaps, wearing dirty jeans and a scruffy old donkey jacket, hair over his collar, hadn't been washed in a while, beginnings of a beard and mustache."

"Fat or thin?"

"Maybe just a little more filled out than you. Certainly not fat, not by any stretch of the imagination."

"The color of his hair?"

"Dark. Black or brown, it would be impossible to say exactly."

"Did he talk on the telephone for long?"

"I don't know. I didn't linger at the window to watch. All I know is by the time I'd finished what I was doing, he was gone again. Say maybe fifteen or twenty minutes."

That didn't quite match the four-minute call that Quinn had received from the box last Tuesday, so perhaps the man had made more than one call. The records from the phone box would tell them what other numbers had been called. If he had phoned Bill Quinn at about nine o'clock on Tuesday, that would have been during quiz night, so perhaps Quinn had missed quiz night because he had been expecting the call. It was a possibility, at any rate. "Is there anything else you can remember about this man?" Banks asked. "How old would you say he was?"

"I have no idea. Quite young. Midthirties, perhaps? The beard may have made him look older, of course."

"Would you recognize him again?"

"I don't know. I couldn't really make out any clear features, if you know what I mean. I'm quite good at remembering faces, though, even if I'm not very good at describing them. I might remember him."

"Do you know where the camp is?"

"There isn't one, really. Not exactly a camp, as such."

Banks's shoulders slumped. "So you don't know where he was living?"

"I didn't say that. I said there isn't a Gypsy camp as such. Giles told me he heard it from a rambler that there's someone living up at the old Garskill Farm. It's about two miles away, on the moors. I can't imagine what the poor fellow was doing walking up near there, even if he is a rambler, as it's well off the beaten track and . . . well . . . it's not the sort of place one wants to be alone."

"Why is that?"

"One hears stories. Old stories. It's a wild part of the moor. Most people give it a wide berth. There's something eerie about the place."

"You mean it's haunted?"

"That's what some folk believe."

"And you?"

"I've no cause to go up there. It's wild moorland. You'd risk getting lost—sometimes those fogs creep up all of a sudden, like, and you can't see your hand in front of your face. And there are bogs, fens, mires, old lead mine workings, sinkholes. It's not safe."

"Good enough reason not to go there, then," said Banks, smiling. "Even without the ghosts. What about kids? Is it somewhere the local kids might go to drink, take drugs or have sex?"

"No. There aren't really any local kids around here, and there are plenty of places nearer Lyndgarth or Helmthorpe for that sort of thing. Less remote, perhaps, but a lot more comfortable."

"So you think this man and the woman you saw might be squatting up at Garskill Farm?"

"It's the most likely place."

"Tell me about it."

"Not much to tell, really. Someone must own it, but I can't tell you who. It's been abandoned as long as I can remember. Falling to rack and ruin. I'm not even certain it was ever a working farm. It's my guess it belonged to whoever owned the lead mines, and when the industry died years back, well, they moved on."

Why on earth, Banks wondered, would someone walk two miles each way twice, eight miles in all, to talk to Bill Quinn on a public telephone if it wasn't important? Clearly whoever had done it didn't have access either to a closer landline or to a mobile, or he feared that someone might be listening in on his conversations. But why? And what, if anything, did he have to do with Bill Quinn's murder?

They heard the sound of the gate opening and dogs barking. Mrs. Boscombe got to her feet. "Ah, here's Giles and the lads. He *will* be glad to see you. You can tell him all about the murders you've solved. I'll just put the kettle on again."

There was no easy way up and over the dale to Garskill Farm, Giles Boscombe had explained, before they managed to cut short his analysis of what should be done about the presence of Gypsies and Travelers. Neither Banks's Porsche nor Winsome's Toyota would make it up the winding track, let alone over the top and across the moorland. There were probably other ways in—from the north, perhaps, or even the east or west—but they would most likely involve long detours and, no doubt, getting lost. Even if mobiles worked, satnavs weren't always reliable in this desolate part of the world. People often mixed up the dales and the moors, but Brontë country was a few miles southwest of where they were, though the moorland landscape on the tops between the dales had many similarities with the moors the Brontës had walked.

There were no village bobbies anymore; like the oggie man, they were a thing of the past. But Banks did happen to know that the Safe Community officer in Lyndgarth happened to drive a Range Rover, and when they raised him on the phone, he sounded only too willing to whiz over to Ingleby and do his best to get them as close to Garskill Farm as possible.

When Constable Vernon Jarrow arrived, they left their own cars by the telephone box and piled into his Range Rover, Banks in the front and Winsome and Joanna in the back. PC Jarrow was a pleasant, round-faced local fellow with the weather-beaten look of a countryman. He said he was used to driving off-road. Banks got out and opened the gate to the winding lane up the daleside, closing it behind him. Jarrow drove slowly and carefully, but the Range Rover still bumped over the rocks sticking out of the dirt and the ruts made by tractors. Some of the bends were almost too tight, but he made them. Banks was reminded of a tour bus he had once taken with Sandra to an ancient site in Greece, hugging the edge of a steep precipice all the way.

"Do you know Garskill Farm?" he asked Jarrow over the noise of the engine.

"I know of it," Jarrow answered. "It's been like that for years. Abandoned."

"Ever been up there?"

"No reason to."

"Not even just to check on it?"

Jarrow gave Banks a bemused sideways glance. "Check on what? There's nothing there."

"Mrs. Boscombe heard rumors there's been some Gypsies or Travelers staying up there recently."

Jarrow grunted. "They're welcome. Long as they don't cause any trouble in the community."

"How do you know they haven't?"

"I'd have heard about it, wouldn't I?"

It seemed like unassailable logic. Banks didn't blame Jarrow for not checking out every square inch of his patch as frequently as possible, but that kind of complacency in assuming that he would know the minute anything was wrong was no excuse. Still, he let it go. After all, the man was driving them to a remote spot, and there was no sense in giving him a bollocking on the way.

When the track came to the east-west lane halfway up the daleside, PC Jarrow kept going straight on, up the daleside, where the road became even more rudimentary, so much so that it was hard to make out at all sometimes, forcing them back in their seats. Soon, they were weaving between outcrops of limestone, bouncing around even more than on the rutted track below. If

Banks had contrived this whole business to irritate and upset Joanna Passero he couldn't have done a better job, he realized as he caught a glimpse of her ashen face in the rearview mirror, hand to her mouth. But he hadn't, and he found himself feeling sorry for her. He had no idea that she suffered from carsickness, and she hadn't said anything. Still, there was nothing he could do about it at this point; she would simply have to hold on.

Soon they were driving across the open moorland, and while it was still as bumpy, at least they were more or less on the flat. This had once been an area of about two or three thriving villages, Banks knew. There was an isolated old house known locally as the Schoolhouse, which was exactly what it had been even as late as the First World War. After that, the moorland had fallen into decline and never recovered. The military had been making noises for years about taking it over for maneuvers, but they already had plenty of land in the area, and they didn't seem to need Garskill Moor yet.

There were roads, tracks or laneways crisscrossing the rolling tracts of gorse and heather, and soon the bumpiness of the ride improved somewhat. Joanna took her hand away from her mouth, but she was still pale. Winsome didn't seem bothered by any of it. Jarrow drove slowly, straight ahead. It was an interesting landscape, Banks thought. People often assume the moorland that runs along the tops between dales is flat and barren, but this landscape was undulating, with surprising chasms appearing suddenly at one side or the other, unexpected becks lined with trees, clumps of bright wildflowers, and the ruined flues and furnaces of abandoned lead mines in the distance. Even in the pale April sunlight, it resembled an abandoned land, an asteroid once settled, then deserted.

"Does nobody live up here anymore?" Banks asked.

"Not for miles. There used to be an old woman in the Schoolhouse. Everybody thought she was a witch. But she died a couple of years ago. Nobody's moved in since, so that's falling to rack and ruin, too."

"Are we almost there?" Joanna asked from the back.

"Not far now, miss," Jarrow assured her. "You just hold on there. It's in a hollow, so you can't really see it until you come right up on it."

They crossed over a tiny stone bridge and bumped along beside a fast-flowing beck for a while, then up the steep bank, along the top, and sure enough, as they turned a corner by a small copse, there, in the hollow, stood Garskill Farm—or rather, the ruins of Garskill Farm.

Actually, it didn't look as bad as Banks had been led to expect. The three solid limestone buildings, arranged around what might have once been a pleasant garden or courtyard, were for the most part structurally intact, though there were slates missing from roofs here and there, and all the windows were broken. Most of them had been boarded up. The two outlying buildings were smaller and had probably been used for storage, while only the central, larger building was meant to house people. Even so, if anyone was squatting there, they had to be desperate.

Jarrow pulled to a halt by the remains of a drystone wall, which had clearly marked the border of the property. They all got out of the Range Rover. Banks felt shaky, as if all his joints had worked a bit loose, and Joanna Passero immediately turned her back and walked a few yards away before resting her palms on her knees and bending to vomit quietly into the shrubbery. Everyone pretended to ignore her. Even Banks felt no desire to take the piss. Only Winsome had had the sense to bring bottled water, and she offered some to Joanna, who immediately accepted and thanked her, apologizing to everyone for her little display of weakness. The wind howled around them and seemed to use the buildings as musical instruments, whistling in the flues and rattling loose window boards like percussion. Mrs. Boscombe had certainly been right about how eerie it was up there.

Banks stepped over some variously shaped stones that had once formed the drystone wall. A lot of skill had no doubt gone into building that wall, he thought, and now it had collapsed, brought down by stray cattle or sheep, or winter storms freezing the water in the cracks and expanding it. Such drystone walls were built to withstand most things nature could throw their way, but they needed a little repair work now and then, a little tender loving care.

Finding himself standing in a garden completely overgrown with weeds, mostly nettles and thistles up to thigh height, Banks paused and turned to address the others. "OK," he said, stepping back. "There doesn't seem to be any kind of an easy way in here, and if anyone was using the place you'd think they'd at least clear a way in and out."

" 'Round the other side?" Winsome said.

"Exactly. So let's make our way around the perimeter and see if we can't find an easier access point. And be careful. There are bloody nettles and thistles everywhere. Winsome, will you take Inspector Passero and check out that first outbuilding, on the left there? PC Jarrow, you come with me, and we'll start with the center building, then we'll all meet up in the one on the far right."

"I've got a couple of torches in the Range Rover," said Jarrow. "We might need them in there."

"Good idea," said Banks.

They waited until Jarrow brought the torches and tested them, then Banks led the way around the remains of the garden wall, just as overgrown on the outside as on the inside, and along the end of the building to their left. They were at the back of the house now, and able to step into the yard over a ruined section of wall. When they arrived at the doorway of the first building, Winsome and Joanna pushed it open and disappeared inside. Banks and Jarrow continued across a stretch of high grass to the back of the house itself.

It was just as dilapidated as the outbuildings from the outside, though it might have been a grand house in its day. Banks stopped before they got to the door and pointed. Jarrow followed his gaze. The pathway worn through the undergrowth from the door to a driveway that crossed the back of the property was clear to see. Obviously, if one or more people had been squatting here, they needed to be able to get in and out, no matter how far they had to walk to the nearest shop or telephone. Ultimately, through a network of unfenced roads, tracks and laneways, if they had any means of transport they could connect with the A66, and from there to Carlisle, Darlington, the M1, the A1 and pretty much anywhere else in the country. But the quickest way to Ingleby was the way Banks and the others had just come.

There were no signs of any cars around, except the burned-out chassis of an old Morris Minor in a back-yard filled with rusty farm, gardening and mining equipment. Banks's father used to drive a Morris Minor years ago. He remembered family outings to the countryside as a child, his mother and father sitting proudly up front, he and his brother, Roy, fighting in the back. They were good memories: hot sweet tea from a Thermos; orange juice and sandwiches and buns in a field by the river, or even on a roadside lay-by; ice creams; swimming in the river shallows if it was a warm enough day.

The implements were nothing unusual. Banks had seen similar things in some of the Dales museums. The closest anything came to transport was an old wooden cartwheel with most of the spokes missing. The silence beyond the wind was even more all-encompassing up here than in Ingleby. A curlew's sad call drifted from the distant moors, but that was all, apart from Jarrow's heavy breathing and the moaning of the wind in the flues, a loose board clattering somewhere.

There was a heavy wooden door with peeling green paint wedged into the doorway at the back, half-way along the building. A simple push from Jarrow's shoulder opened it and they walked inside, switching on their torches. It seemed to be one long room, like the banquet hall of an old Viking dwelling or a school dormitory, and the torchlight picked out two rows of thin foam mattresses. There were ten on each side, all stained and damp. Here and there, two of the mattresses had been pulled close together, as if their occupants were trying to mimic a double bed or huddle close for warmth. There were no pillows. Whoever had been there, it looked as though they were gone. The walls were stone, and there was no ceiling, only bare rafters holding up the roof. In one or two places, the tiles and surfacing had disappeared, letting in the light from outside. Rain, too, no doubt, as the buckets carefully placed under each hole attested. Dirty blankets lay bunched up beside most of the mattresses.

The smell was almost overwhelming. A human smell, only magnified: dirty socks, urine, vomit, sweat. The smell of poverty and desperation. Gnawed bones, chicken legs most likely, and some empty takeaway food cartons and Costa Coffee cups littered the floor. McDonald's. Burger King. Kentucky Fried Chicken. The food must have been freezing before it got here, Banks thought, even though someone must have had a car. The nearest McDonald's was probably the one in Eastvale, at least fifteen miles away. Still, perhaps it was better than nothing. There appeared to be no cooking or food storage facilities here.

At the far end of the room was a trough of murky water with a long spoon on a hook, curved at the bottom so it could be used for drinking. Next to it, behind a ratty, moth-eaten curtain, was a bucket. Banks didn't need the torchlight to show him what was in it. He turned away in disgust. His eyes lighted on a tattered paperback lying beside one of the mattresses. He knelt down and picked it up carefully. It wasn't in English, and he couldn't guess what language it was from any of the words, though the sheer number of consonants, and the odd symbols crowning some of the letters, made him think of Polish. The paper was already faded, and some of the pages were torn. Banks put it back.

"What do you think?" Jarrow whispered.

"I don't know," said Banks, still kneeling by the thin foam mattress. He stood up and brushed off his trousers. "I can tell you one thing, though. I doubt very much we're dealing with Gypsies or Travelers. They don't usually live like this."

"Squatters?"

"More like it. Let's go."

Glad to be outside again, Banks and Jarrow took a few deep breaths of relatively fresh air and watched the women coming over to meet them. "It's a rudimentary loo," Winsome said, "though there's no sewage system from what I can see."

"There's a sort of basic shower, too," Joanna added. "It's hooked up to a cold-water tank. There doesn't seem to be any hot."

"There wouldn't be," said Banks. "Someone would have to pay for that. Maybe they fill a cold-water tank from the beck, or just let the rain collect." He told them what he and Jarrow had found in the larger building.

Winsome and Joanna poked their heads inside and came out quickly. "My God," said Winsome. "What's been happening here?"

"I'm not sure," said Banks. "It looks like a squat, but do you remember that converted barn outside Richmond a few years back? It was in a bit better shape than this setup, but not much. They found a whole bunch of unskilled migrant laborers living there in dreadful conditions. They were mostly Eastern European, and they'd been enticed over here by promises of work. For a fee, of course. Instead they found themselves basically bound in slavery to a gang master, owing so much money they could never pay their way out of it, and what they did have to pay left them nothing to live on—or to run away with."

"The kind of people Warren Corrigan preys on," said Winsome.

Banks gave her an appreciative glance. "So you do listen to the briefings?"

Winsome smiled. "Of course, sir. Sometimes."

"The impression I got was that he operates mostly in the cities, but it's a good point. Keep it in mind. It looks very much as if Bill Quinn's team might have had a man on the inside. We'll have a little talk with pal Corrigan soon." Banks glanced toward the final, and smallest, of the three buildings. The boards were still in the windows, and the back door was shut, though, again, it proved not to be locked, and it wasn't much of a barrier against Jarrow's firm shoulder.

At first, the two torch beams picked out nothing except a pile of dirty bedding, another trough of filthy water, a rickety old chair and a few damp ragged towels and lengths of rope. A broken broom handle leaned against the wall by the door, and Banks used it to poke among the tangle of sheets and blankets on the floor. The handle touched something firm but yielding. Already feeling that clenching in his gut that warned him what was coming, Banks used the stick to hook and pull away the rest of the sheets and blankets, and the four of them gazed down on a man's body. He was naked, and his skin gleamed with a strange greenish tinge in the artificial light. He was thin; he had long-ish, greasy dark hair and the beginnings of a beard; and beside him, among the heap of filthy bedding, was a worn donkey jacket and a pair of dirty jeans.

As the strong fingers worked on the muscles around her neck and shoulders, Annie finally gave herself up to Daniel Craig's magic touch. Her breath came sharply, and her whole body tingled with warmth and pleasure. His hands slid down the small of her back toward the base of her spine. She waited for the touch of his lips and that slight scrape of five o'clock shadow in the sweet spot between her neck and shoulder, then he would turn her over, his lips would continue slowly down her body and his hands would—

"That's it for today, love."

The gravelly voice shattered Annie's erotic reverie. Of course it wasn't Daniel Craig; it was just Old Nobby, the St. Peter's masseur. Old Nobby was ex-navy and a bit long in the tooth, with anchor tattoos on both forearms and enough of the sea dog about him that his other nickname around the place was Popeye. But he had magic fingers and was a damn fine masseur, and Annie found that if she closed her eyes and let herself drift, he could be anyone she wanted him to be for half an hour.

"Thanks, Nobby," Annie said, pulling the bathrobe around her and securing the belt as she sat up. She might not have minded letting Daniel Craig see her charms, but not Old Nobby. Not that he seemed interested. He had his back turned to her, and he was bent over the desk filling out forms. She liked Nobby. He was a bit of an amateur philosopher. He had an open and inquiring mind and often seemed happy to chat for ages about practically nothing at all after sessions. The conversations were almost as relaxing as the massages, though not quite as sexually stimulating. Her skin still tingled pleasantly. Whether he knew of the effect he had on her, she had no idea, and she was certainly not going to ask him.

Now that Annie was back in the real world, she could hear sounds from outside. Though St. Peter's was trying to drag itself back to normal—the regular massage routine, for example—the place was still crawling with police and CSIs. It shouldn't take much longer now, though, she thought. All the guests and most of the part-time staff had been questioned, according to Winsome, some more than once, their backgrounds and alibis no doubt thoroughly checked, and it didn't seem as if anyone from the center either knew anything or had anything to do with what had happened to Bill Quinn. There might still be some connection they hadn't unearthed yet, but Annie doubted it. Whatever fate had befallen Bill Quinn, she believed, had happened because of something outside and had come from outside. It had followed him here, or found him here, without any help from St. Peter's itself. His presence here had been no secret; no tip-off from the inside would have been needed for anyone who wanted to locate him.

"You're doing a grand job, Nobby," she said.

Nobby turned from his paperwork and sat on the only office chair. Annie remained perched on the edge of the massage table.

"Thanks, lass," he said. "Bad business, all this, eh?" He gestured toward the activity outside.

"It certainly is."

"You knew him?"

"No. You?"

"Just professionally, like."

"Did he talk much?"

"Sometimes. You know, I've always thought a good massage can work a bit like hypnosis. Take a person deep down to those long-forgotten places, events and feelings. Sometimes that's where the answer lies."

Sexual fantasies, too, Annie thought. She wondered if Bill Quinn had dreamed of the girl in the photo as Nobby's fingers worked their magic on him. Or was it different for a man, especially when it was another man touching him? "What do you mean?" she asked.

Nobby shifted to make himself more comfortable. His chair creaked. "Must get this bloody thing oiled. I suppose what I mean is that often the root of the problem isn't obviously physical. Even something as simple as neck pain or back pain."

"You mean like when something's psychosomatic?" she said.

"A massage can work both ways, you know." Nobby held his hands up. "Lethal weapons," he said, and laughed.

Annie laughed with him, but she guessed there was more than a grain of truth in what he said. After all, rumor had it that he had been seconded to the SAS at one time.

"You have to be careful not to exacerbate the problem," he went on. "As you can attest better than most, nerves are sensitive things."

"I certainly can. What about Bill Quinn?"

"His neck? There wasn't a lot wrong with it, as far as I could tell. Certainly not the kind of physical problems you had when we first started our sessions."

"Swinging the lead?"

Nobby paused before answering. "No. I don't think so. We can resist getting better for any number of reasons we're not aware of."

"Like what?" she asked.

"The usual. Fear. Despair. Indifference. Indecision. Lack of confidence. Guilt, even."

"And in Bill's case?"

"He was troubled."

"By what? Did he talk to you, Nobby? Did he tell you something?"

"No, not in the way you mean. Not anything you could put your finger on." Nobby flashed her a crooked grin. "Always the copper first, I suppose, eh?"

"Well, I am due to start working on the case officially on Monday. Thought I might get a head start."

"Aye, well. To answer your question, yes, we talked sometimes."

"And you didn't tell the police officer who questioned you?"

"You make it sound like there was something to tell. It was nothing but blethering, smoke in the wind. We had some conversations, as you do. As we're doing now. Our conversations were rambling, vague and philosophical." He snorted. "All the police officer asked me was where I was after dark on Thursday evening, if I knew how to use a crossbow, did I belong to any archery clubs? Had I known Bill Quinn on the force? I was never even on the force, for crying out loud. I was a navy medic, and now I'm a qualified masseur. They asked about practical things. Our conversations weren't practical."

Banks would get along with Nobby very well, Annie thought. He placed as much value in the vague and philosophical as Nobby did. That was why he often went against the rules and spoke to witnesses, even suspects, by himself. He said most detectives didn't know the right questions to ask. "Go on," Annie said. "What were they about, then?"

"Mostly my own thoughts and imaginings, I suppose," said Nobby.

"Will you tell me?"

"No reason not to, I suppose. It's not as if it's under the seal of the confessional, or the Official Secrets Act, or anything. And I'm not his shrink. But only because I like you. There's nothing to tell, really, so don't get your hopes up. Like I said, I got the impression that Mr. Quinn was a troubled man. He said he'd been having these neck pains for about five or six years, and he'd never had any problems before then. It didn't sound as if the cause was ergonomic. You know, too long at the computer keyboard—he hated computers—or even bad posture at the desk. Apparently he was like you, the kind of copper who liked to get out on the streets, and in his spare time he worked on his allotment, went fishing, spent time with his family. Even so, necks are funny things. The vertebrae deteriorate with age, but the X-rays didn't show any serious deterioration in his case. Only moderate. What you'd expect."

"So you're saying the causes were psychological?"

"I'm not a psychiatrist or a physiotherapist, so don't quote me on that. Can you see why it's not something you'd find easy to put into words? I don't even know why I'm telling you. I suppose it's because he's dead, and I've been thinking about him. Just days ago, he was alive as you or I." He held up his hands. "I could touch his skin, the muscle underneath, feel the give and the push, the knots. You know his wife died recently?"

"Yes."

"Of course you do. He was devastated, grief-stricken, poor bloke. I think that was something that brought us together. I knew what he felt like. I lost my Denise five years ago, so I suppose you could say we had something in common. I'm not a grief counselor, so I couldn't help him with it in any way, but it was something we could talk about."

"So you talked about grief, the death of his wife?"

"Yes. Sometimes. And about grief in general. And guilt. Could he have done more? Did he let her down? Was he to blame?"

"He wasn't, was he?"

"Of course not," Nobby said. "That's just the way you think sometimes when you lose somebody you love. You blame yourself. He was out on surveillance, incommunicado, the night she died. He didn't find out until the next morning. The kids were away at university. She died alone. Guilt over things like that can gnaw away at you."

"What did you tell him?"

"I told you. I'm not a counselor. I couldn't do anything but sympathize with him, as I would with anyone in that position, and reassure him that all this was normal."

"What did he want? I mean, why was he telling you all this?"

"Like I said, we had something in common. He seemed to want some kind of absolution, as if he was seeking atonement."

"Atonement for what?"

"Dunno. He didn't say. But it was something that haunted him."

"Something he'd done?"

"Or not done. It's far too easy to regret things you've done. He was drinking a bit too much. One of his kids had said something, and he'd read up on AA. He hadn't joined, hadn't thought he needed to yet, that there was still time to gain control over it. He saw the drink as temporary relief, a crutch, you know the sort of thing. Anyway, I've been there, too, in my long and checkered career, and we got talking a bit philosophically, as you do, about addiction and the whole twelve-step program, and he seemed fascinated by the idea of being given the chance to change the things you can change and let the higher power deal with those you can't, and having the wisdom to know the difference."

"I've heard it," said Annie. "It sounds heavy. And complicated."

Nobby laughed. "It's not so heavy," he said. "It's definitely not easy, though. He asked me if I thought that if a person knew a wrong had been done, and he thought he could put it right, should he try to do it, no matter what the cost to himself or others?"

"What did he mean?"

"I don't know. That's all he said about it."

"What was your answer?"

"I didn't have one. Still don't."

"Was he talking about himself?"

Nobby stood up. It was time for his next patient. "That I don't know. Like I said, he was a haunted man."

Fortunately, Jarrow had a police radio in his Range Rover, but even so, it took over three hours to get a CSI team, police surgeon and photographer up to Garskill Farm. In the end, ACC McLaughlin had to bite the bullet and pay for a helicopter to get Dr. Burns and Peter Darby there, complaining all the while about how expensive the whole business was becoming and hinting that this was somehow Banks's fault.

The CSIs managed a bumpy journey up from Ingleby in their well-sprung van, which looked a bit the worse for wear when it pulled up by the garden wall. They were especially disgruntled as it was the weekend, and they weren't even Eastvale CSIs, who were still busy at St. Peter's. They had come all the way from Harrogate. They also seemed to blame Banks for all their woes, especially the crime scene manager, a particularly surly and obnoxious individual called Cyril Smedley, who did nothing but complain about contamination and bark orders at all and sundry. It made Banks long for Stefan Nowak, who went about his business in a quiet and dignified manner. But Stefan had St. Peter's to deal with.

On the phone, Banks had warned everyone to avoid coming in from the north of the buildings, as there was a driveway leading to a lane, and that was the most likely area they would find tire tracks, footprints and other trace evidence. It needed to be preserved, in case the rains hadn't washed every scrap of evidence away. On a brief reconnoiter, Banks had noticed a couple of sandwich wrappers and an empty paper coffee cup in the grass beside the worn path to the driveway, all of which might prove useful in providing DNA or fingerprint evidence if they had been sheltered well enough from the elements. Whatever these people were up to, they certainly weren't very tidy about it. Already several CSIs were taking casts and collecting whatever they could find on the path and driveway. Peter Darby was taking digital video of the whole show.

Darby had finished photographing the body, and Banks crouched beside Dr. Burns as he examined it in situ under the bright arc lamps the CSIs had set up. The helicopter was waiting beyond the compound to take it to the mortuary when he was finished, but Dr. Glendenning, the Home Office pathologist, was away for the weekend, and there would be no postmortem until Monday. Anything Dr. Burns could tell them today might prove vital.

Banks had already been through the pockets of the discarded clothing and found nothing but fluff. It was the same as with Bill Quinn; everything had been removed from the victim's pockets. Now the various articles of clothing had been bagged and labeled by the CSIs along with the growing pile of exhibits. It was going to be a tough job to get everything out of there. The idea of establishing a mobile murder room at the site was out of the question, but officers would have to be left on guard day and night as long as it was still classified as a crime scene. The CSIs had already divided the area into zones, which the designated officers were searching thoroughly. Banks didn't envy them crawling around in the wet nettles and animal droppings.

"What do you think, Doc?" Banks asked, returning his attention to the body.

"There are signs of violence," Burns said. "Bruising on the shoulders and upper arms, indications that the wrists were bound." He pointed out the red chafing. "But none of these seem to me to constitute cause of death."

Banks pointed to the thighs and chest. "What about those bloody marks?"

"Small animals. Rats, most likely."

Banks gave a shudder. "No crossbow bolt?"

"Not this time."

"What do you think of his hands?"

Dr. Burns examined them. "They seem in pretty good condition. He bit his nails, but not excessively."

"Are they the hands of an unskilled manual laborer?"

"Of course not. There are no calluses, no ground-in grime. These hands haven't been used for anything more strenuous than carrying the shopping home."

"I thought not," said Banks. "What about his general condition? He was living pretty rough."

"Not bad, considering. I'd place him in his late thirties, early forties, generally quite fit, probably runs or works out in some way. The liver's not enlarged, at least not to the touch, so he's probably not a serious drinker. No sign of tobacco staining on the teeth or nicotine on the fingers, so he's probably not a smoker. I can't really say much more from a cursory external examination. I'm only really here to pronounce him dead, you know. And he is. Quite dead."

"I know that," said Banks. "But I also need some indication of time and cause of death."

Dr. Burns sighed. "The same old story."

"I'm afraid so."

"All I can say is that rigor has been and gone, and taking the temperature up here into account, I'd guess three days, probably more. But as you know, there are so many variables. It's not been that cold outside, but it does get chilly at night."

"He died before Bill Quinn?"

"Oh, yes. I'd say he definitely died before the last body I examined. You just have to look at the greenish tinge to see that, especially around the stomach area. That's caused by bacteria on the skin, and it doesn't usually start until about forty-eight hours after death. It spreads outwards and reaches the hands and feet last, and you can see it's there, too. The cool nights may have slowed it down a bit as well, but not much. I'd say between three and four days. Remind me. The first body was found when?"

"Thursday morning," said Banks. "But you said it's almost certain he was killed between eleven and one the night before, and Dr. Glendenning's postmortem confirmed it." Banks glanced at his watch, surprised to see that it was already after four o'clock in the afternoon. "That makes it about two and a half days from then until midday today. Definitely less than three days. Could this one have been dead even longer than you're suggesting?"

"Hard to say for certain, but I doubt it. After about four days the skin starts to get marblelike, and the veins come closer to the surface, become more visible. That hasn't happened yet. There's also not much insect activity. Some signs of bluebottles and blowflies, but they're always the first. Sometimes they come on the first day. The ants and beetles come later. I'd say Tuesday evening or Wednesday morning. That would be my preliminary guess, at any rate."

"Much appreciated," said Banks. If it was the same man who had phoned Bill Quinn around nine o'clock on Tuesday evening, it would have taken him probably about an hour to walk back to Garskill Farm from Ingleby, maybe a bit less, so he had to have been killed sometime after about ten o'clock on Tuesday evening and before, say, eleven on Wednesday evening.

Dr. Burns turned the body slightly so that Banks could see the pooling, or hypostasis, on his back and legs. "All that tells us in terms of time is that he's been dead more than six hours," said Dr. Burns.

"But it also tells us that he more than likely died here and hasn't been moved from that position, am I right?"

"That's right. You're learning."

"So what killed him?"

Dr. Burns said nothing for a few moments as he examined the body again, touched the hair and looked up at the roof. Then he examined the front and back for signs of fatal injuries. "There are no knife wounds or bullet entry points, as far as I can make out," he said. "Sometimes they're hard to spot, especially a thin blade or a small-caliber bullet, but I've been as thorough as I can under the circumstances."

"Blunt-object trauma?"

"You can see for yourself there's nothing of that sort."

"So what killed him? Was he poisoned? Did he die of natural causes?"

"He could have been poisoned, but that'll have to wait until the postmortem. As for natural causes, again, it's possible, but given the bruising, the condition of his body, the rope marks, I'd say they rule it out somewhat." Dr. Burns paused. "You're probably going to think I'm crazy, and I don't want you repeating this to anyone except your immediate team until the postmortem has been conducted, but if it helps you at all, it's my opinion that he drowned."

"Drowned?"

"Yes. He was naked. His hands were bound behind his back." Dr. Burns pressed the chest slightly. "And if I do that, you can just about hear a slight gurgling sound and feel the presence of water in the lungs. If I pressed much harder it would probably come out of his nose and mouth, but I don't want to risk disturbing the body that much." He gestured to the trough of water, the twisted towels, lengths of rope and overturned chair. "In fact, if you ask me, this man died of drowning, probably in conjunction with waterboarding. Those towels by the trough are still wet."

Banks stood up and took in everything Dr. Burns had mentioned. He had never understood the term "waterboarding." It sounded so much like a pleasant activity, something you do at the lake on a lazy summer afternoon, something you do for fun. Along with the rest of the world, he'd had a rude awakening when it hit the news so often over the last few years, especially when George Bush said he approved of it. Now he knew that "waterboarding" meant putting a cloth or towel over someone's face and pouring water over it while they were lying on their back. It was said to be excruciatingly painful, and could cause death by dry drowning, a form of suffocation. "He didn't die of the waterboarding, then?"

"He could have," said Dr. Burns. "Depends on the water in his lungs. Dr. Glendenning will be able to do a more thorough examination than I can. If he finds petechial hemorrhaging in the eyes, which I am unable to see, then you could be right. You would get that in dry drowning, but not in the case of drowning by water. Rarely, at any rate."

"But you can't see any?"

"That doesn't mean they aren't there. Sometimes they're no larger than pinpricks. You'll have to wait for the postmortem." Dr. Burns stood up. "If he was drowned," he went on, "you should be able to find enough forensic information to prove it, to tie the water in his lungs to the water in the trough, for example. On the other hand, if he died of dry drowning as a result of waterboarding, you probably won't find any water. There's always a chance it was accidental. Torture isn't an exact science. But if he was drowned in the trough, then the odds are somebody would have had to hold his head under until he died. It's a natural human reaction to breathe, and we'll use every ounce of strength we have to keep on doing so."

"How come you know so much about it?" Banks asked.

"I've been to some places nobody should ever have to go to," said Burns, then he picked up his bag and walked outside. "I'll tell the helicopter pilot we're ready for him," he said over his shoulder. Banks could remember when Burns was still wet around the ears. Now he had been to places where he had regularly seen the sort of things they had seen here today. Sometimes Banks wondered whether there was any innocence left in the world, and he felt terribly old.

By ten o'clock on Saturday night Banks felt like getting out of the house. He had been home only an hour or so, just enough time to eat his Indian takeaway, and he was feeling restless, tormented by the images of the dead bodies of Bill Quinn and the unknown man at Garskill Farm. He couldn't concentrate on television, and even Bill Evans's *Sunday at the Village Vanguard* CD didn't help. He needed somewhere noisy, vibrant and full of life; he needed to be with people, surrounded by conversation and laughter. He realized that he had become a bit of a stop-at-home lately, cultivating a rather melancholy disposition, importing his solo entertainment via CDs and DVDs, but the Dog and Gun had folk night tonight, and Penny Cartwright was guest-starring. There would still be time to catch a set.

Banks had met Penny on his second case in Eastvale, more than twenty years ago. She would be about fifty now, but back then she had been a young folksinger returning to her roots in Helmthorpe after forging some success in the big city, and her best friend had been killed. Over the years, her fame had grown, as much as a traditional folksinger's fame can be said to grow, and she had recently moved to a larger house close to the river, which always seemed to be full of guests and passing visitors when she was in residence, many of them well-known in folk circles. The wine flowed freely, and the gatherings always ended in a jam session and a mass sing-along. Though Banks had treated her as a suspect on the first case, and it took her many years to forgive him, she seemed comfortable enough with him now and had invited him to her home on occasion. He had joined in with the singing, but very quietly. He had hated his singing voice ever since the music teacher at school made everyone in class sing solo and gave them a mark out of twenty immediately after they had finished. Banks had got nine. He would never forget the public humiliation.

The evening was breezy but mild enough for him to walk by Gratly Beck and cut through the grave-yard, then down the snicket past the antiquarian book-shop into Helmthorpe's high street, where one or two groups of underdressed teenagers wandered noisily from one pub to another. They wouldn't go to the Dog and Gun. It would be too crowded already, for a start, and they didn't seem like the folk music type. There was a disco in the back room of the Bridge and cheap beer at the Hare and Hounds, which was now part of the Wetherspoon chain.

Banks arrived during a break between sets and saw Penny standing at the bar surrounded by admirers, a pint in her hand. She looked radiant, tall, slim, her long black hair streaked with gray. She spotted Banks through the sea of faces in the semidarkness, and he could have sworn her expression perked up, just a little. She waved him over and maneuvered a bit of room for him beside her. They were pushed together by the crush of people trying to order drinks. It wasn't an unpleasant sensation as far as Banks was concerned.

"Hello, stranger," she greeted him, leaning forward to give him a quick peck on the cheek. The young man beside her, in the midst of a rather tedious lecture about the "folk revival," seemed a bit put out by Banks's appearance, but Penny seemed relieved at the interruption and focused her attention on the newcomer. Banks returned the attention. When you were that close to her, looking into her eyes, it was difficult to do otherwise. They sparkled with an inner glow, full of mischief, sorrow and wisdom. The young man trailed off in midsentence and drifted away, crestfallen, back to his mates and more beer.

"He's too young for you, anyway," said Banks.

"Oh, I don't know. I'm not averse to the occasional toy boy," said Penny. "Though I do admit to being more partial to a real man. So what have you been up to?"

Banks realized that he hadn't seen her since the nasty business with Tracy the previous autumn, having been either working or shutting himself away in his cottage for the winter. He told her briefly about his travels in Arizona and Southern California. Penny, it seemed, had been doing quite a bit of traveling herself during the winter, mostly in Canada and the U.S. on a promotional tour for her new CD. There was no mention of a man in her life, and Banks didn't ask.

"I see your son Brian's doing well," Penny said.

"Yes," said Banks. "He's just got back from America himself. I think they had a good tour, then they did some recording in Los Angeles."

"I saw a few posters while I was over there. Impressive. I'm sure the Blue Lamps sell a lot more than I do."

They did, of course. Britpop with a tinge of psychedelia and a smattering of country-folk-blues did far

192 • PETER ROBINSON

better than traditional British folk music in the States. "I'm hoping he'll be able to support me in my old age," Banks said.

Penny laughed. "I suppose that's one use for children. So what have you been doing since you got back? I heard someone was found dead up at Garskill Farm. Is that true?"

"News travels fast," said Banks. "It's no secret. Someone told us there was a group of Gypsies or Travelers living up there, but I'm not so sure."

"How perceptive of you," said Penny. "What an insult. I've got friends in those communities, and they wouldn't stay in a dump like Garskill. It's migrant workers."

"How do you know?"

"I'm a folksinger. I have my finger on the pulse of the folk."

Banks laughed. "Seriously."

"A friend told me. I still have my connections among the local historians and writers, you know."

"But where do they work?"

"There are plenty of places where they're not fussy who they employ, as long as the labor comes cheap enough, and most of these people aren't in a position to complain. Varley's Yeast Products, just north of town, for example. They've been using slave labor for years.

Then there's that slaughterhouse outside Darlington, a meatpacking factory out Carlisle way, the chemical-processing plant south of Middlesbrough. I'm surprised you don't know about all this."

"It comes under Trading Standards or Immigration," said Banks. "At least it did. Now I'm not so sure. Anyway, you seem to know a lot about it. Do you know anything about the people who were living there?"

"Not about any of them specifically, or individually, no. Are you grilling me now?"

"It sounds like it, doesn't it? Actually, I came out to get away from thinking about it. I was up there today, and it's a bloody depressing place. Have you ever been there?"

"Years ago," said Penny. "It was pretty much in a state of disrepair back then. I can only imagine what it's like now."

"Those places were built to last," said Banks, "but I don't envy the poor sods who were staying there."

"It wouldn't have been their choice," said Penny. "They're lured over here by the promise of jobs. It costs them all their savings, then they're paid less than minimum wage for shit work, and they've got no recourse. Most of them don't even speak English. They start out in debt; they get deeper and deeper in debt. Can you believe there are even loan sharks who prey on them?"

Banks could. Once more the name Warren Corrigan came to mind. He would be paying Mr. Corrigan a visit on Monday.

The musicians—acoustic guitar, accordion, stand-up bass and fiddle—assembled onstage again, picking up and tuning their instruments. "I've got to go now," said Penny, touching Banks's arm lightly. "Will you be here later?"

"I don't know," said Banks. "It's been a long day. I'm dog tired."

"Try to last out the set," she said. "Any requests?"

" 'Finisterre,' " Banks said without thinking.

Penny blinked in surprise. " 'Finisterre'? OK. It's been a long time, but I think I can manage that."

And she did. Unaccompanied. Her low, husky voice seemed to have grown richer over the years, with the qualities of warm dark chocolate and a fine Amarone. It wasn't quite as deep in range as June Tabor's, but it wasn't far off. She went through "Death and the Lady," "She Moved Through the Fair," "Flowers of Knaresborough Forest" and a number of other traditional songs. She didn't neglect contemporary works, either. Dylan was represented by the moving and mysterious "Red River Shore," Roy Harper by "I'll See You Again" and Richard Thompson by a version of "For Shame of Doing Wrong" that brought tears to Banks's eyes, the way Penny's voice cracked in its heartbreaking chorus. She finished with what could, in someone else's hands, have been a mere novelty, a slow, folksy version of Pulp's "Common People." But it worked. Her version brought depth out of the anthem and gave its lyrics a weight that was often easy to miss. Everyone sang along with the chorus, and the applause at the end was deafening. What Jarvis Cocker would have made of it, Banks had no idea, but it didn't matter; he'd never been able to take Jarvis Cocker seriously, anyway, though he did like "Common People" and "Running the World." Maybe it was just his name.

As the crowd settled back to drink up their last orders when the band had finished, Penny came over to the corner table, where Banks had managed to find a chair, and sat down. A couple of the band members joined her, and the young man from the interval lurked in the background looking sulky and swaying a little, pint in hand. Banks had met the band members before and said hello. The accordion player was actually a DS from Durham Constabulary moonlighting as a folkie. "You made it," Penny said, smiling. "Didn't doze off, did you?"

"Not once. Thanks for singing my request."

"Pleasure. It's a lovely song. I'd forgotten how lovely. Thanks for reminding me of it. So sad, though."

"Well, there aren't an awful lot of happy folk songs, are there? It's all murders; demon lovers; vengeful spirits; things that have vanished; how fleeting life and pleasure are; love turned cool, died or lost."

"Too true," said Penny. "Look, a few of us are going back to the house. Want to come along? No doom and gloom, I promise."

"I'd really love to," said Banks, "but I fear I wouldn't last long." In fact, he wanted to end the evening as he ended most evenings, at home in his dark conservatory looking at the moon and stars outside, with a nightcap and some quiet music. He felt he could face it now. He didn't feel like a party anymore.

"OK," she said. "I understand. Murderers to catch, and all that."

Banks nodded. "Murderers to catch." If only it were that easy. "Good night."

As Banks left, the eager young man with the theories about the folk revival took his seat, swaying and spilling a little beer as he moved. Penny said hello and smiled politely at him but immediately fell into conversation with her guitarist. Banks didn't think she would be inviting the young man back to her house. She looked in Banks's direction as he was leaving and smiled.

Outside, he noticed a hint of peat smoke in the cool night air, reminding him that it was still only April, no matter how pleasant the days were becoming. No music followed him into the night as he walked the half mile home, mostly along the Pennine Way, with a bright moon and a scattering of stars to light his way. The exercise and fresh air would do him good after a day hanging around in the mire of Garskill Farm.

As he walked along the path that clung to the hillside, which stepped down in a series of lynchets to Gratly Beck, he pictured the migrant worker's body again. Somehow, no matter how many times it happened, he never got quite used to it. He thought of Penny again and knew he shouldn't read anything into her friendly behavior. It was just her way; she was a free spirit, a bit flirtatious, mischievous. Still, he couldn't help but hope. It seemed that nothing had cured him of that. Not Sandra. Not Annie. Not Sophia.

5

Banks got to the office early enough on Monday morning to listen to *Today* for a while as he went through his in-tray. Before long, sick to death of hearing how bad the economy was and how violent things were in the Middle East, he switched over to catch the end of *Breakfast* on Radio 3, where a stately Haydn symphony was playing.

As expected, nothing much had happened on Sunday. Banks had called in at the station briefly, and he found Haig and Lombard working away at the escort agency websites. Doug Wilson and Gerry Masterson were out conducting interviews. He guessed that Joanna Passero would be at home, as would most of the CSIs and lab technicians they so needed to start producing results. Winsome had arranged for the Garskill Farm victim's photo to be on the evening news that night, and it would be shown again the following morning and evening. She had spent most of Sunday asking more questions in Ingleby. There hadn't been many calls made from the telephone box there, and the ones of interest to Banks, made around the time Mrs. Boscombe had seen the man resembling the victim, had all been to mobiles. One was to Bill Quinn; another was a pay-as-you-go, impossible to trace; and the third was an Estonian number they were trying to track down.

Early on Monday morning, the upper floors of the police station were still mostly empty, and Banks enjoyed a little quiet time gazing down on the market square, the gold hands against the blue face of the church clock telling him it was a quarter past eight. He made some notes, answered a couple of e-mails and binned most of the official memos and circulars that had piled up. As Banks worked he could hear people arriving, footsteps on the stairs, office doors opening and closing along the corridor, "good morning"s, brief comments on the weekend's football and television. A normal Monday morning.

By nine o'clock he was ready for a gathering of the troops, but before he could round them up, there was a knock at his door and Stefan Nowak, crime scene manager, walked in. The two had known each other for years. Stefan was unusual among CSIs for being a detective sergeant rather than a civilian. He was working toward his inspector's boards, and he already had a BSc and a number of forensics courses under his belt. He wasn't a specialist but something of a jack-of-all-trades, and his management skills made him perfect for the job. He still spoke with a slight Polish accent, though Banks understood that he had been in England for years. He never talked much about his past or his private life, so Banks was not certain what his story was. He sensed that Stefan liked to cultivate an aura of mystery. Perhaps he thought it made him more attractive to the opposite sex. He had a reputation for being a bit of a ladies' man and dressed as stylishly as Ken Blackstone, though in a more casual, youthful way. He was a lot better looking, too, with a full head of healthy, well-tended hair.

"I hope you've got something for me, Stefan," Banks said. "We could do with a break right now."

Nowak sat down, pulling at his creases the way Ken Blackstone did. "I don't think you'll be disappointed," he said. "I paid a visit to Garskill Farm yesterday and had a chat with the crime scene manager, Mr. Smedley. I must say, he's a bit tense and prickly, isn't he?"

"That's one way of describing him."

"Anyway, I wanted to compare some fibers and tire tracks as soon as possible, and it seemed the best way."

"And were you able to?"

"Not until just now," said Nowak. "The team worked very hard and late up at that dreadful place. The report was in my tray when I got in a little over an hour ago. Someone must have dropped it off late last night." Nowak spent most of his time in Scientific Support, next door, which had been taken over as an annex when Eastvale was the headquarters of the Western Area. It would probably remain as it was, because it was damn useful, and it saved money in the long run. Like most county forces, Eastvale sent most of the evidence collected at crime scenes out to an accredited forensic laboratory for analysis, but there were one or two things they could handle in their own labs here, such as fingerprint and basic fiber analysis, photographic services and documents. Not DNA or blood, though. In the end, most trace evidence went to the official Forensic Science Service laboratory at Wetherby, or to one of the specialist labs dealing with such matters as entomology or forensic archaeology. But having some services in-house saved time as well as money.

"Anything useful?"

"Depends what you mean. The book that someone left behind there was in Polish, by the way. A translation of *The Da Vinci Code.*"

"That's a promising start. Fancy a coffee?"

"Sure."

Banks rang down for a pot of coffee. He still needed about three cups to kick-start him in a morning, and so far he'd had only one at home to wash down the slice of toast and marmalade that passed for breakfast.

Nowak shuffled the files in front of him, picking out photographs of hairs and tire tracks that didn't mean much to Banks. "The long and the short of it is that we can place the same car at both scenes," Nowak announced. "The tracks at Garskill Farm were poor because of the rain, of course, but the ground was very hard to start with, and Smedley's lads managed to get some impressions. There's some very distinctive cross-hatching on one of the tires." He showed Banks two photographs; even he could see that the little scratches on both were the same.

"So hang on a minute," said Banks. "These are photographs from two different scenes, right? You're saying that the tracks from the farm lane near St. Peter's match tracks found in the old driveway at Garskill Farm?"

"Yes."

"Excellent," said Banks. It was the forensic link he had been hoping for. It wouldn't offer an easy solution to the case, and perhaps it wouldn't stand up in court, but it would help them focus, give them a sense of direction and a fruitful line of inquiry. "I don't suppose you can tell the make, year and color? License plate, too, perhaps?"

Nowak laughed. "Not the year. Not yet. It's not a rugged-terrain vehicle, though, I can tell you that much. We've got the wheelbase measurement and identified the brand of the tires, ContiSportContact 2. So now we have to see how many car manufacturers use them, but we should be able to come up with a bit more information soon. Going by the size and wheelbase dimensions, I'd say we're looking at something along the lines of a Ford Focus. All this is still preliminary, of course. Guesswork. We're working from photographs, and we won't be able to state with any more certainty until we get the Dentstone KD impressions done."

Banks scribbled on his notepad. "But you think that what you've told me is accurate so far?"

"Ninety percent."

"That's good enough for me right now."

"Oh, I forgot to mention. It's dark green."

"What is?"

"The car. It's dark green."

"You're having me on."

"Not at all. It brushed against a fencepost and got a little scratch. We're having the paint analyzed as well as the tire tracks. We can probably get you the make, model and year from the paint reference databases, wheelbase and tire type, when we've got it all itemized, but I'm afraid even that won't be able to tell us the license number. Still, taken in combination, it should all help us be a lot more accurate."

"I'm impressed," said Banks.

"You should be."

The coffee arrived. They both took it black, so Banks poured from the metal pot into a couple of mugs and passed one to Nowak. "There's more," said Nowak after he had taken his first sip. "I've just been having a look through the comparison microscope at fibers from both crime scenes. We found quite a few strands of synthetic fiber, most likely from a cheap, mass-produced overcoat of some kind, stuck to the tree from which we think the killer fired his crossbow. Smedley's team found similar fibers at Garskill Farm, in the building where the body was found. Doorpost, chair."

"So the same person was in both places?"

"So it would seem. Or the same overcoat. We still have a fair way to go to be certain—spectrographic analysis, dye comparisons and so on—but from what I can see at first glance, the fibers match. I wouldn't read too much into that as a scientist without all the other things I've mentioned. After all, it's pretty common. These overcoats are mass-produced, as I said, and anyone could buy one from Marks and Spencer or wherever. When we've got a better sense of the makeup of the fiber and the dyes used, we'll start searching the databases and talking to manufacturers and retailers. But all that will take time, and it's still very unlikely to give us a name. I thought you might want a few preliminary signposts as soon as possible. There are footprints, too. Rather too many to be especially valuable, but their expert thinks some of them match the ones you took from the woods at St. Peter's. Same size and distinctive cut on the sole. He was there, in both places."

"You're a wonder, Stefan."

"None of this will stand up in court. I hope you don't—"

"Nothing's going to court. Not for a while. But it sheds a little more light on the cases if we can think of them as definitely connected in this way. Thanks. I'll need to do a bit of thinking about what all this means."

"Smedley's team also found traces of another vehicle on the driveway at Garskill Farm. Seems it has a slight oil leak, so we've got a sample. We've also got tire tracks. This is a larger vehicle altogether, bigger wheelbase and tires. A good-size transit van."

"People mover? Big enough for twenty?"

"Maybe. It'd be a bit of a crush, but when you've seen where they were living, I doubt they'd have minded much."

"I don't think they would have had much choice. Will Smedley's team be able to tell us much more about this other vehicle?"

"Sure. They'll do the measurements, the impressions and analysis. I just thought you might like to know that there was someone else there."

"Now all we have to do is find him."

"Give us time," said Nowak, getting to his feet. "Give us time. By the way, I've been meaning to ask you. Who is that good-looking blonde with the delightful figure I've seen about the place the past couple of days? Is she new? Visiting? Permanent? Why don't I know about her?"

Banks smiled. "She's Professional Standards, Stefan. I'd stay well clear of her if I were you."

"There's nothing wrong with my standards," Nowak said. "Professional or otherwise. Professional Standards, eh? Interesting. She's a foxy one."

"She's married."

"But is she happy, Alan? Is she happy?" He glanced at the coffee mug in his hand. "Anyway, I must get back to work. Can I take this?"

"Of course," said Banks. "Be my guest."

He shook his head slowly at Nowak's departing back.

Though Winsome, Banks and the rest of the team gave Annie a heroine's welcome when she arrived in the boardroom for the morning meeting, she nonetheless felt disassociated from the investigation, from the processes of police work as a whole. As she listened to Banks and Winsome, who did most of the talking, and watched them stick photographs and write names on the glass board, it all seemed very remote and distant from what her life had become, and she found herself drifting away, missing bits and pieces, unsure of the connections. Sometimes the voices sounded muffled, and she couldn't make out what they were saying; other times she would notice that two or three minutes had passed by and she hadn't heard a thing. She didn't even know what she'd been thinking. It was only to be expected, she told herself. She had been away a long time.

Area Commander Gervaise dropped in at the end of the meeting to welcome her, and to remind her to take things easy for the first few weeks, not go running around the county. If Annie felt tired, Gervaise told her, she only had to say so, and she would be allowed to go home. The most important thing was that she make a full recovery. *Bollocks,* thought Annie, making a rude sign at Gervaise's departing rear. The main thing was that she got back on the tracks again before it was too late and she lost all her skills, not only her powers of listening and concentration. She didn't want to be treated like an invalid, like one of those wounded soldiers back from the war whom nobody wants to know or even acknowledge.

She had spent a pleasant weekend reacquainting herself with her tiny cottage in Harkside after over a month at the sprawling artists' colony near St. Ives. The cottage in the heart of the maze, or so Banks had described it when he had first visited her there, years ago. She remembered those days well, the late mornings in bed, the warmth and humor, the lovemaking. Whatever their relationship, however it had ended, at the beginning it had felt like falling in love, full of promise, with that joyous sense of abandon, of falling without a net—feelings that she very much doubted she would let herself experience again, should she be fortunate enough to have the chance. None of those things was a part of her life now, and she had an idea that they weren't a part of Banks's life, either. Maybe she was romanticizing their time together. Perhaps it hadn't been that way at all. *Memory plays strange tricks on us,* she thought. *We often remember things the way we would have liked them to be. Besides, it's foolish to try to rekindle what has gone.* She had ended her last day of sick leave with a long hot bath and a stack of gossip magazines.

In the large open-plan squad room she shared with rest of the team, there were flowers on her desk from Banks, along with a box of chocolates from Winsome. The rest of the squad had had a whip 'round and bought her a fancy teapot, a little gizmo that made it easy to use loose leaves instead of tea bags, and a nice selection of exotic teas, from green to lapsang souchong. It was a nice gesture, and by half past eleven, as she sipped her late elevenses of Darjeeling, sampled a chocolate and looked at the flowers—roses, of course, what else would a man think to buy?—she thought things might not work out too badly after all.

Her main job on her first day was catching up on the Bill Quinn case. Banks had told her a fair bit on Friday night, and at the morning meeting she had learned about the other murder, at Garskill Farm, and its connection with Bill Quinn's murder. Now she had to fill in the gaps, read the witness statements, study the forensic and postmortem reports.

Over in the corner at the spare desk sat two detectives she didn't know. They were on loan from county HQ, Winsome had said. Haig and Lombard. From

210 • PETER ROBINSON

what Annie could see, they were watching porn on their computers, and the most unattractive of the two, wispy haired, shiny suit, skinny as a rake, with bad skin and a Uriah Heep look about him, kept giving her the eye. She couldn't remember from the briefing whether he was Haig or Lombard. All she knew was that they were supposed to be checking Internet sites for the girl in the photo with Quinn. They seemed to be enjoying themselves.

Annie returned to the growing pile of statements, reports and photographs. As she flipped through them, something caught her attention, a blowup from one of the photos found in Quinn's room, and she went back to it. If anyone had mentioned it at the meeting, she had been drifting at the time. She put the end of her pencil to her lower lip and frowned as she thought through the implications.

Closing the folder, she stood up and walked over to Haig and Lombard. The one who had been ogling her averted his gaze like a guilty schoolboy caught smoking or masturbating in the toilets. They appeared furtive, pretending to concentrate on their respective screens. As they both showed images of big-breasted women in lingerie with knowing expressions on their faces, that didn't help the two detectives to appear any more innocent.

"Enjoying yourselves?" Annie asked, arms folded.

"We're working," said the wispy-haired one.

"Who are you?"

"DC Lombard, ma'am." Generally, Annie didn't like being called "ma'am," but these two young pups needed a lesson. She would put up with it.

"Getting anywhere?"

"No, ma'am."

"Where are you looking?"

"Lyon," said Haig. "It's the only place we know DI Quinn has visited in France."

"What makes you think the photos were taken in France?"

"Huh?"

" 'Huh, ma'am.' "

"Right. Huh, ma'am?"

"I asked why France. I suggested to DCI Banks that it had probably happened in a foreign country, but it didn't have to be France."

"It's the beer mat, ma'am," explained Lombard, as if he were talking to a particularly backward child. "You must have seen it. It says 'A. Le Coq.' " He pronounced the last word with the requisite manly gusto and bravado, a smirk on his face. "That sounds French to me."

Annie could see it took them all they had to stop bursting out sniggering. She held her ground. "Did you look it up?"

"What do you mean?"

"The beer, the brewery. A. Le Coq. To find out where it is."

"No need to, was there?" said Lombard. "I mean, it's French, isn't it? Stands to reason. Or maybe Belgian."

"But DI Quinn never went to Belgium, did he?" Haig said.

"I thought so," Annie said with a sigh. "You pair of bloody idiots. You can stop that right now. You're miles off."

"What are you talking about? Ma'am."

Annie leaned over the nearest computer and typed the words "A. Le Coq" into the Google search engine, then she brought up the first site on the list, moved back so the two DCs could both see the screen. "*That's* what I mean," she said. "See how simple it is? Ever heard of Google? And you couldn't be bloody bothered to check. That's sloppy police work."

Annie walked away, leaving the two openmouthed. Time to talk to Banks. She picked up the phone.

Banks found a parking spot on North Parkway and walked to the Black Bull. The road, not far from the big Ring Road roundabout, had a central grass strip dotted with trees, and two lanes of traffic on either side. The houses, set back behind pleasant gardens and walls or high privet hedges, were brick or prefab semis, with a smattering of bungalows and the occasional detached corner house. There weren't many small shops, but he passed a mini Sainsbury's and a Jobcentre Plus, and saw a small church with a square tower across the street. The area had a pleasant open feel to it, with plenty of green in evidence. There was a council estate behind the opposite side, and two tower blocks poked their ugly upper stories into the quickly clouding sky like fingers raised in an insult.

Banks was feeling pleased with himself for getting rid of Joanna Passero for the day. Naturally, she had wanted to accompany him to Leeds, but Dr. Glendenning was performing the postmortem on the Garskill Farm victim, and seeing as she liked postmortems so much, Banks had suggested she should go along with Winsome. The rest of the time she could do what she wanted; there was plenty to keep her occupied. She didn't like it, but in the end she reluctantly agreed. With her along, Banks knew he would have an even tougher time with Warren Corrigan, and he probably wouldn't get anything out of Nick Gwillam at all, even though he wasn't actually a copper himself, not with Miss Professional Standards sitting next to him. Still, it remained to be seen whether he got anything useful on his own.

Before Banks got to the Black Bull, his mobile rang. At first he thought he would just ignore it, but when he checked, he saw the call was from Annie, and he felt he owed her all the encouragement he could give her. He stopped and leaned against a bus shelter. "Annie?"

"I've just been having a word with those two young lads from county HQ," Annie said. "Where on earth do they find them these days?"

"Needs must," Banks said. "Why? Surely they can't be doing any harm on a soft-porn search?"

"No harm, no, but they're wasting time."

"What do you mean?"

"The beer mat."

"What beer mat?"

" 'A. Le Coq.' A blowup from one of Quinn's photos. It came in after you left. I don't think they bothered to check on the brewery's location. They're checking escort agencies in the Lyon area."

"I don't follow. Look, Annie, I've got rather a lot on my plate and—"

"A. Le Coq is *not* a French brewery."

"It's not? Sounds like it to me. Belgian, then?"

"Not Belgian, either."

"OK, you've got my attention. I have no idea where it is. Never heard of it. Enlighten me." A woman, not much more than a girl really, passed by with a two-tier pram in which her twins lay sleeping. She puffed on her cigarette and smiled shyly at Banks, who smiled back.

"If either of them had taken the trouble to find out," Annie went on, "they'd have discovered that A. Le Coq is an old established Estonian brewery."

Banks paused to digest this, work out how it changed things. "But—"

"As I mentioned the other night, I've been to Tallinn," Annie went on. "I've even tasted the stuff. It's not bad, actually. You do know what this means, don't you?"

"That the photos were most likely taken when Bill Quinn was in Tallinn six years ago on the Rachel Hewitt case."

"Exactly. I'll start researching the case immediately. Where are you now?"

Banks explained.

"Will you keep me informed?" Annie said.

"I will. And you me. Thanks a lot, Annie."

"No problem."

"One more thing. Don't forget that one of the calls we think the Garskill Farm victim made from the telephone box in Ingleby was to an Estonian number. You might check if anyone's run it down yet. Or do it yourself. It shouldn't be too difficult."

"Will do."

Banks put his phone back in his jacket pocket and made his way toward the pub, which rather resembled a rambling old house, with a red pantile roof, a white-washed facade and a small area of picnic benches in a stone-flagged yard out front, separated from the pavement by a strip of grass and a low wall. Banks made his way past the empty tables to the door and entered the cavernlike space. The ceiling was high, and the room seemed to swallow up the little groups of tables, even the bar itself, though it was long, and the tiers of bottles reflected in the mirror gave the illusion of depth. The place had clearly seen better days, but there was a certain warm welcome in the shabby velveteen, brass fixtures and framed watercolors of old Leeds scenes on the walls. It smelled of domestic cleaning fluid, but all the Domestos in the world couldn't get rid of the years of stale smoke. A few slot machines flashed and beeped here and there by a nicotine-stained pillar, but no one was playing them. Peter and Gordon were singing "A World Without Love" on the jukebox. It was lunchtime, and there were a few family groups picking away at baskets of chicken and chips or bowls of lasagna, and the usual ensemble of regulars stood at the far end of the bar chatting up a buxom blond barmaid. She looked like a retired stripper, Banks thought. Or perhaps not even retired yet. He walked over to the barman, who was studiously polishing a glass.

"What can I do for you, sir?" the barman asked.

"I'd like to see Mr. Corrigan."

The man's expression changed abruptly from welcoming to hostile. "And who may I say is asking for him?"

Banks showed his warrant card.

"Just a moment, sir."

The barman disappeared. The blonde pulling pints at the far end of the bar glanced over and cocked her hip. A few moments later, the barman reappeared, and a giant materialized beside Banks.

"Curly here will take you to him," said the barman, then he turned away. Curly was as bald as one of the balls on the snooker table at the far end of the room, and about as unsmiling. Banks followed him through a maze of small lounges, past another bar, through doors and down corridors by the gents' and ladies' toilets toward the back of the pub, until they came to a small private function room, perfect for the office lunch. Curly gestured for Banks to enter, and he did. The decor was much the same as the rest of the pub, with plenty of brass and velvet in plush dark shades, with heavy varnished tables, ornate iron legs. Banks had expected an entourage, but one man sat alone at a table, a few papers spread in front of him. He gathered them up and put them in a folder, then smiled and stood up when Banks came in. Banks was surprised at how slight and skinny he was. He had a sort of ferret face, thinning ginger hair, no eyebrows and a high forehead. Banks put his age at about forty. He was casually dressed, wearing a navy sports jacket over his shirt. No tie. He extended his hand in greeting. Banks thought it churlish to refuse, so he shook.

"I know Kelly at the bar checked your ID, but you don't mind if I have a butcher's myself, do you? One can't be too careful."

"Not at all," said Banks, showing his warrant card.

Corrigan examined it. "Detective Chief Inspector Banks," he read slowly. "Impressive. It's a pleasure to meet you at last, Mr. Banks. I've heard so much about you. Sit down, sit down. You're a long way from home. What brings you to these parts? But please excuse my manners. Can I offer you a drink?"

"I wouldn't mind a coffee," said Banks.

"Coffee it is." He called Curly in. "Get Mr. Banks a coffee, Curly. How do you take it?"

"Black, no sugar," said Banks.

"You might think this setup a bit odd," said Corrigan, gesturing around the room when Curly had gone for the coffee, "but I find it far more congenial than some soulless office in a building full of soulless offices. This place has history, atmosphere. And I'm comfortable here. Don't you think it's comfortable?"

"Very," said Banks.

"Of course, I travel quite a lot, too, but when I'm in town, I find it most pleasant to work here. It's also useful for entertaining, too, of course. The chef can put together a decent menu when the occasion demands it, and there's never any shortage of drink. Plus, I find it's a good way to stay in touch with the neighborhood. It's a part of the community."

"You've sold me on it," said Banks. "I'll ask my boss if I can relocate to the Queen's Arms as soon as I get back to Eastvale."

Corrigan laughed, showing rather long, yellowish teeth. The coffee arrived. Corrigan didn't have anything except the bottle of sparkling water already in front of him. "It's a lovely part of the country you come from, the Yorkshire Dales," he said. "You should be proud of its heritage. I'd live there like a shot if I was in a position to retire. Do you know Gratly?"

"I do."

"One of my favorite spots. The view from the bridge, the old sawmill. Picnic by the falls on Gratly Beck on a warm summer's day. I like nothing better than to take the wife and kids there for a day out when I can manage it." He paused. "Still, I don't suppose you've come here to talk about the beauties of the Yorkshire Dales, have you?"

"Not exactly," said Banks. He knew that Corrigan was trying to rile him, or scare him off, by showing that he knew where Banks lived, which he had no doubt checked up on after Bill Quinn's murder, but he was damned if he was going to rise to the bait. "It's about DI Quinn. Bill Quinn."

"Ah, yes." Corrigan scratched the side of his nose. "Poor Bill. Tragic. Tragic. I understand it happened in your neck of the woods. I should imagine that's why you're investigating the case and not the locals here?"

"Got it in one," said Banks. "But I shouldn't worry too much. DI Quinn might be dead, but he'll be replaced so quickly you won't even notice it's happened. I understand he was causing you a few problems?"

"Problems? Bill? Not at all. I enjoyed our conversations, though I must say he was a rather dour man. It was hard to get a laugh out of him. Still, an intelligent man. Well-informed. Well-rounded, too. I like a man who has an interest in outdoor pursuits like fishing and gardening, don't you, Mr. Banks? I think it adds character, dimension."

"Frankly," said Banks, "I couldn't give a toss. What I'd like to know is where you were last Wednesday evening between about eleven and one in the morning."

"Me? I'm assuming this is to do with Bill's death, but I'm surprised you're asking where *I* was. Surely if I had anything to do with what happened—and I assure you, I did not—then I'd hardly do it myself, would I? Do I look like an assassin?"

"Assassins come in all shapes and sizes," said Banks. "And it's murder. Not just death. Bill Quinn was murdered. I think we'd be best calling a spade a spade."

"As you will. Plain speaking. I'm all for that."

"What kind of car do you drive?"

"A Beemer. Some think it's a bit flash for these parts, but I like the way it handles."

"So where were you?"

"At home, I should think. Certainly nowhere near St. Peter's."

"But you knew where Bill Quinn was?"

"Everyone knew where Bill Quinn was."

"Did you tell anyone?"

"Why would I do that?"

"You tell me."

"No."

Banks suspected he was lying. "Where's home?" he went on.

"Selby."

"Any witnesses?"

"My wife, Nancy. Lily and Benjamin, the kids, ten and twelve, respectively. Quite a handful."

222 · PETER ROBINSON

"Anyone else?"

"Isn't that enough?"

"How about Curly out there?"

"We don't live together."

"Where was he?"

"Curly!" Corrigan called.

Curly stuck his shiny head around the doorway. "Boss?"

"Mr. Banks here wants to know where you were last Wednesday night." He glanced over at Banks, an amused expression on his thin pale face.

"At the infirmary," Curly said.

"What happened?"

"Bumped into a lamppost. They kept me in overnight for observation."

"We can check, you know."

"Then check." He lowered his head. "You can still see the bump."

Banks saw it. "Ouch," he said. "Nasty one. Dissatisfied client?"

Curly grunted and walked away.

"So, as you can see, Mr. Banks," said Corrigan, showing his palms in a gesture of frankness, "we have nothing to hide. Our consciences are clean."

"I can't see how that could be," said Banks, "when you prey on the most vulnerable members of the community. You're nothing more than the school bully demanding cash with threats in the playground."

"Unfortunately, there will always be the weak, and there will always be the strong," said Corrigan, "just as there will always be the poor and the rich. The poor are always with us. Didn't Jesus say that, or something very much like it? I know which I'd rather be in both cases. Do you, Mr. Banks?"

"Misquoting the scriptures doesn't help your case," said Banks. "Besides, I think it's more a matter of the decent and the morally bankrupt, and I know which I'd like to be. But that's just me."

"Oh, we have an outraged moralist here, do we? Yes, I remember I'd heard that about you. One of those religious coppers, are you? I provide a service. Do you think these poor vulnerable people, as you choose to see them, are any more decent than the rest of the rabble? Well, let me tell you, they are not. They think this country is the land of milk and honey. For a start, they're greedy. They have no money, no jobs, they're already in debt up to their eyeballs, but they want that new flat-screen television, they want the new car, their wives want to shop somewhere other than Primark for their clothes and their children's clothes. They are also lazy, but they still want to be able to go out to fancy restaurants for dinner, and the younger ones want to go clubbing. All that takes money, and I supply it. I'm doing them a service."

"You make it sound very generous, Mr. Corrigan, if it weren't for your rates of interest."

"High risk, high interest. A businessman has to make a living."

"And the occasional broken leg? What happens when they can't pay, and you come around asking for the money?"

"Now, what good would my clients be to me if they weren't healthy enough to work, should an opportunity and inclination present itself? Ask yourself that, Mr. Banks. Yes, we have had to administer a gentle reminder on occasion, as an example, let's say, but is that so different from any other line of work? Examples must be made. The message soon gets around."

Banks had dealt with criminals like Corrigan before. They didn't really see themselves as criminals, or else they were so cynical about society and human nature that it didn't matter to them what they were, as long as they had the power and the money. On the surface, everything was all very cozy and upper middle class, ponies and piano lessons for the kiddies, cashmere sweaters, Hugo Boss suits, Beemers and Range Rovers, golf club memberships, perhaps even a friend or two on the local council. Underneath, it's another matter. A trail of misery and woe, broken bodies and trampled souls going back as far as the eye can see. Someone had to pay for the Corrigans of this world to live in luxury, after all, whether they be junkies, gamblers or just poor sods who fell for the whole consumer-society deal hook, line and sinker. But there was no point in saying it; there was no point arguing.

"Tell me what you know about migrant-labor camps," said Banks.

"Only what I read in the papers. People come over here seeking jobs, unskilled workers, asylum seekers, illegals, and they don't always find one. Then they start whining about how badly done to they are. Well, that's a big bloody surprise isn't it, given that half our own people can't find a job either?"

"You mean that sometimes they start out in debt to someone like you, are made to work at jobs no one else wants to do, forced to live in squalid dormitories for exorbitant rents?"

"You've been reading the *Guardian*, haven't you? No wonder your heart's bleeding all over your sleeve. I told you, I know nothing about them except what's on the news, and I can't say I pay much attention to that. If they come over here stealing our jobs, they get what they bloody deserve."

"What about the people who bring them here? The agents? The gang masters? The staffing companies? You must have some contacts with them."

"Don't know what you mean."

Banks sensed that he was lying again but moved on quickly, anyway. "Ever heard of a place called Garskill Farm?" he asked.

"No," said Corrigan. "It sounds a bit dales-ish, though. Is it somewhere near you?"

"Close," said Banks. "We just found a body there." He slipped a picture of the victim out of his briefcase and put it on the table. "Recognize this man?"

Corrigan examined it. "No. Not looking very healthy, though, is he?"

Banks followed it with a blowup of the girl Quinn was with in Tallinn. "How about her?"

"Nope. Wish I did, though. She looks good enough to eat." He ran his pink pointed tongue across his upper lip.

There was no evidence that Corrigan trafficked in young girls or acted as a pimp, so Banks couldn't really push him on any of this. It had been a long shot, anyway. All of it. Corrigan was a villain, no doubt, legally and morally, and Quinn had been on to him. But had Corrigan murdered Quinn, or had him killed? Had Quinn been in Corrigan's power and tried to escape? And the man at Garskill Farm? What part had he played? There were still too many unanswered questions.

Leaving the rest of his coffee, Banks stood up. As soon as Curly heard the chair scraping against the stone floor he was in the doorway again. Corrigan gave him an almost imperceptible signal, and he stood aside.

"It's been a pleasure, Mr. Banks," said Corrigan. "Next time you come, let's make an occasion of it. Have a real drink. They've got a very nice selection of single-malts in the main bar. You should enjoy the ten-year-old cask-strength Laphroaig especially."

Banks smiled. "Your information's a bit out of date, Corrigan," he said. "I'm more of a red wine man, these days." Then he left.

Annie had experienced an extraordinary amount of satisfaction after bollocking Lombard and Haig for doing a half-arsed job on A. Le Coq, but now she was feeling guilty. It had been like shooting goldfish in a bowl. After all, they were just probationers, still wet around the ears, transferred in from elsewhere to help out. And they had done a lot of the shit work. For all the jokes made at their expense, it can't have been a lot of fun spending day after day trawling through sleazy Internet sites searching for a face.

On the other hand, if they didn't have what it took to carry out a simple Internet search, a no-brainer, then it was best they should find out now, rather than later, when they had more responsibility and could do more damage. They would get over it and move on. They might even make decent detectives one day. At least now they were checking the Estonian escort sites.

Though Annie had been to Tallinn for a dirty weekend with a DI from Newcastle four years ago, she knew very little about the place. They had done some sightseeing, but not much, sat at tables outside bars in an old part of the city drinking beer—A. Le Coq, as it happened—and eating pasta. The rest of the time they had spent in the hotel room having sweaty sex.

To Annie, that whole part of the world was tainted with the old Soviet curse, and she assumed that the Baltic states were an extension of Russia when it came to crime and Russian Mafia activity. Drugs, people-trafficking and illegal labor scams would be right up there. Perhaps Quinn got involved in something like that, and the Russians were behind it? Weren't they behind almost everything illegal these days? The girl herself could be Russian. There was no way of telling from the photographs, but she did have that certain sad and tragic aspect to her beauty that Annie had associated with Russian women ever since she saw *Doctor*

Zhivago on late-night television. It was one of Banks's favorite movies, she knew, but that was because of Julie Christie.

Anyway, there was no point in speculating further. Whatever his motive, and whoever he was, Quinn's killer had been in the woods at St. Peter's four days ago. They had a few solid leads to him now—the forensics on the tire tracks and fibers, Quinn's involvement in the Rachel Hewitt case, and now the blown-up part of one of the blackmail photos showing an A. Le Coq beer mat. She had Haig and Lombard checking if it was sold in other Baltic countries, too, or anywhere else in such quantities as to justify handing out free beer mats to bars—she wasn't going to make the mistake of assuming too much at this point—but given that Rachel Hewitt had disappeared in Tallinn, and that Quinn had spent a week there working on the case with the locals, she felt pretty certain about it.

There was very little about the Rachel Hewitt case in DC Gerry Masterson's research so far, or in Quinn's old files, which had arrived in the early afternoon. It was hardly surprising, really, Annie thought, as he had been only marginally connected with it. The real stuff would be in Tallinn. In Estonian. Whether it would be possible to get hold of those files if she needed to, she had no idea. In the meantime, she could at least start digging a bit into the background of what happened on that night six years ago.

Rachel Hewitt was to be maid of honor to her best friend Pauline Boyars at her wedding at St. Paul's Church in Drighlington on August 5, 2006. Before that, from July 21 to 24, they were going to Tallinn with four other close female friends for a hen weekend. The girls, all about nineteen years of age, were excited about the trip. They booked their cheap EasyJet flight early and made sure they all got rooms at the Meriton Old Town Hotel, which someone told them was very comfortable and very close to lots of bars and clubs. To save money, the girls asked for twin beds and doubled up; Rachel shared with Pauline.

On the Friday they arrived, the girls met up in the hotel bar for a drink at six o'clock, then walked into town to find somewhere to eat. It was a hot evening, but they were early enough to get a table outside and enjoy some "authentic" Estonian cuisine of pork in beer and elk sausage. The idea was to have a relatively civilized and sedate Friday night out, which is exactly what they did, returning to the hotel around eleven p.m.

Saturday was for sightseeing and shopping, then came Saturday night, the big night itself, party time. They all got dolled up in their microskirts, spangly tops and fishnets, put on a bit of war paint and headed for the bars and clubs. At least they weren't wearing bunny ears and tails, or little whiskers painted on their cheeks, as far as Annie could gather from the reports. They started with a few drinks in the hotel bar, then hit the town. After stopping at a few other bars, they ate steak and frites and drank wine outside at a restaurant, and after that things started to get a bit hazy.

Annie realized that she would have to go through the individual statements made by each of the girls before she could build up a clear picture of the order of events, but according to the newspaper and Internet reports, the girls went on to a couple of dance clubs, getting rowdier as the evening wore on. They were seen talking and dancing with various groups of boys over the course of the evening. Pauline was sick in the street, but soon recovered enough to go on with her friends to another bar on the main square.

Naturally, the boys flocked around them, their predatory instincts sensing the lack of inhibitions that comes with drunkenness, expecting easy pickings. According to all the accounts, though, there was no trouble. At least all the girls agreed on that. They moved on to yet another bar with a group of German youngsters they had befriended earlier at a nightclub, and it was maybe twenty minutes or so after that when Pauline began to wonder where Rachel had got to.

They checked all the rooms and toilets of the bar they had just arrived at, but she was nowhere to be seen. One of the others thought she might have been in the toilet when they left the previous bar and may have missed their leaving, but she was equally sure that they'd told her where they were going. Pauline argued that they couldn't have done, as they didn't decide where they were going until they got outside, and it was the Germans' idea, anyway.

Somehow, Rachel had become detached from her group.

Pauline asked one of the German boys to accompany her back to the previous bar, but in the winding streets of the Old Town they couldn't remember exactly where it was, so they eventually gave up. They tried Rachel's mobile, but all they got was her answering service. The police discovered later that Rachel had forgotten her mobile, left it in her hotel room.

At this point, Pauline said she assumed that Rachel would find her way back to the hotel or get a taxi to take her there. They didn't know the city well, having been there only a day, but although it was winding and confusing, the Old Town wasn't very big, and Pauline thought that anyone wandering around for long enough was bound to return to the place they started from eventually. Besides, Rachel marched to the beat of her

WATCHING THE DARK · 233

own drummer, and whatever she was up to, she would come back when she was ready.

Even so, Rachel's defection put a bit of a damper on the night, so they all returned to the hotel, disappointing the German boys. They expected to find Rachel slumped in the bar, or passed out in her room, but when Pauline went back to her room to lie down, she wasn't there. She said the room started spinning, and she was sick again. Then she fell asleep, or passed out, and when she awoke it was daylight. There was still no sign of Rachel. She felt awful—her head ached; her stomach churned—but despite the ravages of the hangover, concern for her friend gnawed away at her. It wasn't like her to stay away *all* night.

Pauline started to think that Rachel must have got lost somewhere and maybe ended up at another hotel, or maybe got caught up in a group and gone to a party. At worst, she worried that her friend had hurt herself, got hit by a car or something, and was in hospital. She went down to the hotel reception and asked to speak to the manager. The young assistant manager who came out to talk to her was concerned enough to bring in the police, and thus the whole nightmare began. Of course, the girls had drunk so much and visited so many bars and clubs that it took the police close to two days to get any sense of where they had been and what they had done, and by then, anyone who might have been there on the night in question was long gone.

Rachel Hewitt was never seen again, and no clues to her whereabouts were ever discovered.

Annie put aside the clippings and rested her head in her hands. Christ, she thought, what do you do? As a policewoman, she had seen the worst in human nature, and she thought that if something like that had happened to a friend of hers, she would have been down to the cop shop like a shot screaming for some action. But would she?

There had been no real reason to assume that anything bad had happened to Rachel. She sounded like a bit of a character to start with, up for adventure. Annie remembered when her best mate from school, Ellen Innes, had disappeared on a night out in Newquay. It wasn't exactly a foreign country or anything, but there were some wild pubs, and things could get pretty crazy there on a Friday or Saturday night. Annie and her other two friends searched, but they couldn't find Ellen in any of their usual haunts, so they went home, assuming she would come back when she was ready. Annie went to bed without calling anyone.

In the morning, after a few frantic phone calls between the girls' parents, it transpired that Ellen had simply felt tired and decided to go to sleep on a quiet bench by the harbor. She was none the worse for wear, except for a bad hangover and a stiff back. Her parents gave her a strict curfew, and that was the end of the matter. But Annie thought of the things that could have happened, things that probably had happened to Rachel Hewitt. Of course, she realized that she had the benefit of hindsight and the experiences of twenty years as a police officer.

She didn't blame Rachel's friends. Anyone in their position, and their state of mind, would have done the same as they did. And the odds were that if Pauline had insisted on calling the police when she got back to the hotel that night, they would hardly have combed the city for the missing girl. At most, they might have done a sweep of some of the most popular bars, checked the hospitals for accident victims and scoured a few patches of open ground in case she'd nodded off somewhere, but they were hardly going to pull out all the stops for a nineteen-year-old foreign tourist missing a couple of hours at most. They would most likely have assumed that she went off with some boy and was happily screwing her brains out somewhere. In the morning she would be back. Police thinking could be very basic, Annie knew. Especially male police thinking.

Whether she was pregnant when she came back, had been infected with some STD or HIV, or had tried to say

no but had been too drunk to resist was not their problem. Annie understood that much. The police couldn't
be the moral touchstones or guardians of the world,
and to be honest, nobody would want or expect them
to be. It was pointless trying to assign blame, except
to whoever it was who had taken and hurt Rachel, for
Annie was sure that was what must have happened. As
sure as she was that Rachel Hewitt was dead. She could
only hope it had been quick and painless. Annie sighed.
Time to check and see if there was any progress on the
Estonian mobile number called from Ingleby.

She turned to see Joanna Passero standing behind
her, all blond hair and elegant curves. Why did her
appearance always make Annie feel so dowdy and
tomboyish?

"Is everything all right?" Joanna asked.

"Just fine and dandy."

"Are you in pain? Ca—"

"I'm fine. Is there something you want to tell me?"

Joanna seemed taken aback. Annie was aware of
the harshness of her tone and blamed it mostly on the
dark place her mind had been wandering in when she
noticed her standing there. "I'm sorry," she said. "I
was just . . . the Rachel Hewitt case."

Joanna glanced at the computer screen, which
showed a photograph of a smiling Rachel under the

heading WEST YORKSHIRE GIRL DISAPPEARS IN ESTO-
NIAN HEN WEEKEND TRAGEDY.

"Oh," she said. "Did you once know someone who
disappeared like that?"

"We've all worked on cases," said Annie. "It's nothing personal. Just empathy. Anyway, I'm sorry I was
rude just now. Did you have something to tell me?"

Joanna pulled up a chair and sat down. "I've just
got back from the postmortem with DS Jackman," she
said. "It was pretty straightforward, really. The man
was definitely drowned, and Dr. Glendenning is pretty
certain he was drowned in the trough of water at the
scene. They have to do various tests on the samples to
be absolutely certain, of course."

"*Was* drowned, rather than just drowned?"

"That's how it appears. There were bruises on the
back of his neck, on his upper arms and on his shoulders. There were also marks on his wrists, where they
had been bound with some sort of cord. The lab's
working on the fibers. Somebody held him under the
water deliberately. He struggled. And Dr. Burns was
right, he was definitely waterboarded first."

"Jesus Christ, the poor sod," said Annie.

Before meeting Nick Gwillam, Banks ate lunch
by himself at the Pizza Express behind the Corn

Exchange and allowed himself a small glass of Sangiovese to wash down his Sloppy Giuseppe. He had considered giving Ken Blackstone a call to see if he was free for lunch but decided that after his session with Corrigan he preferred his own company for a while. Talking to Corrigan, he thought, had probably been a waste of time, but as with so many similar conversations, he could only know that in retrospect. Just another in the long line of sad, tired, cocky, depressing villains that seemed to be Banks's daily round.

Corrigan was small-time, though there was a chance he had connections with some big players in the people-trafficking world, whose victims provided him with his victims and whom he helped keep in bondage. Essentially, he was a parasite on the bigger organism, but many animals willingly went through life with millions of parasites living on their skin or inside their bodies. It became something of a symbiotic relationship. There was always room for a bit of give-and-take in the world of crime. Especially take.

But that didn't mean Corrigan had anything to do with Quinn's death. Curly's alibi would be easy to check out, so easy it had to be true, and Corrigan's would be impossible to break, even if it were a lie. No doubt he had other minions capable of doing the job for him, and they should be easy enough to round up, but so far his little gang had no history of crossbow use, or of murder. He certainly intimidated people who owed him money, resorted to threats and even to violence on occasion, but he had never, as far as they knew, killed anyone yet. A dead debtor might well be a lesson to the rest, as Corrigan had pointed out, but he was also a loss of income. Why start the killing with a cop and bring down the heat? He was surely under enough pressure already, with the city-wide investigation into his operation and the suicides that could possibly be linked to it. If Corrigan had had Bill Quinn in his pocket, was somehow tied in to the photos and the blackmail, then it now appeared that there was a definite Estonian connection, too. Curiouser and curiouser.

After Banks had finished his lunch, he wandered up to Call Lane, then down Kirkgate. Hands in pockets, walking slowly and taking in the colors, sounds and smells, he cut through the indoor market with its white-coated barkers and stalls piled with scaly fish, marbled red meat and bright shiny fruit and vegetables. No matter how fresh everything was, there was always a faint smell of decay underneath it all.

He came out by the back of the bus station to Millgarth, at the bottom of Eastgate. Though the day had clouded over, it was still warm and was quickly getting more humid. There'd be more rain before nightfall, Banks was sure.

When he presented himself at Millgarth, Nick Gwillam came down to meet him and, not surprisingly, suggested that he'd like to get out of the office for a while, so why didn't they go for a coffee? Banks had had enough coffee for the day, but he was quite happy to enjoy an afternoon cup of tea. They ended up sitting outside the Pret A Manger on the corner of Lands Lane and Albion Place, opposite WHSmith.

"So, you want to talk to me about Bill?" said Gwillam, with a large latte and an egg salad sandwich in front of him.

"You worked with him closely, I understand?"

"Recently, yes. I suppose you know I'm only temporary up here? A civilian, really. Trading Standards."

"Yes. But you worked on the Corrigan case with DI Quinn?"

"For my sins."

"I just had a word with him, and he seemed to know a fair bit about me. Where I live. What I drink. I wonder how he could have found out all that."

Gwillam leaned back in his metal chair and regarded Banks through narrowed eyes. He was tall and lean, with cropped dark hair already thinning and turning gray around the edges, like Banks's own. He wore a pinstripe suit, a white shirt and an old club or univer-sity tie. Finally, he let out a chuckle. "Oh, he played that little trick on you, did he?"

"What trick?"

"See, it's a thing of his. A little trick he likes to play. He rattles off bits and pieces he knows about you. Tries to shock you. I assume he knew you were on the case, Bill's murder, so he'd find out a bit about you."

"Yes, but it's where he gets his information that interests me. He also knew that Bill Quinn was at St. Peter's."

"There was no secret about that. Everybody knew where Bill was. Everybody who had any sort of connec-tion with him, at any rate. He probably told Corrigan himself."

"Why would he do that?"

"No specific reason. Just in conversation."

"Do you think he also happened to mention where I live and the name of my favorite tipple?"

"Everyone knows you're a single-malt man."

"I must say you're very nonchalant about this. But the questions remain. Where does Corrigan get his information, and what else does he do with it other than show it off to impress visiting coppers?"

"Are you suggesting that Corrigan gave away Bill's whereabouts to someone who wanted him dead?"

"It's possible, isn't it? He has to be connected to some pretty violent people in his line of work. If DI Quinn had found out too much, or crossed someone . . . ? But it's just another theory. One of many, unfortunately."

Gwillam sipped his latte. It left a faint white mustache on the top of his lip. "Corrigan talks to a lot of people, mixes a lot," he went on. "People talk to him. Tell him things. He listens. He's like a jackdaw going after silver paper, and he remembers, he absorbs information like a sponge. Sorry about the mixed metaphor, but I think you know what I mean."

"Anyone could have told him?"

"Yes. Even Bill himself."

"And Corrigan could then have passed on the information to anyone himself?"

"Yes. For any reason, or none at all. If he did pass on Bill's whereabouts, it might not have necessarily seemed significant to him at the time. He might simply have done it in passing."

"OK," said Banks. That meant there were two strong contenders for telling the killer where Quinn was staying: the Garskill Farm victim, under torture, and Warren Corrigan, for any, or no, reason at all. Banks also realized with a shock that he had been as guilty as anyone else of giving Corrigan information. At the end of their conversation, he had intimated that he didn't drink Laphroaig anymore, which was only partly true, but that he was more of a red wine drinker, which was wholly true. He had intended it as a put-down of Corrigan's out-of-date source of information, but he realized that through his own showing off, through his need to get one up on Corrigan, he had actually fallen into the trap and told him something he didn't know: that Banks was a red wine drinker. It didn't matter, had no real significance, at least none that he could see, but it shed some light on the way Corrigan worked, and some of the snippets he picked up were clearly very useful indeed.

"What more can you tell me about Corrigan and his business?"

"My interest is mostly in the loan sharking, of course, but we also think he's in a bit deeper with the whole people-trafficking and migrant-labor business. It's quite a wide-reaching racket. Has to be. There are agents and runners all over the place. Even Customs and Excise and immigration officers have to be paid off to turn a blind eye. There are fake visas, passports, too. But it's a connection that's hard to prove. He's nothing if not cautious."

"Drugs?"

"Not yet, at any rate."

"Prostitution?"

"He's clearly got contacts among the pimps, but we don't think he's one himself. Probably thinks it's beneath him."

"And gouging the poorest of the poor isn't?"

"What can I say? Blokes like Corrigan have a skewed version of morality."

"You're telling me. So how deep is he in it? How high up?"

"That's what we're not sure of. We've seen him once or twice with a bloke called Roderick Flinders. Flinders runs a staff agency. Rod's Staff Ltd. Get it?"

" 'My rod and my staff'? Cute. What do they do?"

"They provide cheap labor to whoever wants it, no questions asked. They deal mostly in asylum seekers, illegals of various kinds, unskilled migrant workers. Place them in shit jobs for shit pay."

This was the kind of thing Penny Cartwright had told Banks about on Saturday night, the factories where no questions were asked. "Illegal work?"

"Sometimes. You could certainly argue that it's slave labor. Below minimum wage."

"The same people Corrigan preys on himself?"

"The very same. It would be to his advantage, wouldn't it, to be sure of the supply, know what's heading his way? It makes sense. Helps him expand his markets. You scratch my back, I scratch yours. We suspect that Flinders also helps fix forged temporary work permits for asylum seekers. In some cases he's even got hold of faked passports, which is a bit more difficult, but not so much as you think. He's part of a chain that starts with the agents in the various countries involved and continues through drivers, gang masters, employers, people who rent out the accommodation and the rest of the hangers-on. Everyone takes a slice except the poor sod doing the work. It's a pretty big operation. That's why Trading Standards is involved."

"Why hasn't this Flinders been arrested?"

"He's slippery. Got a smooth front, clever lawyers, and nobody's been able to come up with any hard evidence on the other stuff. Besides, the ones watching him are still excited about where he might lead them. Sometimes I wish we could just seize his phone records and bank accounts, but even I know these buggers are too clever. We've got no cause, for a start. And they use encryptions and untraceable mobiles and numbered bank accounts in countries that don't care where the money comes from."

"He and Corrigan are mates?"

"That's right. Dinner. Drinks. Holidays in the sun."

"And Bill?"

"Me and Bill were just keeping an eye on Corrigan, having the occasional chat, hoping to hook something a bit bigger."

"How long has this been going on?"

"With Corrigan? About eight months."

Banks mulled over what he had been hearing. If Corrigan had these links to organized crime, there was clearly a chance that he was, indirectly or otherwise, behind Quinn's killing, or at least that he knew more about it than he was willing to admit. Quinn could have been bent, as Joanna Passero seemed to think, and suddenly become a liability. But where did the Rachel Hewitt case fit in? What was the connection? And the girl in the photo? Or was all that simply a red herring? Surely it couldn't be? There was definitely a forensic link between Quinn's murder and the murder at Garskill Farm, and there was a link between the two victims; they had spoken twice on the telephone. There was also a possible connection between the Garskill Farm murder and Estonia.

"Just out of interest," Banks asked, "does Corrigan have any connections with Estonia?"

"Estonia? Not that I know of," said Gwillam.

"Maybe through the migrant-labor scam? Through Flinders?"

"I suppose it's possible, but I've never seen or heard anything."

"I was just thinking about the Rachel Hewitt case. Bill Quinn worked on that. He even went to Tallinn in the early stages."

"You think there's a connection?"

"I don't know. Right now, we're just looking more closely at the Hewitt case for various reasons, but as far as I know she was simply an innocent English girl who disappeared abroad. No body has ever been found. But that was six years ago. Where was Corrigan then?"

"No idea, but I don't think he was on anyone's radar that long ago. Maybe mugging old ladies and robbing sweet shops."

"It might be worth a checking."

"Bit of a long shot."

"I know." Banks sighed. "That's the way everything seems in this case. I'm just hoping one of them will hit the mark. Even if Corrigan wasn't involved, he might be doing business with people who were. Did Bill ever talk about Rachel?"

"Not much. It was long before my time, and way out of my areas of interest. It came up once or twice in conversation, but you soon got the sense that it wasn't a good idea to mention it. Bill didn't like to talk about it. He'd get all broody."

"Why do you think that was?"

"He felt he'd failed the girl."

"But he never really got a chance to succeed."

"Doesn't matter. He was just that kind of copper. Took it personal, like."

"But why?" Banks paused to collect his thoughts. "This is something that puzzles me. Everybody I talk to tells me Bill Quinn was haunted by the Rachel Hewitt case, that he felt he failed, but in reality he didn't have very much to do with it. Why did Bill Quinn care so much? He spent a few days in Tallinn, that's all, surely more of a public relations exercise than anything else, by the sound of it, and when he comes back it's as if his life has been blighted by the whole thing. Why?" He wasn't going to tell Gwillam about the added complication of the mystery girl and the photos, clearly taken in Tallinn, too, which might go some way toward explaining Quinn's obsession.

"Like I said, he was that kind of copper," said Gwillam through tight lips. He pushed his cup aside. "And I've worked with all types. Bill took everything seriously. And he happens to have a daughter about the same age as Rachel. He doted on Jessica. Now, if you don't mind . . ."

"Work to do?"

"Something like that."

Gwillam got up and walked down Lands Lane, turning left on Bond Street, out of sight among the crowds of shoppers. Banks swirled the remains of his tea and mulled over what he had just heard. He'd been searching for connections and finding too many, each of which seemed to cancel out or contradict another. He remembered Annie telling him what she had heard at St. Peter's about Quinn's overriding sense of guilt. He had been out on surveillance when his wife died, and that kind of thing could eat away at you. Every copper had missed something important in his family life because of the job—an anniversary party, kid's graduation, a birth, a wedding, even a funeral. Most learned to live with it, but it dragged some of the best men and women down.

Banks glanced at his watch. Time to head back to Eastvale so he could check on developments there before the end of the day.

6

On Tuesday morning, Banks was in his office early again, and this time the first to knock on his door was an excited Gerry Masterson brandishing a sheaf of papers, her wavy red hair cascading over her shoulders in all its Pre-Raphaelite glory.

"It's not that there haven't been a few crimes involving the use of crossbows," she began before even sitting down, "but nearly all of them are domestic, or they involve some nutter going on a spree and getting either caught or killed."

"And the ones that aren't?"

"That's what's interesting. I looked for a pattern."

"And did you find one?"

"I found three unsolved murders overseas involving the use of a crossbow—same make of bolt as used in the Quinn killing, too, by the way—all in one way or another connected with the world of people-trafficking and illegal immigration."

"Now that's interesting," said Banks, taking another sip of coffee. Masterson had brought her own mug with her.

"I thought so. There was one in Vilnius—that's in Lithuania—one in Amsterdam and one in Marseilles."

"How hard is it to get a crossbow across European borders?"

"Not very," said Masterson. "You probably wouldn't want to carry one on a plane, but you could take it apart and put it in with your checked luggage. Or why not just buy a new one in each country, if you're paranoid about getting searched? It's not as if you need a permit or anything. However you look at it, it's a lot less trouble than a gun."

"True enough," said Banks. "The victims?"

"Not known to us, sir, but with definite Interpol profiles. In all cases the conclusion was that the victims were either skimming the profits or about to blow the whistle on a lucrative people-trafficking route, usually connected with Eastern Europe."

"I don't suppose any suspects' names cropped up, did they?"

"Afraid not, sir."

"Pity. You said overseas. What about in this country?"

"I was just getting to that, sir. We've had two over the past three years: a gang master in South Shields, and a hoodie on a housing estate in Stockton-on-Tees. Both unsolved. The gang master was connected with illegals, and local intelligence suggests that the hoodie was attempting to break into the loan-sharking business on his own."

"Interesting," said Banks. "So we've got some sort of enforcer for the people-trafficking and loan-sharking business?"

"It seems that way, sir."

"Any links to Corrigan?"

"No, sir."

"OK. Do we have any idea who this bowman works for?"

"No, sir. I suppose it could be just one person, some sort of crime kingpin who employs him when he's needed. Or he might be for hire. A freelancer."

"Hmm. Anything more on the car?"

"I checked with the local rental agencies. There was a Ford Focus with similar cross-hatching on the front left tire, the same shade of green paint as the scraping we found, rented from Hertz in Leeds last Wednesday and returned on Friday."

"Details?"

"Arnold Briggs, address in South London. UK driving license. But it's all fake, sir. I checked. There's no such address."

"I suppose if these people can forge passports and work visas, they can forge driving licenses, too. So whoever Arnold Briggs is, he's long gone?"

"Afraid so, sir." Her expression brightened. "But the car hasn't been rented out again. It's been cleaned, of course, but forensics might still find something, mightn't they?"

"Indeed they might," said Banks. "It's worth a try, at any rate. Get onto them and—"

"I've already talked to DS Nowak, sir." DC Masterson flushed slightly as she spoke Nowak's name. "I took the liberty. I hope you don't mind. He says he's on it. This does get us forward a little bit, doesn't it?"

Banks admired her enthusiasm, and he didn't want to dampen it. "Yes, it certainly does," he said. "That's good work, Gerry. You showed initiative. Let's go through what we know, or suspect, point by point." He counted off on his fingers. "One: The same car was at both crime scenes. The methods of killing were different, so maybe there are two killers. Two: Quinn and the victim at the farm had spoken twice on the telephone shortly before their murders. Three: we think

254 • PETER ROBINSON

the victim at the farm was also a victim of some sort of migrant-labor scam. Four: Quinn had in his possession a number of photographs of himself in a compromising position with a young woman, most likely taken six years ago in Tallinn. Five: Quinn was briefly involved in investigating the disappearance of Rachel Hewitt, also in Tallinn, at that time. Six: Warren Corrigan, on the surface a petty loan shark, is connected with Roderick Flinders, owner of Rod's Staff Ltd., a front for migrant- and illegal-labor scams. Seven: Bill Quinn was involved in the investigation of said Corrigan. Have I missed anything? I'm running out of fingers. Yes. Eight: there were rumors of a bent copper, possibly Quinn, and possibly through blackmail. It's all giving me a headache."

"Arnold Briggs was the fake name of the person who rented the car," said Masterson. "It's not that easy to kill. I think it would be a bit unbelievable, not to mention too much of a coincidence, if there were two different killers, sir."

"Good point. Now, what could Bill Quinn possibly have in common with the Garskill Farm victim, a migrant worker?"

"Unless he wasn't a migrant worker, sir," said Masterson. "You said yourself he didn't have the hands of a manual laborer. What if he was an informant, or even an undercover police officer?"

"Possible," said Banks. "But I'm certain Ken Blackstone or Nick Gwillam would have brought it up if he was Quinn's informant. But it's an interesting thought. Perhaps our man was at the farm under false pretenses. Either that or he got all the soft jobs."

"Maybe West Yorkshire didn't know, sir? Not if he was an undercover officer from Poland or Estonia or somewhere."

"Maybe you're right, at that," Banks agreed. "One of the numbers called from the telephone box in Ingleby was an Estonian mobile. Again, though, it's bloody untraceable. Annie's tried ringing it, but there's no answer."

"Just the sort of phone an undercover officer might have, or his controller," said DC Masterson. "A throwaway?"

As Banks thought over what Masterson had just told him, there came another knock at his door. When Annie and Joanna Passero walked in, the office started to feel crowded.

"What is it?" Banks asked.

"I just got a call from a woman who says she knows the Garskill Farm victim," said Annie. "She recognized his photo in the paper this morning."

"Why didn't she call before?" Banks said, "It's been all over the papers and TV for the past two days."

"Says she's been away on some sort of retreat."

"Religious?"

"Dunno."

"You think she's genuine?"

Annie rolled her eyes. "We've had a few cranks. I think I can tell the difference. Yes, I think she's genuine."

"Sorry."

"Anyway," Annie went on, "she's in Manchester, but she says she's willing to drive over now and identify the body, tell us all she knows. She was upset, naturally, and I offered to arrange a car for her, but she said she could manage it by herself."

"What's her name?"

"Merike. Merike Noormets. And according to her, the victim's name was Mihkel Lepikson. She said he was her boyfriend."

"Dutch? German? Scandinavian?"

Annie grinned. "Wrong, sir. Estonian. Both of them."

"My, my," said Banks, rubbing his hands together. "This is starting to get interesting, isn't it?"

Before Merike Noormets arrived, Banks and Annie agreed that they would interview her together, preferably in a more congenial environment outside the police station, after she had identified Mihkel Lepikson's body down at the mortuary. But they hadn't reckoned with Joanna Passero, who claimed that she couldn't be excluded from this interview because it impacted directly on the Quinn case. She actually said "impacted." Banks cringed, but there was nothing he could do except let her come along under sufferance. She would only go crying to Superintendent Gervaise if he didn't. Having three people present, four including Merike Noormets herself, would be a bit of an overload, but Banks trusted that Annie knew when to keep quiet and take notes, and he stressed to Joanna that she was present only to observe. He would do most of the talking. She didn't like it, clearly didn't like any of it, but she grudgingly agreed. Annie seemed rather more sympathetic to Joanna's predicament than Banks, but then she had worked for Professional Standards herself.

Merike Noormets was an attractive woman in her early thirties, with hennaed hair and a couple of minor piercings, wearing jeans and a light yellow cotton jacket over an embroidered Indian-style top of some kind. She also carried a stitched leather shoulder bag. She looked a bit hippy-ish to Banks. She had clearly been crying when Annie and Joanna brought her up from the basement of Eastvale General Infirmary.

Banks had waited for them outside in his car, feeling that he had no need to see the man's body again. The rain that had threatened yesterday afternoon had started during the night and was still falling. With it, a cold front had moved in, and the temperature had dropped considerably.

The identification was positive, Annie told him, and now they could get in touch with the parents back home in Tallinn and arrange for them to come over. As soon as the three women had piled into the Porsche, Banks headed out of town. It was a Tuesday lunchtime in late April, so a lot of country pubs and restaurants would probably be closed, but he knew he could depend on the Blue Lion in East Witton.

It was very much a silent journey from the Eastvale mortuary. Banks concentrated on his driving and listened to the lovely strains of *The Lark Ascending* and *Variation on a Theme* by Thomas Tallis. He thought the music might help soothe Merike Noormets and relax her enough to make her open up.

All the parking spots in front of the pub were taken, so Banks parked opposite the long village green, and they walked back over the road to the rambling old building. Merike smoked a cigarette on the way and got through about a third of it before they went inside and found a table in the bar. The menu was chalked on a blackboard over the enormous fireplace. Rain dotted the windows. A few logs burned in the hearth and threw out more than enough heat to compensate for the weather outside. The starters were written on another blackboard over the bar, and to read all that was on offer would have taken all day. Merike said she would like a glass of white wine, and Banks was unable to resist a pint of Black Sheep, but the other two stuck to diet bitter lemon—Annie because of her medication, Banks supposed, and Joanna Passero just to show him up. He bet she was making a note, too: "DCI Banks drinking on duty, during interview of important witness." Well, screw her. Banks knew how to interview an important witness, and it wasn't in a dingy interview room smelling of stale sweat and fear with a Styrofoam cup of canteen coffee in front of you. Especially a witness who had just come from identifying her boyfriend's body.

Merike pushed her hair out of her eyes, pale green flecked with amber, Banks noticed. For some reason he thought of the Jimi Hendrix song "Gypsy Eyes," though she was hardly a Gypsy, and they were hardly Gypsy eyes. There had to be some connection somewhere in his mind, but, as so often these days, he couldn't grasp it. Maybe there was a hint of wildness about her that chimed with the music, he thought; perhaps she had a Gypsy soul, whatever that was.

When the landlord came around to take their orders, Merike said she wasn't hungry. The other three ordered. Banks went for his favorite, smoked haddock with a poached egg, leeks, mushrooms and Gruyère cheese.

"I suppose you want me to tell you everything I know?" said Merike with a hint of irony. Her husky voice was only slightly accented. If she was in her early thirties, Banks calculated, she would have been in her teens when Estonia won its independence from the Soviet Bloc. Old enough to remember life under the old regime. He found himself wondering what her childhood had been like.

"Not everything," he said. "Just what you can. First, I'd like to thank you for coming forward and getting in touch."

Merike seemed surprised. "Why shouldn't I?"

"Not everyone does. That's all. Sometimes people just don't want to get involved."

Merike shrugged. "It was such a shock, seeing Mihkel's photograph in the newspaper like that."

"What was your relationship with him?"

"I suppose he was my boyfriend. My partner. My lover. I don't know. With Mihkel it was always difficult."

"Why?"

"He is the kind of person who comes and goes in your life. Sometimes he disappears for weeks or months. At first, it used to drive me crazy, because he would tell me nothing, but now he tells—he told me—a little more, and we talk on the telephone."

"When did you last talk?"

"On Tuesday. Tuesday evening, at about nine o'clock."

Banks searched for a sheet of paper in his briefcase and showed it to Merike, pointing to a number. "Is this yours?"

"Yes, it's my mobile number. It's a pay-as-you-go I use when I'm over here. Cheap phone, occasional top-ups."

"Did you and Mihkel live together?"

"No. I travel also, for my job, and we are never in the same place together for long enough. It would be too complicated."

"How long have you been seeing each other?"

"Three years now."

"What are you doing in Manchester?"

"I work as a translator. I'm on a two-week course at the university there. Almost finished." She glanced at Annie. "I just returned from a weekend retreat in the Lakes, and I haven't seen any newspapers or television from Friday until this morning. Part of the course.

It was beautiful. Much more grand than our Estonian lakes. But it rained a lot."

"It always does in the Lake District," said Banks. "Your English is excellent, by the way."

"Thank you. I lived in London for many years, in my twenties."

"Do you speak any other languages?"

"German," Merike said, "Finnish, Russian, French and a little Spanish. I'm learning Italian. When you grow up in a small country like Estonia, you soon realize that nobody from anywhere else is going to understand you unless you speak their language. Who learns Estonian except Estonians?"

Who, indeed? Banks thought. He hadn't even known Estonia had a language of its own. He had assumed they spoke Russian there, or perhaps some version of Polish. But languages were not Banks's strong point. "Was Mihkel a translator, too?"

"Mihkel? Oh, no. His English was very good, but he was no linguist. It seems so strange to be talking about him in the past tense. I must get used to it."

"I'm sorry," said Banks.

"Mihkel knew the risks."

"What risks? What was he doing at Garskill Farm?"

"Is that where he was when it happened? I don't know it. I had no idea where he was, except that he was somewhere in England. It seemed so strange to be in the same country and not be able to meet. I couldn't even telephone him. I had to wait for him to ring me."

"Mihkel phoned you from a public telephone box in Ingleby," said Banks. "It's the nearest village to where he was found. It was about two miles away from where he was staying."

Merike smiled sadly. "Mihkel walked four miles just to talk to me? I would never have thought it of him."

Annie gave Banks a sharp sideways glance. He knew that she was hoping he wouldn't spoil Merike's illusion by telling her that she wasn't the only reason Mihkel had walked all that way to the telephone. "Do you know what he was doing there?" he asked.

"He was on an assignment. Mihkel was a journalist. He specialized in investigative reporting. He was freelance, but worked mostly for a weekly newspaper called *Eesti Telegraaf.* They specialize in the sort of articles he liked to write."

"What were they?"

"In-depth, usually about crime. He also contributed sometimes to a weekly column called 'Pimeduse varjus.' In English it means 'In the shadow of darkness.' Very sinister. The idea is looking into the darkness. Watching. It's also about crime."

" 'Watching the dark,' " said Banks.

Merike flashed him a brief smile. "Ah, so you like Richard Thompson?"

"Yes, I do. Very much."

"I like that," she said. "A policeman who admires Richard Thompson."

"His father was a Scotland Yard detective," Banks said. "And a lot of his songs are about murders."

"I didn't know that. About his father, I mean."

"My own son's a musician," Banks went on, unable to stop himself now that he felt he was bringing her out of herself a bit, and enjoying the way the Gypsy eyes were seeing him in a new light, not just as some faceless authority figure. "He's in a group called the Blue Lamps."

"But I know them!" said Merike. "Their new CD is wonderful. The best they have ever done."

"Brian will be pleased to hear that." Banks felt proud, but he could tell from the waves of impatience emanating from Joanna Passero that she wanted him to get the interview back on track. It was one reason he hadn't wanted her around. She didn't understand how important it was to find some common ground with the interviewee, to forge a bond. She was used to interviewing dirty cops, where there was never any possibility of her creating a link because it was an adverse situation from the outset. Annie had been more impatient and aggressive in her interview techniques at first, when she had come from Professional Standards, despite the courses she had taken, but she had learned over the years since then. She knew how Banks operated.

Their food arrived. As they were getting it sorted out, Merike excused herself and went outside for another cigarette. When she came back, they were eating, and her hennaed hair was damp with drizzle.

Merike sipped some wine and made an apologetic shrug in Banks's direction. "Can't smoke anywhere these days, even in Estonia."

"So what assignment was Mihkel working on at Garskill Farm?" he asked.

"I don't know any details, except that he told me before he left it was something to do with migrant labor, and he wasn't sure how long he would be away. That was typical Mihkel. He didn't even dare to take his mobile phone for fear of what would happen if they found it. Not so long ago, a Lithuanian journalist disappeared while he was working on a similar story, all because they found a mobile with a built-in camera among his belongings."

"How did Mihkel deliver his story to the newspaper?"

"I assume he gave it in short pieces to his editor over the telephone. So I am sure he didn't walk four miles only to talk to me, however gallant it sounds. Though I would like to believe he did. He might have risked writing some things down if he had a good hiding place, in the lining of his clothes or somewhere like that."

Banks glanced at Annie, who shook her head. They would have taken his clothes apart already and had clearly found nothing. If Mihkel had hidden any notes, then his torturers had found them first.

"Why was it so secret?"

"The people who run these things are all connected with very powerful and dangerous criminals. It's not a one-man operation. Everything must be in place. Every step of the way must be planned. It takes capital, organization, enforcement, and the ones in the best position to do that are organized gangs. There is much at stake."

"Russian Mafia?"

"Like everyone in the West, you think the Russian Mafia is behind everything. They may be involved, yes, of course, if there is money to be made, but it is not the only one."

"Baltic Mafia?" said Banks.

"Something along those lines. When people speak of the Baltic Mafia, they usually refer to Latvia, Lithuania and Poland, but we are not without our own bad men in Estonia. We don't have to import them all from Russia or Latvia, you know."

"I'm sorry," said Banks. "I don't know much about your country."

"Don't worry. Nobody does. It is very small and has a troubled history. May I have another glass of wine?" She held out her glass.

Banks gestured to Joanna Passero, who glowered but took it to the bar for a refill. "Is there anything you can tell us about the people Mihkel was investigating?" Banks asked.

"All he told me was that he was posing as an unskilled laborer. He started out at an agency in Tallinn, where you go to seek for work overseas, and this place you mentioned . . ."

"Garskill Farm."

"Yes. That is where he ended up. I assume he was with others in the same position, and they would be taken out to their places of work at the start of the day in a van and delivered back to the dormitory at the end."

"Dormitory" was a rather grand word for Garskill Farm, Banks thought. "We think so," he said. "About twenty of them altogether. Unfortunately, they've all disappeared."

"I'm sorry, I can't help you."

Joanna returned with the wine and handed it to Merike, who thanked her.

"What did Mihkel say to you during your conversations?"

"They were very brief. He would just tell me he couldn't talk long, that he might be missed. He told me that he was all right. He told me . . ." She paused and lowered her head down shyly. "He told me that he loved me, that he missed me."

When she looked up again, Banks saw there were tears in her eyes. "I'm sorry if this is difficult," he said. "But we need to find out everything we can if we are to find the person who killed Mihkel."

"I understand," said Merike. "But I have told you all I know."

"Are you certain? Think. Was there nothing else he said to you?"

Merike bit her lip. "He did say something a bit mysterious the last time we talked."

"Last Tuesday evening?"

"Yes."

"What was it?"

"He said he thought he was on the verge of finding a big story to work on. There was something about some photos, too."

Banks's ears pricked up. "A big story? Photos? Was it connected to the story he was already working on? Did he give you any idea what it was?"

"No. He was very guarded. He said I would know soon enough if he was right. Only that it was big, and that it could mean trouble for some very important people. He could say no more about it."

According to the logs from the telephone company, Mihkel Lepikson had rung Merike *after* he had talked to Bill Quinn on Tuesday evening. Within a short while, both Mihkel and Bill were dead. Did their conversation, and their murders, have something to do with this big story he was talking about? It would be too much of a coincidence, Banks thought, if they didn't. Perhaps Quinn was going to pass on the photos to Mihkel, but he never got the chance. But there was also a third number Mihkel had called. "Can you give me the names of Mihkel's contacts in Tallinn, at the newspaper or elsewhere?"

"Of course. He always worked with the same editor. Erik Aarma. It was a close relationship. They were good friends. Erik is a good man. Mihkel wouldn't work with anyone else, and his reputation was big enough that he could make his own rules like that. Erik will be brokenhearted. It was like, how do you say, a spy and his handler. Like in Mr. le Carré's books."

Banks smiled. He was a le Carré fan, too. "I understand," he said. Then he referred to his notes again and showed Merike the Estonian number. "Do you know if this is Erik's number?"

She shook her head. "I have no idea. He would probably use an untraceable mobile. Secrecy was very important, and the work was dangerous, as I have said. Erik might be able to help you with some other names and contacts, people in the organization. Mihkel would have spoken to Erik and only Erik on the telephone. He would also have discussed his ideas for the story first with Erik. In his line of work, you learn not to trust many people, and he trusted Erik."

Banks bet that other number dialed from the telephone box in Ingleby was Erik's dedicated line to Mihkel. "Will Erik reveal his sources?"

"I don't know. I am sure that Erik will help you all he can without compromising himself."

"Will he come over here?"

"Perhaps, if you pay his fare and reserve a room for him at the Dorchester."

Banks laughed. "Not much chance of that, I'm afraid."

"Has Mihkel worked on this kind of assignment before?" Annie asked. "Crime. Migrant labor. That sort of thing. You said he contributed to a weekly column about crime."

" 'Pimeduse varjus.' Yes. But not all the assignments are dangerous. It is true that Mihkel always did like living on the edge a bit too much. He got beat up once when he wrote about the sex trade in Tallinn. Mostly he keeps his head down. He was very good at blending in with the scenery, which is strange when you think how handsome he was. People would notice when he walked into a room, but he could lose himself in a role, be an uneducated, unskilled migrant laborer and nobody would look twice at him. He could be invisible when he wanted. It was very useful in his work."

Except he couldn't hide his hands, Banks thought. And that might have been his undoing.

"So he habitually sought out dangerous situations?" Annie said.

"Good stories," Merike said, correcting her. "There was sometimes danger involved, and Mihkel didn't shy away from the risks. I said he lived on the edge, but he wasn't a fool. He didn't put himself in harm's way without good reason. He wasn't a thrill seeker. Perhaps more of an adventurer, the way he liked to travel to exotic, dangerous places like Somalia, Syria or Haiti. He was very fond of the writings of Graham Greene."

"How do you think the people who did this to him found out who he really was?"

"I don't know. He must have made a mistake. That isn't like him, but it must be what happened. They could have seen something he wrote. Or perhaps they had a spy in their dormitory? An informer in Tallinn?

Or somewhere along the route? Maybe somebody followed him to the telephone box that night. There are
many ways it could have happened."

"Have you ever heard of a policeman called Bill
Quinn?" Banks said, cutting in. "Detective Inspector
Bill Quinn?"

"Bill? But of course. He was a good friend of
Mihkel's."

The three police officers looked at one another. "A
good friend?" Banks repeated. "Close?"

"Well, they knew each other, talked on the telephone sometimes, met on occasion when Mihkel was in
England. But not very close. Mihkel was not very close
to anyone, except perhaps to Erik."

"Did you know Bill? Had you met him?"

"No. But Mihkel talked about him sometimes."

"So it wouldn't surprise you that Mihkel also called
Bill Quinn the same night he phoned you?"

"No. Not really. Why shouldn't he?"

"No reason. I'm just trying to get all this clear. You
see, we didn't know of any connection between Bill and
Mihkel."

"It was before we met," Merike said. "There was
a big case in Tallinn. An English girl disappeared,
and Bill came over to help the investigation. Mihkel
was covering the story. They kept in touch. Mihkel

also came to England to talk to the girl's parents and friends."

At last it became clear to Banks. He hadn't seen the Rachel Hewitt files yet, only got the bare bones from Annie's research, and he hadn't known who Mihkel Lepikson was, or what he did for a living, until just now, so no one had made the connection. Now it made sense. "Was it just the Rachel Hewitt disappearance, or did they have other things in common?" Banks asked.

"Mihkel was mad about fishing," Merike said, smiling at the memory. "I used to tease him about it. That he'd rather be sitting by a river with a hook in the water than be in bed with me. I think they went fishing together once or twice, him and Bill. In Scotland. And there was Rachel Hewitt, of course. Bill kept Mihkel abreast of all the developments over here. The Rachel Foundation. What her friends and her family were doing."

That made sense. A hobby in common. And Rachel Hewitt. But what did it all mean? For one thing, it meant that the Rachel Hewitt case was coming up with such alarming regularity that it was now the number one priority. But he thought they still might find a link to Corrigan, Flinders and the migrant-labor racket. There were too many pieces missing.

Banks reached for the envelope in his briefcase and tipped out the photographs of Quinn with the girl.

"Could these be the photos Mihkel was referring to? Bill Quinn had them in his possession. Do you recognize the girl?" he asked.

Merike studied the photos. "I don't know if these are what he meant," she said, "but I don't know her."

"They would probably have been taken about six years ago," Banks added.

"No. I would remember her."

He pushed the blowup of the beer mat toward her. "I assume that's familiar to you?"

"Yes. Though I prefer Saku, myself. Can I see that one again?" She pointed at the photograph of Quinn and the girl having a drink in the bar. After studying it for a moment, she said, "I think that's the bar in the Hotel Metropol."

"You know it?"

"Yes. I've been there many times for my work, and with Mihkel and Erik."

"Pardon my being a little indelicate here," Banks said, "but is it the kind of hotel where . . . certain women might be found?"

Her eyes widened. "You think I would go to a hotel like that?"

"No, of course not," Banks blustered. He could tell that Annie and Joanna were enjoying his discomfort tremendously, and he was desperately thinking of a way to get out of this without putting his foot any further down his throat. "No. I mean, we think, you know, that . . ."

"This girl?" said Merike. "The one in the photograph?"

"Well, yes. Possibly." He hadn't shown her the bedroom shot, so she wasn't to know the context of the business.

"But she does not look like that sort of girl. Is that how you say it? 'That sort of girl'?"

"I suppose so. Yes. You don't think so?"

Merike examined the photo more closely. "No. Just because she is young and beautiful?"

"And with a much older man."

"Many women prefer older men. I'm not saying it isn't possible. Perhaps you know something I don't. But the Metropol is definitely not that kind of hotel. It doesn't mean you can't have a drink with an attractive woman there, though."

"Thank you, Merike," Banks said. "That's a great help."

The question was: where next? There was one thing Banks was certain of, and that was that if he wanted answers, before very long he would have to pay a visit to Tallinn himself, whether Madame Gervaise liked the idea or not.

It was after seven o'clock when Banks walked through his front door that evening. He picked up the post, gave it a casual glance and tossed it on the computer desk behind the door, along with his briefcase. It had been his habit lately on arriving home from work to put on some music, make a cup of tea and relax in the conservatory with a book before microwaving the remains of yesterday's takeaway, or throwing together a sandwich from whatever he happened to have in his fridge. Today was no exception. He put the kettle on, dug out his old CD of Arvo Pärt's *Fratres*, put it in the CD player and, when the tea was ready, took it and the book he had bought earlier to the conservatory. He wasn't even hungry. The smoked haddock he had enjoyed at the Blue Lion was enough to last him a while, and if he did get hungry later on, he had some Seriously Strong cheddar in the fridge. He could grill himself a sandwich. If that wasn't enough, there was always the leftover Indian takeaway from Saturday.

Banks sipped the green tea and let Pärt's slow repeating piano chords and flurry of strings drift over him; the strings reminded him of Philip Glass. He was due to fly out of Manchester the following morning at 10:25 for Tallinn, changing in Helsinki. Area Commander Gervaise hadn't liked the idea of the trip at all, as he had expected, but after complaining for ten minutes about budget cuts and constraints, she saw that it was the only logical next step in the investigation and approved his travel application, with limited expenses.

The only drawback was that Joanna Passero was to accompany him. Gervaise was quite firm on this. Annie Cabbot had been livid. Having been cooped up in hospital or in St. Peter's for so long, she complained, a nice trip abroad would have done her the world of good. Gervaise argued that someone had to handle the investigation back in Yorkshire, and the budget wouldn't run to three detectives going abroad. Besides, hadn't she just got back from Cornwall? As it appeared that Tallinn was where Bill Quinn had committed his unforgivable sin of adultery and got his photo taken in the act, then Inspector Passero had to be there.

Despite the company, Banks felt excited about the journey. Estonia was a country he had never visited before, and he loved new places, especially cities he could explore on foot. He had picked up the Eyewitness *Top 10 Tallinn* guide from Waterstones before coming home, and he glanced through it as he listened to the music. *Fratres* gave way to the solemn, tolling bell and eerie strings of *Cantus in memoriam Benjamin Britten*, slowly building in volume.

The visit would be mostly taken up with work, Banks knew, talking to the police who had investigated the Rachel Hewitt case and to Erik Aarma, Mihkel Lepikson's friend and editor, but there would always be a free hour or two now and then to take a walk. They had booked in at the Metropol, and he soon discovered from his guidebook that the Meriton, where Rachel Hewitt and the hen party had stayed, wasn't very far away.

Banks had the names of the investigator and the prosecutor on the case. The investigator had now retired, but he had said that he was sorry to hear about Bill Quinn's death and he would be happy to talk to Banks at a place to be agreed upon later. Someone would contact him at the hotel.

Merike Noormets had also told Banks that she was returning to Tallinn the following day and would be happy to help out as a translator, or to drive them around if they needed her. She said most Estonians spoke English, but difficulties might occur with some words or concepts. Banks had her telephone number in his mobile, and he thought he would get in touch. She would be grieving over Mihkel for some time, and perhaps something interesting to do would help take her mind off her loss.

After his talk with Merike, Banks had gone back to his office and looked over the Rachel Hewitt files.

As Annie had already told him, there wasn't much in them because it had been essentially an Estonian case, starting as a local investigation by the Tallinn Central Prefecture, then quickly becoming a case for the National Criminal Police Department when the seriousness of the matter, and the involvement of a foreign national, became apparent.

The investigation itself had gone on for about two months, but the case was still officially open, as Rachel Hewitt was still a missing person, not a murder victim, though most people outside the family believed that she was dead. Banks could glean very little from Bill Quinn's reports, and it seemed to him very much as if the whole thing had been a matter of national niceties and ticking the boxes. Still, Quinn had been there for a week shortly after Rachel disappeared, and he had worked closely with the investigator from the Criminal Police Department, whose name was Toomas Rätsepp, and with the prosecutor, Ursula Mardna.

Annie and Winsome would be questioning Rachel Hewitt's parents and friends from the hen party while he was away. Banks also asked Annie to slip in a few questions about the night of the disappearance to Rachel's friends, to fill in some of the gaps and details, if possible. From what he had read so far, it all sounded very vague and haphazard.

The haunting *Spiegel im Spiegel* was playing when Banks put the book aside and took another contemplative sip of tea. He felt the stirrings of excitement in his chest, not only at the prospect of a trip abroad but at the possibility of making some sense out of this irritating, puzzling and complicated case that had been gnawing at his brain for six days now.

Maybe, with a bit of luck, a bit of help and the right questions, he might just find out what the hell was going on. There was one idea he couldn't get out of his mind now, and that was that Bill Quinn may well have been killed because he found out what happened to Rachel Hewitt. And finding out who killed him might depend on finding out what happened to her.

7

Banks and Joanna were barely talking when they got to the hotel. Banks had spent the long flight from Manchester to Helsinki listening to Arvo Pärt's piano music and reading the only Estonian novel he had been able to find in Waterstones: *Purge,* by Sofi Oksanen. It was heavy going at times but absorbing nonetheless. Sometimes the engine noise drowned out Ralph van Raat's delicate piano playing, but the noise-canceling headphones Banks had bought at Manchester helped. Joanna had sat beside him with her laptop on the tray in front of her, to all intents and purposes working on a report. During the stopover at Helsinki, she went off to do some duty-free shopping, and Banks sat by the gate drinking a latte and reading his book, occasionally glancing out at the planes through the large plate-glass window.

At the Metropol, there was a message waiting for them at reception. It read simply: "Lunch at Clazz tomorrow 1230. Tourists pay." The name was Toomas Rätsepp.

"Cheeky bastard," said Banks. "Fancy a bite to eat now? Discuss strategy?"

Joanna shrugged. "Fine with me. Let's just dump our stuff and get freshened up first."

Half an hour later, map in hand, Banks led the way across a broad, busy avenue, where traffic swarmed and trams rattled by. They brought back childhood memories. There had been no trams in Peterborough, of course, and he was too young to remember the ones in London, but he was sure he had visited one or two cities with his parents and ridden on them. Leeds or Manchester, perhaps, where they had relatives.

The weather was absolutely gorgeous, bright sun low in a clear blue sky, with a faint half-moon in the south. Banks hardly even needed his jacket, which he carried slung over his shoulder because he did need its pockets for his carefully stowed wallet, book, iPod, mobile, pen, notebook and various other bits and pieces. It was all right for women, he thought, glancing at Joanna; they had handbags. Bottomless pits, most of them. Some Frenchmen carried little leather bags with straps, too, but that trend had never caught on in Yorkshire. Banks just used his pockets.

Though it was still light, the evening shadows were lengthening in the cobbled streets of the Old Town, which were lined with three- or four-story buildings with pastel facades of lemon, white, orange, pink or pale green, many of them cafés with tables outside. Some had ornate gables and dormers. Even narrower alleys led off to the left and right, some with signs above doorways indicating cafés or bars, others bare, perhaps with hidden cellar clubs, the kind you had to get text messages to know about. Most of the streets were free of traffic, though the occasional delivery van or utilities vehicle edged its way along, bouncing on the cobbles.

They reached a broad crossroads, almost a square in itself. There seemed to be a few cars and taxis around this area, though they all came to a halt and turned back about where Banks and Joanna were standing, by a large bookshop. Banks guessed that traffic wasn't allowed beyond that point and, indeed, most of the streets were not wide enough for cars anyway.

On their left was the bookshop, and beyond that Banks could see the sign for Fish & Wine, which was recommended in his guidebook. Over the road was a grassy area sloping up to an ancient church. According to his guidebook, the church was called Niguliste and was famous for the medieval painting *Danse Macabre*. By the sloping lawn in front of Niguliste, young people lounged around, smoking and talking, enjoying the early taste of summer, young girls in short shorts and skimpy tops, tanned tapered legs, hennaed or bottle-blond hair.

The church stood in all its majesty, drawing the soft evening light to itself, the top of the white square tower pale orange in the glow.

Joanna stopped for a moment. "It's beautiful," she said.

"You religious?" Banks asked.

She gave him a funny look. "No."

"Me neither."

All the outside seating at Fish & Wine was full, according to the waitress, but they managed to get a table at the end of a bench inside that was right next to the open doors of the side patio. It was a good spot, and they could see the edge of Niguliste and all the people walking by.

They made themselves comfortable and read the English-language menu. Like most places in Tallinn, the restaurant had free Wi-Fi, and Joanna checked her e-mail and text messages before slipping the phone back into her handbag without comment. Banks was curious as to what she was expecting, the way she seemed obsessed with constantly checking her phone. Was it something to do with the job? Coded messages from Professional Standards headquarters? Reports on his behavior? If she wanted to tell him, he assumed that she would do so in her own time.

They both ordered the turbot, along with a bottle of Pinot Grigio. Banks poured the wine. Joanna was wearing an off-the-shoulder frock with a gathered waist. During the flight, she had worn her hair tied back, but now she wore her blond tresses elegantly piled up on top, the way it had been when he first saw her, showing off her long graceful neck to best advantage. She also wore some dangling silver earrings and a locket around her neck. She smelled of the hotel's body lotion and shampoo. She must have checked the Tallinn weather forecast before setting off that morning to know what to pack, Banks thought. It had been raining in Manchester.

"Traveled much?" Banks asked to break the tension that seemed to stretch between them like a taut elastic band.

"I've never really been anywhere before. Well, I tell a lie. I did go to Barcelona once, and I've been to Italy, of course. But that was family, so it doesn't really count."

"Your husband?"

Joanna nodded and twisted her wedding ring.

Sensing that she didn't want to linger on the topic, Banks moved quickly on. "I'd suggest you do a bit of sightseeing, enjoy yourself. Did you bring your camera?"

"No."

"You should have. You can probably buy a cheap one in any tourist shop."

"I'll be too busy working. What are you trying to tell me?"

"I just don't think you'll have a lot to do, that's all. I've got two murders to investigate now, three if you include Rachel Hewitt, and I work better alone, without interference. I don't need someone watching my every move, looking over my shoulder. Also, no foreign cop or prosecutor is going to talk to you. I'll be lucky if they talk to me with you present."

"I—"

"You're Professional Standards. You do what you do."

"Can we clear the air a bit?" Joanna said. "Why are you being so nasty to me? You don't have a reputation as a particularly mean person, so why pick on me? I'm not here to investigate you. Is your ego so big you can't get over that? I've been trying to work with you for six days, and if you're not actively against me, you avoid me, you shut me out. You play silly practical jokes, and now you expect me to go off sightseeing while you do the real man's work. You didn't want me with you yesterday to interview Merike Noormets. You didn't want me to come with you today to Tallinn. You ignored me throughout the entire journey here. You were surly all the way from the airport. What is it with you?" She paused and gave him a level gaze.

"It's just that I can't imagine what there is for you to do here, that's all. Say we find the girl, say she admits she drugged Quinn and put him in a position to be blackmailed. So what? What does that prove? It certainly doesn't prove he was bent, working for Corrigan or anyone else. To find out about that you'd need to be back in England. There's nothing for you here is what I'm saying. I'm sorry."

"No, you're not. You like to humiliate me and make me feel small. Fine. Go ahead if it makes you feel good, if it helps you to think I've got no feelings, that I'm just some sort of robotic persecutor of good honest cops. As a matter of fact, I do have feelings. If you prick me, I bleed. All right?"

"All right," said Banks. "I mean it. I'm sorry. All I'm really saying is that I work better alone."

The food arrived, and they paused to take a few bites before continuing their conversation. The turbot was good, Banks thought.

"Well, I'm sorry, too," said Joanna eventually, "but you're not alone on this one. The point is that I do the job I do, but it doesn't define me. I am not my job. And I'm not made of stone. I meant it. You can be very hurtful, you know. Very cruel. That's not in your file."

"Yet."

"See what I mean? The sarcasm. It's nasty. Mean."

It was what Winsome had said and, if truth be told, what Banks himself had felt. He didn't know why he did it but couldn't seem to stop himself. He felt guilty and foolish now, but he saw Joanna in a new light. She was nobody's fool. She said her job didn't define her, and she was right. This was a living, breathing person, with feelings, as she had made abundantly clear. But he still couldn't forget that she was Professional Standards and, as such, represented a stumbling block to any success he might hope to have.

Joanna glanced around the restaurant, almost as if to check that no one was listening. Nobody was paying them any attention now, as far as Banks could tell. "I'll let you in on a little secret," she said.

Annie and Winsome were skirting the southern edges of Leeds on the M62 toward the Drighlington exit. The Hewitts had agreed to see them that afternoon, intrigued by what little Annie had told them on the phone. "Poor people," Winsome had said. "I didn't intend for them to get their hopes up. But they'll grasp at any straw they think might help them find their daughter alive." And it was true. Pathetic, really, the little tremor of excitement in Maureen Hewitt's voice the moment Annie mentioned she was from the police and wanted to talk about Rachel. If she were in Mrs. Hewitt's shoes, would she accept that her missing daughter was dead after six years? Would she *hope* that she was? Probably not, she realized. When you give up hope, what do you have left? At least if someone found Rachel's body, her parents would *know*, would be able to bury her and move on with their lives, however painfully and slowly. Closure.

"We're almost there," said Annie, checking the signs. "Next exit. Get in the lane."

Winsome edged the Toyota into the exit lane and turned off the motorway toward a large roundabout.

"Not far now," Annie said.

She had read up as much as she could on Rachel Hewitt that morning. Nobody had done a psychological profile of the victim, but Bill Quinn had put together a thumbnail character sketch that described her as an intelligent girl but given to occasional wild flights of fancy and impulsive behavior, a social drinker, a loyal friend, a person who cared for other people and wanted to make the world a better place. Reading that last bit had made Annie feel like putting her finger down her throat and gagging. It sounded like one of those speeches candidates for Miss World or whatever beauty pageant contestants spout in their skimpy swimming costumes. World peace, save the children, the seals and the whales, feed the hungry and all that. But there was a hint of a dark side. Rachel was also a dreamer and something of a material girl. She harbored a fantasy of meeting her Prince Charming one day, but he would have to be rich. It was a common, and possibly dangerous, blend of naïveté and avarice.

Naturally, Quinn had been thorough in his investigation of Rachel's friends and contacts. She could have been targeted for trafficking. Though she didn't seem to fit the usual victim profile, it was a possibility no good copper would fail to check out. A foreign boyfriend woos her, swears undying love and arranges to meet up with her in Tallinn, where they live blissfully together until he reveals his true self and tells her what she has to do to help repay his debts. What she *will* do, if she really loves him. Then the beatings, the rapes, the mental and physical abuse begin, the brainwashing. It happened all too often. But not, apparently, to Rachel. There were no foreign boyfriends in her life, no suspicious characters, no one who didn't check out cleanly. It seemed she had lived an exemplary life with exemplary friends before Tallinn swallowed her up.

They found the house, a compact redbrick semi in a street of compact redbrick semis. There was nothing about it to distinguish it from the rest, no poster of Rachel in the front window or sign in the garden, only a beat-up old Astra in the drive and a lawn that needed a bit of loving care. It was tragic in its ordinariness.

Annie rang the bell and the door was answered almost immediately by a woman she took to be Maureen Hewitt. She was about fifty, Annie guessed, rather on the tall, gaunt side, with a long face and fair hair tied back in a ponytail. She wore no makeup, but her complexion was good, though pale, as if she didn't go outdoors very much. There was an unnatural, brittle brightness in her pale blue eyes that Annie found disconcerting. Someone who lived for hope, no matter what reality presented her with.

She led them to the front room, where her husband was sitting in an armchair.

"It's the detectives who rang earlier," she said.

Mr. Hewitt got up and shook hands with Winsome and Annie. "Very pleased to meet you," he said. "Perhaps . . . some tea before we begin?"

For some reason Annie couldn't quite work out, Mr. Hewitt reminded her of a vicar—not quite grounded, but with a certain aura of authority, weight of sorrow and sense of purpose. He went and made the tea, and when it was done, Mrs. Hewitt suggested they go into the "office" as they were dealing with "official Rachel business."

The office was in the spare bedroom, and this large room was the real heart and nerve center of the operation, Annie felt as soon as she walked in, the mug of tea warm in her hand. In an odd way, the Hewitts seemed somehow more relaxed in the office than they had in their living room. Two of the walls were taken up by desks and office equipment. There were two computers, a fax machine, a photocopier, a couple of laser printers, two telephones, filing cabinets and even a television tuned to a twenty-four-hour BBC world news channel that was on mute. Though the room was generally clean and tidy, there were piles of papers around, many of them flyers with Rachel's picture and a plea for help, in various languages. Framed photos of Rachel lined the walls, from one of her in her mother's arms shortly after she'd been born, to a slightly glamorous studio shot in her teens. She had a half smile on her face, lips slightly parted, and the diffuse, fuzzy lighting you get on glamour shots highlighted her spun-gold hair and her blemishless porcelain skin. Her features were delicate, finely chiseled, but not sharp or pinched, and her cheekbones were high. She looked a bit Nordic, Annie thought, and also a bit like a doll. Fragile, too. But there was more, beyond all that. The intelligent eyes, the serious girl behind the smile. The girl who cared, who wanted to do some good in the world, who wanted to be rich.

"This is our operations center," said Mr. Hewitt, who asked them to call him Luke and his wife Maureen. "Please, sit down."

In addition to the office-style chairs in front of the desks, there were a couple of small armchairs in the center of the room, no doubt kept for interviewers and visitors just like Annie and Winsome.

"You said on the phone you had some news," said Maureen Hewitt, hovering over them keenly.

"Well, it's not really news," said Annie. "But we do have a few questions for you. First of all, have you heard about Bill Quinn?"

"Inspector Quinn," said Maureen. "Oh, yes. Isn't it terrible? And he was so good to us."

"You knew him well?"

"I wouldn't say well, would you, Luke? But we knew him."

"Even after the investigation?"

"We sent him bulletins, let him know what we were doing to keep Rachel's name in the public eye. That's all."

"When did you last see him?"

"Let me think. It was shortly after his wife died, wasn't it, Luke?"

Luke agreed. "About a month ago," he said. "Late March."

"What did he come to see you about?"

"Nothing in particular," said Luke. "It was a bit of a puzzle really. Why he came. We hadn't actually *seen* him for years. Not since he got back from Tallinn six years ago, in fact. He told us what had happened to his wife, of course, and we offered him our condolences, naturally. He was very upset. He said he envied us our strength and belief."

"What did you say?"

"Well, I told him it hadn't been easy. My wife and I are regular churchgoers, and we've had a lot of support from the parish, of course, but sometimes even faith . . ." He shook his head. "There've been times when . . . Anyway, you don't want to know about that. You know, a lot of people think we're just keeping up a front, putting on some sort of a show, that we should long ago have let go and moved on."

"What do you think?" Annie asked.

"As long as there's a chance that our darling Rachel is still alive, then we'll carry on trying to find her," said Maureen. She picked up one of the flyers and handed it to Annie. "Look at this. Latvian. We had a sighting near Riga just last week."

"There must be a lot of sightings."

"You'd be surprised," said Maureen.

"Fewer and fewer as times goes by," said Luke. "The hardest thing is to get anyone to take them seriously and follow up. That's why it's so important to keep her face out there, keep her name on peoples' lips. We have to keep up the pressure, make sure nobody forgets. No offense, but we can't depend on the police. You have other cases, other things to occupy your time. Rachel is all we have. It's up to us to try to keep the investigation going at some level. People think we're publicity seekers. Well, we are. But the publicity is for Rachel, not for us."

"We try to stay on good terms with the media," said Maureen, "but it's difficult sometimes. They can be very intrusive, as you know, if you've been reading the papers and watching TV lately. They're your best friend and helper one minute, then they turn on you the next. We've tried being as polite and informative as we can, but then they turned on us for being too cool and unemotional, not being passionate and anguished enough, for not crying all the time. Honestly, sometimes you just can't win."

Annie had read the stories in the papers about their recent testimony in the hacking inquiry, about how an unscrupulous reporter had hacked into their private telephones and hounded their remaining daughter,

Heather, stealing her diary. At one point, this same reporter had even "borrowed" Maureen's journal and reproduced sections of it in the newspaper, her deepest fears about her missing daughter, a breakdown of communication with her other daughter, her feelings of despair and thoughts of suicide. It had been headline news—MOTHER OF MISSING GIRL ON SUICIDE WATCH—but then so had their evidence against the reporter and his editor later, at the official inquiry.

Heather Hewitt, Annie knew, had gone off the rails at some point during the six years her sister had been missing. Excerpts from her diary showed a troubled teen upset and worried about her big sister but feeling increasingly neglected, sidelined and unloved because all her parents' energy went into the Rachel Foundation and all their time into finding Rachel. It seemed to her that they didn't care that they had a living, breathing, troubled daughter right there who needed them. Heather felt that they wished she had been abducted instead of Rachel, and in her worse moments, she even believed she had heard them saying that, whispering it at night when she was lying in bed trying to get to sleep. She had turned to drugs, become publicly addicted to heroin. From what Annie knew of heroin, it was hardly a surprising choice. Heroin offers a deluxe escape, takes away all your problems, all your worries, all your fears, and wraps you in a warm cocoon of well-being until it's time for the next fix. Hallucinatory drugs throw all your perceptions into disorder and all your fears and worries back at you in the form of nightmares and rising paranoia, and amphetamines and Ecstasy keep you on the move, keep you running, dancing, sweating, feeling good. But only heroin takes all the pain away. The closest Annie had come to truly understanding that feeling was with some of the morphine-derived painkillers they had given her in hospital when she was at her worst.

"How is Heather?" she asked.

Maureen's face clouded. "She's progressing," she said. "I know people said we were being cold and cruel having her put away like that, especially after they leaked her diary in the papers, but the institution was a good idea, for a while at least."

"Until she's ready to face the world again," added Luke.

"Yes," agreed his wife, nodding. "Do you know, she's just the age Rachel was when she went missing."

Annie let the silence stretch for a respectful moment, then she took a photograph of Mihkel from her briefcase. "Have you ever seen this man?" she asked the Hewitts.

They both studied the photo closely, then Luke said, "I think so. Can you tell us his name?"

"Mihkel," said Annie. "Mihkel Lepikson."

"Yes, of course." Luke glanced at his wife. "Don't you remember, love? He's that nice Estonian journalist who came to see us with Inspector Quinn six years ago."

"That's right," Maureen said. "He was writing about the case back in Tallinn. We've kept him up-to-date, too, over the years. He's written updates on the story, tried to help as best he can. They're not all rotten. Reporters."

"He was nice, you say?"

"Yes," said Luke. "Not like the others. At least he was straight with us, and he didn't write about our private grief, or apparent lack of it. It was the case that interested him, the search for Rachel, what might have become of her."

"Did he have any ideas?"

"None that helped," said Maureen.

"Have you ever seen him again recently?"

"Not for years. But we've had e-mails and telephone conversations. He's been helping us to keep Rachel's name out there, and he usually sends us a clipping if he's written anything about her in his paper. It's in Estonian, of course, but you can still see it where he mentions her name, and he writes out a nice translation for us. It's very difficult when you're so far away.

People forget so easily. We've been meaning to get in touch with him."

"I'm afraid there'd be no point," said Annie. "He's dead."

The Hewitts looked at one another in shock. "Dead? But . . . how?"

"He was also murdered. Shortly before Inspector Quinn, we think."

"But why? He seemed such a nice young man."

"Well, his business is a dangerous one. He worked on exposing crimes and criminals, and they don't like it when someone does that. There were probably a lot of people who had it in for him because of the things he wrote."

"About Rachel?"

"That's a possibility we have to consider. Do you have these clippings? Could we take them with us and have a look at them? We'll make sure you get them back."

"Yes, of course." Maureen opened one of the filing cabinets and pulled out a red folder. "They should all be in here. Translations, as well. So you do think Mihkel Lepikson's death had something to do with Inspector Quinn's?"

Annie could have kicked herself. She had gone too far. She didn't want to lie to the Hewitts, but she couldn't tell them the whole truth, either. A good investigation depended on holding back information from the public. "It's possible," she said. "We just don't know. That's why we're asking all these questions. I know it must seem a bit strange to you."

"But don't you see?" Maureen went on. "If the two are linked, they might both have something to do with Rachel. It could all be connected. This could be the sort of lead we've been waiting for. They might have known where she is."

"I wouldn't get your hopes up," Annie said.

"Hopes? What else could I have except despair? Do you know, there isn't a day goes by when I don't imagine the terrible things that could have happened to Rachel over the last six years. That could be happening to her somewhere, even now. Her fear. Her pain. Her desperation. People doing terrible things to her. My little girl alone in the dark with monsters, abandoned. Believe me, I don't sleep much anymore. The nightmares are too frightening."

Her husband touched her shoulder and said, "Or that she's lost her memory somehow, and has forgotten about us, but is living her life happily somewhere. That's what I try to think about, anyway."

Maureen moved toward the doorway. "Come with me. Let me show you something."

Annie raised her eyebrows and glanced at Winsome.

"I mean it. Just follow me," Maureen said. Annie and Winsome did as they were asked.

Maureen took them across the landing and into another, smaller bedroom. "This is Rachel's room," she said in slightly hushed tones. "It's ready for when she comes back. It's always ready. I wash the sheets every week, and her clothes, even though she hasn't worn them for a long time. It's important to keep things clean. *That's* hope. And when our daughter comes home at last, it will all have been worthwhile. I suppose you think I'm insane now, but I don't care. It's one of the things that *keeps* me sane. The hope."

Annie took in the room. It was quite ordinary, not pink or black or anything you might expect from a teenager, thank God, but a neutral tone of blue, with a small writing desk and chair, television and CD player, a few CDs and books in an antique glass-covered bookcase. Posters of Coldplay and Franz Ferdinand adorned the walls. There was also a glossy picture of a sleek BMW standing outside an ugly art deco mansion. Someone, presumably Rachel, had written a thought bubble with the words "MINE ONE DAY!!" in a Sharpie at the top. Annie smiled. Just under the window was a collection of stuffed and fluffy animals, clearly going all the way back to Rachel's childhood. Very girly, she thought.

"She loves fluffy animals," said Maureen, catching Annie's expression. "Collected them. That's Paddy."

Annie glanced at the bed. A one-eyed teddy bear missing a fair bit of stuffing sat propped up against the pillow staring at them. It gave her the creeps.

"Paddy was her first-ever animal, when she was a baby. She took him everywhere with her. He was with her in Tallinn. In her hotel room. Inspector Quinn very kindly got him back for us. Paddy's waiting for her, too. He was her good-luck charm."

"I see she liked cars, too," said Annie.

"Oh, that. That was just a bit of silliness. I can't understand what it was with her and fancy cars. That's more a boy thing, isn't it?"

"Did Rachel still live at home when she . . . ?"

"When she disappeared. It's all right, love, you can say the word. Yes, she did."

"Did she have a boyfriend?"

"Not for a while. She'd been seeing Tony Leach for a couple of years, but they split up about a month before she went away."

Annie remembered the name from Bill Quinn's reports. "Was she upset about it?"

"Of course. Two years is a long time. But she soon got over him. You do when you're young, don't you, though it seems like the end of the world at the time. She shut herself away in her room and cried for two days, then she put him behind her and got on with her life again."

Maureen led them back into the office, but they remained standing. There wasn't really an awful lot more to say. Annie got the names and addresses of Tony Leach and the five female friends who had been with Rachel on that fateful hen weekend, thinking one of the girls might know something and might have kept quiet for reasons of her own. At the door, she turned and asked the Hewitts if there was anything more they could tell her about Bill Quinn's last visit to the house.

"Like what?" asked Maureen.

"What sort of mood was he in?"

"Well, he was very sad, of course. The poor man had just lost his wife. And he seemed distracted."

"Did he say anything odd or surprising? That sort of thing."

It was Luke who answered. "He said one thing that struck me as odd when I thought about it later. We were talking about his wife's death, and one of the comments he made was that it 'changes things.' I'm sure one thinks many things about the death of a spouse, but 'it changes things' seems an odd one to me. I mean, it's sort of self-evident, isn't it, so why say it? Probably nothing, but there you are. And he told us not to give up hope."

"Thank you," said Annie. She knew what Bill Quinn had meant.

"You will keep in touch, won't you?" said Maureen. "If there's anything . . ."

"Yes, of course."

"What little secret would that be?" Banks asked.

"Nobody wants to stay in Professional Standards forever. Annie Cabbot didn't; I don't. As you know, it's not possible, anyway. There's a strict time limit on the job."

"Don't tell me you want to work Major Crimes," said Banks.

"Well, I'd like something a bit more juicy than PS, yes, and something that earns me a bit more respect from my fellow officers."

"And this is a way of getting some on-the-job experience? In the back door, so to speak."

"Something like that. Believe or not, I *asked* for this job. I wanted the opportunity to work with you."

"You were out to get me from the start?"

"No, you idiot. Stop it. I'm not out to get you, I'm out to learn from you. You might not be aware of it, but you have a reputation, whether you know it or not. Yes, you're a bit of a maverick and all the rest, and as I've just found out, you have a cruel and selfish streak, too, but you're generally thought of around the county as a pretty damn good detective. Just don't let it go to your head."

"I should have known. Gervaise is grooming you. She's—"

Joanna waved him aside. "She is doing no such thing. She gave me an opportunity to work with you, said if I was lucky I might pick up a few pointers on how a homicide investigation is conducted. That's all."

"But she does know about your ambitions, and she was willing to encourage them?"

"Area Commander Gervaise is an enlightened woman. We could do with more like her around the place."

Banks liked and respected Catherine Gervaise, but he had never quite thought of her in that way. He sat in silence for a moment, digesting what he'd just heard, joining the dots. Why hadn't he figured this out before, right from the start, at that meeting in Gervaise's office? It gave him choices he hadn't considered before. He could either continue being an arsehole and leave Joanna out in the cold, or he could make use of her, work her hard, test her skills, treat her as a member of the murder team and try to forget the Professional Standards angle, see if she had the makings of a good homicide detective.

But could she forget the Professional Standards angle? Banks doubted it. He didn't care if she found out that Quinn was bent. If he was corrupt, then his corruption deserved to be exposed, especially if it had spread to others close to him and allowed a toerag like Corrigan to thrive. Besides, Quinn was dead. What could they do to him now except cloud his reputation? And what was a dead copper's reputation worth to start with? The ones who found out would soon forget; the rest would neither know nor care. The ones who would be hurt most would be his two children, and they were grown-up enough, resilient enough, to deal with it in time. He already knew that Quinn had probably committed adultery with a woman young enough to be his daughter, and they would no doubt find out about that, too, one way or another. The point was that he now had Joanna Passero to help him rather than hinder him, if he chose to include her. On the other hand, he was in a foreign land lumbered with an amateur wannabe, if he cared to think of it that way. But these days, he was more of a cup-half-full sort of bloke. She had to have some skills he could use. And maybe she could learn.

The waitress came and asked them if they wanted any dessert. Neither did. Banks said they would just stick with the wine, and she smiled and went away.

"So what you're saying is that you want to work on all aspects of the investigation, not just the bent-copper angle?" he said.

"Yes."

"So you'll do what I say, follow my lead?"

"Depends what you say, what the lead is. I won't break any laws, and I won't turn away from any law- or rule-breaking on DI Quinn's part. I'll still do my job."

"Fair enough," said Banks. "I can't really explain why, but I can't get the idea out of my mind that Bill Quinn may well have been killed not because of the photos or Corrigan, but because he found out what happened to Rachel Hewitt. And that finding out who killed him might depend on finding out what happened to her. Can you work with that hypothesis?"

"If you think there's a definite connection between the time Quinn spent here on that case and what happened subsequently," said Joanna, "then I'm with you. Let's find out what it is. But we're not here to solve the Rachel Hewitt case."

"It might not be so easy," said Banks. "I have a feeling that nobody around here is going to want to open up to us about it. Too much wound licking and mudslinging under the bridge, I'll bet. We'll see what we can get from this Toomas Rätsepp tomorrow. If he's like most cops, it won't be very much. Then we'll have a chat with Mihkel's editor, Erik, see if we can get him to talk a bit. Journalists are pretty simple souls really. They can be very close-mouthed, in my experience, but if they think you can do something for them—i.e., give them an exclusive—then they'll bend over backwards to help you."

"What exactly are you after?" Joanna asked.

"Well, ideally I'd like to find Rachel Hewitt alive and well, take her home to her parents, bring her abductor to justice, solve Bill Quinn's and Mihkel Lepikson's murders and have their killer put away for life, then world peace would be a nice bonus. But in reality? First I'd settle for finding out who the girl in the photo is and having a good talk with her, see if I can find out who put her up to it. If she did set Quinn up, I very much doubt that it was her own idea. After that, we'll see where that leads us."

"Do you think anyone knows?"

"I think there's a good chance that someone does, yes," said Banks. "It's more a matter of whether we can get anyone to tell us. If Quinn and Mihkel stayed in touch over the years after they first bonded over Rachel—you know, went fishing together and so on—then I think there's a chance that Quinn was going to meet Mihkel by the lake and tell him the truth about what happened here, and why. He may have been going to hand the photos over to him."

"But Quinn didn't have the photos on him when he was killed."

"That bothered me at first. But remember the mysterious phone call from the pay-as-you-go mobile?"

"Yes."

"What if Mihkel was forced to make that call, to change the time of the meeting or something, or even to arrange it, and what if the different number or something in Mihkel's voice set off alarm bells, made Quinn suspicious?"

"But he still went."

"Yes. It doesn't mean he wasn't on guard, though, cautious. But he clearly wasn't expecting a crossbow bolt through the heart. He may have left the pictures back in the room until he was sure Mihkel was coming."

"That's possible, I suppose," said Joanna. "Do you think this Toomas Rätsepp knows?"

"Why would Rätsepp know? Quinn certainly wouldn't tell him, and I doubt that anyone else would, either. He might be able to give us some general details about the direction of the investigation, but I wouldn't expect much more from him. I still think Erik is our best bet, if he's willing to help."

"What makes you think you can solve this after so long, when everyone else has failed?"

"Because I'm better than them," Banks said, smiling. "Watch and learn. Seriously, though. A lot's happened since then. Are you with me?"

Joanna rolled her eyes and laughed. Then she raised her glass and they clinked. "I'm with you. Seriously, though," she said, leaning forward. "I really don't want us to be working at cross purposes here. I know what you think of me and my job, but we're both concerned with catching Quinn's killer, too, right? Are we OK on all this?"

"We're OK."

8

Thursday turned out to be another warm day, and by lunchtime Banks and Joanna were ready for a cold drink and some food. They had spent the morning getting the feel of the city in which Rachel Hewitt had disappeared and discussing their strategy for the forthcoming interview. They had been all the way up to Toompea and seen the onion domes of the Russian Orthodox Nevsky Cathedral, walked around the Dome Church, admired the views of the city in various directions from the different viewing points and wandered the quiet cobbled streets. There were very few shops and cafés up there, and it seemed remote, even from the rest of the Old Town, quiet and peaceful. Not the sort of area for a hen party.

They found Clazz, back down in the Old Town, opposite a large restaurant Banks had seen mentioned

312 · PETER ROBINSON

in his guidebook called Olde Hansa, a cream-fronted building with lots of wooden benches on its covered patio, which seemed to contain almost as much shrubbery as it did customers. The waitresses were dressed in medieval-themed costumes, and Banks could imagine evening sing-alongs with everyone waving tankards of foaming ale in the air.

But Clazz was much less ostentatious. A man sitting at one of the outside tables waved them over and introduced himself.

"How did you know it was us?" Banks asked when they had sat down.

"Two foreigners looking lost? It does not take much detective skill to work that out, Hr. Banks."

"Please, call me Alan. This is Inspector Joanna Passero."

Joanna smiled and shook Rätsepp's hand. "Joanna," she said.

Banks noticed that he held on to it for a few seconds longer than necessary. Joanna clearly noticed it, too, but she said nothing.

"And I am Toomas. Do you enjoy our lovely weather?" Rätsepp went on. "We often have good weather at this time of year. You are very lucky you come now." His English wasn't quite as good as Merike's, but then he wasn't a translator. It was far better than Banks's nonexistent Estonian.

"It makes a pleasant change," said Banks.

Rätsepp was in his late fifties, overweight, with a head of thinning gray hair; wary, hooded eyes; and bushy gray eyebrows, rather like a pair of horns above his eyes. Banks decided he must have cultivated them that way deliberately, thinking they were sexy or something, because he couldn't fail to see them every time he looked in a mirror. He reminded Banks of the actor who had called Michael Caine "Eenglish" with a sneer in his voice in *Funeral in Berlin.* Oskar Homolka. He was wearing a white shirt, open at the neck, with the sleeves rolled up, showing hairy forearms and throat. A gray sports jacket hung over the back of his chair. There were sweat stains under his arms, and the buttons were tight around his middle.

The waiter wandered over and handed out menus.

"I would recommend the steak," Rätsepp said, "but of course, it is entirely up to you. Perhaps you are vegetarian, yes?"

They ordered steak and A. Le Coq beer for Banks and Rätsepp, and a Diet Coke for Joanna. She had told Banks she felt a little the worse for wear this morning, so he guessed she was laying off the wine for a while.

"I understand you retired recently," Banks said as they waited for their drinks. "How is that working out?"

"Excellent, excellent," said Rätsepp. "It is something I wish I have done many years ago."

314 · PETER ROBINSON

"Why didn't you?"

He rubbed the thumb and fingers of one hand together. "I must work to earn money."

Their drinks arrived, and Rätsepp proposed an Estonian toast. *"Teie terviseks!"*

They sipped their drinks and chatted about police work for a while, then, when their lunch arrived, Rätsepp indicated he was ready to talk.

"It is terrible shame about Hr. Quinn," he said after his first mouthful of very rare steak. A drop of blood hung at the side of his fleshy mouth like a teardrop. Fortunately, he used his serviette a lot while he ate. "He was good man. Very good man. What happen?"

"That's what we're hoping to find out." Banks didn't want to get onto the subject of Quinn's transgressions so early in the conversation, though he hoped that at some point Rätsepp might be able to help him with the photographs, if he felt he could trust him enough to show him them. If, on the other hand, he got the impression that Rätsepp was in any way involved with what had happened to Quinn or Mihkel Lepikson, he certainly didn't want to give too much away. But he would reserve judgment for the moment. He was half-surprised, and very pleased, that Joanna didn't jump in with some comment about Quinn's murder. He figured she must have been learning; she must have listened to him after their set-to the previous evening. "I'm afraid we're all still a bit at sea about it all."

"At sea?"

"Sorry. Confused."

"Ah. I do not really see how an old case will help you, or what it has to do with Hr. Quinn's death," Rätsepp said. "It was long time ago, and Hr. Quinn had only minor role."

"I understand he was over here for about a week?"

"That is correct."

"How soon after Rachel Hewitt's disappearance?"

"Perhaps two days."

"That's very quick, isn't it?"

"There is no real measure for such things." Rätsepp paused and ate more steak. "I think the girl's parents demand he come," he went on. "They call local police in England and ask them to do something. I think the parents are, how do you say, very pushy? It is quite understandable, of course. We do our best, but what can I say? This is beautiful nineteen-year-old girl, young woman, and she is missing forty-eight hours. I know it is very confusing and upsetting for her parents, to be so far away, in foreign country. They do not understand our country. They want someone to communicate what is happening before they come here themselves. Difficult time for everyone."

"What did DI Quinn actually do in the investigations?"

"Nothing very much. What can he do? He is not involved here. He is not Estonian. He attends meetings, of course, so he can go back and tell his bosses what we are doing. But that is all."

"He didn't do any searching, any questioning, any investigating?"

"No. Observing only."

Banks wasn't sure he believed Rätsepp, but he moved on, nonetheless. What reason could he have to lie? "Were there any leads at all?"

"Sadly, no. We check the hospitals, airport, railway station, buses, ferries. We check other hotels. We speak with staff at Meriton to ask if she go back there and go out again. We visit many bars and clubs popular with young tourists. Ask everywhere. Nothing. It is like the girl disappear into air."

"What about since then? Any nibbles? Any traces?"

"For two months we investigate. More. Sometimes now we send out her description again. Nothing. I am sure you also get many mistaken sights, which is all that we have had. From St. Petersburg to Prague, and in the south, Odessa and Tirana. Her parents encourage many of these mistakes. We have also work with an artist on what Rachel look like now. It is not so very big change in six years, perhaps, but it helps."

"What about CCTV?"

"What is that?"

"Closed-circuit television. Cameras. In the streets, in bars. We have them all over England."

"Ah. Yes. We have here, too. But then not so many, of course. We examine all we can find, but nothing show us where Rachel is gone." He paused. "As I am sure you know, many camera images are not so good."

"True enough," said Banks. "Most CCTV's crap, no arguing with that." He gazed around at the other diners. Many were obviously tourists, given away by their cameras or bulging Day-Glo bags. He heard some people speaking German, and some Italian. There were also quite a few young professionals, and he took most of them for locals, who perhaps worked in the Old Town or had come in from the suburbs to have lunch with friends during the spell of fine weather. "This is very good steak," he said.

"I am glad you approve. And the charming lady?"

Joanna, the "charming lady," smiled sweetly at him and said, in her best Morningside accent, "Absolutely delicious, Toomas. One of the tastiest I have ever eaten."

Rätsepp beamed at her. "In what capacity exactly are you here?" he asked, his forehead wrinkling into a slight and, so Banks thought, definitely choreographed frown.

"I'm sorry," said Joanna. "I don't understand the question."

"I apologize for my bad English. You work for Professional Standards, am I not right?" he went on. "But Inspector Quinn's murder is matter for Homicide, no?"

"I can see there are no flies on you, Toomas," Joanna said, waving her fork at him and smiling to take the sting out of her tone.

He checked his arms. "Flies? I do not understand."

"She means you're very quick to grasp a situation," Banks said. "It's just a saying."

"Ah, another of your charming English idioms. I see. It is one I do not know. I will remember. She is here to keep an eye on you, Alan, you lucky man? Have you been naughty boy?"

"It's nothing like that," said Banks. "Inspector Passero is training for her transfer to Homicide and Major Crimes. Her boss thought working on this case with me would help."

"So you are her teacher?"

"Something like that."

"You must be very good to be trusted with such lovely pupil." His eyes narrowed. "I hear things about you."

"All good, I hope?" said Banks.

"But of course."

Banks wasn't sure he liked being such common knowledge. First Corrigan, now Rätsepp. True, one of them was a cop, and it would be only natural for him to find out something about a visiting officer from another country. Even so, it was disconcerting, and he felt it put him at a disadvantage. He wondered exactly how much Rätsepp knew about him, and what.

Rätsepp turned back to Joanna again, still smiling. "But I am not so certain that you tell me complete truth."

Joanna smiled at him again. "Toomas! Would you doubt a lady's word?"

"But of course not." Rätsepp took her hand again for a moment. "It is merely that I understand there is some . . . shall we say . . . confusion over Hr. Quinn's circumstances, some possibility that he was involved in affair of the heart, or perhaps a business transaction of some kind, and you think it happens here." He let go of Joanna's hand and gave it a light pat.

"Well," said Banks, "you've certainly done your homework, haven't you, Toomas? But that's really a nonissue. We're here because we've managed to make a connection between Bill Quinn and an Estonian journalist called Mihkel Lepikson. Have you ever heard of him?"

Rätsepp seemed taken aback at the name, Banks noted, and he got the impression that he was quickly trying to think how to respond. Rätsepp already seemed like a tricky person to pin down, and Banks hadn't expected smooth and easy sailing. How had he known about Quinn and the girl, for a start? There could be a leak in Yorkshire. Or was Rätsepp in touch with the villains themselves? Was he feigning surprise at the mention of Lepikson? He was hard to read. It was entirely possible that he had something to hide, but even if he didn't, the habits of a lifetime die hard. Given his age, Rätsepp must have been a cop during the Soviet era. He would be used to keeping his own counsel. Or lying. Policing must have been a whole different business under the Russian rulers, who would no doubt have brought in their own security organizations. Banks had heard and read many things about the Stasi in East Germany, for example, and he wondered if things had been at all similar here. If so, Rätsepp might be a very skilled dissembler, and he would also make it a point to know everything about everyone. He obviously already knew something about the Quinn case, and the girl, but Banks didn't know exactly how much. Did he know about the photographs, the possible blackmail, the crossbow?

"Lepikson . . . Lepikson . . . ," Rätsepp muttered. "The name sounds familiar, you know. A journalist?"

"The *Eesti Telegraaf.* He wrote about Rachel at the time she disappeared, then on and off over the years. Mihkel Lepikson was found dead under very mysterious circumstances in North Yorkshire, not far from where Bill Quinn was killed, a few days ago. Your government has been advised, and his parents have been located. I believe they have already left for the UK."

"Ah, yes. I can know only what I read in the newspapers, of course," said Rätsepp. "Now I am retired, just private citizen like everyone else, I am out of the loop, as I believe you British say."

"Of course. And I'm sure you can understand that I can't tell you any more, even as one police officer to another, with this being an ongoing investigation."

"Naturally," said Rätsepp. He sounded disappointed and gave Banks the kind of look that seemed to beg for ten minutes alone with him in a soundproof interrogation cell. "I understand completely."

Banks could tell the Estonian was reevaluating him; he could almost hear the cogs turning, new gears engaging. Rätsepp had no doubt expected someone he could get information from easily, but now that this was proving not to be the case, he was having to rethink his strategy. Banks tried to work out exactly where the Estonian stood in this whole business, but he had too little to go on. Was Rätsepp involved with Corrigan, with the crossbow killer, with Rachel Hewitt's disappearance? It was all possible, especially as he seemed to know so much, but there was no evidence to believe so yet. It was more than likely that he had made mistakes in the Rachel Hewitt investigation and was simply covering his arse.

The waiter came around again and asked if they wanted anything else. Banks and Rätsepp both ordered a second A. Le Coq, and Joanna asked for a cappuccino. She pronounced the word deliberately, with what Banks took to be a perfect Italian accent, not the way most Scots or Yorkshire folk would say it.

"I am sorry," said Rätsepp, "but there is really nothing more I can tell you about Hr. Quinn or why he was killed."

"Can you think of anyone here who might have wanted him dead?"

"Here? But why?"

"A connection with the Rachel Hewitt case, perhaps?"

"What possible evidence is there?"

"No evidence, Toomas. Just a gut feeling. Don't you ever have gut feelings?"

"Of course. But not about this."

"Mihkel Lepikson wrote about the case, and Bill Quinn investigated it. That seems like a connection to me. Were there many of you working on it?"

Rätsepp sipped some beer before replying. "I have support investigators, as usual. And I report to prosecutor."

"That would be Ursula Mardna?"

"That is correct. Very senior and very competent prosecutor, of blameless character."

"We'll be talking to her later," Banks said. "I understand that DI Quinn mostly coordinated the investigation back in Yorkshire?"

"Yes. He talk with Rachel's parents and friends. Make some interviews. Communicate with us relevant information."

"Such as?"

"Times, places, minor details."

"Do you have such a thing as a map of the girls' movements that night?"

"Impossible. We try to make one, of course, but it is too difficult. Their memories . . . unreliable. The girls so drunk. The next day also." He made a gesture of disgust. "These girls. They come here and act so indecent and noisy. They must expect . . ."

"What? To be abducted?"

"No, of course not. That is not what I am saying. But they must learn to be more careful and more respectful."

"They were just having a good time, Toomas," said Joanna. "They weren't doing any harm."

"They ruin the peace of our Old Town."

"You should try Nottingham on a Saturday night," Joanna said.

Banks glanced at her, impressed. She was baiting Rätsepp, and doing it with great charm.

"My dear Joanna," he said. "It is not the same. They are visitors. Guests in our country. They should not behave that way."

"Well, it's a bit late for Rachel Hewitt, isn't it?"

Rätsepp looked as if he'd been slapped. His face reddened. "We do our best. We cannot do more. Now you come here and . . ." He waved his hand in the air disgustedly.

Their beers arrived, along with Joanna's cappuccino. Time to put the bridges back together again, Banks thought. He could play good cop when required. "I'm sure you all did your best, Toomas," he said. "But these girls . . . well, as Inspector Passero says, they're young and wild and out for a good time. They don't think about public order and upsetting people. Yes, it's selfish, but you must have been a young lad once. Surely you sowed a few wild oats?"

Rätsepp gave Banks a knowing man-to-man smile. "Certainly I did. But those were very different times. Russian times. You must be very careful what you do and who see you. Much more careful. I do understand it is important, your case, but I do not see connection to Mihkel Lepikson and Rachel Hewitt. I do remember the journalist. He write about case back then. But why do you think the murders were connected to this?"

"It's just too much of a coincidence," said Banks. "Quinn befriended Lepikson while he was over here consulting on the case, *your* case. And both were murdered within about ten miles and ten hours of one another just after they'd been in touch again, just after a telephone conversation in which Bill Quinn told Mihkel that he might have a very big story for him."

Rätsepp frowned. "Big story, you say? What big story?"

"We don't know," said Banks. "I'm just saying it's too much of a coincidence. We also have forensic evidence to indicate that the same man and car were present at both scenes. Most likely the killer. We don't know who he is yet, but we're getting close." Banks realized that he was probably telling Rätsepp too much, but he felt that if he didn't give at least something up, he would get nothing in return. If Rätsepp thought he was getting the best side of the bargain, if he believed that he had succeeded in tricking Banks into giving up too much, it might make his own tongue a bit looser. It was just a matter of exactly what Banks did give away and how valuable it was.

Rätsepp nodded. His chins wobbled. "I still do not understand how I can help you. Our case records are in Estonian, of course, but you are most welcome to see them. Everything is in correct order. We can get translator, though it will take long time. We have nothing to hide. But I assure you there is nothing about Hr. Quinn."

"I'm sure you're right, Toomas. And I don't want to read your case files. All I really want is a general picture of what happened while he was here. And the girls, of course. I know some of the details of the night in question, the drinking, clubbing, no doubt boys following them around. But where did they go, for example? You say you don't have a map, but you must have some idea."

"This was six years ago," said Rätsepp. "So many bars, clubs and restaurants open and close since then that it is impossible to say. And the staff are all new. People have moved on. Even at the time it is very difficult to get an idea of their movements. Yes, we do have list of bars and nightclubs I am happy to give you, but we do not know the times and order of visiting. There are many Irish pubs with names like Molly Malone's and O'Malley's, for example. And many others in Old Town. Nimeta Baar—that is Pub with No Name now. Club Havana. Venus Club. Stereo Lounge. Club Hollywood. The girls go to many of these."

"But not beyond the Old Town?"

"We do not think so."

"Where did they lose Rachel?" Banks asked.

"In Irish pub on Vana-Posti, near south edge of Old Town. St. Patrick's. Nobody see Rachel after there."

"Except her killer."

"Yes," said Rätsepp with a sigh. "The other girls go to bar on Raekoja Plats, main square, with some German boys they meet at Club Hollywood. They notice Rachel is not with them perhaps twenty minutes, half an hour, after they get there. Then it is too late, of course. They cannot find her. They cannot remember where they were before. It is only later that we can put some pieces together."

"And then you went to these places and asked about Rachel?"

"Of course. But we find out nothing."

Annie had already told Banks as much, but he wanted to find out if Rätsepp knew any more. "Rachel didn't know where her friends were going, did she? They had no destination in mind, just picked somewhere at random. She could have just wandered around trying to find them for hours in the Old Town, couldn't she?"

"It is possible," admitted Rätsepp. "But I do not think so. Nobody report seeing her, except a waiter in

St. Patrick's, who say he think she go wrong way, other way from her friends. But he not so certain. As you see for yourself, it is not a very large area. It is very busy that night. We can find nobody who see her. That is because it is two days later before girls can tell us where they go. Tourists go home. German boys gone. Everybody gone." He shook his head in frustration.

"Did no one report seeing her at all after she left St. Patrick's?"

"Nobody. And we do not hear about her disappearance until the following morning. It take us two days to get information from her friends about where they go and what they do. They were so drunk they cannot remember. By then everyone who is there on that night is gone. Nobody knows anything. She is gone. Pouf."

"And that's the last of Rachel," said Banks. "No body. No nothing." He felt a wave of sadness ripple through him as he imagined what fear and pain Rachel must have gone through, whatever had happened to her. His daughter, Tracy, had gone through a terrible ordeal not too long ago, and thoughts about what might have happened to her still gave him nightmares. He could hardly begin to imagine the horrors Rachel's parents must have visualized over and over in their minds, the loop tapes of porn and snuff films. He took a hefty slug of beer.

He remembered the time he had been lost in a foreign city and how frightening that had been. He was fourteen years old, on a school exchange with a French family in Lille. They had all gone to see *Gone with the Wind* in the town center. Banks thought it was boring enough in English, so it would be even worse in French. He found a horror film showing around the corner, one of the old Dr. Mabuse films, and said he would go there and meet them afterward. Naturally, his film was much shorter than *Gone with the Wind*. Finding himself with plenty of time to kill, he bought some Gauloises at the nearest *tabac* and then went and sat in a bar, ordered a beer and waited. When it was time to meet up, he took a wrong turn and couldn't find the cinema. He wandered and wandered, deeper into the back streets, rows of brick houses, little corner churches, washing hanging across the street, the locals giving him strange looks. He knew enough French to ask directions but not enough to understand the answers. The feeling of utter helplessness came over him, verging on panic. In the end, Banks had got to a main street he recognized and boarded a tram back to where he was staying. But Rachel . . . where did she end up?

Rätsepp spread his hands in a gesture of openness. "What more can I say?"

"What do you think happened to Rachel, Toomas?" asked Joanna, cappuccino in her hand. "Just out of interest."

Banks was glad that Joanna had asked the question, feeling he was pushing a bit too hard himself. It was perfect coming from her. Rätsepp seemed to have forgotten her earlier insensitivity, because he favored her with a condescending smile and patted her knee. "My dear," he said, "you must know as well as I do that it cannot be good news. The most obvious theory is that someone take her, some stranger or someone the girls had meet earlier in some nightclub or bar. Perhaps it is someone who has stalked them, or someone she has *arranged* to meet. We have no evidence of this, of course, and it poses many questions and many problems, but it is the best explanation."

"She must have been taken by car," Banks said. "Cars can get into certain streets of the Old Town, can't they? I've seen them."

"Of course," Rätsepp agreed. "Certain streets, certain areas, mostly near the edges. There are many cars around Niguliste, for example, which is not far from the pub where she was last seen. Yes, you are right. It is likely that this person persuade her to get in car. Perhaps she know him from earlier and trust him. We do not know."

Banks remembered the big bookshop, the grass slope and the church, the restaurant where he had eaten dinner with Joanna last night. They were just around the corner from there right now. Somehow, the area was taking on a greater significance in his imagination of what might have happened to Rachel. It was true that a lot of cars and taxis seemed to drop people off there and turn around. It was also quite likely that nobody would notice a girl getting into a car or a taxi. Even if someone was pushing her, it might easily appear he was helping her. "Did you talk to the taxi companies?"

"Of course. We talk to all drivers who work that night. Nothing."

"Could one of them be lying?"

"It is always possible. But we do our best."

"I'm sure you did, Toomas. I'm not being critical, believe me."

"Is all right. I believe she meet someone from earlier. Maybe from Club Hollywood, where they dance and drink before. Is near St. Patrick's. Perhaps he invite her to party or say he drive her back to hotel. She go with him. Then . . ."

"Possibly," said Banks. He remembered Annie telling him that Rachel could be impulsive, and he knew only too well the bad misjudgments that can be made when drunk. "So, however it happened, you think it happened quickly. Someone got her out of there, abducted her, took her away from the Old Town and then . . . ?"

"Otherwise we would surely find body."

Banks gestured around to the three- and four-story buildings. "Some of these places must be like rabbit warrens inside," he said. "There must be old cellars, crypts, attics, places where nobody goes, places nobody's been for centuries. You can't have searched every nook and cranny of an area like this. Could she have been taken inside one of them?"

"Is possible," said Rätsepp. "And there may be such places as you say. We cannot search every room in the Old Town with no information, but we make thorough search."

"Somebody must have seen something," Joanna said.

"No, my dear. Do you think your people in Nottingham on Saturday night see something? A girl get in a car? Is that so unusual there people notice? No. I do not think so. It is not so strange. Do you not agree, Alan?"

"The general public can be remarkably unobservant," Banks agreed. "Even when they're sober." But especially, he thought, a milling, drunken crowd, as had probably been out on the streets of the Old Town at the time of Rachel's disappearance. Rätsepp was right. You could probably commit a murder on the street on a night like that, and everyone would just assume it was part of the fun. Maybe that was what had happened. "Any other theories?"

"We try to consider everything. Perhaps her friends somehow kill her accidentally? Perhaps she fall down some steps, or somehow poison herself through alcohol? They panic, get rid of body and lie. Or they have a fight and she is accidentally killed."

Banks had a sudden flash of the office girls outside at Whitelocks talking of their exploits in Cyprus, laughing about a friend being taken to hospital for alcohol poisoning, joking about another girl who was so drunk she pissed herself in public. Was it only a week ago? Less, even. "And got rid of the body where?" he asked. "You checked all the hospitals and searched all the waste ground and possible hiding places, didn't you?"

"Yes. That is problem with all theories, of course," Rätsepp said. "No evidence. No body. And girls do not have car. We even talk to car-rent companies. Nothing."

"Any other theories?"

"Well," said Rätsepp, scratching his head, "it is not a popular line of inquiry, but we think perhaps Rachel get involved in crime. In drugs, for example. Young girls do such things, for some boy they like, perhaps. They become mules, couriers."

"Did you find any evidence of that?"

"None. But, of course, nobody wishes to think ill of Rachel, and it is not something people talk about. We have cases of foreign girls killed by drug-trafficking gangs they have become involved with, for stealing or for threatening to talk."

"So you still think there might be something in this?"

"Is possible, yes."

"I was just thinking that drug traffickers might also be the kind of criminals who would consider a hit on Quinn, if he was getting too close to the truth."

"It is professional job, Hr. Quinn?"

"We think so," said Banks. "Both killings."

"Then you can perhaps believe that some big drug trafficker did not want to be named. That is another area you must investigate. I understand drugs are big problem in England."

"But why after so long?"

"That I do not know. There could be many reasons. It take Hr. Quinn so long to find him, perhaps? This could be 'big story' for journalist."

"In all these possibilities you're talking about," said Joanna, "Rachel Hewitt is dead. What if she's alive?

Is there anything that could explain what happened to her if she's still alive and well?"

"That is, of course, what her parents wish to believe," said Rätsepp solemnly, "and I do not want to rob them of all hope. But what is the explanation? She hit her head and lose her memory and wander off somewhere? Poland? Russia? She is working in flower shop in Minsk and married with two beautiful little children? Or she do not like her parents and run away from home? This the parents do not wish to accept. They must continue to believe their daughter loves them."

"What if she was abducted and forced into prostitution, trafficked?" said Banks.

"Again, is possible," Rätsepp admitted. "But we are not Albania or Romania. Estonia is not destination for such victims, and is not usually a source. Is a station on the way. Traffic passes through here to England and Finland and Sweden, from the east, from the south. Drugs. People. Girls. Illegal immigrants. So it is possible. But her parents and many others search over the years, send out pictures, and find no trace of her."

Banks thought of Haig and Lombard trolling the Internet sites for the girl in the photographs with Quinn. He had decided not to bring her up with Rätsepp after all; he didn't trust the man enough. He would save her for Erik, Mihkel Lepikson's friend and contact at the *Eesti Telegraaf*. He could think of no more questions.

Rätsepp seemed to sense they had got to the end of their discussion and glanced at his watch. "I must be leaving now," he said. "I have appointment." He took out his wallet and left a card on the table. "If you need to get in touch. Anything." He started to pull out some bills, but Banks held his hand up. "No, Toomas," he said. "Remember, tourists pay."

Rätsepp laughed. "Ah, yes. Thank you very much. I hope to repay the favor in England one day." He stood up, bent gallantly to kiss Joanna Passero's hand, gave Banks a quick salute, grabbed his jacket and disappeared into the crowds around the corner on Viru.

Pauline Boyars lived in a flat above a fish-and-chip shop on the Wetherby Road. She was at home when Annie and Winsome pressed her doorbell at half past two on Thursday afternoon, and she buzzed them up. The fish-and-chip shop was closed, so there was no smell of deep-frying, Annie thought gratefully. It was probably a good thing. Fish and chips was one of her weaknesses and had played havoc with her fading dream of vegetarianism. At least most places didn't use lard for deep-frying any longer.

Whether Pauline overindulged in the services downstairs, Annie had no idea, but she was certainly on the large side, and her complexion was pasty and spotty, as if she ate too much fatty food. Her hair was lank and uncared for and her nails bitten to the quicks. More signs, Annie thought, that Pauline Boyars had very much let herself go. She was only twenty-five or -six, but she looked over thirty.

The flat was untidy, with clothes lying on the floor, piles of gossip magazines and unwashed dishes, but it didn't have that all-pervasive smell of fish and chips Annie had expected. Several windows were open, and she could hear kids playing football in the small park at the back. Didn't anyone go to school anymore?

Pauline cleared some newspapers from a couple of chairs, and they sat down. She didn't apologize for the mess, the way many people would have done, but lit a cigarette and sat on the sofa, leaning forward, elbows resting on her knees. "What's it about?" she asked.

"It's about Detective Inspector Bill Quinn," Winsome said.

"Sounds familiar. Refresh my memory."

"The detective from Leeds who worked on Rachel's case?"

"Oh, yes. I remember him. Worse than useless, like the rest of them."

"He's been murdered," said Winsome.

"It didn't do anybody any bloody good, though, did it?" Pauline went on, as if she hadn't heard. Her right foot was tapping the whole time they were talking. "It didn't bring Rachel back, did it? If you're going to be asking me about all that stuff, I need a drink. I won't offer you any because you're on duty, and because I don't have much left." She got up and poured a hefty shot of vodka into a tea mug.

"Pauline, we're hoping you can help us here," said Winsome in her most soothing voice. "Getting drunk won't help."

"Are you crazy?" She held out the mug. "You think this would get me drunk? If only. What do you want to know?"

"You might have read in the papers that Bill Quinn was killed a few days ago, and his death was suspicious. We've been assigned to investigate."

"Well, bully for you. It was probably some vicious tattooed drug-dealing Hells Angel he put away years ago."

"That's one possibility," said Winsome. "But another is that his death was somehow connected with what happened to Rachel."

"Nobody knows what happened to Rachel. That's the bloody point. She might as well have been abducted by aliens."

Annie saw that Winsome was struggling with Pauline's hostility, so she gave a quick signal and cut in. "You were there that night, Pauline? What do you think happened?"

Pauline stopped tapping her foot and gazed at Annie. Then she stubbed out her cigarette and gulped some vodka. The foot started tapping again. "What good would it do to go over it all again? Don't you think I've been over it a million times with the bloody Estonian police, and with your mate Quinn?"

"I'm sure you must have been," said Annie. "But that was a long time ago, wasn't it? Maybe over the years you've remembered things you didn't say then?"

"Remembered? Some hope. Forgotten, more like. I didn't remember much in the first place. That was the problem."

"It's not surprising," Annie said. "You were out celebrating. Having a good time. You couldn't have had any idea what was going to happen."

Pauline stared at Annie again and sipped more vodka, then stared into the depths of her mug.

"I'm not judging you, Pauline," she went on. "I've been in this job long enough to know that the best will in the world can't stop a criminal getting his way. And I've been pissed often enough to have done more than a few things I'm ashamed of."

"So why do you do it? The job, I mean."

"Now there's a question. I wish I knew the answer."

Pauline managed a brief smile, which changed the whole structure of her face and showed a flash of the beauty that might still have lurked under the ravaged surface. She lit another cigarette.

"Come on, Pauline," Annie said. "Tell us about it."

"They didn't believe us, you know."

"Who didn't?" Winsome asked, picking up the questioning again.

"The Estonian police. Can you believe it? They thought we'd done it and hidden her body somewhere. They kept going on about it, asking us where we'd put her."

"That was probably one of the many theories they developed," said Winsome. "They have to cover all the angles, no matter how unbelievable some of them seem."

"But they never found anyone, did they? They never found Rachel. I think they decided it was us but couldn't prove it, and they didn't bother to look any further."

"This policeman I'm talking about, Bill Quinn," Winsome went on. "He was haunted by the failure to find her. We think he might still have been trying to find out what happened right up until the end, when he was killed last week."

Pauline stared down at her fingernails and nicotine-stained fingers. "I don't get many visitors," she said. "You must forgive me. I seem to have dropped my social skills down the toilet."

"That's all right," said Winsome. "Where's your husband? Is he not around?"

It could have gone either way, and Annie was mentally ready to give Winsome a bollocking later if it blew up in their faces, but Pauline actually softened. Her eyes dampened.

"We never did get married," she said. "Isn't that a joke, after everything that happened?"

"Whose idea was that?"

"Both of ours, really. But I suppose I started it. I stayed on in Tallinn. It seemed . . . I don't know . . . disrespectful to leave before the police discovered anything. I couldn't just leave Rachel like that, could I? But in the end I had to, or I'd still be there, wouldn't I?"

"So you postponed the wedding?"

"At first, yes. It seemed the best idea."

"So what happened?"

"We just postponed and postponed for so long that in the end the whole idea lost its appeal. I was preoccupied with Rachel. I neglected Trevor. He found someone else. They got married two years ago. The old, old story. When I look back, we were way too young in the first place. Young love. What a joke."

"I'm sorry," said Winsome.

Pauline straightened up. "Don't be," she said. "I'm not. Good riddance. That's what I say." She ran the back of her hand over her eyes and glanced from one to the other, then clapped her hands together, showering ash and spilling vodka on the already stained and threadbare carpet. "So, enough of this maudlin rubbish. What is it you want to know?"

"First off," said Winsome, "about Detective Inspector Quinn. Do you have any idea why he would remain interested in the case, and why it might get him killed six years later?"

"Absolutely none at all. I hardly saw him. I mean, I only talked to him once or twice. I know he saw a bit of Maureen and Luke, too. That's Rachel's parents."

"Yes, we've talked to them," said Winsome.

"Well, we keep in touch, like, occasionally. I'm afraid there's not much more I can add. But why do you think it was that? Rachel? Couldn't there be many other explanations for why he was killed?"

"We have our reasons," said Winsome. "Did you like Bill Quinn?"

"Like? I never really thought about it. I must admit, I was a bit of a mess back then, and he was kind enough, his manner, you know . . . nicer than some of those Estonian cops. There was a bloke called Rätsepp. 'Rat's arse,' we called him. He was the one who kept going on about us doing it and dumping her body."

"They were probably all very frustrated," Winsome said.

"I'm sure they were. Sexually, most like, the way some of them were giving us the eye."

"You don't have to go to Estonia to find sexist cops," said Annie. "Come to Eastvale with me now, and I'll show you a few."

"No thanks," she said. "But I appreciate the offer." The kids started shouting down on the playing field, and Pauline went over to shut the back window. When she returned, she poured herself another shot of vodka to replace what she had spilled and lit another cigarette from the stub of the old one. "Noisy little buggers," she said.

"Whose idea was it to go to Tallinn?" Annie asked.

"Mine. I was the bride-to-be, after all."

So much for the idea that Rachel had arranged the hen weekend so she could meet up with a foreign boy-friend in Tallinn. She could have met someone between the decision to go there and the trip, but that seemed too much of a coincidence.

"What was Rachel like as a friend?" Winsome asked.

Pauline paused. "Like? She was full of life, loved to help people, bright, beautiful, funny, stubborn, a bit wild sometimes, spontaneous. Christ, she was just nineteen, you know. What are nineteen-year-olds like? I don't remember. Do you?"

"Did you take drugs?"

Pauline paused and looked at Winsome through narrowed eyes. "We might have done E once or twice, you know, at a club."

"In Tallinn?"

"No way. Far too dodgy getting drugs off some stranger in a foreign city."

"Rachel?"

"No."

"In your opinion, was she likely to go off with a stranger in a car?"

"Maybe, if it was a nice car and she liked the look of him."

"So what do you think happened to her?"

"I think she got lost. Wandered off the beaten track. Some sick bastard abducted her, raped her, then killed her and buried her, or chucked her body in the sea, and it floated all the way to Sweden or somewhere."

"You don't believe she's alive? That she lost her memory or decided to start a new life?"

"No. That's not Rachel. She loved her family and her friends. And her bloody budgie. If she was alive she'd have been in touch. She would have gone home. And this amnesia business is just a load of bollocks. I don't blame Maureen and Luke for clinging on to hope, you know, but sometimes I find them a bit hard to take."

"And why haven't the police found Rachel, or the person who abducted her?"

"Because they're useless."

"But you weren't able to give them much help," Winsome went on. "From what I've been able to make out, it wasn't until the following morning that you reported her missing, and then it took the police nearly two days to get any sort of coherent story out of you about where you'd been, who you'd talked to."

Annie had to give it to Winsome, she was coming along nicely, developing a tough edge. Many others would have shied away from asking an obviously disturbed person like Pauline those sorts of questions.

To her credit, Pauline just shook her head sadly. "Do you know," she said, "since I came back from Tallinn, there isn't a day gone by when I haven't tortured myself with the same thoughts. If only we hadn't forgotten her in St. Patrick's. If only we'd told her where we were going. If only she hadn't forgotten her mobile. If only I had insisted right from the start that we call the police. If only I hadn't passed out in my room. If only I hadn't been so drunk and then so hungover I couldn't remember a single useful snippet of information. If only. If only. If bloody only. And there isn't a day gone by when I haven't imagined what she went through, played the movie in my brain of what he must have done to Rachel and how much pain and fear she must have suffered before she was killed. It varies a little each time, the details, but it's basically the same movie."

"Any chance you would have recognized who did it in your movie?" Annie cut in.

Pauline looked at her in surprise. "That's a bloody clever question," she said. "Nobody asked me that before. But I'm afraid not. No. He's always just a vague shadow. It's only Rachel I see clearly. One of the cops suggested it could have been someone we met during the course of the evening, but we danced with a lot of lads, and nobody stands out as particularly weird. Still, they wouldn't have to, would they? Don't they always say it's the boy-next-door type you have to watch out for?"

"It was worth a try," said Annie. "I just thought it might have been someone you'd seen in the course of the evening, even just from the corner of your eye, and for some unconscious reason, you cast him in that role."

"No. I'm sorry. No."

"Were you aware of anybody following you, or paying undue attention during the evening?" Winsome asked.

"I've racked my brains to dredge up something time and time again, but I just can't do it," said Pauline. "It makes me want to tear my hair out. We talked to a lot of lads that night. Just for fun, nothing serious.

We danced, chatted, had a good time. I mean, I was getting married, so I wasn't interested in other blokes. Rachel had just split up with shit-for-brains dickhead Tony Leach. The others, I don't know . . . I don't even know if I would have noticed if someone *had* been stalking us."

"Do you still see the others?" Winsome asked.

"No. Funny that, isn't it? People used to say we were inseparable. Course, Janine topped herself. Took an overdose. That'd be three, four years ago now."

"Because of what happened?"

"Boyfriend troubles, but that covers a multitude of sins, doesn't it? She was always the sensitive one. Gillian's all right. She got married last year, and she plans on turning herself into a baby factory. First one's out already. She even sent me a wedding invitation and a Christmas letter. I think they're living in Canada. Helen's an alcoholic. I don't know where she lives. On the streets in London, I think. And Brenda's a social worker. She finally got it together after treatment. She's discovered she's really gay, so she's shacked up with some African woman. Our Brenda. Sweet little naïve Brenda. Would you believe it? What a turnup."

Five young lives destroyed, Annie thought. Except maybe for Gillian and Brenda, who seemed to be

349 • PETER ROBINSON

desperately trying to put their lives back together, even if the paths they had chosen were difficult ones.

"How bad was Rachel, really, that night?" Winsome asked.

"Well, she wasn't totally legless. She was a bit wobbly, like, but she could have got back to the hotel on her own, or at least managed a taxi. She had some money. Other than that, it's hard to say. Her judgment was probably a bit fucked-up, but I think if someone had grabbed her, she'd have known what was happening. She was street-wise enough. She wouldn't just have gone along with it."

"She would have struggled?"

"And screamed. I think so. Yes. But if it was some-one strong, with an open car door, or maybe even two people, there wouldn't have been much she could do, would there? All he'd have to do was put his hand over mouth and push her in."

"Is that how you think it happened?"

"More or less."

"What happened in St. Patrick's?" Winsome asked.

"We were just talking to the German lads. They all spoke good English, and they had a great sense of humor. You don't think that about Germans, do you, but they did. It was busy, but not as crowded or hot as that dance place we'd been to. Club Hollywood. I think we even had something to eat."

"A bit of an oasis, then?"

"Something like that. A breather. Then we went off to another bar, and we were thinking of leaving there and going dancing again when I missed Rachel."

"It was you who noticed she was missing?"

"Yes."

"What did you do?"

"First we searched through the place we were in, then we went back to try to find her." Tears welled up in Pauline's eyes. "Me and one of the German boys. But we couldn't remember where we'd been, could we? We were too pissed. Neither of us knew the city, and we couldn't find it again. We didn't remember St. Patrick's until later. Too late."

"So what happened there?" Winsome asked.

"It's all very vague, but I remember someone asked us to leave. Quietly, like. It was one of the places where they didn't like English stag parties, or hens. They had a bit of a reputation for hell-raising by then."

"And did you leave?"

"Yes. We might have given a bit of lip, I don't really remember, but we left. That's why we left. And Rachel had been flirting with the barman. Good-looking bloke. Australian. Can't remember his name. Steve or something."

"They'd been talking?"

"Flirting. On and off. I mean, he was really busy, so he couldn't just stand there and chat, but I remember myself thinking, *I'll bet she's back here again tomorrow.*"

"Did you tell the Estonian police this?"

"Yes, of course. When I remembered. But it was too late by then. When I asked them about it, they said the barman was gone. They didn't know where. Back to Australia, I suppose. Anyway, they couldn't trace him, so that was that. Dead end."

"Do you think he had anything to do with it?"

"I doubt it," said Pauline. "I mean, he was working, wasn't he? He couldn't just disappear. And the police said he didn't have a car. It was just that he might have known where she'd gone, that's all. Rachel might have said something to him."

"Maybe she arranged to meet him later," said Winsome, and she and Annie looked at one another. The three of them sat silently for a moment, thinking over the implications. Winsome seemed to have covered just about everything, Annie thought. She couldn't think of anything else to ask. Pauline's company was becoming depressing and the messy flat oppressive.

"We should be off now, then," Winsome said. "Thanks for your time, Pauline. I'm sure you've got work or something."

"Work? Huh. That went the same way as marriage."

"You packed it in?"

"Sort of. Though I think they made the final decision for me. I'd got my A-levels, but I wanted to start work—like Rachel—and I got a job with Debenhams. In management, not shop floor. Anyway, it was a start. Sort of a management trainee. I got transferred here after things started to go off a bit in Bradford, then . . . I don't know. Couldn't keep up my concentration. Still can't. It was rude of me, I know, but I didn't even offer you a cup of tea. Sure you won't stay and have one?"

Annie could see the desperation in her eyes, but she didn't feel she could stand another fifteen or twenty minutes in this mausoleum of guilt and shame. Luckily, Winsome must have agreed, because she was the one who refused the offer of tea, gently, and led the way out.

Erik Aarma had agreed to meet Banks and Joanna in the hotel lobby at five o'clock, and they spent the time in between talking to Rätsepp and meeting Erik going over their notes and clarifying theories. Both agreed that Rätsepp hadn't been much use and had told them nothing Annie hadn't already gleaned from reading over Quinn's files.

It had taken a long time to set the investigation in motion, Banks thought, but more than likely that was for the reasons Rätsepp had given, the memory of the girls, or lack of it, being paramount. For a start, the police didn't hear about the disappearance until the following day, and the girls were unable to give an accurate account of where they went, what they did and who they talked to, even on Monday morning. Thus, Rachel had been missing for close to thirty-six hours before anything approaching an investigation stumbled into motion. By then, of course, the rest of that night's revelers were long gone.

Perhaps if one of the girls had pushed a little harder a little sooner and reported Rachel missing to the police the night she had got lost, rather than the following morning, something more might have been done. But that was a long shot. Rachel was nineteen, hardly a minor, and there was no guarantee that the police would have started an immediate all-out search for her. Most likely they wouldn't have, unless they had good reason to think something had happened to her. It was natural enough to think that she may have simply wandered off, or met some young man, and would turn up by morning. It was all very well to apportion blame in retrospect, but at the time, nobody thought for a moment that they were never going to see Rachel again, that she was about to disappear from the face of the earth. You don't plan for these things; nobody is ever prepared.

Erik Aarma was a big bearded bear of a man with piercing blue eyes and straggly, ill-cut hair, wearing a baggy checked work shirt and jeans. He was carrying a scuffed leather satchel of the kind Banks used to carry back and forth to school every day, in the days before rucksacks became de rigueur. He wished he had kept his now; it looked cool.

Erik lowered his bulk into the semicircular Naugahyde chair and apologized for being late. He gave no reason, and Banks suspected he was a person who was rarely on time. They ordered coffees and quickly got down to business. Joanna had agreed to make notes, so she took out her notebook and pen. Erik's English was excellent, and it turned out he had worked in London on the *Independent* for a few years. Banks was wondering if he would ever run into an Estonian who needed a translator. That reminded him to get in touch with Merike soon.

As a rule, Banks didn't trust journalists; in the past they had screwed up so many of his cases in the name of people's right to know. But he felt he had no choice as far as Mihkel and Erik were concerned. They were his only allies, and Mihkel was dead. Bill Quinn had clearly trusted Mihkel enough to become friends with him. This from a man who, according to his own daughter, didn't have many friends outside work, followed solo pursuits, preferred his own company. Now Banks was in a position of wanting to trust Erik a lot more than he had trusted Toomas Rätsepp. He hoped his faith would be justified.

Erik's handshake was firm and his anger and sadness over the loss of his friend and colleague clearly genuine. "I do not know how I can help," he said, glancing from Banks to Joanna and back, "but I promise I will do what I can."

"Thank you," Banks said.

"Poor Merike. She must be heartbroken."

"She was very upset, yes," said Banks. "Perhaps you'd like to call her?"

"Yes. Yes, I will."

"How long have you worked with Mihkel?"

"Fifteen years. Ever since he began to work at the paper."

"Was that before 'Pimeduse varjus'?"

"Yes. He worked on general duties at first, then he later came to specialize in crime stories. He started the column in 2001. Sometimes others contribute, but it was his idea in the beginning. Can you give me any idea what happened to him? The stories we heard were very vague."

Banks quickly weighed his options before answering and decided that, given the information he wanted from Erik, it would be best to tell him as much as realistically possible. "He was found dead at an abandoned farm called Garskill in remote North Yorkshire last Saturday morning. We think he had been dead since the Wednesday before. The place looked as if it had been home to a group of about twenty bonded or migrant workers, possibly illegal, most likely Eastern European. We found a paperback book on one of the mattresses, and it turned out to be in Polish. When we found Mihkel, everyone else was gone, and we suspect that they left for work on Wednesday morning and were later directed to new quarters. We haven't been able to discover where they are yet."

"But how did he die? How did you come to find him there?"

Banks paused. "He was drowned," he said. "In a water trough. We know it wasn't accidental because there were bruises to indicate he had been held under. I'm sorry if this is distressing, but you asked, and I'm telling you as much as I can."

"I'm all right. Please go on."

"There isn't much more to tell," Banks said.

"I talked to Mihkel on Tuesday evening," Erik said. "He told me he was calling from a telephone box. He had to be very careful. The men in charge were suspicious because someone had smuggled a mobile phone into another group and used it to take photographs and make calls to a Lithuanian magazine."

"What did you talk about?" Banks asked.

"Conditions there. He said they were terrible. It was cold. There were holes in the roof. They did not get much food, and what they did get was bad. The pay was low."

"Where were they working?"

"Different places. A chicken hatchery. A frozen-food factory. A chemical-packing plant."

"Can I get the full details from you later?" Banks asked. "We'll need to track these places down. That's not my immediate concern, but it will have to be done."

"Of course."

"So he was writing a story for you about this?"

"Yes. We have known about these illegal labor schemes for a long time, but Mihkel thought it would be useful to go undercover, to follow one from the beginning to the end and write an in-depth article. He could not know what that end would be, of course. That it would be his own."

"Did he mention someone called Quinn at all? Bill Quinn?"

"Bill? But yes, of course. They had talked."

"That was all he said, that they had talked?"

"He spoke about another story, a possibly big story, but that was all he could say."

"And this was connected with Bill Quinn?"

"I think so."

"Do you have any idea what it was?"

"No. Not unless Bill Quinn had found out what happened to Rachel Hewitt."

"Or had always known," Banks said to himself.

"What?"

"Sorry. Nothing. So you know about that, about Rachel?"

"Of course. That was how they met, Bill and Mihkel. The Rachel Hewitt case. Mihkel wrote much about it, and he and Bill became friends. They kept in touch over the years."

"The thing is," Banks said, "Bill Quinn was killed, too, around the same time and, we believe, by the same person."

Erik's mouth opened and flapped like a landed fish. He rubbed his forehead. "I . . . I don't . . ."

"I know. It's very confusing," Banks said. "We don't pretend to know what's going on, but there are some very far-reaching connections here. One of them is the Rachel Hewitt case, and another is the migrant-labor scheme you mentioned, the one Mihkel was writing about and Bill Quinn was investigating. Have you ever heard of a man called Corrigan? Warren Corrigan?"

Erik thought for a moment, then said, "No. I'm sorry."

"No matter," Banks went on. "Can you tell me how Mihkel ended up in North Yorkshire?"

"His story?"

"Yes."

"I suppose so," said Erik. "It's not as if he can tell it himself now, is it?"

"It might help us catch his killer."

Erik thought for a moment, then a brief smile flickered through his beard. "I am sorry. It is difficult for me, as a journalist, to give information to police. Old habits die hard."

"If it's any consolation," Banks said, "it's very difficult for me even to be in the same room as a journalist."

Erik stared at him for a moment, then burst out laughing. Joanna joined in. "I have no problem with most journalists," she said. "We'd very much appreciate it if you could give us a few details."

"Of course. As I said, it was Mihkel's idea. Well, mostly."

"Pardon me for interrupting so early," said Banks, "but was that usually the case with his stories, or was he given assignments?"

"It varied. Sometimes, if a subject was hot at the moment, he would be given an assignment like any other reporter. But something like this, something that would take him undercover for some time, and perhaps expose him to danger, that would have to be his own idea."

"I see. Carry on."

"Like most of us, Mihkel had heard about unskilled workers heading for what they thought was a paradise in the UK and other countries, and finding quite the opposite. He wanted to follow the whole process through every stage, find out who the main players were and how it was done. It was actually Bill who told him about this."

"Bill Quinn sent Mihkel in there?"

"No. No. He simply told Mihkel about how the business operated and gave him the name of the agency in Tallinn. It was Mihkel who had the idea to start at the beginning and follow the trail. He was always . . . what would you say?"

"Adventurous? Impetuous?"

"Both," said Erik, smiling sadly.

"Did he send you written reports?"

"No. Not this time. It was too risky. No phones, no cameras, no paper and pencil. We talked on the telephone, and I made notes. He was allowed out, of course, when he wasn't working. They weren't prisoners. At least not prisoners in solid prisons. You understand?"

"I think so," said Banks. "He was living in a very remote place. It was a two-mile walk to the telephone. Did you write up the reports in Estonian?"

"Of course."

"OK. Go on. Can you give me the gist?"

"It's a simple enough story. He first approached an agency here in Tallinn, where they charged him two hundred euros, gave him a telephone number and told him there was a job waiting for him in Leeds."

"Did they say what kind of job?"

"No. But he knew it would be casual labor of some sort, perhaps in a factory or on a battery farm. About fifty hours a week at minimum wage. I think that is about seven euros an hour, perhaps a little more. That's three hundred and thirty euros a week, anyway. He traveled by train and was met at St. Pancras by another agent of the company, who asked for another two hundred euros. So already this job had cost Mihkel four hundred euros and his travel expenses. For all this he had no receipt. The man told him he could get a train to Leeds at King's Cross, just across the road, and he disappeared with the money. Mihkel never saw him again."

"These people, the agents, do you know their names?"

"Yes. The man in London was a Latvian, but he worked with the same agency as the one in Tallinn."

"If it came to it, would you turn these names over to the police or the immigration authorities?"

Erik hesitated. "I don't know," he said. "It would be . . . perhaps unethical. Even though Mihkel is dead. I would have to think."

"OK," said Banks. "No pressure." *Not yet,* he thought.

"Mihkel went to Leeds and contacted the number he had been given. It was a staffing agency."

"It wouldn't happen to be called Rod's Staff Ltd., would it?"

Erik's eyes widened. "How did you know that?"

"Run by a Mr. Roderick Flinders?"

"Yes. The agency said they had never heard of Mihkel, that there must have been some mistake, there was no job waiting for him in Leeds, but they might be able to help him. They gave him a bed in a room shared by ten people in a converted barn outside Otley and told him to wait for further instructions. Four days later he was told he was moving to another area right away. They took him to that farm you mentioned, where he was killed three weeks later."

"What happened during those three weeks?"

"The conditions were terrible, Mihkel told me, and he was sharing with about twenty people. They had only one toilet, a shower that mostly did not function. Filthy drinking water."

"I've seen it," said Banks. "I know."

"Then you will understand. Did you also know that not all the workers were men? There were three young women also, and two couples, all together in the same damp, cold dormitory. Sometimes some of the men tried to touch the women. There were fights. Mihkel said he tried to help. He spoke to a girl from Poland and another from Lithuania. The third girl never talked to anybody. Mihkel didn't know where she was from, but her skin was darker. He thought Kazakhstan, or Georgia, perhaps. For the privilege of living there, they had to pay Rod's Staff Ltd. sixty euros each week in rent. This was deducted from their pay."

"Where did they work?"

"All over the north, from Carlisle to Teesside. Darlington. Middlesbrough. Stockton."

"What sort of work?"

"The worst. Slaughterhouses, chemical-packaging plants, fertilizer factories. You name it. The work was hard and the hours long. Mihkel's first job was at a mushroom farm, picking mushrooms, but that was only for one shift. He never saw any money from that. Then he was sent to a frozen-food factory on day shifts, twelve hours a day, seven days a week, picking any bad beans or peas from the conveyor belt after they had been frozen and before they were packaged."

"A lot more than fifty hours," Banks said.

"Yes. After two weeks he had worked a hundred and sixty-eight hours and he received his first pay slip. It was for sixty-five euros."

"How did they explain that?"

"There were many discrepancies. He was not paid minimum wage to start with, but only five euros for each hour. Would this be easier in pounds?"

"No, it's OK," said Banks. "I can keep track. Besides, there's not a hell of a lot of difference these days."

"Too true," Erik agreed. "Perhaps we should have kept the kroon. Anyway, Mihkel was also told that Rod's Staff Ltd. withholds two weeks' wages and pay . . . what is the word?"

"In arrears?" Banks suggested.

"Yes. Two weeks in arrears. Of course, one hundred and twenty euros for two weeks' rent had also been deducted but had not been included in the deductions on his pay slip. By then, he also owed money to people, and when he had paid them back, he had almost nothing left. This was when someone from Rod's Staff Ltd., perhaps even Mr. Flinders himself, approached him and told him he knew someone who lent money to people in Mihkel's situation and asked if he was interested. Mihkel said yes, he was, as he had no money left for cigarettes or food. Anyway, this was the stage of the investigation he had reached when he was killed. It was on Tuesday evening he told me about the pay slip and the errors on it."

"How did he get to work and back?"

"Someone with a van picked them up in the morning and dropped them off at night. They got weak coffee and stale bread for breakfast. If they were lucky and had enough money, they could just make a dash to the nearest fast-food outlet before the van arrived to take them back, and buy a burger or fried chicken."

"Are you sure he never mentioned someone called Corrigan?"

"No. I will check my notes, but I would remember. I have a very good memory."

It was too much of a coincidence, Banks thought, for someone else to be in the same business in the same general area. Corrigan must have used his minions to reach out to operations like Flinders's, while he remained at the business center in Leeds. The two men knew each other, had drinks together, so it seemed obvious to Banks that they were in cahoots over this. Flinders created and supplied the victims, not only on city housing estates, but also in remote dormitories like

Garskill Farm, which cost him nothing and netted him about a grand a week in rents. To say nothing of the kickbacks he was getting from the employers.

On Wednesday morning, more than likely, the killer had arrived at Garskill Farm and Mihkel had been kept back from work that day. He was tortured, at which time he had probably agreed to the mobile call to Quinn to set him up, arrange to meet in the woods later that night, which had set off the detective's alarm bells, though they had not rung loudly enough to keep him away from the rendezvous completely and save his life. Quinn had, however, kept the photographs in his room, and perhaps had planned, if all turned out to be aboveboard, to go back and get them for Mihkel. But it wasn't Mihkel who turned up in the woods at St. Peter's that night.

"Who knew of Bill Quinn's friendship with Mihkel?" he asked Erik.

"I don't know. It was not something they hid. Anyone could know. Sometimes Mihkel wrote updates on the Rachel Hewitt case, and he often mentioned his connection with the English policeman."

"In the newspaper?"

"Yes."

"So anyone at all could know?"

"It would surely not be of much interest to anyone. What are you thinking?"

"I'm not sure," said Banks. "But someone wanted Bill Quinn out of the way, and that same person also wanted Mihkel out of the way. Can you think of anyone who would want that?"

"No."

"I'm missing something," Banks went on. "There has to be some connection between Rachel Hewitt and the illegal worker scam."

"Why? How?"

"Because we believe someone sent the same killer to get rid of both Bill Quinn and Mihkel."

"But why bring up Rachel Hewitt? You have already said that Bill Quinn was also involved in investigating the workers."

"That's true. Maybe he was working both sides."

"And perhaps with Mihkel's help he was about to become a danger to them, and they knew that? Perhaps they were both killed for the same reason. The Rachel Hewitt case was simply what brought them together in the first place, not the reason for either of the murders."

Banks had always been aware of that possibility, that he could be wandering way off target by taking Rachel Hewitt into consideration. But there was something about her disappearance that bothered him, and something had obviously been gnawing away at Bill Quinn ever since his trip to Tallinn six years ago. There were the photographs with the unknown girl, too. Banks knew, however, that he had to try to keep an open mind on this, that he was in danger of allowing one set of facts to obscure or distort another. Maybe the two events weren't connected, but that didn't mean Banks shouldn't try to find out what had happened to Rachel as well as solve Quinn's and Mihkel's murders. He didn't think he could go through the rest of his days not knowing what happened, the way Bill Quinn had. Look what it had done to him. And her parents deserved better.

Banks took out copies of Bill Quinn's photographs, including the blowups and the cropped version showing only the girl. He laid them before Erik on the table. "We believe that these photographs were taken here in July 2006, when Bill Quinn was over at the start of the Rachel Hewitt case. This is the only real *evidence* that convinces me that what happened to Bill Quinn was connected with Rachel's disappearance, otherwise I'd accept that he and Mihkel were both killed because of the migrant-worker scam. The rest is simply copper's instinct. But the photographs are important. Trust me on that. We believe that someone set him up with this girl. It's possible that she drugged him or got him so drunk he didn't know what he was doing, then got him up to his hotel room so these photographs could be taken. Are you with me so far?"

368 · PETER ROBINSON

Erik looked puzzled, but he said, "Yes."

"We don't know why, but one good guess is that he had somehow or other got close to whoever it was abducted Rachel. Everyone said he was haunted by the case right up until his death. I wonder. One thing that would explain it is that he found out what happened to Rachel and was unable to do anything about it, that he was blackmailed into silence. Bill Quinn was devoted to his wife, but he stumbled this once, and it came back on him in a very big way. When his wife died a month ago, that silence was no longer so important. What he had to do was find a way of making his knowledge public without revealing that he had hidden the truth for six years."

"And to that end, he enlisted Mihkel's help?"

"Yes," said Banks. "I think so. I know it's only conjecture at this point, but it's the only thing that makes sense. The killer knew that Mihkel and Quinn were in touch, knew that Quinn was free now that he was no longer troubled by anyone showing the pictures to his wife. That Mihkel was in England at the time was irrelevant to the killer, really. He could have been anywhere. It simply made things more convenient for the killer, or whoever sent him. Two birds with one stone, so to speak."

"How did the killer know Mihkel was at this farm?"

"I don't know," said Banks. "But it would be my guess that Mihkel slipped up somehow, despite taking such care. I would imagine that all these migrant gangs have spies planted to keep an eye out for infiltrators like Mihkel. They've been stung too often before, as you yourself mentioned earlier. Then someone was sent to tidy up."

"But surely if Bill had discovered anything about Rachel Hewitt, the Tallinn police would know? There was no way he could simply go about and make the investigation by himself."

"That is a problem, I agree. Unless it was something he uncovered on his own, either here or back in England."

"But if it happened here, he would have told someone, surely? The investigator. The prosecutor."

"Yes, he probably would, wouldn't he?"

Erik stared at Banks in disbelief. "Are you saying the police here were corrupt? The Office of the Prosecutor?"

"I don't know," said Banks. "It wouldn't be the first time. But again, it's mere speculation. So much police work is. I'd like you to do me a couple of favors. First, I'd like you to see if you can find out who this girl is. She's probably local, or was in 2006, and may well have been connected with the sex trade or perhaps worked in one of the nightclubs. She might also have been trafficked from somewhere, forced into prostitution. You must have extensive files at your newspaper. You've got the resources, and I don't. Can you do it? Will you help us?"

Erik examined the photos and nodded slowly. "I can try," he said. "If it helps to uncover who killed Mihkel. You mentioned two favors."

"Yes," said Banks. "There's a retired cop called Toomas Rätsepp and a prosecutor called Ursula Mardna. I'd like you to find out all you can about them, too."

After dinner at a Thai restaurant not far from the hotel, at which they discussed their conversations with Toomas Rätsepp and Erik Aarma, Joanna begged off early for the night, pleading that the jet lag and the change of scene were catching up with her. Two hours wasn't much of a time difference, Banks thought, but travel itself certainly was tiring. He didn't know why, as all you had to do was sit there and be delivered to your destination, but it was.

It was only half past nine. Banks felt restless, and he knew it would be no use heading up to his room so early. Besides, having got at least some sense from Toomas Rätsepp of the places the hen party had visited, he wanted to wander the Old Town after dark and get a better feel for the streets, where the cars were, the nightclubs, the bars. It was just around sunset, so he decided now was as good a time as any to set off. Of course, it would have stayed light much later in July, but Banks guessed that the girls would also have been up a lot later than nine fifteen, and that it would have been quite dark when they left St. Patrick's. Some clubs didn't even open until midnight or after, like the ones in cities at home that opened when the pubs closed. He imagined that Tallinn was the sort of place where you could get a drink at any time of the day or night.

It was Thursday, close to the weekend, and the Old Town was much livelier than it had been the previous evening. Walking past the front of Olde Hansa, Banks saw a line of young men shuffling along wearing chain-gang uniforms. A stag party, no doubt. One of them raised a bottle of Saku, smiled and said, "All right, mate?" Banks recognized the northern accent.

Once again he found himself by the large bookshop on the corner of Harju and Niguliste, opposite the church at the top of its grassy slope. He walked along the front of the bookshop, recognizing a few of the English titles he saw displayed in the window; past Fish & Wine, where he turned left; past the corner where he and Joanna Passero had been sitting last night; and continued on, down Vana-Posti.

It was one of the narrower streets in the Old Town, but there were a few cafés and bars, including St. Patrick's, and further down, on his right, an elegant four-story hotel with dormer windows on top and a white facade stood on a corner. It formed a little triangle with benches and fountains, and on another side stood the concave front of a building with soprus written across the top in large letters. It looked like an old cinema, with its steps and massive pillars along the front. There were a couple of large movie posters on the wall, one for *Submarine* and another for a series of classics by master directors. To the left of the second poster was a sign for Club Hollywood, where the girls had been dancing and met the German boys in July 2006. Banks was tempted to go in, just to check out the place, but he realized there would be no point. It would simply be a hot, noisy, jam-packed club, which would stifle his breath and hurt his ears. There were some things worth suffering for the job, but not that.

Instead, he started to walk back up Vana-Posti to St. Patrick's, went inside, stood at the bar and ordered a beer. The place probably hadn't changed much since 2006, he reckoned. Their food was supposed to be pretty good and it wasn't one of the major stag-party haunts. There were no guys in chain-gang uniforms in evidence, at any rate. It was busy, though, and most of the tables and all the chairs around him were taken. There was quite a mix of age groups and accents, from what Banks could make out, and he reckoned it was the kind of place you might kick off an evening, or somewhere you might end up to mellow out for a while. It didn't seem like the sort of establishment that would tolerate rowdy behavior.

There was music playing, but Banks had no idea what it was. It wasn't obtrusive, at any rate. He finished his beer and left, turning right, the way the girls had turned. He turned right again at Fish & Wine, the way he had come, and followed the street straight across Niguliste. In no time he was at the Raekoja Plats, the main square. It had taken him no more than five minutes from St. Patrick's, but the girls and their German friends had probably taken a bit longer. There were plenty of lively bars and restaurants opposite the town hall on the large cobbled square, all with tables outside under awnings, nicely lit by candlelight and dim table lamps: Molly Malone's, Kaerajaan, Fellini, Karl Friedrich. The girls would probably have stayed outside drinking wherever they went in the square, and at some point, they realized they had lost Rachel.

Banks walked back to St. Patrick's, but this time he didn't go inside. He continued past the pub, in the other direction. Rätsepp had mentioned that a bartender thought he saw Rachel go the wrong way when she left St. Patrick's. Maybe he was right. Banks wanted to know what was around there other than Club Hollywood and the My City Hotel. Then he saw, just to his left shortly after passing the pub, one of those long, narrow lanes curving into the distance, mixed facades of four-story buildings on each side, narrow strips of pavement and a cobbled road perhaps wide enough for a car.

Banks turned left and started walking along the street. In places some of the plaster had fallen away from the fronts of the buildings, revealing the stone and brickwork underneath, like the skeleton without flesh, bared teeth and jawbone where the cheek has been ripped away. There were flags hanging above some of the doorways, and Banks guessed most were residences, or perhaps business offices with flats above.

Then he noticed a small illuminated sign above one of the doorways about thirty feet along. It had nothing written on it, only a stylized cartoon of a man in a top hat and tails, who seemed to be helping a voluptuous woman into a carriage. Banks paused and looked at the door. There were no prices or opening times posted—he supposed it was a place you just had to know about—and all he could make out was a vague sort of reception desk and perhaps cloakroom area lit by a reddish glow behind the heavy glass doors. It was elegant, with polished brass and dark wood, certainly not like some of the seedier sex clubs he had seen in Soho, if that was what it was. And it was open.

Would anything have been likely to draw Rachel down here, Banks wondered, assuming she actually had turned the wrong way, unless she perhaps recognized the street, thought it was a shortcut to the hotel or the main road and the possibility of a taxi? Vana-Posti would lead eventually to Pärnu, a broad boulevard with a constant flow of traffic and trams running along the southern edge of the Old Town. But that was not in the same direction as the Meriton Hotel. Still, Rachel might have known she could get a taxi on or near Pärnu. It was a very busy road, beyond the confusing and possibly by now claustrophobic and frightening maze of the Old Town, and she could soon get herself reoriented there. Might something have drawn her down this street, caught her attention? The illuminated sign? Something else? Someone? Had the toilets at St. Patrick's been too busy, and did she still need to go? Perhaps she was looking for a quiet, sheltered doorway to pee in. Or perhaps she had spotted a taxi with its light on down the road and dashed to try to catch it. Then what?

Banks sensed, rather than saw, a shadow entering the street behind him. He had been wary of being

376 · PETER ROBINSON

followed most of the time he had been in Tallinn, but it had been impossible to tell in the busy streets and bright sunshine. If someone wanted to find out where he had been and who he had been talking to, it wouldn't have been too difficult. This was the first time he had been in the Old Town after dark by himself. It could just have been someone taking a shortcut, of course, or someone who lived on the street, but it was still enough to make Banks nervous. More likely than not, Rätsepp had sent a man to follow him and he was in no danger, but he didn't need to make the man's job too easy.

He tried the doors of the mysterious club and found himself in the small reception and coat-check area. The woman standing behind the front desk wore a black bustier that left little to the imagination. Her breasts looked augmented to Banks's unskilled eye. She had a beauty spot painted to the right of her mouth, bright red lipstick and tumbling black waves of hair. Beside her stood two bruisers. Well-dressed, in Armani suits, relaxed, at ease, both giving Banks pleasant nods of welcome, but bruisers nonetheless, with no necks and cauliflower ears.

"Do you speak English?" Banks asked the woman.

"Of course, sir. What is it you require?"

"Can I go in?"

"Are you a member, sir?"

"No. I didn't realize that—"

"If you would just like a drink in the bar, then a onetime membership is available for twenty euros."

"That's just to go in?"

"Yes, sir. Into the lounge."

"There's more?"

She gave an enigmatic smile. "There are many rooms, sir."

"Is there any entertainment?"

"Here, we make our own entertainment, sir."

Already feeling as if he had fallen down the rabbit hole, Banks forked over twenty euros, for which he got a stamped pass, and the woman directed him to a pair of swing doors. "Just through there, sir."

It was a dimly lit lounge bar with leather chairs around low round tables, definitely not built for bottles and liter glasses. Each table bore a shaded lamp with a low-wattage bulb. There was no music and no windows. Waitresses in tastefully scanty clothing with a vaguely S & M theme drifted between the tables, carrying silver trays. Banks had no sooner sat down than one appeared at his side. "What is your pleasure, sir?"

English, it seemed, was the language of choice here, and her accent was impeccable. "Perhaps a glass of red wine," Banks said.

"We have a very good Merlot, sir, a Rioja or Chianti Classico by the glass. We also have an extensive wine list."

"I'll have a glass of Rioja, please," said Banks.

"Very well."

What the hell am I doing here? Banks wondered as he waited for his drink. The conversations around him were hushed, most of the customers in business suits, men from their thirties to sixties. There were no women other than the waitresses. Occasionally, the door at the far end would open and someone would leave or enter.

"What happens in there?" Banks asked the waitress when she brought his drink. Her breasts were not augmented, he decided as she bent to place the wine on a white coaster. She said nothing. "Can I talk to the manager?" he asked.

"Police?"

"How did you know?"

"They're the same the whole world over, sweetie." She held her tray in one hand and pointed to a man standing by the cash register beside the bar. "He's over there. Good luck."

Banks picked up his wine and walked over. He had no idea whether the manager spoke English but was now used to the idea that everyone in Tallinn did. It was a skill, he thought, that the manager of a club like this ought to have. And he did. In fact, he spoke as if he'd just got off a plane from London.

"Can I help you, sir?"

Though he knew it was no use here, Banks flashed his warrant card. Humor twinkled in the manager's eyes. "You can buy those in the shops over here, you know, mate."

"I'm sure," said Banks, "but I figured that seeing as I'm not here to cause you any trouble, merely to ask a couple of questions for curiosity's sake, it wouldn't do any harm."

"There's certainly no harm trying," said the manager. "I'm Larry, by the way. Larry Helmsley."

Banks shook hands. "Pleased to meet you. How did you end up in a place like this?"

"I started working the clubs over in London years back, but I wanted to travel, see new places. Mostly, I see the inside of a dark club and sleep all day."

"What kind of club is this?"

"Private. Gentlemen's. Members only."

"OK. I get it. What I'm interested in happened six years ago."

"Then I'm not your man. I was in Brussels then. Or was it Barcelona?"

"Was this place here?"

"I assume so. It's been through a lot of changes over the years."

"Who owns it?"

"A consortium of interested parties."

"And that's who you work for?"

"I'm more of a freelancer, but they're my employers at the moment."

"How long have they owned the place?"

"About two years. What is it exactly that you're after, mate? What is it that happened six years ago?"

"An English girl disappeared near here. She was leaving a pub around the corner—"

"St. Patrick's?"

"Yes. And she may have taken the wrong direction from her friends and got lost. Maybe she came in here."

"Why?"

"I don't know. Looking for a phone, maybe. She'd forgotten her mobile. To use the toilet. Or trying to find her friends."

"Was she drunk?"

"It was a hen party."

"If it's anything like it is now, she wouldn't have got past the front door. Just a minute. I think I remember the case you're talking about. Her parents have been in the news. Rachel something-or-other, isn't it?"

"Yes. Rachel Hewitt. She was never found."

"Tragic. I didn't know she was near here when she vanished. But I can't help you, mate. Like I said, I wasn't here then, and the present owners have only been around a couple of years."

"It was a long shot, anyway," said Banks.

"I appreciate a man who goes for a long shot. Nothing like it when one pays off. Sorry."

"That's all right," said Banks. He finished his drink, left the glass on the bar and made for the front doors. He passed the waitress on the way, and she touched his arm. "You did quite well with him. You two seemed to hit it off."

"Two strangers united by a common language," he said. "Tell me, is anyone here from Estonia?"

Her accent slipped. "I wouldn't know, sweetie. I'm from Wigan, meself."

Smiling to himself, Banks walked outside, careful to scan both directions of the street. His shadow could easily be hiding in a doorway, like Orson Welles in *The Third Man*, but there was no obvious sign of him. Come to think of it, the whole place had a look of *The Third Man* about it. Banks put his hands in his pockets and strolled watchfully down the curving narrow street until it ended at a square full of packed and well-lit cafés. There he decided to sit and have a final glass of wine before heading off to bed, and to see if his shadow turned up. The Rioja he had paid ten euros for at the club had not been very good, and it had left a nasty taste at the back of his throat.

The person whom Banks thought had been following him was still there, though it was sometimes hard to make him out through the crowds passing back and forth. He was of medium height, about the same as Banks himself, in his late thirties or early forties, already showing signs of thinning on top, casually dressed in jeans and a dark shirt underneath some sort of zip-up jacket. He sat down at the café across the square. Good. They could sit and stare at one another.

Banks ordered a glass of Shiraz, sipped and watched the people go by. A group of girls in red microdresses, carrying heart-shaped red balloons on strings, snaked by in a conga line, giggling and chanting, hips bumping this way, then that, some almost tripping in their impossibly high heels on the cobblestones. When they had passed by, he glanced across the square again, only to find that his shadow had disappeared. He jotted a few notes in his notebook, finished his drink and decided to call it a day. It was two hours earlier in Eastvale, so he could probably still call Annie and get up-to-date when he got back to the hotel. On his way back, he noticed the man once again, about a hundred yards behind him walking down Viru. It didn't matter, Banks decided. He was going to his room for the night. The streets would be well lit and full of people all the way. He would make sure the door to his room was secure. Tomorrow, he would keep his eyes open and his wits about him.

9

Tony Leach lived in an old terrace house off the Skipton Road on the outskirts of Ilkley, where the streets eventually ran into fields, woods and open country. The bay window in the high-ceilinged living room had a fine view of the Cow & Calf, though the rocky outcrops were partly shrouded by mist and low-lying cloud that morning.

Annie and Winsome had driven down from Eastvale, avoiding the A1 this time, to find out what Rachel Hewitt's ex-boyfriend had to add to the picture they were building up. Annie had had a long chat with Banks the previous evening, and he had told her of his talks with Toomas Rätsepp and Erik Aarma, and of being followed in Tallinn. It had been a lot to digest, but Annie was glad to be up-to-date and pleased that things were moving along. She told him to be careful, and meant it. She had shared the information with Winsome on their way to Ilkley. The only other welcome piece of news that morning had been the analysis of DNA from the trace amounts of blood on the tree the CSIs thought the killer used for balance when he shot Bill Quinn. There was no match on any of the databases, but at least if they found him they would be able take a sample and compare them. It probably wouldn't convict him in itself, but it might help. The way this case was shooting off in all directions, Annie thought, it was as well to remember that this was the man they were after: the killer of Bill Quinn and Mihkel Lepikson.

Tony worked at a car dealership in the town center, but that day, his boss had told them on the phone, he was at home with his wife, who was in the final stages of her second pregnancy. The fruits of the first, little Freddie, toddled around in a playpen filled with safe soft toys in the corner of the living room. They looked as if you could eat them, hit yourself on the head with them and jump up and down on them, and neither you nor they would be harmed in any way. Luckily, he was a quiet toddler.

Melanie Leach was lying down on the sofa listening to *Woman's Hour.* When she asked for a cup of tea,

Annie suggested that she and Winsome accompany Tony to the kitchen to chat while he made some. Annie hoped they might get a cup of tea out of it themselves, too, but most of all she didn't want to talk to Tony about his ex-girlfriend while his pregnant wife was in the same room.

Tony was reluctant to leave Melanie alone, at first, but Annie reassured him that he wouldn't be far away and that he had two able-bodied police officers in the house. Why that should comfort him, she had no idea—though they were able enough in many ways, neither Annie or Winsome had any experience in delivering babies or attending to pregnant women— but it did. The only thing Annie knew was to shout for plenty of boiling water. She supposed, if anything happened, they could manage to call for an ambulance without panicking too much, and maybe even persuade it to arrive a bit quicker than it normally would, but she wasn't even sure about that.

"She'll be fine," Tony said nervously, filling the kettle. "She's just a bit jittery because it was a difficult birth last time, with our Freddie."

"I'm sure," Annie agreed. She studied the view from the window, a small back garden full of bright plastic toys, including a blue and yellow tricycle, orange skittles and a purple ball. There was also a swing, which reminded Annie of the swing her parents had put up for her in the artists' commune where she grew up. She had loved that swing. She had very strong memories of her mother pushing her up higher and higher in it when she was very little. At the end of the garden was a brick wall and a privet hedge. "It's just a quick word we wanted, really," Annie went on. "I can see you've got a lot on your plate."

"Oh, don't worry. She'll be all right. Doctor says there's nothing to worry about."

Tony was a handsome lad in his midtwenties, fair hair combed back, a lock slipping over his right eye, tall, footballer fit, a nice smile. He pulled two tea bags from a Will & Kate Wedding tin and dropped them into a large teapot, warming it first with hot water from the tap. The teapot was easily big enough for four cups, Annie thought. She might be in luck. The kettle soon came to a boil and Tony filled the teapot.

"Why did you and Rachel split up?" Annie asked. She had taken a chair at the kitchen table, and Tony was leaning against the draining board by the window.

"Why does anybody split up?" he said. "We stopped getting along. Fell out of love."

"But you were in love once?" Winsome said.

Tony paused before answering. "I thought so," he said. "We'd been going out for two years, after all."

"Was there someone else? Another boy?"

"Not as far as I know."

"Did Rachel go out with other people?"

"Sometimes, in the early days. We both did. We weren't exclusive."

"But you got more serious?"

"I'd like to think so."

"You never got engaged, though?"

"No. It never got that far."

"Sex?" Annie asked.

"None of your business."

"Fair enough. Milk and two sugars for me, please."

Tony brought some mugs down from the cupboard, asked Winsome how she wanted hers and poured them both some tea. Then he put what seemed like half a pint of milk and three tablespoons of sugar into one mug and took it through to Melanie. Annie heard their voices but not what they said. He came back and poured himself a mug of black tea, builder's strength. "I get the impression that you'd rather continue the discussion in here," he said, sitting down opposite Annie. Winsome joined them at the table. "Not that I have any secrets from Melanie."

"All we want from you," said Winsome, "is some insight into Rachel, what she was like. It might help us understand what happened to her."

"But I went over all this years ago with the other detective. Why drag it all back up now?"

"It never went away," Winsome said. "Rachel was never found. Now her name's come up again in connection with another case we're working on, and we have to pursue the line of inquiry."

"What line of inquiry?"

"The 'other detective' you mentioned was murdered a week ago. You might have heard."

"DI Quinn?"

"That's right."

"Bloody hell. I'm sorry. I hadn't heard, actually. He was the one who talked to me back when it happened."

"That's right."

"He was a decent enough bloke."

"So they say. What happened to Rachel might have some bearing on what happened to Bill Quinn. That's why we're going through all this. I can't really tell you any more than that."

"That's all right. I understand."

"Only you can tell us certain things. Her parents have one view—it was their darling daughter—but you might be able to provide a different perspective."

"I don't know about that," said Tony. He glanced at Annie. "I'm sorry. You asked about sex. It was fine. No problems there."

"She enjoyed it?"

"As far as I could tell. Rachel wasn't promiscuous or kinky or anything. I'd say she was pretty normal in that department."

"Did you argue much?" Winsome asked.

"Every couple argues, don't they?"

"What sort of things did you argue about?"

"I don't remember, really. Nothing important. Holidays. She liked beaches, and I preferred cities. Money. We never seemed to have enough to go to all the fancy clubs and shops she liked. That sort of thing."

Annie gestured around the kitchen and garden. "You seem to be doing all right now financially."

"All this came later. I've got nothing to complain about. Melanie and Freddie are happy here. It's even big enough to accommodate Chloe, when she comes along."

"So you already know the gender?"

Tony beamed. "Yes. Ultrasound. We couldn't resist."

"A girl," said Winsome. "One of each. That's nice."

Annie pushed on. "So you're doing all right? Can afford a decent house and two kids to bring up. That's pretty good in these tough times."

"Well, I wouldn't mind a raise and a promotion, but yes, I think I'm damn lucky to have a job I like and I'm good at. The thing is, this would hardly have made it as 'all right' for Rachel."

"What do you mean?" Annie asked.

"It was probably the one thing we argued about most. She liked money and the things it bought. Maybe a bit too much for my liking."

"She was greedy?"

"Not greedy or grasping or anything like that. It was just . . . like the magazines she read, with pictures of fancy cars and houses and yachts and stuff."

"But that's just fantasy, surely?"

"Not to her it wasn't. It was her dream. She was serious about it. The worst thing I could do was criticize her dream."

Annie remembered the photograph of the BMW outside the art deco mansion on Rachel's bedroom wall. "MINE ONE DAY!!"

"How did it manifest itself?" Annie asked.

"She had a lot of rows with her parents. They wanted her to go to university and get a good education—she was certainly bright enough, and they were willing to pay—but she wanted to get right out there and start making money. She said she could learn any job she wanted and make her way up the ladder quickly, as she went along. She could, too. She got a job in a bank. Not as a teller, but at the head office, in the investments department. She was doing pretty well. She was smart, quick, ambitious. I know she would have gone far."

"And by then she would have left you behind?"

"That was always a fear. Yes. Or she would have found someone richer."

"It sounds a bit mercenary. Was that why you split up?"

"Mostly. I just wasn't doing well enough for her, not progressing fast enough. And it didn't exactly sound glamorous—a car salesman. At best you could say I wasn't a *used* car salesman, I suppose. It's true I'm not very ambitious, but is that such a terrible thing? Does everyone have to be pushy and grabbing? I'm happy as I am. She saw me stuck in a dead-end job—I was in a showroom in Drighlington then—and never getting any further, wasting away her life in some dull suburb. It wasn't what she wanted. I told her surely family came first. We could get a mortgage, buy a home, make it our own. But it wasn't a home she wanted. It was one of those bloody mansions she goggled at in the celebrity lifestyle magazines and that other rubbish she read."

"Surely a girl can dream," said Annie. "Was there someone else on the scene? Someone who promised her all this?"

"Not that I know of," said Tony. "No, we didn't split up over someone else. After Rachel, I'll admit

I went wild for a bit. I don't know. I just didn't care. Love them and leave them. Not very nice, but there it was. Then I met Melanie, and she turned everything around. It was like I'd finally found what I wanted in life."

"And Rachel, after you split up?"

"Her ambition made her restless. I don't think she'd found anyone else. She wasn't going to settle for a loser like me next time, that's for sure, and as it turned out, she didn't have to, did she?"

"But as far as you know, there was no one else in the offing, no one she might have invited to meet her in Tallinn, for example?"

"No. Besides, that was a hen weekend. Strictly no boyfriends."

They all paused and sipped tea, then Annie said, "This might be a rather indelicate question, but we think it's important. You say that Rachel was ambitious, liked money and its trappings, that she rowed with her parents about getting a job instead of going to university, right?"

"Right."

"Do you think that might have led her to do anything illegal?"

"What do you mean?"

"Drugs, for example."

394 · PETER ROBINSON

"Not that I know of."

"I mean selling, smuggling. Not necessarily taking them."

"Dealing? Rachel?" He started shaking his head. "No way. Rachel wouldn't get involved in anything like that. Rachel really did want to do good and help people, you know. If she'd realized her dreams and got hold of oodles of money, she'd probably have ended up like Warren Buffett or Bill Gates or someone, as long as she could have her Disney mansion and her magic carpet. No, you're on the wrong track entirely."

"Believe it or not," said Winsome, "we're perfectly happy to know that. It would have made our job a lot more complicated if it were true. But we have to check on these things."

"Leave no stone unturned, right?"

"Something like that. We're just trying to find reasons for what might have happened to Rachel in Tallinn, and falling foul of international drug smugglers was one scenario. They can be very ruthless."

"When did you find out what happened?" Annie asked.

"I suppose it was about three or four days after she'd disappeared. A policeman came around. Uniformed. Wanted to know if I knew anything about where she was. Apparently DI Quinn was over in Tallinn then.

He interviewed me in more detail when he got back a few days later, but I couldn't help him."

"How did you react when you heard what had happened?"

"I was gutted. Naturally. God, it was a terrible time. I went to see her parents, you know, just out of support and friendship, like, but they weren't interested. I was yesterday's news."

"How had you got along with them before?"

"Well enough, I suppose. Or as well as anybody who wanted to steal away their precious little girl."

"What do you mean?"

"It was weird. Sometimes it was like they didn't want her to grow up, and she didn't want to. She was very childlike in some ways. If ever she was away, she had to phone her mother every day. They were always lovey-dovey, you know, with pet names and lots of hugs and kisses. You must have seen those awful stuffed animals if you've been to the house. And there was a stupid budgie she doted on. She'd spend hours talking to the bloody thing. I never thought I'd be jealous of a budgie, but if I'd had the chance I'd have opened the front door and the cage." He smiled. "But it was just a facet of her, that's all. The little girl who doesn't want to grow up, but who wants to be rich, a Disney princess. But she was bright and ambitious, good at her job, and she could be ruthless if she needed to be. At the same time, she couldn't cut herself loose from her mother's apron strings. It sometimes seemed like a tug-of-war between me and them, with her in the middle. In the end none of us won."

It sounded like a nightmare to Annie, who had enjoyed a relatively liberal childhood in the commune. Admittedly, she had lost her mother at an early age, but there had been surrogates, even if there was no replacement. And her father, Ray, always did his best, even if he was a bit forgetful when he was "in" a painting, as he used to say.

"Did the two of you ever go away together?" she asked.

"Once," said Tony. "The year before . . . you know. We went on holiday together. Well, not just the two of us, a group, like."

"How did her parents react?"

"They weren't too keen at first, but Rachel was good at getting her own way. She probably had to promise not to sleep with me."

"Did she?" asked Annie.

Tony gave a wistful smile. "It was one of the best times of my life," he said.

"I'll take it she did, then. Where did you go?"

"An all-inclusive on Varadero Beach, Cuba. We'd been saving up for it. It was expensive but worth it."

"Cuba hardly sounds like the sort of environment for a girl like Rachel," said Winsome.

"You're right about that. She hadn't much to say for the political system or the cleanliness of Havana. But she did love the beach and her Danielle Steele. And she phoned her mother every day."

"Dutiful daughter," Annie commented.

"Look, I know some of this is coming out all wrong," said Tony. "But Rachel was a good person, despite it all, the ambition, the love of money. She had the biggest heart of anyone I've known. She'd do anything for you. She wasn't greedy, and she wasn't selfish. In the end, I suppose we just weren't meant to be together."

"Did she make any friends over in Cuba, at the hotel, on the beach?"

"Like who?"

"Europeans, perhaps? Especially Eastern Europeans. Russians or Estonians, for example?"

"Not that I know of. We pretty much stuck together the whole time." A sound came from the front room. "Is that Melanie calling?"

Annie heard the voice, too. "Sounds like it," she said. "I think it's time for us to go now." She was certain that when Tony took in the tea they had prearranged some signal to bring the interview to an end, and this was probably it. Annie looked at Winsome, who just shrugged, and they followed Tony through to the front door, wished him and Melanie well, and left.

"**I am** not at all sure how I can help you," said Ursula Mardna. The Office of the Prosecutor General was in a neoclassical-style two-story house on Wismari, a peaceful, tree-lined street, not far from the parliament building and the British embassy. The place was an old private house, and Ursula Mardna's office had probably been the master bedroom. It was a large space, with all the trappings of an important and powerful government official. Banks had been watchful on their walk over there, and he didn't think they had been followed. If his theory was correct, and Rätsepp had put someone on his tail to keep track of the progress of his investigation, then he probably already knew that Banks would be visiting Ursula Mardna this morning.

You couldn't really compare the function of the prosecutor here that closely to the Crown Prosecution Service back home, Banks thought. From what he had read, the relationship was a lot more complicated and political, rather than just a matter of decisions being made on whether there was enough evidence and whether the evidence was good enough to merit a prosecution. The prosecutor guided an investigation in a very hands-on way, including the collection of evidence and use of surveillance. In some ways, he imagined, the prosecutor was more like the American district attorney, but perhaps even more complicated. Prosecutors would also turn up at crime scenes. Of course, the disappearance of a young English girl in Tallinn was a high-profile case, especially when she hadn't been found after several days, or years.

"We're just trying to cover all the angles we can," said Banks, "and you were instrumental in the Rachel Hewitt investigation."

Ursula Mardna waved down Banks's comment. "Please. It was not a most glorious success. I wake up still and think about that poor girl some nights." She had a strong accent but her English was clear, and for the most part correct. Banks placed her at about forty, or just over. That would have made her in her midthirties when she worked the Rachel Hewitt case. Quite young. It could have been a career-making case, if it had been solved. As it was, she didn't seem to be doing too badly. She was stylishly dressed and attractive, with an oval face, lively brown eyes and reddish-blond hair cut short and ragged around the edges, in a rather punkish, pixie style. She had no piercings that Banks could see but wore some rather chunky rings and a heavy silver bracelet.

"You don't believe she might still be alive somewhere?" he asked.

She gave Banks a pitying glance. "No more than you believe it, Hr. Banks. Or you, Pr. Passero."

"It would, indeed, be a miracle," Joanna said, and turned a page in her notebook.

"We got most of the details from Hr. Rätsepp," Banks went on, "but we were just wondering if you have a different view of things. Perhaps there were things he didn't tell us?"

"Toomas Rätsepp was a fine investigator," said Ursula Mardna. "One of our best. If he could not solve the case, nobody could."

"What about his team?"

"Fine officers."

"So in your opinion, everything that could possibly be done was done?"

"Yes. We were most thorough."

Banks wondered about that. Rätsepp had said the same thing. He also had to keep reminding himself not to expect too much, that he was talking to a lawyer, basically, however high ranking and however close her role was to that of the investigator. What was she going to say, that Rätsepp was a sloppy copper and the investigation was a shambles? No. She was going to defend her team, especially to an unwelcome foreign detective. "Do you remember DI Quinn?" he asked. "That's really who I'm here about."

She tilted her head to one side. "Of course I do."

"What exactly was his role?"

"His role?"

"Yes. The part he played, his function in the investigation."

"Ah, I see. I think he was ambassador from the British police, no?"

"But he must have got involved somehow?"

"He was here for only one week."

"But quite soon after Rachel's disappearance, I understand?"

"Then you will also understand that there were many obstacles in the beginning of the investigation. The girls themselves, they could not remember."

"I understand that," said Banks. "Hr. Rätsepp said the same thing. But DI Quinn was in at the start?"

"You could say that. He was allowed to accompany a junior investigator to get some feel of the city, to observe the investigations we were starting to make."

That was the first Banks had heard of it. Another thing Rätsepp had neglected to mention. In fact, he had told Banks and Joanna that Quinn had played no active role in the investigation, had merely attended meetings. "Who was this investigator?"

"I cannot remember his name. It is so long ago."

"Would it be in your files?"

Ursula Mardna gave him an impatient glance and picked up the telephone. "It would."

A short scattershot phone conversation in Estonian followed, and several moments later a young pink-faced man in a pinstripe suit knocked and walked in with a file folder under his arm. Ursula Mardna thanked him and opened the folder. "His name is Aivar Kukk. According to this file, he left the police force five years ago."

"A year after the Rachel Hewitt case. Why?"

"To pursue other interests." She pushed the folder away. "It happens, Hr. Banks. People are sometimes lucky enough to find out that they have made a wrong choice in life early enough to correct it."

"Do you have his address?"

"I am afraid we do not keep up-to-date information on ex–police officers. Even if we did, there would be much red tape involved in giving it to you."

"Of course."

She favored him with an indulgent smile. "We have come a long way since the Soviet era, but red tape is still red tape."

"Never mind," said Banks. "I'm sure we'll be able to find him if we need to."

Ursula Mardna gave him an assessing glance, as if trying to work out whether he would be able to, or perhaps whether it mattered.

"What were your impressions of DI Quinn, Ms. Mardna?" asked Joanna.

"He seemed a good man. Very serious. Dedicated."

"Did he change at all during the course of the week he was here?"

"Change?"

"Yes. His attitude, his feelings about the case, his commitment, his mood. Anything."

"I did not see much of him after the first two days," she said, "but I did get the impression that he placed himself more in the background. Is that how you say it?"

"He stood back?" Joanna said.

"Yes. When he started, he was so full of energy that he did not want to sleep. He just wanted to walk the streets looking for the girl. I suppose he became tired, and perhaps depressed when he realized there was so little he could do here. I think he perhaps lost hope."

Or he gave up when someone showed him the compromising photos, Banks thought.

"I suppose so," said Joanna. "It must also have been intimidating, a foreign city, different customs, different language."

"As you can see, the language is not much of a problem here, but the other things . . . yes. I think he came to feel, how you say, out of his depth? That things were best left to us. The locals."

"That would explain it," said Joanna, making a note.

Ursula Mardna seemed a little alarmed. "Explain what?"

"The change in him."

"Oh, yes."

Banks showed her a photograph of the girl who had been with Quinn. He hadn't shown her image to Rätsepp because he hadn't trusted him. While he thought Ursula Mardna might well be erring on the side of caution and self-protection in all her responses, he took that as the reaction of a canny lawyer, not a bent copper. But he still didn't want her to see Quinn and the girl together. There was something rather too final and damning about that. "Do you recognize this girl?" he asked.

She studied the photograph closely, then shook her head and passed it back. "No," she said. "I have never seen her. Who is she?"

"That's something we would very much like to find out," said Joanna.

"I am sorry I cannot help."

"Was there any possibility that Rachel Hewitt's disappearance was connected with drugs?" Banks asked.

"Naturally, it was a direction we explored. We found no evidence of such a connection, but that does not mean there was none. Perhaps back in England. I do not know . . . Why do you ask?"

"I suppose you kept, still keep, pretty close tabs on the drug-trafficking business around here?"

"Tabs?"

"Keep an eye on. Watch."

"Yes, of course."

"And there was no link between Rachel or her friends and drug smuggling?"

"We did not reveal any such link."

"Could it be possible that any . . . er . . . uncovering of such a link might have been, shall we say, diverted, suppressed, avoided altogether?"

"What are you saying?"

Banks leaned forward and rested his arms on the table. "Ms. Mardna," he said, "I've worked as a police officer for more years than I care to remember, most of that time as a detective. I have worked undercover, vice, drugs, just about anything you would care to name, and if there is one thing I have learned, it is that there is *always* the possibility of corruption and intimidation, especially when drugs are involved, mostly because of their connection with organized crime. Now, can you honestly sit there and tell me there has never been a whiff of corruption in the Tallinn police?"

Her face reddened. "I cannot tell you that, Hr. Banks," she said. "But I can tell you that in this case, the possibility of drugs was thoroughly investigated by Investigator Rätsepp and his team, and reviewed by myself. The girl had no connections with any of the known drug traffickers at that time, and as far as I know, investigations back in Britain found no hints of any such a connection there either. All of which led us to believe," she went on, "even in the absence of a body, witnesses or forensic evidence, that we were dealing with a sex crime."

"Stands to reason," said Banks. "Attractive young girl, alone in a strange city. Odds are someone might take advantage of her. But why kill her?"

"We worked on the assumption that whoever abducted her—or whoever she arranged to meet during the evening—also killed her to avoid identification and disposed of the body somehow."

"Why should somebody she arranged to meet do that?"

"I can only speculate. Perhaps things went too far? Something went wrong? The girl became nervous, tried to back out? Protested, struggled. I do not know. There could be many explanations."

"And the body?"

"Estonia is a small country, but there are many places to get rid of a dead body. Permanently. And before you ask, we did search as many of them as we could."

Banks scratched the scar by his right eye. "It seems the most convincing scenario," he said. "In which case we're probably wasting our time here." He gestured to Joanna and they both stood up.

Ursula Mardna stood up with them, leaning over the desk to shake hands. "You would never waste your time in Tallinn, Hr. Banks. Especially as we have such wonderful weather this week. Good-bye. Enjoy yourselves."

That, Banks thought, was what Rätsepp had wanted them to do, too. Have a holiday, don't bother chasing ghosts. But it only made Banks all the more suspicious.

"Since when has it been illegal to beg in the street?" Annie asked PC Geordie Lyttleton, who had just nipped into the Major Crimes office to report an incident.

"It isn't," said Lyttleton, "but she was getting quite aggressive, ma'am. She scared the living daylights out of one old lady, following her down the street shouting some sort of gibberish after her."

"And what sort of gibberish did it turn out to be?"

"Polish gibberish, ma'am. She can't speak English. Jan from Traffic speaks a bit of Polish, though. His mum's family's from Warsaw. Anyway, he got it out of her that she has hardly eaten since last Wednesday. She lost her home and left her job. She was in a bit of a state. What she actually meant was that she was squatting up at some ruined farm and—"

"Garskill Farm?"

"She didn't know what it was called. I just thought, with the murder and all . . . well, there might be a link of some sort."

"Excellent thinking, PC Lyttleton. Good work. We'll make a detective of you yet. Where is she now?"

"Well, ma'am," said Lyttleton, scratching his head, "she was bit, erm, aromatic, if you catch my drift, rather ripe, so I took her down to the custody suite and got WPC Bosworth to show her to the showers and fix her up with one of those disposable Elvis suits."

Annie smiled. He meant the coveralls they gave to prisoners while their clothes were being examined for trace evidence. A bit of embroidery in the right places and they might look a bit like the jumpsuits Elvis Presley wore in his Las Vegas shows. The basement had been modernized recently, and there were decent shower facilities for the use of anyone being held there. Letting the girl use them was stretching it a bit, but if Lyttleton was right, it beat sitting in a small warm room with her as she was. "Did you arrest her? Charge her?"

"No. Not yet. I thought I—"

"Well done, lad." She thought of the starving girl, set the vestiges of her vegetarianism aside, put some money on the table and said, "Go and get her a Big Mac, large fries and a Coke, will you, and get someone to send DS Stefan Nowak over from next door, if he's not too busy. I know he speaks Polish."

"Yes, ma'am. What shall I—"

"When she's finished with the shower, take her up to interview room two and let her eat there. Try to put her at ease. Tell her she's nothing to be frightened of."

"She doesn't understand English, ma'am."

"Do your best, Constable. A kind smile and gentle tone go a long way."

"Yes, ma'am."

Interview room two was no different from any of the others, except that it had a viewing room beside it, with a one-way mirror. Annie wanted to see what sort of shape the girl was in before Stefan arrived, so she installed herself in the tiny room and waited there.

The girl was shown into the interview room. A lost, pathetic figure in the overlarge jumpsuit, small and frail, skinny as a rail, clearly scared, wide-eyed, starving and exhausted, damp brown hair clinging to her cheeks and neck, she seemed no older than fourteen, though Annie estimated she was probably eighteen or more. When the door closed and the girl thought she was alone, she flicked her eyes around the room as if checking for monsters in the corners and then just sat there and started to cry. It made Annie want to cry herself, it was so bloody heartbreaking. Just a frightened, hungry kid, and there was no one here to comfort her, to hold her and tell her that she was loved and everything would be all right. You didn't have to be a *Guardian* reader to raise a tear or two for that predicament.

Lyttleton entered the interview room and handed over a McDonald's package. Before Annie even had the chance to feel guilty and wish she'd sent her a salad sandwich or a tofu burger instead, the girl fell on it and ripped off the wrapping paper. Annie had never seen anything quite like it, but it reminded her of one of those nature shows on BBC with David Attenborough. In a matter of moments, burger, fries and Coke were gone. Lyttleton had been decent enough to leave her alone to eat—he must have suspected it would not be a pretty sight—and Annie now felt guilty that she had been riveted to the spot by such a personal degradation as someone eating like there's no tomorrow. She felt like a voyeur, or a participant in a sick reality TV show.

When the girl had finished, she carefully picked up all the scattered wrapping paper and put it in the wastepaper basket, then she used one of the serviettes to wipe the table where it was stained with grease or ketchup. *Christ,* Annie thought.

A few moments later, DS Stefan Nowak arrived in the viewing room. Annie explained the situation. "Can you help?" she asked him.

Nowak looked through the one-way mirror at the girl. "I can speak the language, if that's what you mean. I'm not a translator, though. It's a special skill I don't have."

"This isn't official," Annie said. "We'll get a statement and all the rest the correct way later. Right now, I need information."

"Does AC Gervaise know?"

"I'm sure she would agree if she were here."

Stefan grinned and held up his hands. "OK, OK. Only asking. Come on, then. Let's have at it."

The room still smelled of McDonald's, and it made Annie feel slightly queasy. Fish and chicken she could handle, but she always avoided red meat. The girl jumped up when they entered, but she stopped short of running away and curling up in the corner. Instead, she regarded them sullenly and fearfully and sat down again slowly. She had a sulky, downturned mouth, lips quivering on the verge of tears and dark chocolate eyes. Her fingernails were badly bitten down, some showing traces of blood around the edges. All in all, she was probably a very pretty girl under normal circumstances, Annie thought, whenever she was lucky enough to experience them.

"Could you ask her name, please, Stefan?" Annie said.

A brief conversation followed. "She says it's Krystyna," Nowak said. "After her grandmother. She wants to know when you are going to let her go and what she is accused of doing."

"Tell her she's got nothing to be afraid of," Annie said. "I just want to ask her a few questions, and then we'll see what we can do to help her."

Nowak translated. Lyttleton came in with a pot of hot coffee and three Styrofoam cups, powdered milk and artificial sweetener. Annie guessed the girl might crave real sugar, but then she'd just had a large Coke. It was a wonder she wasn't bouncing off the walls.

"Ask her how old she is," Annie said.

Stefan talked with Krystyna and said, "Nineteen in July."

She's of age, then, Annie thought. Though of age for what, she didn't know. For the life she had been leading? "Where does she come from?"

Nowak spoke to Krystyna, and the answer came slowly, hesitantly.

"She's from a small town in Silesia," he said. "Pyskowice. Industrial. Coal mining." He paused.

"She . . . I mean, she doesn't speak very good . . . Her Polish is very . . . provincial. She's not well educated."

"Spare us the Polish class distinctions, Stefan. Just do the best you can, OK?"

Nowak's eyes narrowed. "OK."

Annie had always thought Stefan could be a bit of a stuck-up elitist prick at times. He was well educated and probably descended from some Polish royal family. Maybe he was a prince. She'd heard there were a lot of Polish princes about. Maybe it was a good line for getting laid. Stefan did all right in that department, she'd heard. She wondered if a line like that would have worked on Rachel, with her dreams of wealth and opulence. Then she got back to the matter at hand. "Ask her why she came here."

Annie watched Stefan translate. Krystyna's expression turned from puzzlement to surprise.

"For a better life" was the answer Stefan translated. There was no irony in Krystyna's voice or her expression. "Why do they all think we owe them a better life?" Stefan added.

Annie ignored him and paused for a moment, then asked, "Where was the farm she lived on?"

"In a wild place," came the answer. "There was nothing to do. No shops. No movies. No television."

"What was it like?"

"Cold. The roof leaked. The garden was all over-grown with weeds and nettles. There was no proper place to wash and no real toilet."

"It sounds like Garskill to me," Annie said. "Can you ask her when and why she left?"

"Wednesday morning," the answer came. "They were all told to pack up their belongings—not that they had any, apparently—and that they wouldn't be coming back there after work."

"Where was she working?"

Nowak and Krystyna conferred for a while, then he said, "A yeast factory. There was a sign outside that said 'Varley's,' she said. I think I know the place. They make yeast products for animal feed and for prisoners, diet supplement pills and suchlike."

"A yeast factory? Sounds bloody awful," said Annie. "How did she end up living at Garskill Farm and working there?"

This time the conversation in Polish was longer, with a clearly frustrated Nowak asking for more rep-etitions and clarifications. Finally he turned to Annie and straightened his tie. "She went to Katowice, the nearest large town, but there were no agencies there, so she went to Kraków and found someone who took her money and gave her an address in Bradford. I think she said Bradford. It was all phony, of course. These people are so gullible. Anyway, she ended up at the farm with about twenty other hopefuls doing a variety of rubbish jobs until they found somewhere to place her permanently, or so they said. And they kept most of her earnings back for bed and board and to pay off her debt to the agency."

It was a familiar story. Annie looked sympathetically toward Krystyna. "Where is this yeast factory?" she asked Nowak.

"Northern edge of Eastvale. That old industrial estate."

"Ask her why they had to leave." She thought she knew the answer, but she wanted to hear Krystyna's version, nonetheless.

"A man came to the farm in the morning," Nowak said a while later. "Different man. She hadn't seen him before. He came in a dark green car. A shiny car, I think she said. It looked new. The other two men, the regular ones who drove them to their jobs and back in the white van, seemed frightened of him. He told everyone to pack up, that they wouldn't be coming back tonight. That was it. She didn't mind so much because she didn't like living there. Apart from everything else, men kept trying to mess with her. That's what she said."

"What language did this man speak?"

"English," Stefan translated. "At least, she thinks it was English. She actually does know a few words. And then someone translated for the workers who couldn't understand."

"Did he have an accent of any kind?"

Annie saw Krystyna shake her head before answering. "She doesn't know. She couldn't understand much. She'd hardly be likely to know if he had a Scottish accent or something."

"Can you describe this man?" Annie asked Krystyna. Nowak translated.

Krystyna nodded.

"Excellent. We'll see if we can rustle up a sketch artist after our little talk. If the worst comes to the worst, I can always have a go at it myself."

"Do you want me to translate that?"

"No. Don't bother," Annie said. "Ask her what happened next."

Nowak asked Krystyna and translated her reply. "They all piled into the van as usual. All except for Mihkel. They held him back. He had told her his name was Mihkel. He was from Estonia. She liked him. He was nice to her, and he didn't . . . you know . . . want anything." Stefan cleared his throat. "Some of the men tried to touch her at night. They were very crude. Apparently, there were two couples at the farm, and everyone could hear them when they made love, however quiet they tried to be. These men imitated them, made funny animal sounds and laughed. Mihkel protected her and her friend Ewa. She would like to see her friend Ewa again. She is sorry for leaving her, but she was scared."

"That's probably how Mihkel gave himself away, the poor bastard," Annie said. "Being nice to people and asking too many questions. At least one of the men in the work gang was probably a plant for the other side. Don't translate that. Did she ever see Mihkel again?"

"No," said Nowak after another brief exchange. "They were taken to work, as usual. She was to be picked up outside the factory at six o'clock, but she says she got out early and ran away."

"Why?"

Krystyna seemed confused when Stefan translated the question. She muttered a few words. "She doesn't really know," he said. "She was unhappy at the farm. She thought she would not see Mihkel again, and the new place would be worse."

"Was there anything else?" Annie pressed.

After a while, Krystyna cried and told Stefan that the regular van driver had been pressing her to sleep with him, and that he wanted her to go on the streets to make more money. He said she could earn money very well that way and pay off her debts in no time, but she didn't want to do it. She ran away.

Annie found some tissues in her bag and handed them to Krystyna, who thanked her politely in Polish. Even though she had nothing, Annie thought, Krystyna had chosen to flee the work gang rather than stay there and suffer their mauling and end up deeper and deeper in debt, trawling the streets for prospective clients. What had she thought would happen to her, on the run, alone in a strange country? She had been desperate enough not to care. "Do you know where they are now, the others?" she asked.

When she understood Stefan's translation, Krystyna shook her head. Then she spoke again.

"She doesn't know where they were taken," Nowak explained. "She's been in Eastvale ever since. She walked from the factory. She has no food or money. Since then she's been living on the streets, sleeping in shop doorways and alleys."

Krystyna spoke again. A question, this time.

"She wants to know if she can have a cigarette," Nowak said.

"Afraid not," Annie replied. "But tell her I'll buy her a whole packet when we've finished in here."

Krystyna merely nodded at that.

"She says Mihkel asked her about herself," Annie went on. "Did they talk much? How did they communicate?"

"They couldn't speak the same language," Nowak said after listening to Krystyna for a while. "But Mihkel knew a little Polish, so they managed a few basic exchanges. His accent was funny."

"What did he ask her about?"

Annie could tell by Krystyna's gestures and facial expressions that she wasn't going to get much of answer.

"Just her life in general," said Nowak finally. "She said mostly he asked about her, like you. How did she get there? Where was she from? Why did she come? He wanted to know her story. She asks if he was a policeman, too."

"No," said Annie.

"She also asks where has he gone."

Annie sighed. *Bugger it.* This just wasn't fair. Should she tell Krystyna the truth? That they suspected the man in the dark green Ford Focus had tortured and drowned Mihkel? If she did, she risked scaring the girl so much that she might balk at giving a description of the man. If she didn't tell her, she was being dishonest. She topped up everyone's coffee and moved on. "Can you ask her if she ever saw anyone else around the place who wasn't part of the normal furniture and fittings?"

420 · PETER ROBINSON

Krystyna seemed surprised at the lack of an answer to her question, and the change in direction, but she listened to Stefan's translation as she sipped her coffee.

"A man came once who seemed to be in charge," Stefan translated. "He was dressed better than the driver and his friend, who brought them stale bread and weak coffee in the morning before work. He was wearing a hat and an overcoat with a fur collar. He was English, she thought. Probably half the people there were Polish, and some of them spoke English, so word got around that he wanted them all to know that if they needed money, there was a way. A friend of his would lend them money, and they could pay him back when they got more pay for their jobs, after they had paid off the agency."

No mention of interest, of course, Annie guessed. She bet the boss man was Roderick Flinders himself, or one of his men, and that Corrigan was involved somewhere down the line. She excused herself for a moment, reassured Krystyna that she would be back soon and went to her office. She had photographs of both Corrigan and Flinders, which she took back with her and set in front of Krystyna. "Do you recognize either of these men?" she asked.

Krystyna studied the photographs and pointed to Flinders. "This one," Nowak translated. "He was the one who came and told them he could get them money. She hasn't seen the other man."

It figured, Annie thought. Corrigan wasn't likely to venture out into the trenches when he had others to do that for him.

"Excellent," said Annie. "I'm going to see if I can rustle up a sketch artist. We can use Menzies, from the art college, if he's available. He doesn't live far away. I'll send a car. I know it's upsetting for her, but I don't want her to leave here until we've got sketches we can use. This is the first time we've got anywhere close to a description of our man, and I don't want to lose it. Do you think you can entertain Krystyna for a few minutes while I'm gone? I promise I won't be long."

"Sure," said Stefan. "We'll have a laugh a minute."

Annie gave him a cold look as she stood up. *Some people,* she thought. Krystyna's eyes followed her, as if she wanted to go with her, too, but Stefan's voice was soothing enough when he started to speak Polish, and Annie turned at the door, smiled and gave Krystyna a thumbs-up sign.

Erik Aarma said he would be happy to have dinner with Banks and Joanna that evening, and that he would like to bring his wife, Helen, along. Nobody had any objection to that, so it was arranged for half past seven.

In deference to the tourists and the fine weather, Erik said, they would eat in the Old Town, something he rarely did, and a nice treat for Helen, too. She loved pasta, and they didn't have it very often. They had an apartment in Kristiine and usually ate locally or at home. Perhaps an evening out would dispel some of the gloom they had been feeling over Mihkel's death.

It was a Friday night, and getting quite busy, as they took their table at a small Italian restaurant on Raekoja, quite near the main square, and just around the corner from Clazz, shortly after half past seven. The revelers weren't out in full force yet, but the chain gang was back, and a group of girls dressed as Playboy bunnies tottered by on their high heels, attracting many wolf whistles, searching for a bar in very loud Glasgow accents. Whenever Banks saw groups of girls such as that now, he thought of Rachel. In a way, he felt that since he had been in Tallinn, he had drifted away from his starting point, the murder of Bill Quinn, then the discovery of Mihkel Lepikson's body at Garskill Farm, and his case had turned into a quest for the truth about what had happened to Rachel. Not that he believed she was still alive, but her body had to be somewhere, even after all this time. Annie was doing the real work, back in Yorkshire, he thought, getting closer to identifying Quinn's killer with every moment. It would be a great success for her to have on her first case after the injury. A real confidence booster. Banks had not entirely lost sight of Bill Quinn, or of Mihkel Lepikson, but it was Rachel he sought in the winding cobbled alleys and long evening shadows of Tallinn's Old Town.

Erik seemed pleased with himself, so Banks was hoping for good news. Joanna was chatting happily away with Helen, only pausing to glance at her mobile every now and then. Helen was almost as large as her husband, but minus the facial hair, and quick to laugh. A fresh breeze had picked up during the day, and Erik said it might mark the end of the warm spell. It was still pleasant enough to sit outside, but they definitely needed to wear jackets. Joanna had a wool shawl wrapped around her shoulders. Where did she get these things? Banks wondered. She had the perfect item to wear for all occasions. Every once in a while, Banks caught a whiff of burning tobacco as a smoker passed by.

"I am not going to beat about the bush, as you say," said Erik as they clinked glasses and toasted absent friends. "I will not keep you in the suspense. I have found your girl."

Banks almost dropped his glass. He looked at Joanna, whose eyebrows shot up so far they were almost lost under her blond fringe. "Are you sure?" he asked.

"I am sure."

"But . . . how?"

Erik tapped the side of his nose. "Ah, but we have our resources. People say sometimes we have more files than the Stasi did."

"Seriously?" said Banks.

"Do you want to know who she is?"

"Of course we do."

"Her name is Larisa Petrenko."

"Like the conductor?"

"Vasily Petrenko? You know of him? Yes, like that."

"She's Russian, then?"

"It is a Russian name. But that should not be a surprise to you. Forty percent of Tallinn is made up of Russian-speaking citizens. Helen is Russian-speaking, but we speak Estonian. The most popular last name in the whole country is Ivanov."

"I thought people were changing their names to Estonian to have a better chance of getting on here?"

"You should not believe all you read in the newspapers, my friend. The next thing you know they will have us dragging Russian-speaking Estonians away at midnight and locking them up in Patarei."

"You don't do that already?"

Erik laughed. "Not for some time."

It was clearly a touchy subject, though, Banks sensed. The whole Russian-Estonian thing was beyond his comprehension, though he knew the basic facts, the history of the relationship. He felt it was something you had to live through, grow up with. "You don't happen to know where she lives, do you, this Larisa Petrenko?"

"Of course. She lives in Haapsalu. She has a restaurant there with her husband."

"I can't believe this," Banks said, shaking his head slowly. "Where is Haapsalu?"

"On the west coast. About one and a half hours to drive. We will not be able to join you, I am afraid. Family matters. But Merike is back. I have spoken with her. She will pick you up at your hotel after breakfast tomorrow. Is ten o'clock too early?"

It was all moving so fast. Banks glanced at Joanna, who shook her head. "Not at all."

"Merike is very sorry she could not join us tonight also," said Erik, "but there you are. You will see her tomorrow."

"I'm still rather taken aback by this," Banks said. "What you're telling me is that you found the girl in the photo with Bill Quinn, and she lives an hour and a half away, and runs a café with her husband, right?"

Erik beamed. "That is correct. You pay attention. A restaurant. Haapsalu is a tourist town. Nice. You will like it."

"So she's not a hooker in Budapest or a stripper in Belfast?"

"Not at all. She is a most respectable young woman, which makes me think she might not enjoy to talk about her past."

"We'll manage it somehow," said Banks. "I have to know how you found her, Erik. Come on, you can't just leave us guessing like this."

Erik tilted his head to one side. "I could," he said. "You only asked me for the information. Not how I found it. Should I give up my trade secrets so easily?"

"I'm not asking—"

Erik waved his large hairy hand in the air. "It is all right, my friend. I am only kidding. Is that what you say? 'Kidding'?" He winked at Joanna.

"Damn right, it is," said Banks.

A pretty dark-haired waitress appeared to take their orders. She wore a name tag that identified her as "Irena." Nobody had had a chance to study the menu, as they had all been too busy talking, so they took an extra minute to scan the list, then Irena came back and they all ordered pasta and a bottle of Chianti. It was starting to get dark now, the shadows long and deep in the narrow cobbled streets of the Old Town. Someone was singing in the distance. A glass smashed a little closer. Banks fancied he could hear a zither playing somewhere.

"We have some very good facial-recognition software," Erik said. "Perhaps you do not know this, but

Estonia is very famous in high technology. We invented Skype."

"I had heard that," said Banks. "So that's how you did it?"

"Not exactly." Erik pointed to his head. "I also have a fantastic memory."

Helen laughed. "He does," she said. "It is true. He has memory like steel hat."

"I think that's 'steel trap,' Helen," Joanna said, correcting her.

"Yes. That is right. Like steel trap."

"So how did you do it?" Banks asked.

Erik paused for dramatic effect, then he said, "I'm a newspaperman. It is in my blood. The ink. The hot lead. Which we do not use anymore, of course. When I first saw the photograph, I knew the face was familiar, but the context was not. I do not know any escort girls or prostitutes. Only through news stories, and that was not where I had seen her. No, it was something else. Two years ago there was a big celebrity wedding in Haapsalu, which is unusual in itself. This beautiful Russian girl, who had just graduated from university in Tartu, married one of Estonia's most famous artists, Alexei Petrenko. Very handsome. He had a reputation for being a ladies' man but he seemed to have settled down at last. We reported on the wedding, with photographs. Not me, of course. And not Mihkel. But a reporter who writes such celebrity stories. But I am editor for many different reporters." He tapped the side of his head. "And that is how I remember."

He seemed exhausted by his long speech in English, took a long swig of wine and leaned back in his chair.

"You are certain?" Banks asked.

"Yes. As soon as I stopped thinking she was an escort or a hooker, I started to remember and looked through file photographs." He pulled a photo out of his inside pocket and slid it over the table to Banks. "This is her, is it not?"

Banks studied the picture. There was just enough light at the table to make it out. The happy couple. It was definitely *her,* all right. There was no mistaking those cheekbones, those eyes, even though her hair was shorter and styled differently. Banks felt a frisson of excitement. He showed the photo to Joanna, then made to pass it back, but Erik waved it away. "Keep it," he said. "I made a copy for you. I don't need it."

"That picture was in the newspaper?" Banks asked.

"But of course. All the newspapers. It was big news."

If anyone had been searching for the woman, Banks thought, the photo would have been a giveaway. But if anyone had been after her, he told himself, she would have known not to invite public scrutiny that way. Which meant that she probably had no idea what she had done, or why. The problem was that things had changed over the last month, since Quinn's wife's death, and that might include her situation, too. There was no reason why she should become a liability if she knew nothing—if all she had done was play a seduction game six years ago with a man she didn't know while someone took photographs—but she could be a loose end, and it seemed as if someone had been tidying up loose ends. Banks felt no reason for undue alarm, but the fact that two people had been killed already, and that he had been followed around Tallinn, made him a little nervous. Ten o'clock the following morning hardly seemed soon enough. Still, if she had survived unharmed up until now, there was no reason to fear that tonight she would meet her doom. Banks quelled his concerns and thanked Erik profusely for the information.

"My pleasure," said Erik. "Especially if it helps to catch whoever killed Mihkel."

"It could help," said Banks. Their food arrived, and there was a short break in conversation while everyone got settled with serviettes, side dishes and knives and forks. Irena smiled at Banks and refilled their wineglasses.

"I think she fancies you," joked Joanna.

"Get away with you," said Banks. "My charm only works on the over-sixties."

"I don't know. She may have visions of an English husband, an English passport, an English country house." She turned to Erik. "Irena? Is that a Russian name?"

"Probably," Erik said. "Could be Polish, too. Or Slovakian. Many names are common to more than one country."

"There you are," she said to Banks. "An exotic Eastern European bride."

Banks twirled up a forkful of spaghetti and smiled at her. "Rather like an exotic Italian husband."

Joanna seemed to freeze for a moment, then she blushed. "Not at all," she said. "Not at all like that."

"Anything on Toomas Rätsepp and Ursula Mardna?" Banks asked.

"The prosecutor's clean as a whistle. High-flyer. Tipped for even bigger things. The Rachel case set her back a bit, but she's more than made up for it since then. Feared and respected."

"She seems so young."

"It is a young woman's job."

There were plenty of young women around the CPS offices, too, Banks realized, but he had never really thought about it that way. "What about Rätsepp?"

"Nothing definite. No dirt that sticks, so to speak. There are those who think he mixes too closely with the wrong elements. Not real gangsters and criminals, you understand, but businessmen, rich and powerful people who might need occasional favors, who sometimes move very close to the edge."

" 'Businessman' is a word that covers a multitude of sins, I've always thought," said Banks.

"He has a very nice apartment in Kadriorg, which is most unusual for a retired police officer. It is an expensive area."

"Wouldn't he be more careful if he had something to hide?"

"Of course. That is why there is no dirt that sticks. He would not dare to be so open, as you say, if he could not explain the money."

"How does he explain it?"

"Inheritance. It is true that his father was quite wealthy. He began with one small shop and ended up running a chain of electronics stores. He died around the time Rätsepp retired. Rätsepp didn't get everything, of course—he had brothers and sisters—but he ended up with a decent share."

"And that explains the flat, the money?"

"To the satisfaction of most people," said Erik. "You must draw your own conclusions."

"Was Rätsepp involved with anyone who might be responsible for what happened to Rachel Hewitt, for Bill Quinn and Mihkel?"

" 'In the right circumstances, don't you think, everyone is capable of anything.' "

"*Chinatown*," said Banks. "Or close enough. Is there any way of finding out more?"

"Not without ruffling too many feathers. The wrong feathers to ruffle. We have a free press, but with freedom comes responsibility."

"That's a lesson we're still learning back home," said Banks.

"Yes. I know."

"Thanks for all you've done."

"You are welcome. As I said, it is for my friend Mihkel. And now to other things. Vasily Petrenko. Is he still with the Liverpool Philharmonic?"

Joanna pulled a face, and Helen started questioning her about her job, investigating bad cops. "Yes," Banks said to Erik. "Yes, he is." And as he went on to talk about the young conductor's successful career, he noticed a familiar figure sitting outside across the small square. It was the man who had been following him the previous night.

Banks returned to his conversation, and when he looked again a few minutes later, the man was gone.

But Banks knew he was around somewhere, watching, watching the dark.

It was getting on toward the end of Friday afternoon, and the working week for most people would soon be over. It wouldn't be much of a weekend for Annie— she would still have plenty of tasks to keep her busy— but things slowed down when the people you relied on weren't around. It was hard to get any lab work done, for a start, let alone a rush job. Thankfully, they had Stefan Nowak and Vic Manson and the team next door, but they weren't equipped to do everything, and they liked to keep as normal hours as possible if they could.

The question of what to do with Krystyna remained paramount in Annie's mind. They had got Rick Menzies, their sketch artist from the art college, and between them, Rick, Krystyna and Stefan had come up with a good description, which Annie thought translated into a more-than-usually-clear sketch, from the five o'clock shadow to the cropped hair and crescent scar by the hairline, to the bulbous nose and ears slightly sticking out, to what Annie could only describe as a cruel mouth.

Annie glanced briefly at the notes and message she had received over the afternoon. The most interesting item was that Vic Manson had managed to get a couple of fingerprints from the inside of the glove compartment of the Ford Focus they thought the killer had hired under the name of Arnold Briggs. Of course, there could be no guarantees they were his at this point. Like the DNA, the fingerprint was not in any of their databases.

AC Gervaise poked her head around the door. "Got a minute, Annie?"

"Of course," said Annie, following her out into the corridor. She was surprised when Gervaise led her toward the staircase down to the ground floor and the exit, rather than up to her office. She was even more surprised when they crossed to the corner of Market Street, heading straight for the Queen's Arms.

"I guessed you might feel like a break," said Gervaise. "It's been a long week."

"Yes, ma'am."

"And you can stop that. I enjoy it about as much as you do."

Annie grinned and followed her through the door. The place was busy, a popular destination for the postwork crowd on a Friday, but a lot of people liked to stand at the bar and relax, so they found a quiet, round, copper-topped table by the window looking out on the market square, which was in that in-between twilight period after work, so few shoppers were around, but before play, so the young revelers hadn't arrived yet. The chairs and tables were outside, on the wooden stand, but nobody was sitting there at the moment. A brisk wind was blowing, and if Annie wasn't mistaken she could see a drop or two of rain on the windows.

"My shout," said Gervaise. "What's it to be?"

"Am I off duty?"

"As far as I'm concerned you are."

"Right, then. I'll have a pint of Cock-a-Hoop, please."

"Excellent."

Gervaise came back a few minutes later with two pints. Judging by the color, Annie guessed them both to be Cock-a-Hoop. The name made her think of A. Le Coq, and of Banks and Joanna Passero, no doubt enjoying another nice open-air dinner in Tallinn.

"Where's DS Jackman?" Gervaise asked.

"She's talking to some of the other girls who were at the hen weekend, to see if they remember anything Pauline Boyars didn't."

"I'm not sure about this sudden concentration on Rachel Hewitt. I hope you remember we're looking for the man who killed DI Quinn and this Estonian journalist."

"Of course. And we're getting close. But they're connected."

"Hmm. We'll see, no doubt. Anyway, how was your first week back at work?"

"Fine," said Annie. "Busy, of course, but it's great to be back."

"I did advise you to take it easy."

"With all due respect, I've been taking it easy for long enough already. It's time to get back in the saddle."

Gervaise sipped some beer. "You've got a point. How did you get on with the Polish girl?"

"Krystyna? We got an excellent sketch of the suspect," Annie said. "I've sent it off to everyone I can think of. NCS, Trading Standards, Force Intelligence Unit, SOCA, the Human Trafficking Centre and Interpol. Not to mention the county forces nationwide. Wanted: handy with a crossbow, interested in waterboarding."

"That should do it," said Gervaise.

"I'm not too sure," said Annie. "I mean, there's definitely foreign involvement in this. Estonian and Polish for starters. If our man was sent to kill Quinn and Lepikson, there's every chance he doesn't live in the UK, and if that's the case, the odds are that he's left the country. Who'd hang around after a double hit? He could be anywhere."

"Interpol's got pretty good data these days. They'll pull something up on him if there's anything there."

"Let's hope so. They drew a blank on the DNA. Anyway, I'm not expecting a lot until after the week-end, but I'm trying to stay hopeful."

"What have you done with Krystyna?"

"That's the problem," said Annie, leaning forward and resting on her elbows. "She's down in the cells right now. She's not under arrest or anything—she hasn't really done anything wrong except yell at an old woman in Polish—but I want to keep her around until we find our man, then see if she can make a positive identification. Besides, she's got nowhere to go, poor thing. She's got no fixed abode, and if immigration get their hands on her, they'll whisk her away from us."

"I see your problem. We might be able to stretch to a B and B for a couple of days."

"I'm not sure she'd stay. She's scared. It took me and Stefan a while to put her at ease and convince her she wasn't going to be locked up. She's got no clean clothes to wear, either. I mean, you can only get so far in an Elvis suit."

"A wha—" Gervaise said, then stopped herself. "Oh, I see. That's what you call them. Well, no. You're right about that. You could take her to Oxfam or Sue Ryder and buy her a few things." She checked her watch. "Though you'd probably have a job at this time."

"And then what?"

"Well, short of taking her home yourself, lending her some of your castoffs, I don't really know."

"Don't think I haven't thought of that. She doesn't speak any English."

"People get by. I had a Spanish roommate once, when I was at police college. She didn't speak a word of English, and I know no Spanish, but we managed all right. I'm not saying you should do it, if the idea bothers you, though. I suppose we can accommodate her in the cells for a few days at the taxpayers' expense, though let's hope it doesn't get leaked to the local press, or we'll have swarms of homeless heading up from the cities."

Annie laughed at the image. "Think what the press would say if a female police officer took a young girl home with her. Not that I care."

Gervaise paused. "Do we know for certain she's illegal?"

"We know nothing except that she's Polish, and Poland is a member of the EU. I don't know if she has the right documents or filled in the right forms. She has no identification now, no passport, no money, nothing. God knows where they are. I'm thinking of ordering a raid on Roderick Flinders's business offices and home. Krystyna identified him from a photograph as someone who came around with offers to lend money, so that clearly links him with Corrigan's nasty little business. He'd probably be too canny to keep anything incriminating there, but I might just do it anyway, just to put the jitters up the bastard. And for my own pleasure, of course."

Gervaise finished her pint and glanced at Annie's glass, still about a quarter full. "Another?"

"No, I shouldn't. I'd better—"

"Oh, come on with you. How often do we get a chance to take a break from the station and have a good old natter?"

"Well, seeing as you put it like that." Annie drained her glass and handed it over. "I'll have the same again, please."

As Annie sat waiting for Gervaise to come back with the drinks, she thought of poor Krystyna shut in the cells. Though an inner voice warned her about getting involved, perhaps, she thought, it wouldn't be a bad idea to take Krystyna home. Just until the dust settled and she could get her life sorted out. They could communicate through sign language. She could sort out some clothes for her. Nothing would fit her well, of course, as she was so thin, but there were ways of making do, a little nip here and a tuck there. Anything was better than the oversized Elvis suit. Best of all, Krystyna would be in a clean and comfortable house, not a cell. Annie would order a pizza. They would watch television. Krystyna could sleep in the spare room. Annie saw Gervaise talking into her mobile at the bar. When she came back her hands were empty, and her face was serious.

"I'm afraid that second pint will have to wait," she said. "I've just received notice from West Yorkshire. Warren Corrigan's been shot."

10

Saturday morning was a little cooler than it had been earlier in the week, with a fresh wind off the Baltic bringing in a few ponderous clouds. Merike was wearing a patterned jumper that reminded Banks of Sarah Lund's sweater from *The Killing*.

"Haapsalu is a spa town, right?" she was saying as they drove through the outskirts of Tallinn on a major road, all apartment blocks and shopping centers. "Like Harrogate and Bath."

"I understand," said Banks, sitting next to her in the front of the messy yellow VW Bug. He was keeping an eye on the rearview mirror. It was perhaps too early to tell, but he didn't think they were being followed.

"It has an old castle, the Episcopal Castle, some beautiful old wooden houses and a nice waterfront.

Peter the Great used to go there. And Tchaikovsky. There's a bench dedicated to Tchaikovsky."

"I'd like to see that," Banks said. "But this isn't exactly a day at the seaside."

"I know," said Merike, casting him a sideways glance. "I am hoping we are successful, too."

The plan, such as it was, was for Merike to first talk to Larisa, try to set her at ease, assure her there would be no comebacks or consequences, and then for Banks to question her, with Merike's help as a translator, if necessary, about her past. If her husband didn't know, and if he was there, they would get her away from him for a while. Joanna Passero, who had a special interest in this part of the investigation, would be taking notes and asking questions whenever she felt it necessary. Banks could hardly sideline her on this. They had not telephoned in advance. There were many reasons why Larisa Petrenko might want to forget her past, and they didn't want to scare her away before they got there.

The suburbs of Tallinn gave way to fields and woods. Here and there, a narrow unpaved lane led between rows of hedges to a distant village. The road they were traveling on wasn't very busy, though it was obviously a main east-west route, with bus service and all, so they made generally good progress. Merike had the radio tuned quietly to some inoffensive pop program. In deference to her passengers, she refrained from smoking, though Banks assured her she was welcome to do so in her own car, which was pretty thick with the smell of tobacco anyway. Joanna sat in the back gazing out at the scenery. She didn't seem ill, the way she had on the way to Garskill Farm, but then the road here was much smoother. Banks was thinking about the phone call he had received from Annie late last night. Warren Corrigan had been shot. She said she would call when she had more news. He wondered whether that triggered bad memories, or whether she could disassociate from what had happened to her.

Soon they were entering a town—Haapsalu itself, Merike announced—with a few modern buildings dotted around grassy areas, all very low-rise, then rows of old wooden houses as they drove slowly down the main street. Merike found a place to park and pulled to a halt. She pointed out of the window to a restaurant. "There," she said. She glanced at her watch. "They should be open for lunch. It is very popular because the restaurant is above Alexander Petrenko's gallery, where he has some paintings for sale."

"It seems a good business idea," said Banks. "Have a stroll around the gallery, see something you like, head upstairs for a nice meal and a couple of drinks to think it over."

"He does very well, I think, but he is so rarely there, of course. His studio is elsewhere in town."

Banks could sense, if not smell, the fresh sea air when he got out of the car. He took a deep breath to rid himself of the tobacco smell that lingered in the upholstery. The first thing Merike did when she got into the street was light a cigarette. "You want me to go in alone first, right?"

"Yes, please. I don't think we should all go traipsing in there at once and scare the living daylights out of her," Banks said. "You go have a word with her, tell her what we have in mind. See if she can get someone to cover for her for a while, and we'll all go for a walk on the seafront. Sound OK?"

"OK," said Merike, stamping out her cigarette. "I feel like a cop."

Banks smiled. "There's no need to take it that far. Just be yourself."

"Who else could I be?" said Merike, then she checked for traffic and wandered across the street. Banks and Joanna hung back by the VW. There were a few tourists walking about, checking antique and gift shops. "It's famous for shawls, Haapsalu," said Joanna. "Beautiful shawls of knitted lace."

"Maybe later," said Banks, thinking something like that might make a nice present for Annie, though on second thought, she didn't seem much like a lace-shawl kind of girl. Still, there were plenty of gift shops in the Old Town. Some amber jewelry, perhaps, or ceramics.

Joanna wandered a few yards down the street to look in a shop window while Banks kept his eye on the door of the restaurant. It was about ten minutes before Merike came out. At first Banks thought she was alone, then he saw the woman behind her. Larisa Petrenko. She was a slighter figure than he had imagined—for some reason he had thought her a tall, leggy, exotic beauty. The closer they came, the more he could see that she was definitely a beauty, though in a very natural way. She wore her hair tied back in a ponytail. Her jeans were not the kind you had to put on with a shoehorn, but they certainly showed off the curves of her hips, rear end and legs. She had put on some weight since the photograph with Quinn had been taken, but not much. She was still slim and petite, and very young-looking. And she was nervous. Banks gave Merike a quizzical glance.

"This is Larisa," Merike said. "She is willing to talk to you. Her husband is not here today. He is at his studio working. She does not believe she can tell you very much, but she will help if she can."

Banks smiled at Larisa and offered his hand. She shook it. Her grip was firm, her skin soft. "I cannot be gone for long," she said in clear but accented English. "Kaida is by herself, and we should be busy soon."

"Can we walk?"

Larisa led them down some quiet streets of wooden houses, and they soon came out at the sea. There was a large white wedding-cake-style building on the water in front of them with a covered walkway all around it, like the covered porches in the southern USA. To the right was something resembling a white bandstand sticking out from the shore. They walked along the waterfront path. Larisa had already told them on the way about her simple life in Haapsalu with her husband and her café, about how she had gone to university to study modern languages and wanted to teach but changed her mind. Now she made pottery and ceramics and ran a successful restaurant in a tourist spa.

"I take it that's a long way from your old life?" Banks said.

"Yes."

"Do you want to tell me what happened?" Banks had already shown her the photographs, which had embarrassed her.

Banks saw a polar bear in the water near the shore, then he realized it was just a statue of a polar bear. Haapsalu's version of *The Little Mermaid*, he guessed. They came to a stone bench that was inscribed P. I. TSAIKOVSKI 1840–1893 under a circular etching of the man himself. "Let's sit here," said Larisa. "I like to sit here when I walk by the sea."

"Do you like Tchaikovsky's music?" Banks asked.

"Not particularly. But I like the idea that he was here. I like to think of him enjoying the same view and hearing great music in his mind."

Banks liked that idea, too, and he also liked Tchaikovsky's string quartets and symphonies very much. The four of them sat in a row, Banks half-turned toward Larisa. "Do you remember that night when the photographs were taken?"

Larisa gazed out to sea, screwing her eyes up against the glare from the water. "Pieces of it," she said. "I met him in the hotel bar. I was pretending to get change for the telephone, and I caught his eye, as was planned."

"So you didn't approach him directly?" Joanna asked from beside Banks.

"I smiled at him. He came up to the bar and asked if he could help. He gave me some change. A few minutes later I came back in to thank him, and he offered to buy me a drink. After that, it was easy."

"But at no time did you proposition him?" Joanna asked.

"What kind of girl do you think I am? Of course I did not proposition him. We talked. He was nice. He was lonely. He had nobody to meet, nobody to talk to."

"What did you talk about?" Banks asked.

Larisa frowned. "I do not remember. Wait. We talked about fishing at some time. He did. I remember how intense and alive he became when he talked about fishing. The rest is gone. Small talk. How he liked Tallinn. The sights. That sort of thing."

"Did he talk about his job?"

"I do not know what his job was. Perhaps he did."

"He was a police detective."

"I would have remembered," Larisa said. "And I would have left. In those days I avoided the police."

Banks let that one go by. "So you talked," he said. "Then what?"

"Dinner. I said I was hungry, and he took me to dinner. And we drank some wine. And we talked some more."

"When did the subject of going to his room come up?"

"Towards the end of dinner. We were perhaps both a little drunk. He said it would be nice to continue the conversation up in his room. I agreed."

"You did this all of your own free will?" Joanna asked. "Not for money?"

"Yes, of course for money," said Larisa. "But not from him. I am not a prostitute. Not even then."

"So someone paid you?" Banks said.

"Two thousand kroon. It was a lot of money."

"Do you know who paid you?"

"Of course I do. It was the same man who gave me the powder to put in his wine."

There had been no point heading down to Leeds on Friday evening, as it was West Yorkshire's crime scene, and they would only be in the way, so Annie had given in to her softer nature and taken Krystyna home to her little cottage in Harkside. They had spent the evening in companionable silence watching American cop shows on Channel Five while sharing an Indian takeaway and a bottle of chilled Sauvignon Blanc. Annie's clothes hung on Krystyna, but she seemed to appreciate just having something clean to wear. She had spent over an hour in the bath and used most of the scented salts that Banks had bought Annie for Christmas. She never touched the stuff herself. He was crap at presents, Banks, but at least he tried.

Annie had got Stefan Nowak on the phone that morning and had him explain to Krystyna where she was going and that she was coming back soon, where the food was, and so on. She could tell by the coolness and distance in his voice that he didn't approve of her taking Krystyna home with her, but Annie didn't care. Stefan said he expected to be in the lab all morning, barring another murder scene, so Annie left his number for Krystyna in case there were any problems. She promised to be back by late afternoon. When she thought about it, she realized that she actually expected Krystyna would still be there, and that she would be disappointed and sad if she weren't. Then she shook that feeling off and got into Winsome's car, come to pick her up for another drive to Leeds.

The way Annie managed to piece it all together later, this was what happened: Late on Friday afternoon, Corrigan was in his "office" in the Black Bull with Curly, finishing up for the day and counting the take brought in by several of their debt collectors that afternoon. It had been a lucrative day, and Corrigan was in a festive mood, ready to take his wife to Anthony's in central Leeds. Curly was about ready to head off to his local in Wortley with his mates for a Friday-night darts match. They were both enjoying an end-of-the-week drink, as was their habit, a pint of bitter for Curly and a double Glenmorangie for Corrigan.

A man walked into the Black Bull at about five forty-five p.m. Of medium height and build, with a short dark beard, he was wearing a navy blue overcoat and a woolly hat. None of the staff had ever seen him before. He bought a half pint of Guinness and a packet of pork scratchings and sat down at a table by the far side of the public bar. He didn't remove his overcoat, though it was warm in the pub. Nobody paid much attention to him. The Black Bull wasn't very busy at that time. Apart from one or two punters dropping by for a stiff one on their way home from work, it was too early for the two-for-the-price-of-one dinner crowd and the karaoke-night regulars.

Somebody noticed the man get up and go to the toilet shortly after he had arrived. He was gone for about five minutes. The theory was that he had spent that time checking out the lie of the land. At 6:05 p.m., he went back to the bar and bought another half pint of Guinness and a packet of salt-and-vinegar crisps, with a new ten-pound note, fresh from the cashpoint. Getting up his nerve, so the theory went. The barmaid who served him noticed that he had a foreign accent, but that wasn't so rare around those parts. His hands were also shaking slightly, and he spilled a little beer when he picked up his glass.

It was about 6:15 p.m. when he went to the toilet a second time, or so the woman at the next table, who was the only one who noticed, assumed.

According to a barmaid who was walking past the office on her way from the staff room to the main bar, the man negotiated the maze of corridors and bars in the back of the pub and approached Corrigan's office. Both Corrigan and Curly were sitting on the banquette

sipping their drinks. Hence, there was no one to pre-
vent the man from walking straight into the office.

Curly got immediately to his feet and moved forward to stop the man coming any closer. "Hey, you!"
he said. "Private office. Nobody's allowed back here."
Startled by his loud voice, the barmaid paused to see
what was happening and glanced into the room.

Before Curly could get any further, the man pulled
a gun from the pocket of his overcoat and shot him.
Curly fell to the floor, clutching his side. The man then
turned his attention to Corrigan, who was now cow-
ering on the banquette, pleading for his life, trying to
shield his body with his briefcase. The waitress was
terrified, but she said she was rooted to the spot; it was
like watching a road accident in slow motion. Corrigan
picked up a handful of money and held it out, telling
the man to take what he wanted and leave. The man
fired again, and Corrigan jerked up off the banquette,
holding his arm out, trying to make a dash for the door.
The man shot him again, this time in the stomach.
Corrigan fell to the floor and groaned, trying to hold in
his oozing insides. The man stood for a few moments
and surveyed the scene, perhaps enjoying the sight
of Corrigan suffering before he died, then he raised
the gun again and emptied it into the prostrate body.
Corrigan jerked with each shot, but not another sigh or

groan escaped his lips, only a final bubble of blood that slid down his chin and hung there.

By this time, the waitress had snapped out of her trance and made a run for the back exit, which proved no problem. Nobody tried to stop her. The shooter wasn't interested. It would appear that once he had completed the deed he set out to do, he sat down on the bench where Corrigan had been sitting and simply waited for the police to come.

It didn't take long. The manager had heard the shots and phoned 999. The customers had all dashed outside before anyone could stop them, and most of them had gone home by the time the police arrived, about ten minutes later.

When Annie and Winsome met Ken Blackstone there the following morning, the pub was still taped off as a crime scene, and the CSIs were still busy, but there was no sign of Corrigan. His body had been removed from the back-bar office, though his blood had spread in great stains across the floor like a map of the world, and the CSIs would have the time of their lives deciphering the spray patterns that had spurted over the nicotine-stained walls. Curly was in Leeds General Infirmary.

"It's Killingbeck's patch, of course," explained Blackstone, "but they know we have an interest, and of course, we know you have an interest. Besides, I'd say this counts as Homicide and Major Crimes, if anything does. Nice to see you again Annie, Winsome."

"Yeah," said Annie. "We must stop meeting like this. People will talk."

"Not Warren Corrigan, it seems."

"The other bloke?"

"Curly? A.k.a. Gareth Underwood. Last I heard, they had some hope for him."

They stood and surveyed the scene of carnage for a while, before the CSIs shooed them away, after which they took a table in the main bar.

"Drink?" Blackstone offered. "Manager says to help ourselves."

"It's a bit early for me," said Annie.

Winsome agreed.

"Suit yourself," said Blackstone. "The sun must be over the yardarm somewhere. I'll have a small brandy, Nick. Get one for yourself as well, then come and join us."

The man did as Blackstone said. When he came back, he sat down opposite Annie.

"This is Nick Gwillam," said Blackstone. "Trading Standards, Illegal Money Lending Unit."

"Where's your boss?" asked Gwillam.

"Tallinn," said Annie.

"Lucky for some."

"So what's the story?" Annie asked Blackstone.

"Not long ago, a young girl called Florica Belascu topped herself here in Leeds. She'd borrowed money from Corrigan, or one of his minions, and it had come time to collect. Naturally, she couldn't pay, and she had a small drug habit to support. Corrigan suggested she try going on the game, make a bit of money from curb crawlers. He wasn't into that line of business himself, he said, but he thought he could fix her up with some-one who'd take good care of her. She refused. Seemed she hadn't sunk so low that she'd sell herself on the street. A couple of days later, the minion and one of his underlings came back and raped her, gave her a bit of a slapping around and left. Reliable witnesses bear that out. Next morning, she was found hanging from an old wall fixture in the bathroom. CSIs had little doubt she did it herself, despite the rape and beating. Either way, the finger points at Corrigan."

"Who was the minion? Curly?"

"No. Curly's mostly for show. Like a guard dog. It was a scumbag called Ryan Currer. We've already got him banged up for an assault on another estate."

"Who found the body? How did you find out about all this? Surely the girl didn't tell you?"

"Florica was too scared to talk, but her girlfriend wasn't. She had no debts, and she hated what Corrigan was doing. Florica was a lezzie, but she wasn't out of the closet. They lived together but kept it low-key. Tatyana, the girlfriend, was the smarter of the two. She'd managed to keep herself hidden during their visits. They didn't know about her. She'd tried to help Florica with the money, but she didn't earn enough herself, even though her employment was legitimate. She'd witnessed a lot of what had happened, though not the rapes and beating. She'd been at work then, cleaning offices in the city center. We checked. She found Florica afterwards, which is how we know she was still alive when she went to bed that night. Florica didn't want the police involved, and she refused to go to hospital. Tatyana patched her up. In the morning, Tatyana found her hanging in the bathroom."

"She talked to me, Tatyana did," said Gwillam. "Me and Bill."

"Is this connected with Bill Quinn's death?"

"Don't think so. Can't be a hundred percent certain, but I don't think so. This is a family matter. A matter of honor, of vengeance. The man who walked in here last night and did us all a favor is called Vasile Belascu. He's the girl's father. He said he shot Corrigan in revenge for his daughter's death. They believe in vendettas where he comes from, apparently."

"How did he know what happened and where to find him?"

Gwillam winked. "A little bird told him."

"You're sailing a bit close to wind, aren't you?" Annie said. "You, too, Ken."

"We contacted the girl's father in Romania," Blackstone said. "We told him his daughter had committed suicide, and we wanted him to come and identify the body. We had no idea what he would do."

"So who told him about Corrigan?"

"Same person told us, I should think," said Gwillam. "We didn't tell her not to tell anyone else. But we might never know. She's gone back to Odessa now, it seems."

"Christ," said Annie. "This just gets better and better. I think I will have that drink, after all."

"You'd better tell me who it was," said Banks. "Who told you to seduce Bill Quinn and drug his wine?"

"It does not matter," said Larisa. "The man who instructed me was not the man who wanted it done."

"How do you know?"

"I heard him on the telephone."

"Who was it, anyway?"

"The club manager at the time. I do not remember his name. Marko or something."

"Where was this?"

"I was working in a nightclub. Not doing anything wrong, you know, just a waitress, coat-check girl, sometimes hanging out and talking with the customers. Downstairs was a big noisy bar and a dance floor with spinning balls of light and strobe shows, but upstairs was just a quiet bar where people could relax and have a drink."

"Where was this club? What was it called?"

"Here in Tallinn. On a small street off Vana-Posti. It had no—"

"With just a sign outside showing a man in a top hat and tails helping a lady into a coach?"

"That is right." She seemed surprised. "You have seen it? It is still there?"

"I've seen it," said Banks. It was the place just around the corner from St. Patrick's, where Rachel Hewitt had possibly been spotted going the wrong way by the Australian barman. "It may have changed quite a bit since your day. It's a sort of exclusive sex club now, or at least that was the impression I got. What sort of club was it back then?"

"Just a nightclub, for dancing, parties. Mostly young people. It was very good class. More expensive, perhaps, than Hollywood and Venus, more popular with Estonians than with tourists. As I said, it has no name. We just called it the Club."

"How does Bill Quinn come into this?"

"It was just fun, really. A joke. I was given his picture and the name of the hotel where he was staying, told to seduce him, to pretend we were making love. We never did. It just looks like it. But we never did have sex. He was asleep by then. It was all really very funny. Someone took photographs. I got two thousand kroon. That was that."

"You didn't know who ordered it?" Joanna Passero asked.

"No."

"You didn't know why you were doing it?"

"No."

"Weren't you just a little bit curious?"

"Two thousand kroon was a lot of money."

Joanna looked at Banks and shook her head as if to say a promising lead had turned to dust right in their grasp. Banks wasn't too sure.

"Were you taking drugs then?" he asked.

Larisa hung her head. "Yes. My life was a mess. I was only eighteen. I had run away from home. I drank too much. But soon after, maybe one, two months, I left, left Tallinn, went home to Tartu, became sober. When I was well again, I enrolled in the university. After three years I met Alexei, and here we are. I left that life behind me, Hr. Banks. Now I am only twenty-four, and I sometimes feel I have lived a whole lifetime. I am sorry if I cannot help you more. I have done nothing wrong."

Except drug a man and set him up for blackmail, Banks thought. But he said nothing. He couldn't see any point in trying to ruin a young woman's life over a misguided act committed six years ago, no matter what its consequences had been. "You said the man who actually instructed you and paid you was not the man who ordered it done, that you overheard a telephone conversation."

"Yes."

"Do you know who he was talking to?"

"No, but it was someone who was . . . I do not know how to say this. His boss? Someone who told him what to do?"

"Do you have any idea who that might be?"

"No. I only know the club manager who told me. Perhaps other people employ him."

"Why did you leave the club, Larisa?"

Larisa paused and picked at a fingernail, as if struggling to find an answer. "I had a friend there, a friend called Juliya. She was from Belarus. She was a very beautiful girl, very funny, clever, and very nice. She was good to me. She made me laugh when I felt bad. She showed me how to live in that world. We shared a flat together."

"Did something happen to her?" Banks asked.

"She ran away."

Banks and Joanna looked at one another. Banks also noticed Merike's eyes open a little wider. "Ran away?" Banks echoed.

"Yes. Just like that. One day she was there, then she was gone. All her clothes and belongings—not that she had much—gone. Not a word of good-bye, not a note to say where she had gone. Nothing."

"But she took all her things?"

"Yes."

"What did you think happened to her?"

"I think she went back to Belarus. She had a boyfriend who came to the club a lot. He was very rich and handsome. What do you call it, like a playboy? He always had good drugs, the best clothes, a fast car, and women were drawn to him. He was charming, but I think underneath he was dangerous. Young, rich and wild. For him there were no boundaries, no rules. There were many rumors about him. I do not know if they were all true. Juliya did not go into details. Wild orgies. Kinky sex. Every drug you can imagine. He had friends in St. Petersburg, people said, criminal friends. Russian Mafia."

"And this was Juliya's boyfriend?" Joanna said.

Larisa gave her a sad smile. "We were living in a very strange world back then. Very unreal. It all feels like a dream, sometimes like a nightmare. At first he excited her, but soon I think she became frightened of him."

"So you think Juliya left to get away from this boyfriend?" Banks asked.

"Perhaps. I just knew that was the end for me after she had gone. I was alone. I had to get away, too."

"Why? Because of Juliya?"

"Because he was turning towards me. I always thought I was safe. He liked blondes. But I realized soon that he was not so particular as I thought. When he turned his attention to me at the Club, asking me to go away with him for weekends in St. Petersburg or Helsinki, that was the end. I disappeared quickly, too."

"Just like Juliya?" Banks said.

"Yes. But I went first to Tartu," Larisa said. "I think Juliya went home to Minsk. I never heard from her again until I got married. She must have seen something in the newspaper because she sent a postcard with congratulations to Alexei's studio. It was from Athens."

"What about the man? Weren't you worried he'd try to find you?"

"No. A man like him has no attention span. Someone else would come along. A new toy. He would forget what I looked like in a few days."

"Do you remember his name?" asked Banks.

"Yes, of course. It is Joosep Rebane."

"That's an Estonian name," Merike said.

"Oh, yes," said Larisa. "He is Estonian. Not all the bad people here are Russian, you know."

"Do you know where he is now?" Banks asked.

"I have no idea. I turned my back on that life. He is not a man who seeks to have his picture in the newspapers, or his name, I think. Then he was just rich and spoiled, but now I suspect he is in the criminal underworld, trafficking drugs, girls, perhaps in St. Petersburg. Maybe even in Tallinn. But he keeps out of sight. And perhaps he behaves differently from when he was younger."

"Do you think he could have been the one who ordered the club manager to get you to set up Bill Quinn?"

"I do not know. Perhaps. But why?"

"I have a few ideas about that," said Banks. "When did all this happen?"

"It was six years ago. Summer."

"Around the time the English girl disappeared?"

"I think so. I do not remember. I really . . . I did not hear much news."

"You never linked the events in your mind? The English girl disappearing? You being asked to seduce an English detective?"

"I did not know he was a detective. This Quinn man. He did not talk about his work. And my brain did not make link."

"OK," said Banks. "Can you remember whether Juliya disappeared before or after you went to the hotel to meet Bill Quinn?"

"I think it was just before. Can we go back now?" Larisa asked. "I do not know any more. I cannot leave Kaida alone for too long."

"Of course," said Banks, standing up. "We'll walk with you. It's a lovely town."

Larisa smiled. "Yes. Is very small, but in summer many tourists come. There is much business. Much to do."

"Perhaps we can eat at your restaurant before we return to Tallinn?" Banks said.

Larisa looked alarmed.

"Don't worry," he went on. "I only say that because we're hungry. If I think of any more questions, I will be very discreet. We have no intention of spoiling the life you have made here."

Larisa gazed at him seriously for a while, as if trying to decide whether he was telling the truth, then she said, "Yes. Yes, that will be nice. I will cook for you myself."

Annie and Winsome managed to fit in a quick sandwich at Pret with Blackstone and Gwillam before they got a call from Leeds General Infirmary saying that Gareth Underwood wanted to talk to them. It took a moment for the penny to drop: Gareth Underwood was Curly.

There was a police guard on the private room in which Curly was being kept for observation after a bullet had been removed from his left side the previous evening. As far as the doctor was concerned, it was nothing but a flesh wound, having missed all the important organs, though it had done some minor tissue damage, and one always had to keep an eye open for infection.

Curly was lying propped up on his pillows, connected to various machines that displayed his heart rate, blood pressure, oxygen levels and other bodily functions comprehensible only to doctors and nurses. Annie swallowed as she walked into the room, her mouth dry. It brought back too many memories, most of them bad. Curly was also hooked up to an MP3 player, with his eyes closed. He had a large glass of water with a bent straw on his bedside table.

Neither Curly's doctor nor Blackstone wanted to crowd the room, so only Annie and Ken Blackstone went in, leaving Gwillam and Winsome outside. Gwillam seemed put out by his exclusion, perhaps because he felt it was because he wasn't a real copper, being Trading Standards, but Winsome took it in her stride.

Curly seemed to sense someone in the room. He opened his eyes and took out the earbuds. "Woz is a goner, isn't he?" he said as they sat beside the bed in the hospital chairs.

"Woz?" said Blackstone.

"Mr. Corrigan. Warren. It's what I called him. Woz."

"Yes, Curly, he's a goner."

"Would you mind calling me Gareth? I always hated Curly."

"What do you want, Gareth? We're busy."

"It's that copper who came to see Woz on Monday I want to talk to. Where is he?"

"DCI Banks?" said Annie.

"That's his name."

"I'm afraid he's out of the country," said Annie. "I'm his partner. You can talk to me." She checked with Blackstone, who nodded. Her dry mouth had turned into a tightening sensation in her chest when she entered the hospital room, and she wondered whether it meant the onset of another panic attack. They happened sometimes when she skirted too close to her recent experiences. Careful, slow breathing soon brought it under control. This was nothing like what happened to her, she told herself. Curly, or Gareth, seemed fine. He'd be back out in a day or two, right as rain, not spending months in and out of places like this, having operations, fearing for his legs. But she was past that now, she told herself. It was over; she was fine. And Gareth might well be spending the next few months and more in a place even less pleasant than a hospital room.

"First off," said Gareth, "before I tell you anything, I want to do a deal."

"What sort of deal?" Blackstone asked.

"I want immunity. I know all about Woz's business. I even know where he keeps his books. I can name names. I know a lot, and I'm willing to tell it all, but I don't want to go to jail. And I want protection. A new identity."

"I don't know about all that, Gareth," said Blackstone. "It's not up to me. We can put in a word for you."

"You'll have to do better than that."

"Gareth," said Blackstone, "you haven't been charged with anything yet. You're not even under arrest. No doubt you have done many bad things, but they're not our concern at the moment. Corrigan's shooting is."

"It's not as if you don't know who did it, and why."

"Tip of the iceberg, Curly, tip of the iceberg."

"Gareth. And some of these bad things you think I've done might just become your concern if I start talking." He rested back on the pillow and grimaced with pain. "Bloody painkillers they give you around here are useless."

Annie could certainly relate to that. There never seemed enough painkillers available when you were really in pain.

"Why don't you just tell us, Gareth?" Blackstone pressed on. "You know it can only count in your favor. Otherwise, you'll be spending countless hours in detention, in smelly interview rooms. No painkillers there."

"You can't fool me, Mr. Blackstone. I know my rights, and medical attention is one of them. But I'll admit you've got a point. See, the thing is, I want to go straight. I've had enough of this."

"Of what?"

"This life. Woz, and what he was doing. Robbing the poor to pay the rich. It's disgusting. He was scum. I've got a conscience, you know."

"A bit late for that, isn't it?"

"It's never too late to repent."

"Don't go all religious on us, Gareth."

"Don't worry, I won't. I just think that every man should be given a second chance, that's all. I want to go straight. I want to go back to my old line of work."

"What was that?"

"Club bouncer."

"That's a step up in the world."

"At least it's honest work."

"That's debatable." Blackstone leaned forward. "Gareth, I appreciate your change of heart, I really do. But I'll appreciate it a lot more if you actually tell us something useful."

"What did you want to talk to DCI Banks about?" Annie added.

Curly paused for a moment. The mental turmoil was clear for even Annie to see, as he debated whether to open up or not. "I want a lawyer first," he said. "I'll make a deal, but I need some guarantees. On paper."

"So what do you think of it all?" Joanna asked Banks that evening. They were dining alone this time, and as it had been a long day, and the weather had turned a little chilly, they had decided to eat at the hotel but changed their minds when they heard the noise from the karaoke bar. Instead, they skipped over to the steakhouse at the bottom of Viru, near the gate, away from most of the parties and noisy groups. They found that wearing jackets or sweaters, and with the help of the well-placed heaters, they were fine outside, and plenty of others seemed to agree. The steaks were a bit more pricey than Clazz's but excellent quality.

"I liked her," Banks said.

"I expect most men would agree with you."

"Hey, now, wait a minute before you start getting all women's-lib on me. I admire what she's done. She was on a downward slope—drugs, sex clubs, bad boys, the lot—and she pulled herself up by the boot strings. She's got guts, and a fair dollop of common sense. Not a bad-looking broad, either."

Joanna nudged him playfully. "Bastard," she said.

Banks drank some more wine. "You don't believe her story?"

"Most of it," Joanna said. "I'm inclined to think she abridged it, and censored it a little here and there for general consumption."

"Oh, you're such cynics in Professional Standards. Don't you believe anybody?"

"I've always found it's a good starting point."

"So what are you going to put in your report?"

"Which one?"

"What do you mean?"

"The one on Bill Quinn, or the one on you?"

"If you're planning a report on me, I can guarantee you'll have met with a mysterious accident before you get to the airport."

Joanna laughed. "Oh, you're not as bad as you like to make out. There'd be no point doing a report on you. Nothing to put in it. Boring."

"I don't know what's worse," said Banks, "being a fit subject for you or not."

"Oh, take my word for it, not is best. As for Bill Quinn . . . I don't know. He's dead. I think that whatever I have to say, I'll do my best to make sure it remains internal, depending on how far he went. Unless anyone else, anyone still alive, that is, turns out to be involved. There's still the possibility that someone was manipulating him, though, that he was a rotten apple."

"Do you think that's the case?"

"I don't know. Tell me what you think. Instruct me, oh great homicide cop."

Banks finished his glass and poured another. Joanna held her glass out, too. He emptied the bottle. They were both a little tipsy, partly with the success of the day and partly with the wine. "Larisa worked at that club I saw just around the corner from St. Patrick's. A waiter in the pub said he thought he saw Rachel turn the wrong way when she went out after her friends, but later he said he wasn't certain."

"She didn't even know where her friends were going."

"Let's assume she went the wrong way. The others turned right. Rachel turned left."

"OK. I'm with you so far. But after that?"

"After that, it gets a bit speculative, of course, but I think I'm assuming that Juliya's boyfriend was involved somehow, by the sound of him. Joosep. Perhaps Rachel wandered into the club, intrigued by the sign, the lack of a name, whatever, and she bumped into him. He liked blondes, remember."

"He liked anything in a skirt, according to Larisa."

"But blondes especially. Rachel was a very pale blonde. And very lovely. I think he turned on his charm, or he did the caveman routine, one or the other, and he got her away from there, back to his flat, or wherever. Maybe she felt she was in a new exciting city, so she should have an adventure. Everyone seemed to think she was an impulsive and spontaneous sort of girl. I don't know the details. But I think she soon realized what a big mistake she'd made, and perhaps she struggled. He didn't like to let her go. He liked his own way. I think he had it, and then he got rid of her."

"How? Where?"

"I don't know the answers to that yet."

"How does DI Quinn come into it?"

"I think Bill Quinn and Toomas Rätsepp came to the club asking questions. That's the link we've been missing. That's what Rätsepp lied to us about. They ruffled too many feathers somehow, got too close, and Joosep Rebane had to think what to do pretty fast. I think he bribed Rätsepp, but he couldn't do that with Bill Quinn. He was a foreign cop. Another kettle of fish entirely. So he made a few inquiries. No doubt friend Rätsepp would have helped, for a fee, and found out that Bill Quinn was a happy family man with a wife and two kids he adored. But Bill Quinn was also human, and you've seen Larisa. So Rebane got the club manager to pick the prettiest girl in the club to set a honey trap for him. The rest is history. They showed him the photos, told them what they wanted of him, and that was that. He didn't like it, but what could he do? When Quinn's wife died, word got back that the hold was broken, and perhaps that Quinn had been haunted by guilt at not being able to do anything all those years. We know Joosep Rebane likely has connections with a rough crowd, gangsters, whether in St. Petersburg or Tallinn, Russian or Estonian, and he sent one of them over to deal with Bill Quinn and Mihkel Lepikson, who was going to help Quinn get his story out without incriminating himself."

"But how did this Joosep Rebane come to have so much power over a senior police investigator?"

"That I don't know," said Banks. "I don't know how the system works here, but I can guess there's just as much corruption as there is back home. Maybe you should get a job here?"

"No, thanks. Do you think the prosecutor, Ursula Mardna, was involved?"

"Probably not. I don't think she would have told us about the young cop Bill Quinn went out investigating with if she was involved. Aivar Kukk. I'd like to talk to him. There must be something there. Rätsepp neglected to tell us about that. But there are obviously a lot of connections we don't get yet."

"And what about Mihkel Lepikson?"

"Mihkel was the journalist on the original story, and he became friendly with Quinn. He's an investigative reporter and contributes to a column on crime in *Eesti Telegraaf* called 'Pimeduse varjus.' 'Watching the Dark,' or something along those lines. Joosep Rebane would have known this. He would also have kept an eye on him. Mihkel didn't know anything, not at the time. Quinn didn't confide in him about the photos and the blackmail. He didn't tell anyone. Joosep Rebane nipped the investigation in the bud when it had only got as far as Rätsepp and Bill Quinn. But when Rebane found out Lepikson was also in England, he got nervous and commanded a double act. No point only killing Bill Quinn, if Mihkel Lepikson was going to blast the true story on the front page of *Eesti Telegraaf.*"

"And the bonded-labor scheme?"

"It wouldn't surprise me if Joosep Rebane doesn't have his finger in that little pie, too. I'll bet you he knows Corrigan and Flinders, at any rate. Drugs, people. It's all the same to some, as long as the profits are good. What do you think?"

"There's a lot of holes," said Joanna. "Like how Joosep Rebane knew Mihkel Lepikson was in Yorkshire and in contact with Bill Quinn. But it's not bad, as theories go. From my point of view, Bill Quinn obstructed the full investigation of a disappearance, perhaps a murder, for six years. I'd hardly say he comes out of it smelling of roses, no matter what his reasons. God knows what else he did, too."

"True," said Banks. "But you can't crucify a man who's already dead."

"As I said before," said Joanna. "I'm not out to crucify anyone. It'll be an internal report, I hope, but there will be a report." She paused and swirled some wine in her glass. "There's still one big question we haven't answered yet," she said.

"I know," said Banks.

"What happened to Rachel Hewitt?"

"I wish I knew. I wish I could think of a way to find out. I'm pretty sure she's dead, but . . . ?"

"Erik might be able to help."

"How? We still need a starting point."

"The nightclub," Joanna said. "You seem to know a bit about it."

"I've been there," said Banks.

"You've *what?*"

"I went there after dinner the second night we were here. I was wandering around, trying to follow what I imagined might have been Rachel's footsteps on the night she disappeared, and I just stumbled across it. Rachel might have done the same, too."

"You didn't tell me you'd actually been *inside*."

"You're starting to sound like my ex-wife. Do I have to tell you every time I go to a sex club?"

Joanna flushed, then saw Banks was teasing her, and smiled. "What did you find out?"

"Nothing. That's why I didn't tell you. There was nothing to tell. I talked to the manager, Larry something-or-other, and a buxom waitress from Wigan. That's it. Oh, and I had kinky sex with a lady-boy from Bangkok, but that was nothing to write home about. The place has changed ownership God knows how many times in the last six years. There's no connection left to the old days, or none that I could find."

"But there *is* a connection to Larisa and probably to Joosep Rebane."

"And possibly to Rachel," Banks said. "I'm sure Erik will be only too happy to do a bit more digging, maybe even find out what happened to Aivar Kukk, if we ask him nicely."

It took close to two hours, but Blackstone and Annie managed to rustle up a lawyer from the CPS and a duty solicitor, who thrashed out a deal for Curly between them. There was no way he was getting a new identity, but they found they could keep him out of jail if he told everything he knew and if he was guilty of no major indictable offense. Curly thought about this for a while, no doubt going over in his mind exactly what he was guilty of, and agreed. When it came to it, he had probably done no more than intimidate a few people and administer a minor beating or two. When everything was signed, the lawyers took a backseat, and Blackstone and Annie pulled their chairs close to the bed. Annie had phoned Stefan and asked him to tell Krystyna she would be late, and she was worried because he had got no answer. She tried to tell herself that Krystyna had just gone to the shop for some food or cigarettes, but it gnawed away at her even as she listened to Curly's story.

"So give," said Blackstone.

"I saw him," he said.

"Saw who?" asked Annie.

"The bloke who killed Bill Quinn and that foreign reporter."

"You know about Mihkel Lepikson?"

"Course. Woz knew he was up at Garskill Farm. Flinders had a bloke on the inside keeping an eye out for things like that. They've tried it before. The reporter was just too good to be true. Always asking questions. Making friends with the others. Always off to the telephone box. That's what they said. Flinders came down for a chat with Woz, who gets on the blower to Rebane. Flinders is another cunt, by the way. I can tell you things about him would make your hair curl."

"Hang on a minute," said Annie. "Slow down. Are you telling me that Warren Corrigan gave the order for the deaths of Bill Quinn and Mihkel Lepikson?"

"Not him, no. Not directly. He was what you might call a station on the way, but it went through him, if you see what I mean. He supplied the crossbow, I can tell you that. Had me go and get it, actually. But he was doing it on orders."

"Whose orders?"

"Bloke called Joosep Rebane, or something like that. Not sure how you pronounce it or spell it. Russian or something."

Annie made a note of the name, though she was also far from sure about the spelling. "And who's this Joosep Rebane when he's at home?"

"The boss. Kingpin. He says jump, Woz asks how high. Like I said, he's Russian Mafia or something, but he's behind all these migrant-labor schemes, the phony agencies, bonding them with debt, all that stuff. It's also a front for drugs. That was going to be the next big thing. Woz was gearing up for it. Flinders and Woz both worked for Rebane, when it came right down to it. They didn't see him very often—he liked to keep a low profile and was paranoid about secrecy and security—but I can tell you, they were shit scared of him. He had a reputation as a bit of a wild man, which I think he liked to cultivate. You know, like in those Mafia movies. Horse's head under the bedclothes. Kind of bloke who'll be asking about your dear old mother one moment and laying into you with an axe the next. I must say, he gave me the willies."

"Did you meet him?" Annie asked.

"Only twice. At the pub. Back way, of course. Car waiting, dark windows."

"Can you describe him?"

"Youngish bloke, about thirty, maybe a bit over. Tall, good-looking. I suppose the girls would find him attractive, if you know what I mean. Wears nice expensive suits, Armani, Hugo Boss, that sort of thing, hair always cut perfectly. Dark brown. Brown eyes. More like black. Charming on the surface, but there was something in his eyes that told you you wouldn't want to upset him."

Annie took out the sketch of the man Krystyna had described, hoping to God that nothing had happened to her. "Recognize him?" she asked.

"He's the one Woz gave the crossbow to. He's done a couple of jobs for him before."

"What's his name?"

"Robert Tamm."

"Nationality?"

"I don't know. He had one of those sort of Russian accents, too, but it might have been Bulgarian or Slovakian for all I know. I can't tell one of those buggers from another."

"Do you know where he lives?"

"Aye. Glasgow. He came down on the train and picked up a rental car. But he's not Scottish. No way. I could spot a Jock accent a mile off."

"Arnold Briggs," said Annie. "OK, let's get back to Mr. Big. You say you met this Joosep Rebane on two occasions. When was the most recent?"

"About six months ago."

"Do you know what the meeting was about?"

"No. Woz sent me out to the main bar."

"But he was hardly a frequent visitor."

"No. I should imagine this was one of the far-flung outposts of his empire. He communicated by phone and through the agents mostly. Untraceable mobiles, of course."

"So what were these recent developments you want to tell us about, whatever resulted in death warrants for Bill Quinn and Mihkel Lepikson? I assume this Robert Tamm worked for Joosep Rebane?"

"That's right, far as I could tell. Enforcer. Hit man. What have you. Did his dirty work."

"So you acquired the crossbow that Warren Corrigan gave Robert Tamm, on the orders of this Joosep Rebane, to kill Quinn? And the same man tortured and drowned Lepikson?"

Curly swallowed. "Yes. But it sounds bad if you put it like that. I didn't know what he was going to use the crossbow for, did I?"

"A spot of grouse hunting, perhaps?" said Blackstone.

Curly looked toward the solicitors again, who both seemed fascinated by the discussion. "See what I mean about me wanting some guarantees here?"

"You've got all the guarantees you're getting," said Annie. "Go on."

Curly sighed. "See, Joosep Rebane always let on that he had a cop in his pocket, had something on him. Bill Quinn. But when Bill Quinn's wife died, Rebane started to get worried. Woz got more phone calls from him. Rebane asked him to keep an eye on Quinn, then . . . well, you know what happened."

"Did you know why he was worried?" Annie asked.

"Not at the time, no. We didn't know what Rebane had on DI Quinn."

"And now?"

"Well, I've only really been able to work it out while I've been in here, but remember I mentioned that things started to go pear-shaped around the time Bill Quinn's wife died?"

"Yes."

"Well, it must have meant that Rebane didn't have anything on him anymore. Stands to reason. So I reckon it was probably a woman. That was the only thing that made sense, really. Why Rebane would get worried and all. If Quinn didn't have a wife, then he didn't have to worry about Rebane telling her he'd been playing away from home, did he? And he obviously had videos or photos or some sort of proof. Again, it stands to reason."

"You're not as thick as you look, are you, Curly?" said Annie.

"Gareth. And no, I'm not."

"Are you telling me that Bill Quinn was bent?" said Blackstone. "Alan mentioned the possibility, but I . . ." He shook his head.

"I'm telling you that I think Quinn was being black-mailed by this Joosep Rebane to go easy on Woz," said Curly. "I'm not saying Quinn liked it, but he had no choice. He was in a position to warn Woz about raids, and anything else that might act against his interests. But something put the heebie-jeebies up them all around the time Quinn's wife died. Not immediately, like, but over a couple of weeks. If you think about it, and if Quinn was being blackmailed, then he couldn't just suddenly go to his boss and say, 'Guess what, guv, I've been passing information on to Woz Corrigan and doing my best to keep him out of jail this past while.' Could he? Anyway, when they found out that this reporter had infiltrated the migrant group, and that Quinn knew him, it was double trouble. They figured Quinn had put the reporter onto the operation in the first place, to give him a good story like, but that the real story was going to be what Joosep had been up to. Apparently Quinn and the reporter had been bud-dies for years. Quinn was looking for a back door to spill the beans without getting any comeback, and the reporter was it. The way Woz explained it to me was that if Quinn could find a way to use the reporter to get his story out, then Rebane and Woz and Rod Flinders wouldn't be safe anymore. So they both had to go."

Annie rubbed her forehead and stood up. "What a tangled web we weave," she said. Her thoughts returned immediately to Krystyna. She wanted to get back to Harkside as soon as she could, but there was one more stop to make on the way, something Banks had asked her to do.

As Winsome drove, Annie phoned home again but still got no answer. She phoned Stefan and managed to get through to him at the lab, but he had heard nothing from Krystyna. Annie cursed and ended the call.

"What is it?" Winsome asked.

"Krystyna. She's gone."

"I shouldn't worry too much. She's probably just gone for a walk or a drink."

"She's been gone for hours. She's got no money."

"We'll be home soon. Sure you want to make the stop?"

"We're almost there now. Might as well."

Pauline Boyars was already well into a bottle of vodka, and the place was still a tip.

"It's just a little thing," Annie said without even bothering to sit down, "but we were wondering if you remember a nightclub in Tallinn that didn't have a name. All it had was a sign with a man in top hat and tails helping a woman into a coach."

"I don't think we ever went to such a place," said Pauline, "but it does sound awfully familiar. Just give me a minute, will you?"

She brought a tin down from one of the bookshelves and scattered its contents on the table. It was full of all kinds of rubbish, a key chain with a plastic Eiffel Tower on one end, an old cigarette lighter, a ticket for an exhibition at the Prado, a postcard from Rhodes. And there, amid the detritus of Pauline's travels and memories, was a small laminated card that bore an image of a man in top hat and tails helping—or pushing?—a woman into a carriage.

"I don't think we ever went there," said Pauline. "Though I can't be sure. I think someone was handing these out in one of the other clubs."

Annie thanked her and they left, grateful as before to get out of the cloying atmosphere.

"What was all that about?" Winsome asked.

"Something Alan asked about. Apparently this club has come up in connection with Rachel's disappearance, and he wanted to know if any of the others knew about it."

"Well, he's got his answer, hasn't he?"

"Yes," said Annie. "I'll phone him when I get home."

When they arrived at Annie's cottage, Winsome got out of the car and went up to the door with her, and they both went inside. Everything looked normal, but there was no sign of Krystyna. Annie checked upstairs and Winsome checked the kitchen.

"You'd better see this," she said when Annie came down.

Annie went into the kitchen and saw the cocoa tin where she kept her petty cash. It was open, and there was nothing but a brief note in Polish inside.

"How much was in there?" Winsome asked.

"About thirty quid."

"She won't get far on that."

There was also a note in Polish stuck to the fridge with a magnet shaped like a buttercup. Winsome put the kettle on and Annie returned to the living room, flopped on the sofa and started to cry.

11

On Sunday morning around eleven, Banks took the lift down to the Metropol lobby and went out to meet Erik and Joanna for coffee in Viru Keskus. Last night he had spoken for a long time with Annie on the phone. She had been worried and upset by the disappearance of a young Polish girl who had been staying at Garskill Farm with the migrant workers. She had run away on the day Mihkel Lepikson had been killed, and Annie was worried that someone might think she knew too much and try to harm her. He had reassured her as best he could, but he could tell it hadn't done much good. Annie had also told him about Curly's lengthy, and quite perceptive, deposition, and that Rachel's friend Pauline remembered the club with no name, that she even had a card bearing its sign. Rachel, too, might have been given such a card, Banks thought, and if the place looked familiar to her, that might well have tempted her to go inside. Perhaps she had thought it was where her friends had gone after St. Patrick's. Bit by bit, he felt, he was getting closer to the truth of what happened.

Annie had also come up with some more names Banks could try on Erik, including the name of the killer, Robert Tamm. Surely it could only be a matter of time now? Perhaps most importantly, Joosep Rebane's name had come up in her inquiries into Corrigan's business, as well as in Banks's inquiries about the nightclub. Larisa had named him as Juliya's boyfriend. Now they had a direct link between Rebane, Corrigan, Flinders and the whole migrant racket. But he still had to find out if, or where, Rachel fit in.

He made his way inside and up the escalators. The shops were open, and the shopping center was busy, even though it was Sunday. After a few wrong turns, he finally found the café in the large bookshop, where Erik had arranged for them all to meet. *Estonians must be great readers,* Banks thought, *with so many huge bookshops in the capital.*

Erik was sitting at a table alone drinking Coke from a bottle and reading a newspaper. Banks went and bought himself a coffee and joined him. People bustled all around them, carrying bags, looking for tables, heading to the shops.

"Where's your charming colleague?" Erik asked.

Banks checked his watch. "Shopping," he said. "She'll be here soon. I want to thank you once again for that information you got for us the other day."

"It helped?"

"A lot."

"I spoke briefly with Merike last night, and she said you seemed happy with your talk with Larisa."

"Interesting woman," Banks said. "And she was able to give us— Ah, the wanderer returns."

Joanna bent down and set her bags and packages on the ground around the third chair, like presents under the Christmas tree. Banks noticed designer names he didn't recognize: Marc Aurel, Ivo Nikkolo. There would be no carry-on-only going back for Joanna, Banks could see. She might have to buy a new suitcase. Ever the gentleman, Erik offered to go and get her something to drink, but she insisted on going herself. They waited politely until she returned with a bottle of fruit juice.

"We've got a few more names for you to check out, if you will," said Banks.

"It's getting to be like a hall of mirrors," said Joanna. "Every time we get one name, it leads to another, and so on."

"It's always like that when you're getting close," said Banks. "The storm before the calm."

"Don't you mean—"

"No. It always gets more and more confusing until it settles down, when you know. The storm before the calm."

"A good story can be like that, too," Erik said. "Mihkel knew that. He always talked of so many balls in the air. Like a juggler. Give me the names. I will try tomorrow. I feel like I am working for the British police."

Banks laughed. "We'd snap you up like a shot. First of all," he said, "I'm curious about a bloke called Robert Tamm. He lives near Glasgow, but my source thinks he's Eastern European, perhaps Estonian."

"It could be an Estonian name," said Erik.

Joanna looked puzzled, and Banks realized that he hadn't had a chance to talk to her since Annie's phone call. She had been in her room sleeping, he assumed, when Banks took the call, and he hadn't seen her so far that morning. This time, it was simply circumstances; he wasn't deliberately keeping her out of the loop. He explained to her briefly what he had learned, including that Joosep Rebane claimed to have DI Bill Quinn in his pocket.

"So we're pretty sure this Robert Tamm is the killer?" she said when he'd finished and she had scribbled some notes.

"So it would appear."

"That's the case over, then, isn't it? I mean, I know we have to get the Glasgow police to go—"

"Hang on," said Banks. "Wait a minute. Are you going to abandon Rachel Hewitt, just like that? Like everyone else?"

"That's not fair. She's not our case."

"Dismissing her isn't fair, either. She deserves more than that. She became our case. You said you were with me on that."

"Yes, but only if it helped lead us to Quinn's killer. It has done, so we're finished now."

"You can do what you want, but I'm not leaving Tallinn until I find out what happened to Rachel."

"Don't be so melodramatic."

"I'm not being melodramatic. We owe her. You know what your problem is? You lack—"

"If you will excuse me for interrupting, children," Erik said, holding up his hand. "Perhaps you two can save the argument for later? I do have to go home soon. My mother-in-law is coming for dinner."

"Sorry," said Banks, giving Joanna a dirty look, which she returned with bells on. "Robert Tamm, yes. Perhaps you can find out if he has any Estonian under-world connections. Also, there's a nightclub on an alley off Vana-Posti. It doesn't have a name, but there's a sign of—"

"A gentleman helping the lady into a coach?"

"That's right. You know it?"

"I've passed by. I just assumed it was some sort of exclusive sex club."

"It is now. Well, not that exclusive. They let me in. And there's a waitress from Wigan."

"Then what do you need to know?"

"Its history," said Banks. "Specifically what sort of place it was and who owned it, or ran it, six years ago, when Rachel disappeared."

Erik made a note. "OK. Now you mentioned another name."

"Joosep Rebane," said Banks. "We think he's the one who hired Tamm to kill Mihkel and Bill Quinn. He said he had Quinn in his pocket but started to get nervous as soon as Quinn's wife died." Banks paused and waited for Erik to catch up, but he put down his pen. "Well, aren't you going to write it down?" Banks went on. "Joosep Rebane. I think I've got it right."

"Oh, you have got it right, my friend," said Erik. "I don't even need to go to my files for that one. Where do you want me to begin?"

Annie had slept badly on Saturday night. She had tried to phone Stefan to see if she could beg him to come over and translate the note for her—or she would even drive out to his place—but all she got was his answering machine. She even got hold of Jan from Traffic, but he explained politely that whereas he could manage a few phrases in Polish, he certainly couldn't read and translate the language. Annie realized when she got up that she had been lying awake waiting most of the night, waiting for a knock on the door, for a phone call that she wouldn't be able to understand. She tried Stefan's number again. Still no reply. *Bastard,* she thought. He must have picked up some slut or other and was still at her place for a morning shag. She wished it wasn't a Sunday, then she might be able to gather a posse, get an official search or something going. On the other hand, Krystyna wasn't a criminal; she was a victim. Annie didn't want to frighten her, make her feel she was being hunted and chased. God only knew what she would do then. She might also be a witness, able to help against Flinders and Robert Tamm, when the Glasgow police found him. But mostly she was a victim. She had no papers, no passport, but she was a citizen of the EU. Annie could report her missing, she supposed, but Krystyna was over eighteen, and they wouldn't exactly pull out all the stops so quickly, unless perhaps she stressed that the girl might be in danger because of something she knew. That was what worried Annie most, that Krystyna didn't realize the danger she was in, that she might go back to these people. The inactivity was driving her crazy. She needed to do something.

Krystyna hadn't known where her colleagues were being taken after leaving Garskill Farm on Wednesday morning, but Annie remembered that she had spoken of another Polish girl, Ewa, who had been her friend at the farm and, Annie assumed, had also worked with her at the yeast factory. It didn't prove very difficult to locate Varley's Yeast Products in the phone directory, and given the hours that Flinders's agency demanded of its workers, it also seemed likely the place would be operating seven days a week.

Before she left, Annie tried Stefan one more time. Nothing. She left a message for him to call her as soon as possible on her mobile and took Krystyna's note with her in case she got a chance to meet up with Stefan before going home again.

It wasn't a long drive to the northern edge of Eastvale. The shops soon gave way to housing estates, several leafy enclaves of the wealthy and, finally, after a stretch of wasteland, the old industrial estate where the yeast factory was located. The weather had turned wet, and wind lashed the rain against her car windows. Those few brave souls who had ventured outdoors, most likely on their way to or from church, struggled with umbrellas, many of which had blown inside out.

Annie arrived at the factory gates shortly after eleven in the morning, and she was pleased to find them open. There was a little gatehouse where visitors were required to report and sign in. Annie wound her window down and flashed her warrant card at the man on duty. He barely glanced up from his newspaper before waving her through. As soon as she had opened her window, she could smell the yeast, and she wondered what it must be like to work there day in, day out. It must have permeated everything. How could you even get the smell off your skin or your clothes when you got home? Even if you had a decent bathtub or a shower, which the workers at Garskill Farm didn't.

There were several buildings scattered about the compound, and the yard was filled mostly with pallets, some of them loaded down with containers, others waiting, all getting wet. She found a place to park outside what appeared to be the offices, which must have been working on a skeleton staff on a Sunday. She noticed a couple of people standing outside one of the other buildings having a smoke and went over to introduce herself. One of them told her she needed to talk to one of the white hats. She wouldn't find one inside the building they were closest to, he added, as that was where the yeast grew in vats. The white hats would most likely be over in the main building, where the yeast was processed.

Annie entered through a door at the far end and soon found herself in an open area, where several giant rollers, like the front wheels of bulldozers, turned slowly as the yeast coated them, dried and was shaved off by a fixed razor-sharp blade into large boxes, and then no doubt fed into the other machines. The smell was even stronger inside.

She found a white hat, which happened to be a trilby. He was also wearing a white coat and carrying a clipboard. He seemed to be standing around doing nothing, so she went over and showed her identification.

"Can I have word somewhere?" she asked over the noise of the factory.

He jerked his head in the direction of a row of small offices, and when he closed the door behind him, the volume level dropped considerably. It was a shabby office, furnished only with a cheap desk, chair and gunmetal filing cabinet. There was an ashtray on the desk with several cigarette stubs in it. The room felt uncomfortably small to Annie with the two of them in there. "Len," as he was called, was a red-faced, paunchy man in his fifties who, to Annie's eye, was fast heading for a coronary, if he hadn't had one already. He rested one buttock on the desk, which creaked in complaint. Annie remained standing by the door.

"I've come about some migrant laborers you employed here recently."

The man's eyes narrowed. "They come and go. That's nothing to do with me."

"Are they here now?"

"Not anymore. They wouldn't be in here, anyway. Most of them usually work over in the extracting department."

"In particular, I'm trying to find a Polish girl. I think her name is Ewa. She's friends with another Polish girl who worked here until a week ago last Wednesday."

"I don't know anything," Len said. "Like I said, they come and go. I don't know their names. As long as they do their jobs, I don't give a fuck what they're called. You'll have to try Human Resources, and they don't work on a Sunday. It's not my department."

"Said Werner von Braun."

"What?"

"Never mind. Thanks for your help." Annie left the office, muttering "arsehole" under her breath. She stood for a moment in the doorway watching the people work. Most seemed absorbed in their tasks, such as they were, and they didn't return her gaze. Krystyna certainly wasn't there. Not that Annie had expected her to be.

Before leaving the factory altogether, she thought she might as well drop by the extraction department and see if she could find out any more there. As there was only one large building left, she assumed that was it; dashed across the yard, avoiding puddles as best she could; and headed inside.

The factory floor was quiet, no thrum of machines or banging of gears and metal drums. There was one man, sans white hat, walking around the equipment, checking things and jotting notes on his clipboard. Annie coughed loudly enough that he could hear her, and he turned, surprised to see her there.

"Yes?" he said.

"Police." Annie came forward and showed him her warrant card.

He put his clipboard down. "What can I do for you?" He was younger than Len, and a lot more trim, as if he played football in a local league on Saturdays maybe.

"I'm looking for someone who works here, or used to work here," Annie said. "Len over in the other building said I'd have a better chance here."

The man, who introduced himself as Dennis, laughed. "Len's very old-school. There's nothing much he doesn't know about yeast."

"How can you stand the smell?" Annie asked.

Dennis shrugged. "You get used to it, like anything else."

"Hmm. Anyway, I understand you employ a number of migrant laborers around here?"

"That's right, though I don't actually do the employing. That would be the personnel officer, or Human Resources as they call it now. I believe we have a contract with Rod's Staff Ltd., who supply most of the workers."

"Do you know anything about them?"

"What do you mean?"

"The conditions they live in, the wages they're paid, that sort of thing."

"No. I just make sure they do their jobs, and they're treated well enough on the shop floor, get their tea breaks and all. There's quite a turnover. As you can imagine, nobody wants to do this sort of work for very long."

Annie took in the row of industrial washing machines and the racks of hanging canvas sheets, about twenty of them in a row, stretching from one side of the room to the other. "What kind of work would that be?"

"As you can see, we're not in operation normally today. We have to do maintenance and equipment checks once in a while. That's me. As a rule, we make the yeast extract here. Basically, you force the yeast through those canvas sheets and collect what gets through to the far end. It's concentrated and thick by then, sort of like Marmite."

500 · PETER ROBINSON

Annie felt her stomach churn. She hated Marmite, more because of its consistency than its taste. "What do you do with the used canvas?" she asked.

"That's what the big washing machines are for. You flip them in there and wash them. It's a dirty job because by then they're covered in slime. It's sort of the consistency of—"

"I can guess, thanks," said Annie. "You don't have to spell it out."

"They usually wear neck-to-toe leather aprons."

"I'll bet they do. Do you remember a young Polish girl, very thin, short dark hair, pretty if she had a chance? She could hardly lift one of those canvases."

"She sounds familiar, but as I said, they come and go. A lot of them are thin and seem none too healthy."

"Haven't you ever wondered why?"

"Not really my business. I assumed it was because of where they come from. Poor national diet."

"As opposed to the north of England, where we all eat so well?"

"No need to be sarcastic. I'm only saying."

"Sorry." Annie scratched her head, thinking a visit from Trading Standards might be in order. Or Immigration. "Sorry. It's just a bit frustrating, that's all."

"There was a girl hanging around the gates this morning about the time the shift started. She sort of fits your description. She might have worked here at some time."

"Did anyone talk to her?"

"I don't think so. We get quite a few Eastern European girls here. Poles, Ukrainians, Lithuanians, Estonians and Latvians."

"That'll be Rod's Staff connections."

"I suppose so. If it's illegal immi—"

"No, no," said Annie. "I know we're all one big happy family now they're all in the EU. They might not all have the correct or up-to-date permits and visas, but we won't worry about a little thing like that."

"Then what is it?"

"Murder."

Dennis swallowed. "I knew something was up," he said.

"What do you mean?"

"When they didn't turn up for their shift yesterday."

"Who didn't?"

"The nine people we've been employing from Rod's Staff. The van usually drops them off at eight o'clock. Yesterday it didn't turn up."

"Why not?"

"No idea. The boss was furious. They've always been reliable before. That's one reason we use Flinders. But the boss got no warning at all. He couldn't get in touch with the Rod's Staff office. Mind you, it is a weekend, and most offices are shut."

"So none of the casual labor turned up for work yesterday, but this girl you think might have been Polish, and you might have seen working here, was standing at the gate this morning?"

"Yes."

"Could she have been one of the Rod's Staff girls?"

"She could have been. Yes."

"What happened to her?"

"A car came, and she got into it."

"Whose car?"

"Roderick Flinders. I know because I've seen him here before."

"What make of car?"

"A gray Clio."

"What happened?"

"I don't know. I wasn't watching. I was just crossing the yard, coming here, as a matter of fact, when I saw her walk out of the gatehouse and get in the car."

"Did she get in of her own free will?"

"I suppose so. I mean, I think I'd have noticed a struggle. I can't really say I paid a lot of attention. I had other things on my mind."

"It's all right, Dennis," said Annie. "I've finished now. You can put it out of your mind again. For the moment." Then she turned away and walked off.

When she got in her car, out of the rain, Annie thought things over and realized that Flinders would certainly have heard about what happened to Corrigan, and that would have shaken him up a bit. He wouldn't necessarily know *who* had shot Corrigan and Curly, that it was an angry parent of a girl their organization had exploited, or why, so he might well have imagined that it was something to do with the murdered policeman and journalist, and that the whole enterprise was falling apart. Perhaps he thought that he himself was next for the chop. The sensible thing to do would be to abandon ship.

And no doubt Joosep Rebane back in Estonia, or wherever he lived, would have heard the news by now, too, and his most sensible course of action would be to extricate himself as completely as possible from the whole business. Three murders meant way too much pressure and scrutiny. Best to wash his hands and walk away.

But where, Annie wondered, did that leave Krystyna? And how had she got to the yeast factory? She probably knew the name of the place, Varley's, having seen it day after day, and she had enough money for a taxi. She thought she would find Ewa there, but she had found Roderick Flinders instead.

Annie stopped at the gatehouse on the way out. The man was still reading his paper.

"Got a minute?" she asked.

He acted as if it were a great hardship to tear himself away from the Sunday Sport.

"What is it?"

"There was a young girl here earlier this morning. She was seen coming out of your office and getting in a car, Roderick Flinders's car."

"That's right."

"Want to tell me why?"

"Because Mr. Flinders asked me to get in touch with him if I saw any of them. They weren't supposed to be here, see. He'd placed them all somewhere else, but I suppose not all of them knew. She couldn't speak English, anyway."

"You work for Flinders?"

"No. Varley's. But he treats me well, and I keep an eye on his crews. It's good for everyone."

"What did she want?"

"I think she was looking for someone. She kept saying a name. Sounded like 'Eva.' I told her to come in out of the rain and sit down for a minute and I'd try to find out for her."

"And you phoned Flinders."

"Yes."

"What did he say?"

"To keep her there, and he'd be over as soon as he could. He only lives about fifteen minutes' drive away.

I gave her a fag and a cup of tea. She seemed content enough. A bit nervous, maybe."

"And Flinders took her away?"

"She went with him. He nodded when she said 'Eva,' to let her know he knew what she meant and he could help her, like."

"Where did he take her?"

"Now, how the hell should I know?"

"So, am I to understand that Joosep Rebane is something of a celebrity?" said Banks, lowering his voice. Joanna had stopped sulking and pricked up her ears now.

"Celebrity criminal, you might say," Erik answered, scratching at his bushy beard. "Nothing proven, of course."

"Of course," said Banks.

"It does not harm his reputation that he looks like a rock star and has the lifestyle to match," Erik went on.

"But I'll bet he doesn't play an instrument."

"He plays many. The gun. The knife. The baseball bat."

"A veritable symphony," muttered Joanna.

Banks sipped some coffee. It was cold but strong.

"Thirty-one years old, and for the past four of them, he's been the leading man in the drug-dealing and people-trafficking rackets and, clearly, also is involved in these migrant-labor schemes that your friend and Mihkel have been investigating. Baltic Mafia. Estonia is not a destination, you understand, but it is a route. Rebane is a skilled fac— What is the word?"

"Factotum? Facilitator?" Banks suggested.

"Facilitator. Yes. He has connections with all the organized criminal groups in Eastern Europe, especially the Russians, but in some ways he stands very much alone and aloof. Very Estonian."

"Have the cops ever got close to him?"

"It is possible," Erik said. "But I do not know. My guess would be that he always has someone powerful on the inside. He greases the palms. Is that how you say it?"

"That's how we say it."

"We have corruption here, like everywhere. Police, local government—parliament, for all I know."

"You say he's been in the business for about four years?"

"Yes. Before that he was just another wild, spoiled, rich kid who got away with far too much and spent his time with the wrong sort of people. He came to prominence in his own right when a storage container full of illegal immigrants was found at Southampton docks. A container that was discovered to have shipped from Tallinn. You may remember the incident. Two of the people inside were dead. Of course, there was no evidence to link him to the crime, but his name was whispered in many circles, and it soon became something to fear."

"Was the newspaper involved?"

"We could not name him, but we came as close as we could without risking a libel suit. His father is Viktor Rebane, a very famous and powerful businessman. He was fortunate enough to be able to buy into utilities after the Soviets left and everything was privatized."

"I wonder what he thinks of his son."

"Viktor Rebane has never spoken publicly on the subject. He is a very well-respected figure himself, but he must be aware of his son's activities. Sources, however, say he becomes furious every time Joosep's name is linked to some crime or bad behavior, but he can do nothing to stop him. Joosep is headstrong."

"Did Mihkel write about Joosep?"

"Yes. In 'Pimeduse varjus.'"

"So there was no love lost between them?"

"Pardon?"

"I mean, they didn't like each other."

"I do not know if they ever met. I do not think so. But no. Mihkel recognized Joosep Rebane for what he was, a thug come into power. And Mihkel could be merciless in his attack, so that everyone knew who he meant."

"Does Joosep have a reputation with women, too?"

"There have been complaints. Rape. Violence. All withdrawn."

"Any deaths?"

"None that could be directly linked to him."

"His name comes up six years ago," Banks explained, "when Larisa worked at the club, and her friend Juliya was Joosep Rebane's girlfriend for a while. Juliya left town rather suddenly around the time Rachel disappeared. Larisa thinks she went back to Belarus. His name has also come up more recently in connection with Warren Corrigan, Roderick Flinders and their migrant-worker scheme. Rebane probably runs the agencies here, Flinders does the staffing and accommodation in northern England and Corrigan puts them all in debt. Nice little scam. Robert Tamm is probably Rebane's enforcer, or one of them. Can you search around for any links?"

"I can try," said Erik. "But as I told you, he's low-profile. He manages to keep his name out of the newspapers. Even ours."

"Yes, but people know things. You, for a start. You know things you can't print. I'm not after evidence I can use in court, just something that might help me sort this whole mess out and find out what happened to Rachel. I'd also like to know where I can find Joosep Rebane."

Erik laughed. "That is very unlikely to happen," he said. "Rebane has the money and contacts to disappear, and if he has any sense that is exactly what he will do the way things are now."

Joanna sighed. "The case is over," she said again. "Or it will be when the Scottish police pick up Robert Tamm and deliver him to Eastvale. My priority, after what you just told me, is to get back home and interview this Gareth Underwood."

"Fine, then," said Banks. "Why don't you go home? Be my guest. You'd have found out more if you'd stayed there in the first place, wouldn't you?"

"Maybe I will go back if you keep playing the tough guy, going off hunting hardened criminals. What is this, a pissing competition?"

"My job."

"Well, don't expect me to scrape you up off the street."

"Please," said Erik. "You must stop quarreling. People will think you're in love. And while you're here, you should try some real Estonian food. It will help you make peace. There is a very good restaurant on Vana-Posti called Mekk. Have you tried it?"

They both said no.

"Go there tonight, eat some smoked eel and roast duck and bury the hammer."

"It's 'hatchet,'" said Joanna. "And I don't like eels."

"Whatever. Veal cheeks, then. I will make a reservation for you myself. Seven o'clock." He wagged his finger. "Do not be late. And be thinking of me having dinner with my mother-in-law." He picked up his newspaper, put on his cap and waved good-bye. "I will be in touch."

Joanna gathered her shopping bags, and they followed Erik down the stairs and out of the Viru Keskus. They were just across the road from their hotel, but it was a wide road and the system of traffic lights was a little haphazard.

Banks stole a glance at Joanna as they waited for a light to change, a tram rumbling by. "What do you think?" he asked.

"You know what I think."

"I mean what Erik said. Mekk. Burying the hammer. Seven o'clock."

"I suppose I've got to eat."

"Once more with enthusiasm."

They arrived at the hotel. Joanna favored him with a small smile. "I'll meet you in the bar here at half past six," she said, and headed for the lift, maneuvering her packages. Banks made for the bar, but before he got very far the receptionist called his name. "Hr. Banks?"

"Yes."

"I have message for you." She took a small envelope from under the desk and handed it to him.

"Did you see who delivered it?" he asked.

"No. Sorry. I just come on."

"It doesn't matter. Thank you." Banks tapped the envelope against his palm thoughtfully as he took a stool at the bar and ordered a beer. Who was it from? Rätsepp? Merike? Ursula Mardna? There was only one way to find out. He was thirsty from the day's walking and from the sticky, unpleasant taste of cold coffee. When he had taken a few sips of chilled beer, he turned the envelope over in his hand and opened it. There was no signature, just a short message in block capitals. "MONDAY 1400 PATAREI. COME ALONE."

Stefan Nowak lived in one of the new luxury apartments about half a mile outside town, down by the river. The building used to be an old monastery, but it had been gutted and converted into a number of apartments of all shapes and sizes. Stefan's was one of the smaller units, but he had a balcony and fine view down to the riverbank and the woods beyond.

His answer to Annie's message had been brusque and clipped, but he had agreed to see her if she would drop by. This she did after she left the yeast factory. His flat was, as she expected, immaculate and tasteful, with

framed prints of art exhibitions and classic movies on
the wall, module or Ikea-style furniture, and not a speck
of dust to be seen. She had to admit, whatever he had
been doing last night and this morning, he didn't seem
at all the worse for wear. Casually dressed in jeans and a
black polo neck, he looked every bit as cool and elegant
as ever. The room smelled vaguely of cinnamon, and
Annie wondered if Stefan had given his date cinnamon
buns for breakfast before kicking her out. Did he bake
them himself? That would be too good to be true. The
smell reminded her that she hadn't eaten anything since
last night. She had been so worried about Krystyna.

Stefan frowned as he read over the notes. "I'm afraid
the grammar and spelling aren't very good," he said.
"And her handwriting . . ."

Annie was sure her mouth flapped open. It felt as if
it did. It was hard to get the words out. "You bloody
complain about the spelling in a language that as far as
I can see has nothing but consonants with funny squig-
gles on them?"

"It matters," Stefan said. "And if you understood
anything at all about the Polish language, you would
know it's not as simple as that." He waved the note.
"This girl is barely literate."

"What do you expect?" Annie said. "She's from a
poor working-class area, and she ran away hoping for

a better future here and ended up working in a bloody yeast factory. I've been there. Believe me, Stefan, you wouldn't want to set one Camper-shod foot in the place. Can you just please translate the fucking note?"

Stefan stared at her, perplexed and annoyed, but he started to translate, anyway, stumbling and correcting himself here and there to make his point. "This first one's quite easy," he said. "It says, 'I owe you thirty-two pounds sixty. Sorry. I will pay back.' In the other note she says she's very sorry and she thanks you for all you've done for her. Also the clothes and money that she promises to pay back. She stole money from you, Annie?"

"Borrowed. The poor creature couldn't even go to the shop and buy a chocolate bar or a packet of fags, for Christ's sake." Krystyna must have seen Annie take some cash from the old cocoa tin in one of the kitchen cupboards to pay for the takeaway, and she had stolen the rest, but she wasn't going to admit that to Stefan. "Carry on."

"There's not much more," Stefan went on. "She wants to find out what has happened to her friends, to Ewa particularly, and she can't sleep until she knows they are all right. She was foolish to run away without saying good-bye. She will be in touch with you when she can. There's a heart and—"

"Yes, I could read that bit, thank you," said Annie, snatching the note back.

Stefan shook his head. "Annie, why are you getting so involved? It's not like you. Do you know what you're getting yourself into? You're letting this get to you, you know. It will only end badly."

"What do you mean?"

"The girl. She's a user. Probably a junkie as well as a thief."

"She's no junkie."

"But she is a thief, isn't she? She stole that money from you, didn't she?"

"What makes you say that?"

"Her words. The way she says it in the note. I didn't translate exactly, but she says something about being sorry for money she *took*."

"You bastard!" Annie felt her face burning. She had no answer for Stefan's questions. Had no idea why she was going out on a limb for this pathetic young girl, who had lied and stolen and taken advantage of her hospitality, and left without so much as a by-your-leave. Perhaps it was because she had watched the way she ate the Big Mac and fries in the interview room, and then cleaned up after herself with the serviette. Or the way she had watched the American cop shows intently while eating her takeaway, although she didn't understand a word. It was true that she was unsophisticated, but that didn't mean she had no manners or breeding. Or feelings. It was true she was a thief and liar, but those are habits that are easy to come by when you are exploited and have nothing of your own. Did Annie want to change her? Maybe. But all she had really wanted to do was offer the hand of friendship in a world that had so far proved unfriendly.

She grabbed her jacket, thanked Stefan grudgingly and went back down to the car. After she had sat down and taken a few deep breaths, gripping the wheel tight, she phoned Winsome, who, as she had guessed, was at the station. "You did say to call if I needed anything," she said. "Are you up for an adventure?"

"I know you don't approve of my direction on this," Banks said between tastes of smoked eel, "but I just feel that we've got so close to solving the mystery of Rachel Hewitt, it would be a disservice to her parents, for a start, if we just turned away now."

"I'm not as heartless as you think I am," said Joanna. "I'm just not used to the ways of . . . the ways you . . . I mean, I haven't been involved in this kind of investigation before. When you explained it to me the other night, that finding out what happened to DI Quinn might depend on finding out what happened to

Rachel Hewitt, I understood. It made sense. But we know who killed Bill Quinn now. It's just a matter of finding him and bringing him in. Rachel Hewitt isn't your case. Never was. We should go home. But you're all over the place. Usually things are a lot more focused and straightforward in my job."

"True. But you're here to learn, aren't you? You do want to make a move out of Professional Standards. We do things differently there."

"You're telling me."

"What I was going to say back at the coffee shop was that you lack breadth of vision. That's the difference between your job and mine. And if you want to make a move, you're going to have to learn to think in a different way. Yes, you could argue that you've solved your case. Or Annie has. We know who killed Bill Quinn and Mihkel Lepikson, and he'll no doubt soon be in custody. There's probably enough forensic evidence to put him away even if he doesn't sign a confession. We also know that Quinn was bent, in thrall to Joosep Rebane, and through him to Warren Corrigan. For you, it stops there. That completes your chain of thought. But Rachel Hewitt hasn't been found, and we have several leads on what might have happened to her. Now, you might worry about expenses and justification, but I'd pay my own hotel bill and airfare to stay here and settle my curiosity about what happened to Rachel and, with any luck, give her parents a bit of peace. That's the difference between us."

"What? You're a romantic, a knight in shining armor, a tilter at windmills?"

"I've been called worse."

"I'll bet. But isn't it someone else's job now?"

"Probably. Technically. Officially. But I'm doing it. You can either come along with me or go back to Eastvale and write your report."

Banks ate some more smoked eel. It was delicious. He had to admit that Erik had done them proud. Not only a reservation but attentive service, a table for two in a quiet corner far from the kitchen and toilet doors. He must have told the maître d' that they were VIPs. The restaurant was a joy, with its modern decor, dark orange walls, muted lighting and unusual food. Banks's smoked eel came with potato cakes and a horseradish sauce, among other things. Joanna Passero's artichoke soup came with pork crisps and rye bread.

"What do you think about your precious DI Quinn, now you know a bit more about what happened?" Joanna asked.

"Bill Quinn let himself get compromised. He was a fool. He should have known to stay away from Larisa, that she was a honey trap. It's not the first time that trick's been used. They caught him off his guard, just like Robert Tamm did at St. Peter's. Do I feel sorry for him? Yes. Do I condone what he did? No. There were other ways out."

"Like telling the truth?"

"That's one strategy. Not necessarily the best in his case."

"But whatever strategy he used, it got him killed."

"Yes. Like too many other people in this case. But we also have to think of the good ones left alive. Rachel's parents. Erik. Merike. Larisa. Even Curly, if what Annie tells me is true about him wanting to go straight."

They finished their starters and sipped some more wine, then the mains came: duck fillet for Banks and baked cod for Joanna. Much as Banks spent far too much of his time microwaving Indian takeaways, eating fish and chips on the move and munching on Greggs pies, he loved a fine meal when he got the chance. Joanna made sounds of delight at her first mouthful, then stopped to check her mobile. Whatever it was she saw, it made her frown.

"What is it with that?" Banks asked.

"What do you mean?"

"Your mobile. I know people get obsessed with checking their e-mail on the go, and all that—it makes them behave rudely at dinner parties—but you're never off it. It's as if you're waiting for the announcement of the end of the world or something. What is it that's so important?"

Joanna gave a sound halfway between a sniff and a snort. "It's nothing," she said, snapping the case and putting her mobile away. "It's personal. Private." She wouldn't meet his eyes. "None of your bloody business."

"Don't you think we know each other well enough by now, even if no one could call us the best of friends? And if we're working together, it is my business. It's a distraction."

Joanna raised her eyes, and Banks saw a vulnerability and pain in them that he had never noticed before. She must have realized because she quickly reasserted her usual ice-maiden manner. "It's nothing."

"Come on, Joanna."

"Why do you want to know?"

"My curious nature."

"So you can laugh at me, make fun of me?"

"What? Why would I do that?"

"You've been doing it right from the start."

"So what is it? Come on. Tell me. I promise I won't make fun of you."

Joanna toyed with her food, obviously trying to decide whether to tell him or not. In the end, she averted her eyes and said, "It's my husband. I think he's having an affair."

"So who keeps texting you?"

"A colleague. I asked her if she'd keep an eye on him, see if anything unusual happened."

"And has it?"

She nodded. "The bastard."

Banks could tell that her eyes were welling up by the way she kept her eyes down on her food. He didn't say anything for a while, but when he sensed she was in control again he rested his hand on her arm and said, "I'm sorry, Joanna. Really, I am."

She looked at him then, and he thought she seemed surprised by his words and his tone. At least she didn't jerk her arm away. "The thing is," she said, "I should have seen it coming. He's Italian. He's always maintained that it's perfectly OK for the husband to take a mistress. I feel such a fool. I always thought he was teasing, you know, but . . ."

"What are you going to do?"

"I've been trying to decide. I'll have to have it out with him when I get back, of course, then I'm leaving him. We don't have any children, so that's one less thing to stand in my way. I can't bear it. I can't bear living like this. Some people might be able to put up with such behavior, but I can't do it. I've got a nice flat in Northallerton, I like it there, so I might as well just stay up north." She smiled. "I'd still like to work in some other unit. Maybe I'll chase after your job."

"You're welcome," said Banks. "Do you still love him?"

"What kind of a question is that?" Joanna said nothing for a while, just stared down at the tablecloth. Then she spoke so softly that Banks could hardly hear her. "Yes."

They ate on in silence, Joanna quaffing her wine rather quickly now and needing a refill well before Banks. "So now you know everything about me," she said when she was able to manage a cavalier, fuck-it-all tone in her voice.

"I doubt that," said Banks. "But I am sorry to hear about your problems. I've been there. If you ever want—"

She waved her hand. "No, it's fine, thanks. I don't need to talk about it. I don't suppose your wife was unfaithful to you, was she?"

"As a matter of fact, she was. Knocked me for a six."

She looked at him as if seeing him for the first time. "Well, well. Wonders never cease. And I'd have thought . . ."

"That I'd be the one at fault?"

"Yes."

"I'm not saying I wasn't at fault."

Joanna studied him for a moment. "For some reason," she said, "I find myself unusually hungry after this conversation. Have you got room for pudding?"

"I think so," said Banks. "And I've got a little job I'd like you to help me with tomorrow."

There was a gray Clio parked in front of the newish, detached house outside Eastvale, and the man who answered the door seemed very nervous indeed. When Annie and Winsome showed their identification, he kept the door on the chain while asking them what they wanted.

"Mr. Flinders?" Annie asked. "Roderick Flinders of Rod's Staff Ltd.?"

"What if I am?"

"Mind if we come in for a moment?"

"As a matter of fact, I'm busy. It's not convenient."

Annie gave him the scathing look she reserved for the most obvious liars, and after a thirty-second staring match, during which she could swear she saw sweat break out on his brow, Flinders shut the door, fiddled with the chain and opened it to let them in, ushering them toward the living room at the front. The furniture was all slightly old-fashioned, as if it had been bought at auctions. The large plasma TV was probably worth a small fortune. Flinders himself was not quite what she had expected of the sleazy exploiter of unskilled labor, but an overweight, red-faced, balding man in his early fifties, wearing a chunky-knit cardigan, who looked as if he would be more at home behind a desk in an insurance office than shepherding poor migrant workers around from factory to factory. His skin was baby smooth and had the sheen of wet plastic. Still, Annie realized, he didn't do much of the shepherding himself; he had minions and gang masters to work for him.

"What is it?" he said, turning to face them. "As I said, I'm very busy."

"With what?" Annie asked.

"Pardon?"

Annie glanced around the room. "What are you so busy with?" she asked. "I don't see anything in here to occupy your time."

"A business matter. In my home office."

"Ah, I see. Then we'll get straight to the point. Winsome?"

Winsome consulted her notebook. "We're investigating a series of infringements of the law under the Asylum and Immigration Act, and the Anti-Slavery Act," said Winsome. There was no Anti-Slavery Act, but it sounded more dramatic than the Coroners and Justice Bill, under which such matters came.

"What are you talking about?" Flinders cried. "I'm a legitimate businessman. Everyone who goes through my company is closely vetted. We have no truck with asylum seekers or illegal immigrants."

"They don't need to be illegal, sir," Winsome went on. "All we need to prove is that violence, intimidation or deception were used to bring a migrant worker into the country."

"And, of course," Annie added, "moving people around the country without their consent is also a form of trafficking under the law, and is therefore prosecutable under the act. Sentences can be rather excessive, as many judges take a dim view of these activities. In other words, mate, you could get banged up for a long time."

"But I've done nothing wrong."

"Do you know a man called Warren Corrigan?"

Winders averted his eyes. "I've met him."

"Perhaps you've heard he was shot on Friday evening?"

"I . . . yes . . . I . . . on the news. It's terrible. Just terrible."

"Indeed it is," said Annie. "A real tragedy. Do you know the circumstances under which he was shot?"

"No. I don't know who did it, either. I was here at home. It was nothing to do with me."

"We know that, sir. But we understand that you met with Mr. Corrigan on a number of occasions?"

"We did some business together, yes."

"What sort of business would that be?"

"Business of a financial nature. Warren was a financier."

"That's a nice name for it, isn't it?" said Annie. Winsome nodded.

"For what?" Flinders demanded.

"Loan shark."

Flinders did his best to appear indignant but succeeded only in looking more scared. "I know nothing about that. As far as I was concerned, Warren Corrigan was a legitimate businessman, like myself."

"'Like me,'" Annie said, correcting him. "What about Mihkel Lepikson?"

"Who?"

"The Estonian journalist found murdered at Garskill Farm."

"I know nothing about that."

"But you know Garskill Farm, don't you?"

"Yes. The company used it as temporary accommodation for some of our workers."

"The 'company' being you?"

"Well, yes."

"I'm glad to hear it was only temporary," Annie said, "though it turned out to be a bit more permanent for Mihkel Lepikson."

"I told you, I don't know him."

"Did you visit Garskill Farm the other Wednesday morning?"

"No, I didn't."

"I'm not sure if I believe you," said Annie. "Still, we'll leave that for the moment. Mind if we have a look around?"

"Have you got a search warrant?"

"No, but I'd be happy to wait here with you while Winsome goes and gets one." She glanced at her watch. "I must remind you, though, it's Sunday, and magistrates can be awfully hard to find on a Sunday. It's unlikely we'd be able to get hold of one until tomorrow morning, at the earliest. In the meantime, we might as well take you to the station, and you can spend a night in the cells. Don't worry. It's not as terrible as it sounds. It might not be as comfortable as this place, but you get three square meals a day, there's a working toilet and the showers are hot."

"All right. Get on with it then."

"Like to give us the guided tour?"

Flinders led them around the house—his office, first, with the filing cabinets and computer, which would definitely be worth a search warrant in itself—then a large well-equipped kitchen complete with island and pots and pans hanging from a ceiling fixture, too spick-and-span to have been used recently; a cloakroom; plenty of cupboard space; dining room with heavy dark wood table and over-stuffed chairs. Upstairs were four bedrooms, two of which were empty and one of which was set up for guests.

"Do you live here all alone?" Annie asked.

"My wife and I have separated," said Flinders. "I've been thinking of selling the place and moving somewhere smaller, but the market is poor."

"Oh. Sorry to hear that. About your wife, I mean."

The final room was Flinders's bedroom. He seemed reluctant to open the door, but he clearly sensed that he wasn't in much of a position to refuse. Two suitcases lay open on the four-poster bed, half-filled with clothes and toiletries.

Annie glanced at Winsome and raised her eyebrows. "Going somewhere, Mr. Flinders?"

"If you must know, I was planning on taking a short holiday. It's been a stressful time at work lately. My heart . . . angina, you see."

"Somewhere nice, I hope?"

"Acapulco."

"Very nice. All alone?"

"Yes."

"What about the business?"

"It can run itself for a little while. I have helpers. One needs to recharge one's batteries every now and then. Even a police detective should know that."

Annie laughed. "I've been recharging mine for the past few months. They're in pretty good shape by now. Right, Winsome?"

"Right," said Winsome, smiling.

Flinders's chin started to wobble. "You can't possibly read anything into this," he said. "It's a coincidence, that's all."

"What's a coincidence?"

"Well, you know . . ."

"No. Tell me."

"You coming here just before I was about to leave. I know it might appear bad, but—"

"And here's me thinking you meant us coming here after Warren Corrigan was shot, and after Mihkel Lepikson was murdered by a hired killer called Robert Tamm, in your presence."

"I wasn't there, I tell you!"

"We think you were." Annie actually doubted that Flinders had the bottle to watch Robert Tamm torture and drown Mihkel Lepikson, but she was aiming for maximum discomfort. People seemed to think the police fitted people up all the time, so why not let Flinders believe that he was going to get fitted up for conspiracy to murder?

Flinders licked his lips. "I should go. I have to get to the airport. I have a flight to catch."

"I don't think that's going to happen," said Annie. "You might as well relax and get used to the idea. I hope you took out some cancellation insurance."

"But you can't . . . I mean, I have freedom of movement. I—"

"Like your workers?"

"I resent that."

"Shut up, Mr. Flinders. I'm sick of your whining. Where's Krystyna?"

"Who?"

"Krystyna? The girl you picked up this morning at the yeast factory where some of your migrant crew used to work."

"I don't know wh—"

"You were seen. Your car was seen. Your man in the gatehouse told me everything. Didn't seem to think he'd done anything wrong. We know that nobody showed up for their shift yesterday morning, the morning after Corrigan was killed. We think you're running scared because you're worried that what happened to him might happen to you. You cut the crew loose, but the guard on the gate phoned you when he saw Krystyna hanging around the gates. She was looking for her friend Ewa. Krystyna had been gone for over a week, since the day Mihkel Lepikson was killed, in fact. You were worried she knew something. What have you done with her?"

Flinders was very red. He flopped into an armchair beside the bed and his head sank to his chest. His breathing sounded labored. Annie glanced at Winsome, a little alarmed, worried that he'd had a heart attack or something. He fumbled in his pocket, brought out a little cylinder, then opened his mouth and sprayed lightly under his tongue. "Nitroglycerin," he said, patting his chest.

Annie knelt so that her eyes were level with the top of Flinders's head and spoke softly. "Take it easy. It's all over now, Roddy. Tell us where she is and things will go better for you."

"I never wanted any of this," Flinders said. "Nobody was supposed to get killed. Nobody. Do you understand? That wasn't part of the plan. I abhor violence. Nobody was supposed to die. I had nothing to do with any killing."

Annie felt a chill run through her. Was he referring only to Corrigan, Quinn and Lepikson, or did he mean that Krystyna was dead, too? "That's what you get for playing with the big boys. You can't just pick up your toys and go home whenever you want. You're in, and you're in deep. Accessory to murder. It'll help if you tell us where Krystyna is."

Flinders raised his mournful, tear-stained face to hers. "I told you, I don't know. I haven't see her."

"But you do know her?"

"If you say she's one of my workers, then I suppose I must do. I don't know them all by name. Can't even pronounce most of them."

"Have you hurt her, Roddy?"

"I haven't hurt anyone."

They went back downstairs. Annie looked toward the open kitchen. "Is there a cellar here?"

"No." Flinders answered just a little too quickly and sounded just a little too desperate.

Annie pointed to a door beside the stainless-steel fridge. "Where does that door lead?"

"Nowhere. It's just a larder."

"I'll go see," Annie said to Winsome. "Why don't you stay here and keep Mr. Flinders company? He still seems a bit peaky to me. We don't want him having a coronary or something, do we?"

"You can't do this. It's private. It's—"

But Annie had already opened the door, and what she saw was a flight of stairs leading down to a basement. It probably wasn't a cellar in the old sense, coal cellars having been out of fashion for many years now, but a lot of modern houses had basement areas that could be used for storage, entertainment rooms or even extra living space. Annie flicked the light switch, but nothing happened.

She turned to Flinders across the room. "No lights?"

"I never go down there."

"Got a torch?"

"No."

Annie searched through the drawers and cup-boards in the kitchen and finally found a small torch, along with a box of candles and matches. She checked to make sure the battery worked and set off down the wooden steps. The basement floor was concrete, and the large area under the house was separated into a number of rooms or storage areas by wooden parti-tions. Annie could make out some lawn furniture, an old barbecue, a bicycle with flat tires, an upturned wheelbarrow, some camping equipment, an ancient radiogram.

She stood still, shone her torch into the dark corners and walls and called out, "Krystyna!"

She thought she heard a sound. Hardly daring to breathe, she listened closely. It could have been a mouse or something, though it sounded more like a muffled voice trying to speak. She couldn't be completely clear where it was coming from, so she began a systematic search in the general direction.

In the third partitioned area she entered, the torch-light picked out a small bundle curled on the floor in the fetal position. On examination, this turned out to be because Krystyna's feet and arms were tied in such a way that she could stretch neither without tightening the rope around her neck.

Annie dashed over and tore off the sticky tape that covered Krystyna's lips, then she pulled out the rag that had been shoved in her mouth. Krystyna gagged and coughed while Annie worked on the ropes, which she finally managed to untie. When Krystyna was free at last, she threw her arms around Annie's neck and buried her face in her shoulder, crying and muttering thanks or prayers in Polish. Annie got her to her feet, and together they made their way upstairs. When Annie appeared with Krystyna in the kitchen, Flinders held his head in his hands and wept.

"What were you going to do with her while you buggered off to Mexico, Rod? Leave her down there to starve or suffocate to death alone in the dark? She's half starved to start with. It wouldn't have taken long. Or had you been in touch with Robert Tamm? Was he going to come down and take care of her after you'd gone, do your dirty business for you? Like he killed Mihkel Lepikson and Bill Quinn?"

"That wasn't my idea," said Flinders through his tears. "None of it was my idea. I told you. Nobody was supposed to get killed. Nobody was supposed to get hurt."

Annie stood up. For the first time in many a year she wanted to kick someone hard in the balls. But she suppressed the urge and tightened her arm around Krystyna. "We'll sort out the blame later," she said. "First we'll get you to the station and see how sweetly you can sing."

12

*S*tone walls do not a prison make / Nor iron bars a cage. The lines from the old poem came to Banks as he got out of the taxi in front of Patarei. *Perhaps in some cases that was true,* he thought, *but nobody had mentioned it to the builders of this prison.* Beyond the rusted, graffiti-covered gates, a guard tower stood commanding a view over a prison yard overgrown with weeds and scattered with rubbish. The long, gray brick building stretched alongside it.

Banks followed the signs to what he thought was the entrance, all the while keeping his eyes open for a tail. But he saw no one. Eventually he came to the entrance. Beside it stood a small ticket office in which an old woman sat alone. She took some euros from him, gave him a guidebook, then smiled, showing a relatively toothless mouth, and pointed the way in. Banks thought she was probably the first Estonian he had met who didn't seem to speak English. Perhaps she didn't speak at all.

Though it was warm and sunny outside, the interior of the old prison was dank and chilly. There were puddles on the floors and damp patches had discolored the walls and ceilings. In places, the whitewash and plaster on the arched roof and the institutional green paint on the walls had peeled away to expose red brick underneath.

And the place smelled. Probably not as bad as when it was a functioning prison, but it smelled. Damp. Rot. Sweat. Fear.

Banks was alone, or so he thought until he walked into one of the cells to get a better look and saw a young couple already there, guidebook in hand. They might have been a honeymoon couple, handsome young man and pretty girl, and Banks wondered what the hell they were doing visiting such a place. They smiled, and he smiled back.

On the wall of the cell were head-and-shoulders shots of young girls, along with a few nude models. Further along the corridor, Banks passed what must have been an office. It was impossible to get in the doorway now, as it was piled almost to the top with rubbish, mostly old telephones, radio parts, bits of desks and chairs, papers, various broken circuit boards, and in front of it all, a rusty old mechanical typewriter. Banks crouched and saw that the keyboard was in Cyrillic script.

The next floor seemed to be have been devoted almost entirely to the prison hospital. The cells were larger, more like wards for ten or twelve people, with tubular-metal-frame beds and thin stained mattresses. It reminded him of Garskill Farm. In the doctors' offices, medical forms, sheets of handwritten figures and old newspapers still littered the desks, next to old typewriters, again everything in Russian. One of the newspapers had a color photograph of a beach and palm trees on the bottom corner, and Banks guessed it was probably an advert for vacations in the sun.

Worst of all were the operating theaters. Metal gurneys slatted like sinister beach recliners stretched under huge bug-eyed lamps beside old-fashioned machines with obscure dials and buttons, like something from a 1950s science fiction movie. The glass-fronted cabinets still housed bottles of pills, phials, potions and boxes of ampoules and syringes. The tiles had come away from the walls in places to reveal damp stained plaster. The dentist's chair with the old foot-pedal drill just about did it for Banks. He moved along quickly, tasting bile.

He had been wandering for about fifteen minutes and was standing in an eerie room with splotchy brown and red walls when it happened. The sudden but surprisingly gentle voice came from behind him.

"They say it was used as a pretrial holding facility, but have you ever seen an execution room in a pretrial facility?"

Banks turned. The man behind him was youngish, midthirties perhaps, prematurely balding, with a goatee beard and mustache. He was slightly taller than Banks, and skinny, and he didn't seem in the least threatening. Banks recognized him immediately as the man who had been following him around Tallinn.

"You get my message, then?" he said in heavily accented English.

"Who are you?" Banks asked.

"My name is Aivar Kukk. I was policeman many years ago." Even though he spoke softly, his voice still echoed in the cavernous corridors of the decaying prison.

"Why have you been following me?"

"To make certain that you were not being followed by Hr. Rätsepp or his men."

"And am I?"

"Not that I have seen. Perhaps he does not see you as much of a threat."

"To him? I'm not."

"But you may be when we have finished talking. Even so, I do not think it is Hr. Rätsepp you need to fear. Shall we be tourists? This is an interesting place. The execution room was used before it became a pre-trial holding facility, of course. It was first a sea fortress, but is most famous as Soviet-era prison. Many were executed and tortured here. Now art students work on projects, and there are exhibition openings and many other functions. People even get married here. It was to be an art college, but nobody can get rid of the damp."

There seemed to be no one else around except the young couple about fifty yards down the corridor, Banks thought as he walked along with Aivar Kukk. He wondered if the young couple were thinking of getting married here. The arched corridors seemed to stretch on and on ahead for miles, and the chilly damp had seeped into his bones. Banks gave an involuntary shudder. "I can believe it. So what's all the cloak-and-dagger stuff about?"

"I do not understand."

"I mean why the note, and following me? And why meet here?"

"We will not be disturbed. You were not followed here. Patarei has just opened again for the tourist season. Nobody will come here at this time. Do you not think it is an interesting place?"

"All prisons give me the creeps."

"This one certainly should."

As they walked and talked, Banks wasn't paying quite as much attention to the crumbling decor and the claustrophobic cells, but in some places he noticed there was so much graffiti and paint splashed over the walls and floors, as if someone had let loose a bunch of drunken art students. "How did you know I was here in Tallinn?" Banks asked.

"I read what happened to Bill Quinn in the English newspaper, and then Mihkel Lepikson. I knew it would be a matter of time. If nobody came soon, I would have sent a message. I still have friends in the department and at newspapers. We meet, drink beer, gossip, and they keep me informed. Tallinn is small city. Estonia is small country. Is not too difficult to know when a policeman comes from England, or what he is doing here."

"And what *am* I doing here?"

"You are looking for killer of Bill Quinn and Mihkel Lepikson."

"How do you know that?"

"Is not difficult. You have talked with Toomas Rätsepp, Ursula Mardna and Erik Aarma."

"Anything else?"

"Yes. You are looking for Rachel Hewitt."

"What makes you think that?"

"I saw you go in club, remember? Club with no name."

Banks tried not to show how perplexed he was by all this. "Seeing as you know so much of my business," he said, "perhaps you can tell me where Rachel is?"

"I am afraid I cannot. I do not know."

"Then why are we here?"

"Please come here," Aivar said, entering another open cell with rows of bunk beds in it. Banks followed him over to the window and saw through the bars the beautiful pale blue waters of the Baltic dancing with diamonds of sunlight, the undulating line of a distant shore across the bay. It made him think what the view must have been like from Alcatraz. He had looked out on the prison island from Fisherman's Wharf just last year, but he hadn't taken the boat out and seen the San Francisco skyline from the inside. He hated prisons, and he wouldn't have come here today if he hadn't been curious about the note.

"I think that must have been the greatest punishment of all," said Aivar. "To look on a view like that and to be locked in a cell."

They remained silent, admiring the view that had represented unattainable freedom to so many. "I can help you," Aivar said finally. "I was junior investigator. I work with Bill Quinn on original case."

"I know," said Banks. "Ursula Mardna told me."

"Ursula Mardna was good prosecutor. Toomas Rätsepp was lead investigator. Boss. I was junior. But I work with Bill, all night we are asking questions, walking streets, just two, three days after girl disappear, as soon as we have some information where they had been drinking."

"What really happened?"

"I have never told anyone."

"Why not?"

"Fear. First for my job, then for my life. But now it is too late."

"What do you mean?"

"I mean I no longer have anything to fear. Nothing anybody does can stop truth coming out now. Too many people know things. Too many people are asking questions. Murder was a desperate move."

"We think Bill Quinn was killed because his wife died, and he got in touch with Mihkel about what really happened over here. There were photographs," Banks said. "A girl. Bill. Here in Tallinn. He was blackmailed. With his wife dead, they didn't matter."

Aivar gazed out over the water, a sad, wistful look in his eyes. "So that is what it was," he said. "I wonder how they get to him. They cannot use the same threats they use with me."

"What do you mean?"

"Let's walk again."

They left the cell. Banks just caught from the corner of his eye the figure of a blond woman disappearing into a cell several yards away. Joanna Passero. Aivar clearly saw her, too. "Your colleague?" he said, smiling.

"Inspector Passero."

"A good idea. I approve. I do the same in your position. Perhaps she need to learn how to keep better hidden, but let her follow. Very beautiful woman, is she not?"

"What happened?"

Banks saw a small room off to the side that looked as if its walls had been splashed with blood from a bucket. Someone had drawn red hearts and written LOVE in big dripping red letters. In the old library, there were still books on the wooden shelves, piled haphazardly, all in Russian, or so it appeared from their covers. On one window ledge stood a big old reel-to-reel tape recorder, its innards partially exposed. And everywhere the damp and the smell.

Aivar leaned against a rickety wooden desk. "We walk around Old Town, Bill and me, asking questions. Tuesday night. We know they are in St. Patrick's bar because girls have remembered some things. That is last bar they are all together. Australian boy, bartender, he tell us he see Rachel leave after her friends and turn in the wrong direction. I think he likes her, so he quickly runs after her to warn her, and he sees her turn corner into side street. Not far along is nightclub with no name, where I see you."

"What happened?"

"Outside is a car, very expensive car. Mercedes. Fill whole street."

"What color?"

"Silver-gray. Barman, his name is Steve, he sees Rachel go in club. He thinks to go after her, then he thinks perhaps she meet someone, she is not so lost after all."

"He was sure it was Rachel?"

"She wears short yellow dress. Blond hair. He can see."

"Jesus," said Banks, glancing toward the window. "I knew there was something about that place."

"You have hunch, yes?"

"Something like that. So what happened?"

They left the library and walked back down the arched brick corridor. There was no sign of Joanna, but Banks knew she was not far away. Not that it mattered now; he didn't feel he was in any immediate danger.

"Nothing," said Aivar. "It was late. We go in club, but nobody knows anything. No silver Mercedes. Nothing. Do not like cops. We report to Investigator Rätsepp in his office, and he says to leave it with him. Next day. Next day. Nothing happen. We hear no more. When I ask, he tell me it was not a good lead, that barman was mistaken. We look for Steve again, even though Rätsepp says not to, but we cannot find him. His friend in St. Patrick's tell us he return to Australia."

"So let me get this clear," said Banks. "You get a lead to where Rachel went after St. Patrick's, probably the last place she was seen alive. You take it to your boss. He tells you to leave it with him. It evaporates."

"I am sorry?"

"It disappears. Nothing more is done. No follow-up."

"It disappears. Yes. Goes nowhere. No further action. Hr. Rätsepp insist."

"Did you talk to Bill about it?"

"Next day, I try. He is very quiet. Says Rätsepp must be right and barman must be mistaken, and it is not worth following. I do not understand. We are both excited when we talk to Steve. Then Rätsepp call me in his office and tell me I must never question his orders or judgments if I care about my career. I do care then, but not later. I leave after a year. Second day I am at home, two men come and, how do you say . . . they beat me up."

"How bad?"

"Not so badly I need hospital, but they know how to hurt. Then they tell me if they ever find out I mention Rachel case or club again, they will kill me. I believe them."

"So you told no one until now?"

"No. I get job in tourist business. Learn better English. Mind my own business. Keep my head down. But I never forget."

"Did Ursula Mardna know?"

"No. I do not believe Rätsepp tell her."

Banks felt some relief that his suspicions about Ursula were probably wrong and not everyone on the case was bent or intimidated. But she hadn't known about the lead. Rätsepp hadn't passed it on to her. It stopped with him, and he was Rebane's man.

They passed the execution room with the hole in the floor, where the Russians used to hang people before the Second World War, before the Nazis took over for a few years. Banks had had enough of Patarei by now and suggested they get out of the place. Aivar said they must leave separately, as they came.

"There is just one thing," Banks said as they shook hands.

"Yes?"

"The silver Mercedes. I don't suppose the barman got the number?"

"Only part."

"Did you ever find out who owned it?"

Aivar shuffled his feet in the grit. "Hmm," he said. "That was another reason to do as Rätsepp told me."

"Why is that?"

"I cannot help be curious, so I check. Not so many silver Mercedes. A name comes up."

"Let me guess," said Banks. "Joosep Rebane."

"No. It was Viktor Rebane. His father," he said, then he turned and walked off toward the exit.

Krystyna looked a little nervous, as well she might, thought Annie, as she sat in front of the large-screen television and watched the VIPER display. With any luck, she was about to identify Robert Tamm as the man who came by Garskill Farm on Wednesday morning over a week ago, the morning that Mihkel Lepikson was murdered. She had already identified Roderick Flinders as the man who had abducted her, tied her up, gagged her and locked her in the basement of his house. Flinders was in custody, and a whole range of charges was being prepared against him. The CPS was having a field day. Annie and

Winsome thought they would let him sweat for a while longer before talking to him. All the better to let him contemplate his options, which were getting more limited by the hour.

Of course, Krystyna's identification wouldn't prove that Tamm murdered Mihkel Lepikson, only that he was at Garskill Farm on the morning in question, but taken in concert with the rest of the forensic evidence, including fabrics and the DNA tying him to the woods where Bill Quinn was murdered, and the tire tracks and fingerprints in the glove compartment of the rented Ford Focus tying him to both crime scenes, it would go a long way toward helping convict him. The Glasgow police had found a crossbow in Tamm's cellar, too. So Krystyna was about to bear witness against a hardened hit man.

Luckily VIPER, the Video Identification Parade Electronic Recording, had replaced the old line-ups, where a witness walked in front of a row of people of similar description to the suspect and picked out the guilty one. She didn't have to face that sort of confrontation with Tamm. But she was nervous, nonetheless, especially after her experience with Flinders.

Eventually, it turned out to be a simple matter. He was the fourth individual to be displayed on-screen, and she recognized him immediately. Every little bit helped.

The Glasgow police had located Tamm and picked him up easily enough, and the two officers who delivered him to Eastvale had seemed happy to dump their prisoner and head off for a night on the town on expenses. Annie wished them luck. She knew what a night on the town in Eastvale was like. Glasgow, it wasn't.

Krystyna had returned with Annie to the Harkside cottage on Sunday night after a mandatory stop at the hospital for a quick examination. She was no worse for wear but a little tearful and contrite. Annie had pampered her with a long bath, pizza, wine and television. Krystyna had even learned a few more words of English, and, to Annie's eye at least, she was putting a bit more meat on her bones with every meal. At Annie's suggestion, Krystyna had actually telephoned her parents in Pyskowice, and there were more tears and talk of reconciliation and going home, or so Annie gathered from the tone, and from Krystyna's sign language at the end of the conversation. Krystyna seemed more cheerful after the phone call, at any rate, though Annie had a feeling that she wouldn't stay very long in a small town in Silesia. But she did hope that perhaps the next time Krystyna left home, she would do it the right way, with a real job in hand. There might even be something in Eastvale to suit her, if she improved her language skills.

Leaving Krystyna with Winsome in the squad room, Annie took Doug Wilson with her—he needed the experience—and they went into interview room three, where Robert Tamm was sitting as still as a meditating monk and as expressionless as a stone.

Annie spread her files on the table and leaned back, tapping her pen on the metal surface. "Well, Robert," she said. "Quite a pickle you're in, isn't it?"

Tamm said nothing. Whether he understood her or not, she couldn't tell. She thought "in a pickle" might be too obscure an expression for a foreigner. "You're in a lot of trouble," she said.

Tamm still said nothing. He hadn't asked for a lawyer yet, but they could get a duty solicitor for him quickly enough if he did. He had already been cautioned, and he had indicated that he understood, but he still wasn't saying anything. Clearly he had another plan. Silence. He wasn't the kind to blurt out a confession.

It had been a long day, Annie felt. She and Winsome had done about as much as they could do. She thought they could probably get a conviction on the murders of Bill Quinn and Mihkel Lepikson, especially with the testimony of Gareth Underwood, a.k.a. Curly; Krystyna; and Roderick Flinders, but they still had nothing to link Tamm to Joosep Rebane. Doug Wilson seemed bored with the lengthening silence already.

So much for learning from experience. For that you needed experience of something other than silence.

As for Rachel Hewitt, Annie knew that was not their case, but she also knew that it had become a personal mission for Banks, and she knew what he was like when he got his teeth into something. She wished she were with him in Tallinn, not in a romantic way, but helping on the case. She had seen the trail of damage that Rachel's abduction had left behind—Maureen and Luke Hewitt; Pauline Boyars, the bride that never was. She wondered how Banks was getting on with the Professional Standards woman. Were they still speaking? Was she getting under his feet all the time? Could they possibly be sleeping together? The woman might have been married, but she was an icy blonde, after all, and Annie never trusted icy blondes. Not even to be icy.

The case was over bar the formalities now. They had Robert Tamm and Roderick Flinders in custody, and the next few days would be a matter of working with the forensics experts and the CPS to build up a solid case. Flinders was a weak link. He had already talked plenty, and he would probably talk a lot more tomorrow if he thought there was a chance of saving his own skin. A night stewing in the cells would do him good. There were still a few migrant workers from Garskill Farm on the loose, but they would find their ways home, or into the hands of the police, wherever they ended up. Krystyna's friend Ewa had turned up in Liverpool, and Annie had arranged for her to pay a visit to Eastvale sometime over the next few days. Krystyna herself was safe now. Warren Corrigan was dead, and Curly was going straight. He was happy with his deal. He would talk, too, and he knew a lot. Result, then, Annie told herself, as she gestured for Doug Wilson to leave the room with her. Tamm was a dead loss. They'd get no confession from him. She told the officers on duty outside the interview room to take him back to the cells, and she and DC Wilson headed back to the squad room.

Haig and Lombard, the DCs on loan, were long gone, but Winsome and Geraldine Masters were still there, along with Krystyna.

"Come on," said Annie, dropping her file on the desk. "It's celebration time. Let's all go and get pissed." When Krystyna looked puzzled, she said, "You, too," and mimed drinking. Krystyna nodded and smiled, and they picked up their coats and filed out to the Queen's Arms.

13

"Viktor Rebane and Toomas Rätsepp grew up together in the fifties in Narva, near the Russian border," said Erik on the way out to Viimsi on Tuesday morning. Ursula Mardna had arranged a meeting between Banks, Joanna and Viktor Rebane, from which Viktor would walk away as free as he arrived. Joosep, as expected, had disappeared from the radar. Banks was now certain that Ursula had known nothing of the lead that Bill Quinn and Aivar Kukk had passed on to Toomas Rätsepp six years ago, or she wouldn't be helping him so much to uncover the truth. She wasn't in thick with Viktor Rebane; that, as Erik was explaining, was Toomas Rätsepp. Ursula was so angry about what had been done that she swore Rätsepp would go down, despite his friendship with Viktor Rebane, and Banks believed her.

Erik carried on with his potted history. "It was a very strange time there. Much bomb damage, many Russian immigrants. They came to Tallinn together with their families as young men and remained friends. When he was old enough, Viktor worked for state industry, and after independence he bought into utilities. Toomas first joined the militia, then he became policeman. At the time Rachel disappeared, Viktor also had a major interest in the nightclub around the corner from St. Patrick's. It is said that he never went there, himself, that he was not interested in such pursuits, only in the profits. He had many cars, and his son liked to use the silver Mercedes most of all. Viktor spoiled and indulged him then."

"And he's powerful enough to get away scot-free."

"He knows a lot of secrets. But it is not only that. You must understand, Viktor Rebane is really not a bad man. Everyone knows that his son is psycho crazy and feels sorry for Viktor. He has done a lot of good for this country since independence. Much charity work. Many jobs. Remember that. He is a respected citizen. We are close now."

They had driven from the Metropol and were skirting Kadriorg Park, turning onto the coastal road to Viimsi. Everything had happened so quickly after Ursula Mardna had made the phone call that Banks's head was still spinning. He was sitting in the front of the VW beside Merike, with Erik and Joanna in the back. Joanna had been very terse and offhand with Banks since they had dinner at Mekk on Sunday evening, and he guessed she was wishing she hadn't opened up and told him her personal problems in a moment of weakness. That often happened. You tell someone something that shames you, reveals you, makes you vulnerable, then you close up and wish you'd kept quiet in the first place. It feels almost as if they've got something on you, got a hold over you, the way Joosep Rebane and Warren Corrigan had over Bill Quinn. He wanted to tell her he didn't feel that way, but it wouldn't go down well. Instead, he kept quiet on the subject. If she was still annoyed about trying to solve the Rachel Hewitt case, she was hiding it well now and had been as excited as Banks at the latest revelations and the forthcoming meeting with Viktor Rebane. He felt that she could scent the end, as he could, and the aroma intoxicated her. She might make a homicide detective yet.

Viktor Rebane had agreed to meet the foreign police detectives, who had no power or jurisdiction over him, as a courtesy in a public place of his choice, and they were heading for a restaurant. Apparently he lived in Viimsi, where he had a large modern house on its own grounds, with tennis court and swimming pool.

"So why has he agreed to see us?" Banks asked Erik.

"He is an old man. Sick with cancer. He is tired, and he wants to make amends before he dies. I think he has much on his conscience. He also has assurances from the very top that nothing will come back on him."

"Even murder?"

"We will see," said Erik. "As a journalist, I would give a lot to be at your meeting, but he specified only you and Joanna. We will wait in the car in the parking lot. Perhaps you can help me with a story later, let me interview you? An undisclosed police source?"

"Perhaps," said Banks. "If there is a story."

Merike pulled into a car park off the road, by the shore. "It's up there." She pointed ahead to a path by the beach. "It's called Paat. That means 'boat.' It looks like an upturned boat. Good luck."

Banks and Joanna walked toward the path. It was another fine day, blue sky striped with milky white cloud, and the sea lapping at the breakwaters. The beach was mostly pebble, with a few sods of grass here and there. Over the other side, to the left, they could see the Tallinn shoreline, and straight ahead was a large island.

The path led them into the restaurant's outside area, where a few sheltered picnic-style benches were set out against the low seawall. The restaurant itself was nearby, and it did resemble an upturned boat. Banks, however, found his eyes more drawn to the outside area, where an old man in a windcheater sat alone at one of the picnic tables, a mug of tea or coffee steaming in front of him, while two neckless bruisers stood, hands clasped in front of their privates, scanning the grounds. Probably ex–KGB agents, Banks guessed.

When Banks and Joanna approached the table, the bruisers stepped forward and patted them down. They were gentle and discreet enough with Joanna, Banks noticed, but she clearly didn't like it, and he didn't blame her. They were a little rougher with him, but not enough to hurt. When they were satisfied neither had a weapon or a wire, they stood aside, and Banks and Joanna sat opposite Viktor Rebane.

He was a hunched figure, and his chin was tucked into his throat in such a way that he looked permanently on the verge of a particularly noxious burp. His bald head was liver-spotted, as were his lizardlike hands. Frown lines had eaten deep into his brow. He must have been about the same age as Rätsepp, Banks guessed, if they grew up together, but he seemed a good ten years older. The ravages of cancer, no doubt. Or its treatment.

"First, let me not forget my hospitality," Viktor Rebane said. "May I offer you both a drink?"

"Why not?" said Banks. "I'll have beer, please. A. Le Coq if they have it."

"Excellent choice. And the lady?"

"Just a cappuccino, please," said Joanna, clearly still smarting from her patting down.

Rebane snapped his fingers and the closest no-neck went off to the bar. As if sensing Joanna's mood, Rebane said, his yellowish eyes twinkling, "I do apologize about the body search, my dear, but man in my position cannot be too careful. Beautiful woman is often most dangerous weapon."

"Is that an old Estonian proverb?" said Joanna.

Rebane smiled. "No. Is old Viktor Rebane proverb. The reason I agree to see you now, so soon," Rebane continued, "is I have appointment at hospital this afternoon. I am very tired and sick after chemotherapy, for many days. I am sure you understand."

"Of course," said Banks. "And we're very grateful you took the trouble to talk to us. Perhaps you can help us answer a number of questions?"

"Perhaps. First thing I tell you is I do not know where my son is, so please do not ask. Joosep and I have not spoken for many years now. He is always difficult child. Wild, unpredictable. Especially after his mother die. He is only ten at the time. He keep very bad company. Perhaps I spoil him. It is fashionable to blame parents, is it not? Do you have a son, Hr. Banks?"

"I do," said Banks. "He's a musician."

"Is good. In Estonia we love music. My son is drug dealer, people trafficker and gangster. But he is still my son. Do you understand that?"

"I think so," said Banks.

"How far you go to protect *your* son?"

Banks thought for a moment. "Probably a long way," he answered. "But I might draw the line if he raped and killed women."

An expression of pain passed across Rebane's face, and immediately Banks felt guilty for being so brutally cruel; it had been unnecessary. No-neck came back with the drinks.

"Joosep tell me the girl die of a drug overdose," Rebane whispered.

"What girl?"

"The one you are interested in. I am a father. I have daughter, too, with my third wife. She is twenty-one. I am proud of her, and I love her. That is perhaps the real reason I am talking to you. I feel something for the parents of this girl."

"It's taken you a bloody long time."

Rebane gave an impatient shake of his head. "It is easier to forget when nothing reminds you. There are always many other things to think about. I regret most of all the things I did not do, not the things I did. But now . . ." He shook his head slowly. "Too much has

happened. Old wounds have reopened. I am a businessman, Hr. Banks. I am not interested in your moral
judgments. I have perhaps done many wrong things for
my business interests. I have made many enemies. Do
you understand?"

"I think so."

"Six years ago Joosep is my beloved son. Now he is
a stranger to me."

"Will you tell me what happened six years ago?"

Viktor remained silent for a few moments.
Seagulls squealed over a shoal of fish close to shore.
"Joosep come to see me. He is very upset. Most agitated. When I ask him what is wrong, he tell me a
girl die of a drug overdose at his party. An English
girl. He tell me he is sitting in nightclub. You know
which club?"

"I know."

"He is sitting in nightclub with friends. My nightclub. They are ready to leave, and this beautiful girl
comes in. A vision. She has lost her friends. Joosep, he
tells me he ask her if she want to go to party, and after
he will drive her to her hotel. She says yes, and they
go in his car. But at party, girl drinks more and takes
drugs, and in morning they find her dead. She has . . .
how do you say . . ." He pointed to his throat, what
little there was of it to see. "Choke."

"Asphyxiated," said Banks. "'Choked' will do. Choked on her own vomit?"

"Yes."

"So what happened?"

"He is in trouble, and he wants me to help him. Then, on Wednesday morning, Toomas, my old friend, telephones to tell me that Joosep's name, my name, and the nightclub also, have come up in the investigation, and I ask my friend Toomas to stop it, if he can, to make sure it goes no further. It is not too late. Toomas will do that for me. He will help Joosep. And for money, of course. He know I will be very grateful."

"Of course," said Banks. "It's comforting to know that corruption's no different here than anywhere else."

"Perhaps. I am not so certain. Or you are being ironic, yes? You English."

"Maybe just a little bit. So Toomas Rätsepp shut down the investigation?"

"He close off that direction. Yes. Is easy because not many people know. Barman from St. Patrick pub, of course. But he is easy. Threat of beating and ticket back to Australia. And junior investigator who report his findings to Toomas. Also easy if he want to stay in job, have promotion. Beating, too. English policeman is problem."

"Bill Quinn," said Banks.

"Yes. We cannot warn him to stop or threaten him. Is madness to assassinate foreign cop on Estonian soil. We need different solution."

"And you thought of one."

"I have trusted colleague pick out pretty girl from club and give her money. You know the rest. Accidental meeting arranged in the hotel bar. Drinks. A sleeping powder. Dinner. Photographs. Easy."

Joanna charged in now, as Banks had expected she would. This was the part of the story that interested her the most. "So you're saying that you arranged with the girl to have Bill Quinn seduced, drugged and photographed in a compromising position, then you blackmailed him?"

Rebane nodded, which made him look even more as if he were about to burp. "It is only way to save my son. I help him out of many difficulties. Back then I always had hope he would change, that he would stop being wild and foolish. But he has gone other direction. I can help him no more. He is lost to me. But you will never find him. Despite everything, he is still my son, and I will not have him locked in prison or mental hospital."

"And when Bill Quinn's wife died, your blackmail didn't work anymore."

"No," said Rebane. "By then Joosep know what I have done, and he has taken photos some years before.

He now has business, criminal business, in United Kingdom, and he think it useful to have policeman . . . how you say?"

" 'In his pocket'?" Banks suggested.

Rebane didn't quite seem to understand but grunted his agreement anyway.

Banks said, "But Bill Quinn was going to tell all after his wife died, wasn't he, so you had to find another way of dealing with him. You sent Robert Tamm."

Rebane seemed puzzled. "Robert Tamm? He does not work for me. He work—"

"For Joosep?"

"I do not kill Detective Quinn, or order kill. I have nothing to do with murder."

"Of course not. But your son does, doesn't he? He has already used blackmail against Quinn over the years to smooth his illegal operations in the UK, and suddenly they're threatened. He finds out that Bill Quinn and an Estonian journalist called Mihkel Lepikson are planning to tell the whole sorry story. So Joosep has them both killed. You might not do it yourself, but you're quite happy to leave him free to murder and maim and rape and ruin as many lives as he wants, aren't you?" said Banks.

Rebane banged his skinny fist on the table. "He is my son! What would you have me do? I tell you I am not interested in your cheap morality. Take what you are given and be grateful. Like scraps for the dogs. Georg!" One of the no-necks came over. "Georg. Help me. We will leave now. I am tired." Viktor Rebane struggled to his feet with Georg's help.

Banks and Joanna remained seated. "I have one more question," said Banks.

Rebane stared down at him, still shaking with fury. "You have great deal of nerve, my friend," he said through gritted teeth.

"Where is Rachel Hewitt?"

During the three hours it took to drive to Võrumaa, Banks sat in the back with Joanna and dozed or gazed out on the scenery, going over the whole case in his mind, especially the end of the meeting at Paat where Viktor Rebane had glared at him for so long he was certain the old man was not going to tell him anything. But Rebane finally whispered a location, then hobbled off with Georg's help.

Erik and Merike sat up front navigating and chatting quietly in Estonian. The radio played quiet jazz.

Perhaps, Banks thought, he had been too hard on Viktor Rebane, but he didn't like gangsters who pretended to be respectable. Maybe Viktor was a respectable businessman who had done a lot for his country, but Banks was willing to believe he had done more than a few things that needed sweeping under the carpet, too, and that Toomas Rätsepp had helped him more than once. You don't keep company like the no-necks Viktor was with for no reason. But he was untouchable, and that didn't really matter too much; he was clearly dying. Joosep Rebane was out of sight, perhaps hiding in St. Petersburg with his Russian gangster friends, Banks guessed. There would be plenty of police forces watching out for him across Europe, but it was more of a waiting game than a chase or a hunt.

Banks had a suspicion that Joosep would most likely meet a sticky end at the hands of his criminal colleagues once the story came out. Gangsters could be a very moral lot. Murder and mayhem were fine in the service of business. Torture, arson and maiming all had their place in the pursuit of profit, but anything to do with young girls or children was frowned upon. At best, Joosep's colleagues would view him as careless, at worst as a possible rapist and murderer of an innocent young woman. Either way he would become a liability, if he wasn't one already. The odds were also that Joosep had pissed off enough people already and that this would be the last straw.

The countryside rolled by outside the car window, forest and farmland, along with the occasional village and small town. The woods were thick with evergreens, Banks noticed, which must have made it beautiful in winter, especially under a blanket of snow. Everyone was quiet, perhaps contemplating the hours ahead or thinking about the past. He recalled his telephone conversation earlier with a slightly hungover Annie. She seemed pleased with the way things had wrapped up in Eastvale. He hadn't known then, of course, that he was close to the end of his own investigation in Tallinn.

Viktor Rebane had told Banks that his son had not taken Rachel Hewitt to a party in Tallinn but to a lake house, which happened to be in an area of small wooded lakes called Võrumaa, in the far south of the country, about a three-hour drive from the nightclub. Joosep often held late-night parties there, parties that sometimes went on for two or three days. Cocaine and amphetamines kept people awake, and barbiturates put them to sleep. The lake house belonged entirely to Joosep, Viktor had stressed. Nothing was in his name, and he had never been there. No doubt he had his own secret playgrounds.

Banks couldn't help but wonder whether Rachel had quickly sobered up when she found herself being driven out of the city, far away from everything she knew, unless Joosep had somehow drugged her the way Larisa had drugged Bill Quinn. Rohypnol, or some such thing. Or had she agreed to go? Was it adventure she was seeking? Did she really think it would be fun? By all accounts, Joosep Rebane was a rich, handsome and charming young man, with rock-star charisma and a fancy silver Mercedes. Rachel wasn't a party girl, according to everyone who knew her; she wasn't promiscuous, but she was spontaneous, and she was certainly attracted by wealth and its trappings. Did she believe that Joosep Rebane was the Prince Charming she had been looking for?

Immediately after Viktor and the no-necks had left Paat, Banks had phoned Ursula Mardna, who had pinpointed the location of the lake house for them and said she would arrange for a local CSI team to get over there and start work immediately. If Banks wished, he could set off from Viimsi and meet up with her at the scene.

Merike had a little trouble finding the particular lake once they had left the main highway, and they spent some time driving along unpaved roads through thick forest, stopping to read signs, before they arrived at the end of a long, winding entrance road that led to the simple wooden lake house, with a lawn stretching down to the water's edge. Banks couldn't see any other cottages around, though there were a few outbuildings that clearly belonged to the main house. It seemed the ideal, isolated place for Joosep Rebane's antics.

The path to the house and lake were taped off, and a surly uniformed officer stood on guard. Erik tried to talk to him but got nowhere. Fortunately, Ursula Mardna arrived within half an hour of them and sorted everything out. Erik and Merike were not allowed past the tape, though, only the police, and that infuriated Erik, as he had come so far. He stayed in the car for a while, sulking and smoking with Merike, then they walked as close as they could get. No doubt, Banks thought, he would keep his eyes and ears open for a story, and his mobile phone would have a decent camera. Banks had no problem with the story being told, and he doubted very much that Ursula Mardna would. She was assuming control now, directing the CSIs. If her initial failure in the Rachel case hadn't done her career much harm, finally solving it after all these years could only do it good.

The CSIs were busy inside the house, and outside two of them were digging up areas of the lawn they had decided offered the most potential for buried bodies. Viktor had said Joosep told him he had buried Rachel's body in the garden, but not exactly where. Banks wondered why he hadn't just dumped her in the lake, but dead bodies in the water all float eventually, and perhaps he had worried that there was more chance of someone seeing her, even in such an isolated place as this. Others must live not so far away, and surely ramblers, cyclists or boaters came by occasionally.

Banks and Joanna stood on the deck with Ursula Mardna, watching over the scene. A small motorboat lay moored to the dock at the end of the garden, alongside a rowboat. The opposite shore was about a quarter of a mile away, and as far as Banks could see, there were no lake houses or dwellings of any kind over there. It seemed as if Joosep and his friends had the lake to themselves. Banks could smell the fresh pine and hear the birds singing up in the trees.

There were no signs of recent inhabitation, the Crime Scene Manager told Ursula Mardna; in fact, he said, there were no indications of anyone's having been there at all recently. Other than the occasional discussions between CSIs, it was perfectly quiet, much like Banks's own cottage by the beck outside Gratly. The lake house itself was large enough for four bedrooms upstairs and a poolroom in the basement, and the outbuildings were fitted with bunks for extra guests.

The main floor consisted of one large open room incorporating a living area, dining table and kitchen. It smelled musty and stale, as if it had been locked up for a long time, and dust motes danced in the rays of sunlight as Banks walked the uncarpeted floor. A few rugs had been thrown here or there, but mostly it was bare boards. There was a wood-burning stove in the living area, which must have been nice and cozy on a winter's night. There were a few battered armchairs, a decent stereo setup, along with a pile of punk and heavy metal CDs, a collection of hash pipes, a large flat-screen TV with DVD player and a pile of martial arts movies and Korean bootleg porn. The walls were covered with stylized prints from the Kama Sutra mixed in with cubist and abstract expressionist works.

Banks was happy to go outside again, and when he did, one of the CSIs digging in the garden called out. Banks and Joanna hurried over with Ursula Mardna to join him, as did several of his colleagues, standing around the edge of a three-foot-deep pit. Banks could see Erik straining his neck behind the tape, no doubt snapping away with his smartphone camera.

The CSI, a forensic archaeologist, Ursula Mardna explained, carefully brushed away soil from an empty eye socket. The bones had darkened from years underground, where various compounds had leached into the soil. The CSI worked carefully with his brush, and Banks and Joanna watched as the skull slowly came into view. It was going to take a long time, he explained, so there was no point in their standing over him. He would call them when he was finished, then would begin the difficult and painstaking process of getting the body from the earth to the mortuary. Only the photographer remained as the archaeologist continued his delicate work.

Banks, Joanna and Ursula Mardna paced the deck as they waited. Someone had a flask of hot coffee, and Banks was grateful for the loan of a plastic cup to drink from, even though it was a warm day and he would have preferred a cold beer. It was at times like this that Banks also wished he still smoked. When Ursula Mardna brought out a packet of cigarettes and a small tin to contain the ashes, so she wouldn't contaminate the scene, he was tempted to ask her for one, but he controlled the urge.

Everyone seemed vaguely interested in the arrival of the English detectives, especially in Joanna Passero, casting them curious glances every now and then, but nobody paid undue attention to them. Fewer people seemed to speak English here than Banks had encountered in Tallinn. It was early evening, and though it was far from dark, the shadows were lengthening over the water, and the light through the trees was taking on that muted, filtered evening quality.

Eventually, the archaeologist and his assistants called the three of them over. The skeleton Banks looked down on could have been male or female as far as he was concerned, though the pathologist, who also now arrived at the graveside, quickly assured them it was female.

When Banks and Joanna stood at the edge of the shallow grave with Ursula Mardna, Banks knew he had found what he had come for, though he felt no sense of triumph, just a kind of sad relief. It was impossible to see the yellow color, of course, but fragments of the dress still clung to the darkened bones, as did the white open-toed high-heeled shoes, though they were no longer white and pieces had disintegrated. There were also the remains of a small handbag, a metal clasp and decayed leather strap. Everything looked as if it might have been tossed on top of the body, and Banks wondered if Rachel had been naked when she was buried.

After all the photographs had been taken, and soil and vegetation samples carefully removed and packaged, one of the CSIs very carefully retrieved the handbag. The fabric had rotted, but some of the contents were still intact: a tube of lipstick; a tattered, mostly rotted leather purse; a plastic hairbrush; keys; some loose coins, mostly Estonian kroon, along with some British pounds; and a Meriton Hotel ballpoint pen. If there had been anything else, it had decomposed over the years, like the flesh.

The pathologist knelt by the body and borrowed the CSI's brush to clear more soil from the neck area. After much umming and ahhing, in addition to the use of a magnifying glass and a delicate physical examination with gloved fingers, he stood up. Banks heard his knees crack. The man spoke with Ursula Mardna in Estonian. She turned to Banks and said, "He cannot say for certain, but he thinks she was strangled. There are many small bones broken in the throat."

"However she died," Banks said, "somebody buried her. There'll be an investigation, I assume?"

Ursula Mardna nodded. "Of course."

Banks asked whether he could examine the purse, and after a quick glance at Ursula Mardna, who nodded briefly, the CSI handed it to him, after first having him put on a pair of protective gloves. It wasn't because of fingerprints, Banks knew—none would survive after so long—but simply crime scene protocol.

With Joanna Passero by his side, Banks opened the purse carefully. The one thing you could usually depend on surviving most of the elements except fire was plastic, and sure enough, there it was. Or there they were. Tesco, credit and debit cards, Co-op, Boots, Waterstones and half a dozen others. All in the name of Rachel Hewitt.

He had found her.

The last thing Banks took out of the purse, stuck in a slot behind one of her credit cards, was a small laminated card inscribed with an image of a man in tails and a top hat helping a voluptuous woman into a coach. Or was he pushing her?

14

Late June sunshine flooded the market square as
Banks looked down from his open office window
on the shining cobbles, smelling coffee and freshly
baked bread, listening to the ghostly harmonies of
Erkki-Sven Tüür's *Awakening* from the iPod dock.
The gold hands against the blue face of the church clock
stood at a quarter past five. A group of walkers drib-
bled into the square in ones and twos, gathering at the
market cross after three or four hours out in the dale,
all kitted out with the latest boots, red and orange anor-
aks, rucksacks and walking sticks, trouser legs tucked
into their socks. One of them was clearly the leader, and
he carried an Ordnance Survey map in a clear plastic
cover around his neck. Already the little wooden plat-
form and tables with umbrellas had been set up on the

cobbles outside the Queen's Arms, reminding Banks of his evenings in Tallinn, eating out in the Old Town with Joanna Passero.

It seemed like years since then, but it was only a month and a half. Annie was back at full throttle, as if she had never been away, especially as she had solved Banks's case while he had been off tilting at windmills. She also told Banks with great glee that she had got a letter in very basic English from Krystyna, who was now living in Kraków and working in a traditional Polish restaurant, studying English in her spare time.

Joanna Passero was still at county HQ, about to leave Professional Standards for Criminal Intelligence. Banks thought often about their trip to Tallinn, the city, the people they had met, the discovery by the lake in Võrumaa. They never had got to see the *Danse Macabre.*

Another time, perhaps. As Banks had expected, Joanna's report on Bill Quinn leaked to the press, and there had been a minor furor about policemen and prostitutes. But the brouhaha hadn't lasted long; celebrity phone-hacking had once again taken over most of the media's attention.

Erik Aarma's story, which appeared in late May over two weekly issues of the *Eesti Telegraaf,* did a great deal to restore Bill Quinn's reputation. Erik opened with the murders of Quinn and Mihkel Lepikson, then worked his way through the migrant-labor scam and Corrigan's shooting, and all the way back to the disappearance of Rachel Hewitt, making connections with Joosep and Viktor Rebane wherever he could legally do so. Soon the article appeared in translation, sometimes in digest form, in newspapers all over Europe. After all, Rachel's disappearance had been a major story six years ago and had been kept very much in the public eye since then by her parents' efforts. Though many of the players had to remain anonymous, there were few readers—in Tallinn, at any rate—who could remain in any doubt about to whom Erik was referring when he wrote of a rich and wild young man and his wealthy businessman father.

Viktor Rebane died of lung cancer in Tallinn in the first week of June, just after the article appeared. His son did not appear at his funeral. The following week, a body was pulled out of the Neva River outside St. Petersburg with two bullets in the head, and there was little doubt in anyone's mind that it belonged to Joosep Rebane, a conclusion soon borne out by DNA analysis. His criminal masters had clearly taken the moral high ground when they learned that he had been responsible for the death of an innocent young woman. They had no doubt already known he was something of a liability,

Banks thought, and his days had probably been numbered anyway.

Ursula Mardna came out of the whole affair triumphant, her earlier lack of vigilance forgotten, and Toomas Rätsepp was prosecuted for a number of serious offenses under Estonian corruption and bribery laws.

Banks returned to his desk and picked up the three sheets of paper he had received in the post that morning, along with a brief covering note from Erik explaining that he had received the letter in response to his article, and Merike had translated it from the Russian. The quiet music, with its drifting harmonies, long notes and high strings, seemed both peaceful and tense at once. Banks sat down, sipped some lukewarm tea and read:

Dear Mr. Aarma,

It was with great interest and curiosity that I read your article in a national newspaper recently, and I feel it is my duty to clarify one or two important points for you. Why now, you may ask, after so long? I have no excuses except cowardice and self-interest for not coming forward until now. You say in your article that though certain facts are clear, perhaps nobody will ever know exactly what happened at the lake house in Võrumaa on that July night six years ago. But that is not true. For, you see, I was there.

I worked at a nightclub in the Old Town of Tallinn. It had no name, and we called it simply the Club. I was sharing a flat with another young woman who worked there, a rather naïve Russian-speaking Estonian girl called Larisa, who was not at work on the night I am about to describe.

There was a crowd, or a clique, at the Club, centered around Joosep Rebane, son of Viktor, one of the Club's owners. You refer to both these men in your article, or at least it seems to me from your descriptions that they could be nobody else. Joosep had that "aura of glamour" you mention, of the movie star or rich playboy, about him. He did not work. He did not have to. He had money. He was intelligent, but not well read or educated. He had charisma, but it was laced with cruelty. He liked to humiliate people, exercise his power over them, and yet people gravitated toward him, especially women. Why? I can't explain. I couldn't then, and I can't now. The excitement? The edge of danger he always seemed to generate?

On weekends, we would often congregate at the Club and then go somewhere else later. The core group was five or six strong, and sometimes others joined up with us later, came from outside the city, even from as far as St. Petersburg and Riga. Sometimes Joosep would drive us all down to his lake house in Võrumaa. There we were so isolated we could do anything, and we did.

One night in July six years ago—I do not remember the exact day of the week, or the date, but your article says it happened between Saturday, July 22, and Sunday, July 23, so I must trust you—a young girl walked into the Club just as we were about to leave. The girl was drunk. She looked lost. Joosep immediately sensed she was vulnerable, and he went to her to ask if he could help. She was just his type, a blond vision in a short yellow dress, with full lips, pale skin. I could not hear all their conversation, but soon he had persuaded her to have a drink, into which I thought later he must have put some Rohypnol, something he had done before, even when the girls were willing.

When we all went outside—there were I think five of us by then—Joosep tried to get the girl into the car. She did not want to come with us at first, but Joosep is very persuasive. The drug had not started working by then. Joosep said we would go to a party at his flat nearby for a while, and then he *would drop her off at her hotel. She seemed to like this idea, or at least appeared half-willing, and Joosep bundled her into the back of the car. Then we were off. No party. No hotel. But the lake house. Võrumaa.*

I do not remember much about the journey. I think the English girl whimpered a little as she realized we were leaving the city, then she fell silent. I know that Joosep had to practically carry her out of the car when we arrived, and he immediately put her in one of the outbuildings. I have no recollection of him coming back to the main building. It was after four o'clock in the morning by then and starting to get light. We were all somewhat the worse for wear. Time did not matter. We would often sleep for a few hours, then start a party at ten o'clock the following morning, or three in the afternoon, if we felt like it. Sometimes people would turn up unexpectedly, and we would have a party to welcome them. There was always lots of booze and drugs. And sex. That night I believe we smoked one joint, then everybody passed out quite quickly. There was always tomorrow.

It must have been a couple of hours later when I awoke, having heard a sound. Everyone else in the main building seemed to be still crashed out. I went to the window, which was open to the warm night air, and I heard another sound, like a muffled scream, then a gurgling sound and a fist thumping against thick wood, then silence.

Something about the sounds made my skin crawl. I ducked down, so that I could not be seen from outside. Time passed. I do not know how long. The morning light grew stronger. Then Joosep walked out of the outbuilding with a bundle in his arms. I saw the yellow dress, the little handbag hanging from her hand, one white shoe dangling.

He looked around and sniffed the air like a wild animal. I felt fear prickle through me. I thought for certain he would see me or know instinctively that I was there. But he didn't. He looked at the lake, as if contemplating something, then carried on, walking just a few more feet to a spot near where the woods started. There was a spade propped against one of the trees for gardening, and he started digging. The girl lay on the ground beside him. I could not tell whether she was alive or not, but she did not move.

I watched Joosep dig a shallow grave, drop her body into it, and shovel back the earth, tapping down the grass sods on top to make it appear *undisturbed. It didn't, but who would care? Who would notice? Soon the turf would knit together again and it would be hidden forever.*

He went back into the outbuilding, and I lay down on my mattress again trying to decide what to do. I did not think he had seen me. If he had, I reasoned, he would probably have come and killed me, too. But I could not be certain. Joosep's mind moved in strange ways. All day he kept catching my eye and smiling. He told us that the English girl had run away during the night, and everyone just laughed. Did nobody realize there was nowhere for her to run? When Sasha decided it was time to go back to Tallinn, I asked if he would take me along as I was working at the Club that night. I could not be certain that Joosep believed me, but he let me go.

When we got to Tallinn, I went immediately to my apartment. Larisa was not there. I packed a few clothes and personal things, just one suitcase, and made sure I had my passport. I did not have a car, so I had to hitchhike. It is not difficult if you are a reasonably attractive young woman. I soon got to Riga, then Vilnius, then Minsk, then . . . But that is where my story ends.

Please do not try to find me. I am sorry for what I did, or did not do. That night has haunted me ever since. There was nothing I could have done to save the English girl, except perhaps run into the outbuilding and try to stop Joosep. But no one can make Joosep change his mind once it is made up, and he is much bigger and stronger than me. Perhaps I could have told my story sooner to spare her friends and family the agony of not knowing. I hope you will understand why I felt I could not do that until I read your story.

Juliya K.

Banks folded the sheets, put them back in the envelope and massaged his temples. "The Wanderer's Evening Song" was playing now, and Banks let the strange choral harmonies flow over him for a few moments. As he did so, his mind went back to Rachel's funeral in late May, the crowded crematorium, hordes of media outside with their handheld cameras and boom microphones, oblivious to everyone's pain and loss. As the coffin slipped away, Coldplay's "Fix You" had played over the music system. It had been Rachel's favorite song around the time of the hen weekend, her best friend Pauline said.

Banks went with Annie to the funeral tea afterward at the Hewitts' house, where they sipped Harvey's Bristol Cream and ate little triangular sandwiches with the crusts cut off. The media were consigned to the pavement beyond the garden gate, though occasionally an adventurous reporter managed to sneak closer and press his nose up against the window behind the lace curtains.

Banks managed to get Maureen Hewitt alone for a few moments, though her daughter Heather stuck close to her. The young girl made a ghostly presence, pale-skinned, dressed wholly in black, and Banks didn't recollect her ever saying a word. Her expression remained unchanging, too, a sort of blank grief mixed with anxiety, as if she were always on the verge of tears, or of jumping up and running away.

Maureen Hewitt thanked Banks for getting to the bottom of the mystery of her daughter's disappearance and assured him that, while she and her husband were devastated that they had not been right about Rachel's still being alive, all their lives were much better for the sense of closure that knowing the truth brought. Banks assured Maureen, as best he could, that her daughter's death had been quick and painless, that she had died of a drug overdose on the very night she had disappeared, probably without regaining consciousness. Maureen refused to accept that her daughter would take drugs willingly, and Banks told her that they were probably administered without her knowledge, though he had no real evidence of this at the time. It helped Maureen a little. She said that she and her husband would continue with the foundation and its work for the sake of all the other missing children out there.

Pauline, the would-be bride at the hen weekend, was the only one of Rachel's old friends to turn up. She had clearly had too much to drink, even before she arrived. Her voice soon became too loud, and when she smashed a glass, Mr. Hewitt had a quiet word with her. She left in tears. Banks and Annie made their excuses and left shortly afterward.

Banks looked at the envelope one more time, then he got up, put it in his filing cabinet and walked over to the window again. Juliya's letter and the questions it begged would still haunt him tomorrow, and the day after that. For the moment, though, it was a beautiful late afternoon, the best of the year so far. The tables were fast filling up outside the Queen's Arms, reminding him of the Old Town in Tallinn, and he wanted nothing more than to sit by himself with a cold beer in the cobbled market square and watch the world go by.